Turned Out Saga

Turned Out Saga

Angel M. Hunter

www.urbanbooks.net

Urban Books, LLC
300 Farmingdale Road, NY-Route 109
Farmingdale, NY 11735

ISBN 13: 978-1-62286-511-6
ISBN 10: 1-62286-511-1

First Mass Market Printing June 2017
First Trade Paperback Printing June 2016
Printed in the United States of America

10 9 8 7 6 5 4 3 2 1

Distributed by Kensington Publishing Corp.
Submit orders to:
Customer Service
400 Hahn Road
Westminster, MD 21157-4627
Phone: 1-800-733-3000
Fax: 1-800-659-2436

Chapter One

"Shining Star"

Earth, Wind & Fire

At the age of twenty-nine, you would think Champagne Rose had it all. She worked as a publicist in New York City and was engaged to the man of many women's dreams, Zyair Truesdale. Not only was he a wealthy entrepreneur, but he was kind, supportive, and willing to do anything for her. Even with the picture-perfect life, Champagne felt that something was missing, and she was ready to make changes in her life and in her relationship.

She didn't believe in moving in with someone before marrying them, up until Zyair convinced her otherwise. Now five years later, she and Zyair still lived together, unmarried.

The funny thing was, he wanted to get married, but she was comfortable with what they had. She enjoyed having her own bank account. She enjoyed the independence that came with not being married. Champagne watched her friends' relationships fall apart right after they got married, for one reason or another, and didn't want that to happen to her and Zyair.

She wasn't ready to get married, but she also wasn't ready to break up. It's just that they'd been together now for so long and things were starting to wear thin. The chemistry just wasn't there. The sex had become routine, the same shit over and over—You lick me, I suck you, you put it in, and then I'll ride you. You cum, and I'll cum, maybe . . . if I'm lucky. At least that's how she perceived it.

Champagne yearned for more caressing, kissing, cuddling, and talking. She knew she still loved him but the passion was gone. She often found herself avoiding sex altogether.

If it was bothering her, it had to be bothering him.

Was it her? Was it him? Was it their busy life-styles? Whatever it was, she knew it had to change, and fast. She wanted to feel his fingers in her hair, moving down to her neck, where his fingers would be replaced with his lips. She wanted him to tease her with his tongue, tease her with his manhood, putting just the tip in and pulling it out. She wanted to beg for it, to demand that he enter her. She was tired of him putting it in, whether she was ready or not, tired of the rollover sex, the moving-in-and-out, up-and-down momentum of it all. She was just plain tired.

Champagne wanted things to change. She needed things to change. She still loved him, for goodness' sake. She just wasn't in love. *Were you supposed to stay in love,* she wondered, *or did this happen to every couple?* If it did, the thought frightened her. She was determined to gain back what they once had.

Sometimes late at night as they made love, she would lay in their king-sized bed and let her mind wander. She pretended to instruct him, tell him what to do, where to kiss. She'd ask him if he forgot her secret spots, and he would then ignite the slowly fading fire.

She chose to hold these thoughts in. She realized thinking something and saying it were two different things. She was afraid. She didn't want to hurt his feelings, and she definitely didn't want him going off to be with some other woman, just to prove he still had it.

So she put up with the mediocre sex and wondered if he was doing the same.

Little did she know, Zyair was getting bored with their sex life as well. The fireworks and the umph was gone. It wasn't like he wasn't attracted to Champagne anymore. He was. To him, she was still fine and sexy. He was still drawn to her, still interested. Heck, he was ready to marry her. So why wasn't their sex life the way it used to be? Why wasn't it as intense as it used to be? He remembered when they used to have to dry their bodies off because of the steam they created together.

They used to have sex in every room, and everywhere. She'd even given him a blowjob in the car not once or twice but a number of times. Now he could count the number of times she'd suck his dick in a month on one hand. What the hell was going on with them? He wished he had the answer.

Sometimes while they were making love, he would feel his dick go soft. He would then have to close his eyes and fantasize. Normally, that fantasy included another woman. So common, he thought, but he couldn't help it. He didn't have this fantasy because he wanted to sex someone else down. He did because he believed it would enhance what was slowly fading. He also knew it was an ego thing. He wanted to be "the man," the one to satisfy two women. He also wanted to see his woman being pleased. He loved how she looked when she was at the point of no return, the way her eyes would close and her mouth would part, and she would arch her back and let out a soft moan.

The other reason was because, honestly, his mind did stray and he did think about new pussy every now and again, and this way he could actually get it without cheating. So, on second thought, maybe he did want to sex another woman down.

Just like Champagne, he didn't say anything. He didn't want her to kick him out or kick his ass. She might even have accused him of having an affair, which wasn't the case. That was in the past, where it belonged. He'd been there, done that, got caught, and won't do it again.

Zyair Truesdale owned his own business. Well, actually it used to be his parents', and when they'd retired, they turned it over to him. Both parents were now deceased. His father had died four years earlier of a heart attack, and his mother less than a year later, of heartache. At least, that's what he believed.

Being the educated brother he was, he capitalized on it in a big way. Because of his business sense, Zyair was able to live comfortably. He thanked his parents in his prayers and knew they would've been proud of him and what he'd done with the business.

Private Affairs, an upscale restaurant and catering service, had two locations, one in New Jersey, the other in Georgia. His plan was to open a third in Miami within the next two years. Only the rich or well-off could afford the prices, and that's how Zyair wanted to keep it. The food was not only delectable but the ambiance was classy. And on Thursday through Sunday, he showcased live bands.

It was where Zyair and Champagne met. She was wining and dining one of her potential clients,

Jackson Davis, an up-and-coming actor who'd just landed a movie with top billing stars, and he was looking for someone to get his name and face out there. He'd heard that Champagne was the one.

Jackson was flirting with her, trying to get the message across that he was interested in more than business but she pretended like she didn't notice.

From across the room, Zyair couldn't take his eyes off her but didn't want to say anything, not knowing if they were on a date. It was obvious that the gentleman she was with wanted more than she was willing to give. Every now and then, he would try to take her hand, and she would pull back. He'd lean in a little close, and she'd lean away. Zyair chuckled to himself. "Damn, brother, can't you take a hint?"

Finally, Champagne stood up to go to the ladies' room.

Zyair saw this as his opportunity. He walked a short distance behind her, and paced a short distance from the bathroom door, waiting for her to come out.

When she stepped out and started heading toward her table, he approached her. "Excuse me, are you and your date enjoying your meal?"

Champagne placed her hands on her hips and playfully asked him, "Are you a restaurant critic or something?"

Laughing, he told her he was the owner of the establishment and was just checking on his most attractive customer.

Flattered, Champagne smiled. She liked the fact that he was straight to the point. She had noticed him watching her and already knew who he was. After all, she worked in the public relations field, and it was her business to know everyone with status, especially in the African American community.

A month earlier, she went out to lunch with Alexis, her best friend since college. She'd just read a feature article on him in Black Enterprise and was impressed. After showing his picture to Alexis, she joked, "This man is fine as hell. Rich and smart. I'm fine, going to be rich, and bordering on brilliant. Don't you think we'd make a good couple?"

Alexis laughed. Little did she know, that prediction might be coming true. Would she laugh when she heard that she might stand a chance?

"Well," Zyair said, interrupting her thoughts, "are you and your date having a good time?"

"He's not my date, he's a client. And, yes, we're having a good time." Champagne glanced toward the table and noticed Jackson looking their way.

"I have to get back."

"What's your name?"

"Champagne Rose."

"Really?"

"Yes, really."

Placing her right hand in his, he brought it to his lips and placed a soft kiss on it. "Well, Champagne Rose, can I call you or see you again?"

Looking him in the eyes and shaking on the inside, Champagne said, "How about I call you?"

"You don't know my name or my number."

"Zyair Truesdale," she told him, "and I'll call you here." On that note she walked away and left him with a smile.

"She knew who I was all along," he said to himself.

He liked a woman that played hard to get.

Sometimes Champagne would think back to that moment and recall the rush of talking to him the first time. She wished they could go back and start all over again. Maybe not all over, because they'd overcome a lot and some things she didn't want to repeat. What she did want a repeat of was the energy of a new relationship. Realistically, she knew it was too late for that, but it wasn't too late to make some kind of change.

Chapter Two

"Let's Wait Awhile"

Janet Jackson

Champagne was irritated by the waiter's rudeness and intended on telling him so. Then again, maybe she was just on edge considering she and Zyair were out to dinner to have "a talk," the two most dreaded words in a relationship.

Lately they'd been having a lot of disagreements about nothing and at the most inopportune times. Sometimes it would start first thing in the morning, putting a damper on the rest of her day and leaving her unable to focus and with her mind racing.

Zyair would be doing the same.

Each would think of what they should have said or how they could have handled the situation better. If the disagreement wasn't first thing in the morning, it was right before bedtime, leaving them unable to sleep, but faking it for fear another disagreement would start up.

Everything one of them did seemed to irritate the other. It didn't matter what it was, from leaving the plate on the table, to leaving the toilet seat up, or talking loud on the phone. There was entirely too much tension in the house, and it was time to bring it to a head.

Earlier that day, fed up with the nonsense, Champagne suggested they go out to dinner to "talk and discuss some things."

Zyair agreed, figuring it would be an opportunity to get some things off his chest as well. He was ready to get out of this rut they were in and move forward.

They sat at the Soul Africana cafe, having cocktails and waiting on their appetizers.

"So," Zyair said, making a weak-ass effort to break the ice.

"So?" Champagne replied.

Zyair loosened his tie. "What's on your mind?"

Champagne took a deep breath. "I feel like our relationship is at a standstill. I feel like it's taken a turn for the worst, like something is missing, like we're stuck in a place I don't want to be in. I don't want to continue feeling this way, and I need to know if you're feeling the same way." There she'd said it. Now all she had to do was wait on his response.

For a moment Zyair didn't respond. He'd suspected what this talk would be about but for her to blurt it out, putting it out in the air that way took him off guard. He wondered if it was his fault or whether they were both to blame. He knows that it takes two to make or break a relationship. Was theirs broken or in need of slight repair? "I agree," he told her. "So what do you propose?"

Since he agreed, Champagne wondered why didn't he bring this up before she did, and how long he'd been holding back.

"I don't know. Maybe a vacation, maybe counseling, maybe time apart."

"Time apart?"

That threw Zyair for a loop. Why would they need time apart? A relationship can't be fixed with time apart, you needed to be together to make it work. Maybe what she really was saying is that she wanted to break up? Damn, could that be it? Could that be the real reason behind this talk? He didn't want that. Despite their differences, he couldn't imagine growing old with anyone else. That whole getting out there, meeting new people, learning their quirks, their likes and dislikes was a lot of work, and he had enough work on his plate. He'd had his share of gold diggers and wasn't ready to experience the drama again.

"Time apart? How is time apart going to help us?"

"I suggested more than time apart, and if you felt the same way why didn't you say anything?"

"Honestly . . . because I didn't know what to say. I couldn't pinpoint what was wrong."

"But you knew something was?"

Zyair sighed and reached across the table, and Champagne placed her hand on top of his. "Yes, Champagne, I did. Listen, I don't know what you want me to say. I don't have any solutions, but I do know that time apart is not what we need. Maybe what we do need is time together on some exotic island, away from the pressures of work and other outside sources."

Before Champagne could say anything, the waiter returned, placed their appetizers on the table, and walked away. Didn't even ask if they needed anything else.

Champagne tried to pull her hands away to call the waiter over, but Zyair, knowing how she was about service, squeezed her hands. "What do you think the problem is?"

"I don't know either. I just feel like things have gotten routine, and that we got too contented."

"Contented? You say that like it's a bad thing." He removed his hands.

"I'm not saying that at all. What I'm saying is, sometimes I wish we still had that I-can't-wait-to-see-you and-want-to-be-around-you-every-minute-of-the-day anticipation we had when we first got together."

"Champagne, is that realistic?"

"Probably not but the thought is nice."

***

Zyair smiled because he remembered that feeling like it was yesterday, the anxiety of the first phone call one week after their initial meeting at Private Affairs. Thoughts of her overwhelmed him, and he just couldn't stop thinking about her. He wondered if she would call or if she just played him.

Right when he'd given up hope, she called. He was unavailable at the moment, busy going over a contract with the new chef, and told his assistant to tell her he would call her back within the hour.

"Zyair?" she asked, when he said hello into the phone.

"How did you know it was me?"

"You're unforgettable," she flirted. It was because of caller ID and the fact that his voice and his lips were unforgettable.

"I'm glad you called. For a minute there I was giving up all hope," he told her.

After leaving the restaurant that day, she thought of him often. She wished she had given him her cell phone number instead of taking his.

"Girl, call the man," Alexis told her, "Remember, he asked you if he could see you again . . ."

"Yeah, you're right." Champagne dialed the number, full of anxiety and feeling like a child about to go the candy store, only to be told he'll call her back within the hour. She tried her hardest not to watch the clock but found herself doing it anyway.

"So how's your week been?" he asked.

"I've just been busy trying to make a dollar," Champagne said.

"You're a publicist, right?" He'd done his research. That's one of the perks of being rich. You can find out almost anything about anyone. He knew he was wrong for having her investigated, but before he took someone out or got too involved, he had to know a little bit about them.

Champagne didn't recall telling him. "Yeah. How did you know that?"

He lied, "One of my waiters recognized you. He worked an event for one of your clients."

She tried to recall his staff and couldn't. "Oh."

"Would you like to go out sometime?"

She thought he would never ask. "Sure. When?"

"Tomorrow around seven p.m. We could do dinner and perhaps a show."

"I'd like that."

They chatted for a short while longer and agreed to meet at Private Affairs and leave from there. Champagne wasn't ready for him to know where she lived.

That first date was like a fairy tale. He had a limo waiting outside for them.

"You go all out for all your dates?" Champagne asked, not really caring because she was the one getting the special treatment tonight.

"No, I wanted to impress you," he told her honestly.

"I also didn't want to have to concentrate on driving. I wanted all my attention to be on you."

Damn, a brother was smooth and fine.

Every date after that, they looked forward to with excitement. Maybe it was the newness of it all, getting to know one another, or the anticipation of the lovemaking they both determined would come sooner rather than later. It could have been the fact that when they met, they were both looking for someone to share their lives with and found it in each other.

Whatever it was, it had up and disappeared, and it was now time to address the issue.

"Let's take this opportunity and discuss the pros and cons of our relationship," Zyair suggested.

Champagne rolled her eyes. "This isn't about business, this is about us. Our relationship. Pros and cons? What kind of mess is that?"

"Well, you're the one who said you wanted to talk."

"I do."

"Well, I was just making a suggestion."

"Well, make another one."

Zyair sighed. "Okay, let's do it this way. You say one thing that needs to change or has been bothering you, and I'll do the same."

"We can't get mad at each other either, okay," Champagne said, not wanting this to turn into something ugly.

"I agree. This is about bettering us as a couple, not breaking each other down as individuals."

"Okay, I'll go first," Champagne volunteered. "Maybe we've gotten bored with one another."

"Bored? I don't know if that's it. Maybe we've gotten more like routine. Everything is the same. It's stagnant, our work schedules, what we do when we get home, even the sex."

"The sex?" Champagne panicked. She knew it and wanted to be the first to address it, but to hear him say it brought up all sort of insecurities.

"Why are you picking up on that one thing? You're the one who said we wouldn't get offended or anything."

"I know you're right. It's just that—never mind. You're also right about the sex thing."

It was now Zyair's turn to be offended. "Are you saying I don't please you?"

"Are you saying I don't please you?"

They just looked at one another, Champagne thinking of him straying, Zyair wondering how many orgasms she's faked.

Champagne broke the silence. "You please me, Zyair. It's just that we barely kiss, we barely touch. You just go right for the gusto." *Even when you do that, I'm not wet enough. And when you go down on me, you act like it's not something you want to do. You just go straight for the clitoris. Whatever happened to licking around, tasting every inch of it?* Champagne thought to herself. There was no way she was going to say that part out loud.

Zyair frowned. "The reason we don't kiss is because you turn your head. The reason we don't touch is because you're always tired. And the reason I always go for the gusto is because I thought that's what you wanted." *Plus, you barely suck my dick. I feel like I have to force-feed you, and when you take it upon yourself you just lick it and put the head in. You don't devour it like you used to.*

"I guess we're both to blame for what's happened to us." Champagne tried to recognize.

"Yeah, I guess we are. So the question remains, what are we going to do about it?"

Champagne cleared her throat. "I have some suggestions."

"Go ahead."

"Let's make one day a week our date night. We have to do something together outside the house, something we normally wouldn't do."

"Like?"

"Take dance lessons, go to a play. We haven't done that in a while. Let's try a new restaurant. We almost always eat at yours, which isn't a bad thing but a change would be nice. We could play games, maybe even do things with other couples."

"Other couples like who?" Neither of them knew many.

"Alexis and whoever she's dating." Which, at the time was, no one.

Zyair frowned. He liked Alexis and all but she acted holier-than-thou, always talking about, "the Lord this, and the Lord that." Don't get him wrong, he believed in God and even attended church occasionally, but he just felt like she went overboard.

Besides, he didn't feel like hearing the when-are-you-two-going-to-get-married question. He was ready but it seemed like Champagne wasn't. And he couldn't pressure her because when she was ready for marriage he wasn't.

"We can do all those things. But why don't we do something real wild and go to Hedonism?"

"Hedonism?" Champagne asked.

"Yep."

"Isn't that the all-nude resort?"

They had watched a special on it together. Zyair was ready to pack his clothes and go by the time the first commercial aired. He was afraid to say anything because he thought Champagne would ask him if he was crazy. His best friend Thomas went and said it was off the hook. People were fucking everywhere, and you could actually sit there and watch. Heck, some folks even let you join in. Now that he wasn't too sure about, but the watching part he could get with.

Champagne surprised him by saying, "It does sound interesting. Let me think about it."

"Are you serious? You're really going to think about it?"

"Yes, but we also need to work on doing some of the things I suggested as well."

The rest of the evening went without incident. Both of them felt a sense of relief about getting some things off their chest.

That night when they arrived home, Zyair made the effort to be romantic. While Champagne was in the shower, he dimmed the lights and tried to create a soft, seductive setting. He pulled out a bottle of wine, made a pallet of pillows near the fireplace and turned on some Luther. Then he went to join her.

Stepping into the bathroom, he asked, "Do you mind if I join you?"

Surprised, she told him, "Of course not." Actually she was about to get out, but knew what he was trying to do and decided that, instead of pulling back, she would embrace this gesture.

A few seconds later, Zyair pulled back the doubled glass sliding door and took her in with his eyes. He loved what he saw.

Five years later, she was still beautiful, her skin flawless, smooth and tight, not an ounce of fat anywhere. How he could neglect her, he didn't know. His woman possessed what most men desired. Not only was she smart, sexy, beautiful, and compassionate, but she was also self-aware and selfless. She was also body and health conscious.

He roamed her body with his eyes and appreciated it once again. "I'm sorry I've been neglecting you. I'm going to start making it up to you from this day forward." He got undressed and stepped in the shower.

"The same here."

Champagne reached over with the washrag to rub his chiseled chest and washboard stomach. She teased him by moving her hands below his waist but stopped suddenly and said, "Turn around. Let me wash your back."

"This isn't supposed to be about me. This is supposed to be about you." Zyair took the buffer and placed it to the side. He then took the lavender-scented body wash and placed his hands on her shoulders. "I love you, you know that, right?" He moved his hands from her shoulders to her breasts, letting the suds build up. "I can't imagine not being with you." He started massaging her nipples with the palms of his hands. "You're my future wife." He moved his hands down her stomach to her thighs, as the soap washed away, and got on his knees. "The mother of my children." He pushed her knees apart and Champagne leaned against the wall, the water still running.

Zyair palmed her pussy. "Do you want me to kiss you here or on your lips first?"

Champagne looked down, lust in her voice. "Those lips."

Zyair pulled her pussy lips apart and placed one of his fingers deep within her. "How's this?"

Champagne nodded.

"I don't understand that. Tell me, how's this?" He took his finger out and stuck his tongue deep inside her, causing her legs to give.

"What about this?" He took his tongue out and started playing with her clitoris, flicking it back and forth, then licking it.

Champagne grabbed his head and tried to pull it into her pussy. "I thought you forgot about that."

He looked up at her. "Let me do this my way. I don't want you to tell me that I just go for the gusto ever again."

"And I don't want to have to tell you that."

That night ended with a passion they both thought they wouldn't get back. Maybe this would be the new beginning they both desired.

Chapter Three

"Just Got Paid"

Johnny Kemp

Champagne walked into her office, excited to start her day; only to find her boss, Charles Jackson, chilling in her space, behind her desk, like he belonged there. This irritated the hell out of her. She stopped in her tracks and started to curse his ass out but had to remind herself that him paying her was what paid her bills.

She loved her job. Maybe not where she worked and who she worked for, but she enjoyed doing what she did. She made people more famous than they already were. She came up with different ideas to do so, such as press conferences, dates with other stars, and magazine interviews. She also helped throw parties. Basically, she did what she had to do to get her clients more recognition.

In return she also received gifts, trips, and recognition, not to mention the friendships she developed with quite a few well-known actors, actresses, and singers.

Champagne started working for Jackson Publicity seven years ago as an assistant, and had worked her way up to becoming one of the top publicists. She would have gotten there even sooner, had she slept with her boss, who'd tried on numerous occasions, only to have her turn him down. But, like a true trooper, he wouldn't give up.

"Champagne," Charles Jackson said.

"Jackson," Champagne replied. When she'd first started working there, she called him Mr. Jackson but he kept insisting that she call him Charles, which was too personal for her liking, especially after his advances. Tired of the back-and-forth banter in regards to his name, she finally settled on calling him Jackson. "Do you mind if I take my seat?" she asked in a tight tone that let him know she was annoyed.

"Oh, of course not." He stood up and moved from behind her desk, brushing up against her in the process. She knew he did it on purpose and just wasn't feeling it today. Actually she was getting tired of it. Champagne looked at him with contempt. "So, what can I do for you?" She wanted him to get to the point of his visit and out of her sight. She knew there was a point, because he didn't come into her office often.

"Well, I'm getting you a partner."

Champagne looked at him.

"What?" She'd heard him, but wanted him to repeat it. He knew she worked alone.

The other publicists had assistants and interns but she didn't because she liked the flexibility of doing what she wanted, when she wanted, and not having to look over someone's shoulder or have them look over hers.

"I said, I'm getting you a partner."

"I've told you before, I don't want a partner."

"No, what you've said is that you don't want an assistant; there's a difference."

"I don't—" She was getting ready to say understand but decided not to give him the satisfaction of seeing her upset.

"The person's name is Camille Ferguson, and she'll start in one week. On your desk is her resume and an outline of what I want you to show her."

"Fine. Whatever." Champagne knew in her gut that if she'd slept with him at the last conference they attended, this shit wouldn't be happening.

"Do you have a problem with my decision?" he taunted.

"Yes, Jackson, I do. I don't think I have to tell you that."

A month earlier, Champagne, Charles, and Tiffany Sweeps, one of the other women in the office, attended a Minority Business Conference in Washington, D.C., where they took a number of workshops and networked extensively. On the second night there, they joined a few other participants for drinks, and everyone got a little past tipsy.

Champagne knew this wasn't kosher and decided to head back to her hotel room to get some rest. She told the others that she would catch up with them tomorrow.

"I'll grab a taxi and head back with you," Jackson said. "It'll be my treat."

"Oh, no, you don't have to do that."

"I know I don't have to. I want to."

Champagne thought nothing of it and accepted.

In the car, only a few words were exchanged. When they arrived at the hotel, she said good night and started heading toward her room, only to find Jackson following behind her.

She turned around. "Are you following me?"

"Yeah. I was hoping we could stay the night together."

Jackson was less than a foot from her, and for the first time that night, she realized just how drunk he was. "I don't think so." She placed her key into the keyhole.

"Why not, Champagne? You know I want you and have been waiting for quite some time." He was up in her face. "No one has to know. It'll be our little secret."

She knocked his hand down as he groped her breast. "I told you I'm not interested."

"Aw, come on." He leaned over and tried to kiss her. "Don't you know how far I can take you?"

She pushed him away. "You know this is sexual harassment, and you've been doing it for quite some time. I'd advise you to stop."

"Are you threatening me?"

"Do I have to?"

He took a step back. "Why are you so high and mighty? Just because you got a rich boyfriend don't mean shit. I've got almost as much money as he does."

"Please, just go away and leave me alone."

Jackson started walking away. "You know I can get pussy anytime. Don't think yours is special."

Champagne didn't feel a need to respond, she just shook her head, went into the room and avoided him for the rest of the conference. She spoke to him only if necessary.

When they returned to New York, the air was tight with tension, so she knew this was payback. It couldn't be anything else. She worked her ass off for him and got him the best clients possible. Even when he continued to be an asshole, she recruited for better clients and basically made his company the success it was today.

The time had come and Champagne knew what she had to do. It was time to move on. She'd been thinking about starting her own business anyway, and he'd just given her the opportunity.

She didn't want to react emotionally and up and quit in that moment. She had to sit down and plan her shit out. She wanted to take two clients with her, and she needed to prepare them.

Just knowing in that instant what her plans were calmed her down. She looked at Jackson and surprised him with, "Do what you have to do. If you think I need a partner, so be it. Now, if you don't mind, I have some phone calls I need to make."

Jackson was thrown off. He just knew she would be pissed. All the other women in the office kissed his ass but not Champagne, not even after all these years. He figured he would have worn her down by now. He was in love with her, and was angry that the love wasn't being returned.

"I'm planning on having a staff meeting the end of this week before Camille starts, so check your schedule."

The second he left her office, Champagne was on the phone with Alexis. "Girl, are you busy for lunch? I need to talk."

"Never too busy for you."

"All right, let's meet at our spot in the village around one p.m."

"I'll be there."

For the rest of the morning, Champagne made phone calls, confirmed a few interviews, and started putting together a plan for her new venture.

What she had in mind was a dual public relations/personal assistant business that would cater to the wealthy, famous or not. If you could afford her services, she would take you on as a client. Her goal would be to make the client's life easier by arranging their schedules, setting up appointments, booking vacations. Basically managing their lives. Champagne knew this wasn't something she could do on her own and would definitely have to hire people.

Damn, I hope I'm not getting in over my head, she thought to herself.

Champagne and Alexis met at Bojo's, a vegetarian spot. Alexis didn't eat anything that lived and roamed the earth. This cracked Champagne up because she knew that Alexis grew up on ham and bacon.

As always, they sat outside. They loved to take in the sights and talk about the people that walked by. This day, they wouldn't be doing that. Champagne had some serious business at hand she needed to discuss.

"Would you like something to drink?" the waitress asked.

"Some water and the menu," Champagne replied.
"With lemon."

The waitress walked away.

"So, what's up, lady? What's new?"

"Beside the fact that I'm leaving my job?"

"Get out!"

"Girl, I can't do it anymore."

"What happened? Don't tell me Jackson came on to you again. I told you, you should have told Zyair a long time ago."

"And I told you, I had it under control. But that's not why. He had the audacity to tell me he hired a partner for me."

"A partner? Do you need a partner?"

"No, I don't need a damn partner. I know he's only doing this because I won't sleep with him."

"Well, sue his ass."

"I don't feel like going through all that. Plus, I have a better plan."

Alexis was all ears.

"I've brought him most of the top clients, and I'm going to take them with me when I leave."

"What about the contract you signed saying you couldn't do that?"

"Girl, I haven't signed a contract in over a year. I think it slipped his mind, because I've been there so long."

"You've got to do what's best for you."

Before Champagne could say anything else, the waitress placed their water on their table along with the menus.

Champagne waited until she walked away. "You know, me and Zyair had a talk."

"The talk?"

"Yeah, girl, the talk."

"It's about time. I was getting a little tired of you complaining to me about the same things over and over."

"I was not."

"Yeah, you were. You just didn't realize it. You were starting to sound like a broken record."

"Well, how come you didn't say anything?"

"Because I'm your friend, and that's what I'm here for, to listen."

Alexis and Champagne had been friends since childhood, going back as far as the fourth grade. They grew up in Neptune, a small town in New Jersey, and lived next door to one another.

Just as in any relationship or friendship, the two had been through their ups and downs. During their elementary, middle and high school years, you couldn't keep those two apart. They did everything together. They joined the same club, coordinated their clothes, calling each other the night before to find out what the other was wearing, and sometimes even liked the same boys. When that happened they both chose to leave it alone, because no man was gonna come between them.

Then there was the "thing" neither of them would ever discuss, playing house with one another. One would be the mommy, and the other, the daddy, and they would take turns kissing, rubbing up against each other, feeling each other's breast, and occasionally fingering each other. This went on mostly during the middle school years, until they both became interested in boys. You would never think this took place, because they never acknowledged it.

They were different in personality and looks, total opposites but both beautiful. Alexis was a yellow girl, as the boys called her, and shapely, so she usually received most of the attention. It never caused a problem because, unlike most light-skinned girls back in the day, she didn't flaunt it. She just wanted to be regular. It was already bad enough that she could barely walk down the street without some asshole yelling obscenities.

Not one to take any shit, she'd always speak up and tell someone what was on her mind, causing many fights in her youth. Things hadn't changed. As an adult, she still did this. The only change now was that she was saved, sanctified, and filled with the Holy Spirit.

Champagne felt like she went overboard with it, "The Lord this, the Lord that . . ."

It started when they went away to college in New York. Alexis met this guy called Brother. Yep, that was his real name. He wanted to be a minister and attended church regularly. When he and Alexis started dating, he invited her to church.

From that point forward, Champagne thought Alexis had joined a cult. She started being judgmental, quoting Bible verses. She'd stopped going out and drinking, acting like Champagne wasn't good enough. It was to the point that they stopped speaking for over a year.

One evening Champagne went out and was a little hungover with a headache. She went to Alexis's dorm, thinking she would find some comfort and support, only to have Alexis pray for her.

After listening to Alexis try to pray the demons out of her, she told her, "Listen, I love you and all, but I can't take you judging everything I do and say. So maybe we need to chill a little. If you really need me, I'm here for you, but other than that, our friendship has reached a point where I no longer feel comfortable. I have to watch what I say and what I do. I'm always on guard and I feel like I can't be myself around you."

It was a heart-wrenching moment but something Champagne had to do for her peace of mind. It felt like a breakup. She cried for several days. She'd gotten used to picking up the phone and hearing her best friend's voice almost every day.

Often she'd find herself picking up the phone, and dialing the number only to hang it back up. Homegirl was having withdrawal symptoms. She didn't realize how much she'd come to depend on Alexis.

It was Alexis who needed Champagne first. Brother broke her heart. She'd caught him cheating with one of the sisters in the church. At the time, Alexis still considered herself a virgin, as far as penetration. Orally, no.

She came crying to Champagne, "I thought he was perfect for me. He was saved, he went to church, and he didn't pressure me to have sex."

I don't care how much church a man attends, Champagne thought. *If he's not getting the sex from his woman, he's getting the sex from somewhere.* But she didn't say anything, not wanting to kick a sister when she's down.

Alexis was still saved and she still had judgmental ways but thank God, no longer went overboard with it. So when Champagne told her about her and Zyair going to Hedonism, Alexis didn't tell her she was going to hell, she just said, "Are you out of your mind?"

There was no way in the world she would take her man to a place filled with beautiful, naked women. She certainly didn't want to be around a bunch of naked men running around with their dicks hanging out. It just wasn't something she wanted to see and she couldn't understand why Champagne would either.

"Have you two lost your natural minds? I can't believe Zyair would even suggest such a thing. And for you to accept, what were you thinking?"

"I was thinking that it's time to add some spice into my relationship."

"That's the only plan you two could come up with?"

"You're judging, Alexis," Champagne told her in a tone that reminded her how far they'd come.

"I know, and I'm sorry. But there has to be some other way to add a spark to your relationship. Going to the freak beach? I don't know, girl. Something about it just ain't right. Plus, you ain't never walked around nobody naked, so how are you going to feel walking around strangers naked?"

"They won't know me, I won't know them. That's what's going to make it easy."

"You might be biting off more than you can chew. What are you going to do when his dick gets hard?"

"What do you mean, what am I going to do? Hop on it. Plus, there isn't too much he can do while I'm right there."

"Well, what are you going to do when you see some Mandingo-looking man and he turns you on?"

"What do you think I'm going to do? Stare with my tongue hanging out."

They shared a laugh, easing the tension that was forming.

"You're sick, you know that?"

When Champagne returned to the office, she found a note on her desk from Jackson. He wanted her to put together a list of her clients and any pertinent information she wanted to share with Camille.

"To hell with that," Champagne said and packed up for the rest of the day.

Chapter Four

"Boys"

Mary Jane Girls

Zyair was sitting in his office, a huge smile plastered on his face. He recalled the way Champagne surprised him by sucking his dick the last night and did it like it was the best tasting dessert on this earth. He'd arrived home from work late that night because of a party for an up-and-coming male fashion designer that wasn't scheduled to end until after one in the morning. Zyair was tired, and the only thing on his mind was climbing into the bed.

To his surprise, Champagne had other things in mind. "Hey, sweetie," she greeted him when he walked in. Looking sexy as hell, she was relaxed in the sitting room in a short black negligee and a glass of wine in her hands.

From an earlier conversation, he knew she'd had a rough day at work and was surprised to see her up. "Why aren't you in the bed?"

"I was waiting for you to come home."

"That's sweet but you didn't have to do that."

"I know I didn't have to. I wanted to." Champagne stood up and gave him a kiss, took his hand, and pulled him toward the bedroom. "Now go and take your shower, and I'll be out here waiting with a surprise."

Zyair questioned her with his eyes but she wasn't giving anything away.

"Wash up good too," she told him. "Don't miss an inch."

While in the shower, Zyair wondered what she had planned. She did say, "Don't miss an inch." That meant a blowjob was in order, so he took extra care in cleaning his penis, under his balls, and his ass. One never knows.

Zyair stepped out of the shower and into the bedroom. He dried himself off with the towel. On the nightstand next to the bed were some items. He took a closer look at them—Honey Dust Body Powder, Motion Lotion, and some weird-looking vibrator. "What the hell is that?" he asked.

"It's called a cyberflicker."

"And what is it supposed to flick. I know you don't plan on that going anywhere near me."

"Come here. Just relax and let me do my thing."

"I don't know."

"Trust me, I'm not going to do anything I'm sure you won't like."

Zyair sat on the bed cautiously.

Champagne straddled him and pushed him back.

"Don't you want to talk about your day?" he asked, playfully.

"No. I have something better in mind." Champagne kissed him on his eyelids, causing him to shut them and then traced his lips with her mouth. She pushed him back on the bed, moved her legs to rest between his, and placed her hands on his penis, massaging it.

Moving down his body with her tongue, she reached over for the Motion Lotion and ran her tongue over his shaft.

Zyair had his eyes open and watched her every move. She rubbed the lotion over his penis, and with each hand movement it was heating up.

Zyair moaned. "That feels good."

"Well, this is going to feel even better." Champagne blew on his penis, causing a heated sensation and then draped her mouth around it and circled it with her tongue, up to the head.

"Oh, girl, what are you doing?" Zyair tried to sit up but she pushed him back down.

Instead of answering him, she proceeded to suck and lick every inch of him.

Zyair had his eyes closed and was giving his I'm-about-to-explode-at-any-moment face, when he heard this buzzing sound. "What the hell!" He opened his eyes in time to catch Champagne holding that "flicker thing" between his balls and ass. When she placed it there, his whole body tightened up.

"Come on, baby, relax. We said we wanted a change."

When he realized that she wasn't trying to put anything in him, he relaxed and enjoyed the feeling of the vibration, which ran up and down the length of his body. When she started licking his balls, he knew it would be over any minute.

"I'm going to cum any minute now. Let me inside of you."

Champagne wasn't hearing it. She was enjoying the moment.

"Ugh!" Zyair yelled out. "I'm about to cum." Champagne replaced her mouth with her right hand, dropped the flicker and massaged his balls with the left, while he exploded.

Afterward Zyair looked at her with love. "That was the bomb." He didn't even question her about the new items. He'd just had the best orgasm in quite some time. If she'd only swallowed, that would have topped it off.

Champagne went to wash her hands and get a rag to wipe Zyair down. When she returned he was sound asleep. Smiling and wishing she could pat herself on the back, Champagne was pleased with herself.

So here Zyair sat, recalling last night and thinking to himself, *I couldn't believe I let her put a damn vibrator anywhere near my ass.*

Shaking his head, he tried to clear his thoughts and concentrate on the work that lay before him, but before he could even do that, there was knock at the door.

"Who is it?"

His employees knew not to bother him, especially if his door was closed. Every other Friday, he took care of the financial end of the business, paying bills, reviewing his cash flow and paying his employees, and this was one of those days. He did this religiously. It enabled him to know, on a consistent basis, what he was bringing in and what he was putting out. No one could or would ever try to cheat him out of a penny. He knew where every cent went.

His business allowed him the luxuries of his Cadillac, Jeep, and Mercedes coupe that sat in the garage of his estate. It also allowed him to purchase Champagne the three-carat engagement ring she wore on her finger. Heck, it allowed him to be rich beyond his dreams and become richer in the upcoming years. Even his parents would be pleased at the success of the restaurant. Yes, it was a little more lavish than they'd initially planned but to make money, you had to spend money. And he expanded on their dreams, bringing to fruition what they couldn't.

"It's Thomas, nig—" Thomas stopped short. He almost slipped up and said the whole word.

"Hold up." Zyair got out of his chair and let Thomas in.

"What's up?" Thomas greeted. They gave each other a pound.

"Nothing. Just taking care of business as usual."

"Want to go out for lunch?"

Zyair gave Thomas a long, steady look.

"What? Whacha lookin' at me like that for?"

"Today is the second Friday of the month. What do I do the second Friday of every month? My finances. You know this, and still you drop in and expect me to—"

Thomas stood up. "How about this? I have free lunch while I'm here and we go out tonight instead, go to a strip club, see some naked ass, have a couple of drinks. I'ma call up Trevor and Wise and see if they want to join us."

Zyair really wasn't feeling it but he knew he'd been neglecting his boys for the last month. He glanced at the calendar and recalled that it was Thomas's birthday. Not letting on that he forgot, he said, "Cool. Anything for the birthday boy."

"Aww, nigga, I thought you forgot."

"You're my boy. I wouldn't forget your day."

"Yeah, okay. I saw you take a peek at the calendar."

Thomas and Zyair met during their first year of college. They attended Rutgers University in

New Jersey together, and hung out with the same crowd. One evening when they were standing in the hall, Thomas overheard Zyair talking about his sloppy-ass roommate that was pledging a fraternity. "I'm about to go upside his head."

Thomas was going through the same thing with his roommate and was in the process of finding an apartment off campus. He'd need a roommate if he wanted extra cash to spend on the ladies. He decided to approach Zyair. "Yo, man, I'm about to get an apartment off campus, if we split the cost, we can get a two bedroom and it'll save me a few dollars."

"Yeah, but what will it save me?" Zyair asked.

"I don't know what it'll save you, but you just might get peace of mind."

Zyair looked at him and tried to sum him up. He recalled seeing Thomas around campus talking to the finest ladies. He also knew that Thomas wasn't a slouch in the academics department. Although he dressed like a thug and talked liked he was from the streets, he ran track and stayed on the dean's list. He'd appreciate a change because his roommate was a slouch, loud, and irritating. Peace of mind was definitely something he could use.

"Yo, man, thanks. It sounds like a plan but I need to see the place first." Zyair wasn't stupid. He knew that college students could only afford so much. He knew what he could afford, and he wasn't too sure if he wanted to give up safety for comfort.

The apartment turned out to be in a decent area of New Brunswick, close to downtown and near public transportation, so he moved in.

Thomas and Zyair got off to a smooth start. Both of them were neat freaks. Nothing was ever out of place. When they had women over; they were always impressed, especially when they learned they kept the place up themselves. They also never had any major disagreements, especially when it came to women. Zyair liked them attractive and smart, while Thomas liked them ugly and dumb. His theory was ugly women treat you better because they want to hold on to you and would do just about anything to make that happen. Zyair didn't have a theory. He just wanted someone he could carry a conversation and be seen in public with. It wasn't long before they became the best of friends.

They'd stay up late at night and talk about any and everything under the sun. They had each other's back. Where one might slack off in studies, the other picked up. They complemented one another, balanced each other out.

They became like brothers. Zyair's parents would send Thomas necessities when they sent Zyair's, who never felt cheated because he knew Thomas grew up in a foster home without family.

Thomas and Zyair still had each other's back. They'd drink together and even go so far as to have sex in the same room. Well, that was before Champagne came along.

Occasionally Zyair would recall with disdain an incident that took place their senior year. They'd had a party to celebrate their upcoming graduation. Drinks were flowing, and weed was being passed back and forth like water. Everyone was having the time of their lives.

As the clock ticked and hours passed, the crowd started to disburse, until there was about ten people left. And what was a party with people dancing, laughing, and having a good time became an orgy.

How it happened is still beyond Zyair's knowledge. All he knew was that one minute he was kissing this girl on the couch, and two minutes later he looked up to find a group of five having sex near the fireplace, and two other couples off to the side doing their thing. Dicks were being sucked, people were fucking doggy style.

There was no pussy eating. Back then, that was something the brothers denied doing, so to actually be seen doing it was out of the question.

Full of liquor and weed, Zyair decided to see just how far he could go with his female friend. It ended up being all the way.

Later that night, after everyone left, Zyair lay semiconscious out on his bed. He could barely move. His head was pounding. That night was his first night experimenting with weed, and he recalled hearing someone say it was laced with something.

Feeling a little out of it, he found himself falling asleep. He woke up with someone's lips wrapped around his penis. Not even bothering to open his eyes, he figured it was the girl he'd been with earlier. He decided to go with the flow and take the pleasure ride. He started moving his hips and grinding into the person's mouth and went to reach for their head when he heard his door open.

"What the fuck?" Thomas yelled out.

Zyair opened his eyes and looked down to find Ty'ron, a classmate and fellow partygoer with his dick in his mouth. Shocked, embarrassed, and confused because it was feeling so good, Zyair's initial reaction was to jump up and push Ty'ron's head away. He then kicked him in the chest, causing him to fall back. Zyair was about to beat his ass to pulp but Ty'ron got up to run out the room.

"Close the door!" Zyair called out.

Thomas did as he was told.

Zyair looked at Thomas and tried to convince him. "Yo, man, I'm not gay. I was in here passed out. I wake up and this motherfucka has my dick in his mouth." Zyair took a step toward Ty'ron.

Ty'ron covered his face, like the punk he was, and immediately started apologizing.

Zyair was up on him when Thomas said, "Wait! Wait!" and stood between them.

"Move out of my way, man, or you're going to get hurt too."

"Nah, man. I've got a better idea. Let's humiliate him instead. That's what we used to do in foster care."

"Fuck humiliation! He needs his ass kicked!"

Thomas started to unzip his pants and turned toward a frightened Ty'ron. "You want to suck some dick? Here's a dick for you."

Zyair was shocked. "Yo, man, what the fuck are you doing?"

"Let him finish his job on the both of us."

Zyair looked at Thomas like he'd lost his mind. "I ain't gay, man."

"And neither am I. He started it, let him finish."

Zyair, not being sure what to do and caught between confusion and anger, decided to just follow Thomas' lead, and together they forced Ty'ron to do them both. They knew he wouldn't say anything for fear of what it would do to his reputation.

This incident stayed their secret. They never told a soul about it and discussed it only once, and that was the following day.

"Yo, man, what made you come into my room?" Zyair asked.

"Well, when you were doing Sarah, I saw Ty'ron watching, and it looked like he was watching you harder than her. When you went to your room, he said he was going to the bathroom. Something just didn't feel right. He was taking a long-ass time to come back, so I thought I'd check on you. Shit, you better be glad I did because ain't no telling how far he would have tried to go."

"How come you just didn't let me beat his ass?"

"That would have been too easy."

"I don't know, Thomas. I don't feel right about what we did. I'm not gay, and the shit feels wrong."

"Man, please . . . just because you let another man suck your dick don't make you gay. When I was in foster care, it was either that or get beat down. Which route would you have taken? Don't even worry about it. It's between us. We don't even have to talk about it anymore."

To Zyair, just because it wasn't talked about didn't mean it didn't happen. It was something he thought about occasionally but never discussed ever again with anyone. He decided that the incident was something he would take to his grave.

Later that evening Zyair and Champagne sat on the couch discussing Champagne's business plan. Suddenly Zyair glanced at his watch. "Oh, shit."

"What's up?" Champagne asked.

"I forgot I told Thomas and the boys I'd hang out with them. Today is Thomas' birthday."

Champagne didn't know whether to believe him or not. It's funny how insecurity can creep up on you at any given moment. Ever since they'd had their we-need-a-change-in-our-relationship talk, she'd been second guessing herself. Then out of the clear blue sky, Zyair informed her that he was hanging out that night, which didn't make it any better. She knew that he was anal about his schedule.

"Where are y'all going?" she asked.

"I'm not sure, but I'll call you while I'm out."

That made her feel a little better, because he couldn't be doing too much if he telephoned her.

"What time do you think you'll be back?"

Zyair stood up. "Why the third degree?"

"What? I can't ask you any questions?"

Not in the mood for an argument, Zyair chose not to answer. Instead, he just leaned over and kissed her on the forehead. "I'll call you while I'm out."

Chapter Five

"Friends"

Whodini

Zyair and his boys had taken to doing something at least once a week.

While in the mall shopping, Champagne admitted to Alexis that she was a little jealous.

"Girl, please . . . don't be jealous. A man needs his space, just like a woman does. I'm sure you don't want to be cooped up under some man all day every day. You need to be you and let him be him."

"I know, but I've gotten spoiled. It's just been me and him for the past couple of months."

"Reality check! You've also been miserable. Plus, you're going to have him for the rest of your life. What's a couple of hours here and there?"

Champagne knew Alexis was right. She also knew she was going through some emotional shit right now. She felt like she was on some sort of roller coaster. She was definitely leaving her job.

She was going to start a new company, and to top all that off, Jackson expected her to train the new girl. She was feeling a little sensitive and a lot overwhelmed.

Camille, her new partner came in making demands, acting like she was Whitney or some other diva. Champagne knew that Camille and Jackson were fucking. The way he was rolling out the red carpet for her, there couldn't have been any other reason. He was even paying her a higher starting salary than normal, and as if that weren't enough, what really broke the camel's back was when he tried to hand over one of Champagne's better clients, who politely told him that the only person he was interested in working with was Champagne.

Thank God, she had already talked to some of her clients and informed them she was leaving. Most of them said they would like to continue having her service them, no matter where she was employed. She informed them that she would have to look over their contracts first. She didn't want to get into trouble legally by stealing clients under contract. If she discovered she couldn't be held liable for them leaving, so be it.

"You know, tomorrow is the day I'm officially handing in my resignation."

Alexis didn't hear her because she was looking at a pair of shoes. Champagne knew not to repeat herself because nothing came between Alexis and her shoes.

"What do you think of these?" Alexis held up a pair of white three-inch heels.

"I don't like white shoes, you know that."

"Well, humor me."

"Anyway, I'm resigning tomorrow, and I'm a little nervous about it."

"That's understandable." Alexis looked at the cashier and told her she'll take the shoes in a size eight. "Champagne, honey, you're about to embark on a big project. Starting your own business isn't something small. You have a right to be nervous. I believe in you, though. You're smart, and you're a go-getter. It'll all work out."

Champagne heard what Alexis was saying. She knew she was right about her being a go-getter. Shit, mostly everything in life she wanted to achieve she'd achieved. She and her brother Sir were raised by a single mom, who tried her damnedest to instill in them a sense of pride and self-esteem. She told them over and over that they could be whatever they wanted to be and do whatever they set their minds on doing. Champagne believed her. Sir didn't. Growing up, neither of them knew their fathers.

Sir was two years older than Champagne and always seemed to have a hard time, as a child and as a man. It was like he was cursed. He just couldn't seem to get it together. He did average in high school, flunked out of college, couldn't find a job, and turned to drugs.

Champagne blamed it on the fact that there wasn't a male figure around, someone to guide him and be an example. Champagne and her mother tried to help him the best they knew how but to no avail. Sir committed suicide at the age of twenty-two. It devastated Champagne. She went into a shell for over a year, not talking to anyone or doing anything. School was all that mattered to her. She was determined to graduate at the top of her class.

Champagne became an overachiever and sometimes she still found herself falling into the am-I-doing-enough, am-I-achieving-enough trap. Every time you turned around there was something else she wanted to do. First, she wanted to be a teacher, then a counselor, then in the arts. She went back to school to get her master's and was considering going back to get her doctorate. Why? Because she could. She often wondered, *Why settle, when the world has so much to offer?*

What drove her were memories of her brother and his unhappiness, his insecurities, his failures and, most of all, his suicide. There was no way she would be so displeased with her life that she

would take her own, so her response was to con-
sume herself with work and Zyair. She knew it was
unhealthy, but she didn't know what else to do
about it.

After her brother's death, she and her mother
barely spoke. Whenever she tried to initiate a
relationship, she was pushed away. Eventually she
gave up but her plan was to correct that soon.

"You know what? You're right, I can do this. I'm
intelligent, I'm talented, I've made some of the clients more popular than they ever believed possible.
Most of them want to come with me when I leave,
so what do I have to be concerned about?"

Alexis smiled. "Now that's what I like to hear."

"What's on your agenda this evening?" Champagne
didn't have anything planned, Zyair was working
late, and she didn't feel like being by herself.

"I've got a hot date, girl."

"Get the hell out of here. When was the last time
you've been on a date? Does he go to your church
or something?"

"No, he don't go to my church. And why you
gotta rub in the fact that I haven't been on a date in
some time? Actually I met him at the Laundromat."

"The Laundromat? What were you doing at
the Laundromat? You have a washer and dryer
at home."

"Something is wrong with the dryer. Anyway, let me finish. I had just finished putting my clothes in the dryer and was about to walk out when this fine, with a capital F, brother strutted in. I was about to leave, but I hesitated."

"You hesitated?" This surprised Champagne because Alexis never ever made the first move. She was a Christian and believed that women shouldn't go looking for men, that men are the hunters.

"Yeah, girl, that's how fine he was. Not only that but there was this magnetism about him that just drew me."

Champagne couldn't believe what she was hearing.

She laughed. "Magnetism?"

Ignoring her; Alexis continued, "So I turned around and decided to wait until my clothes dried and see if he would strike up a conversation."

"Did he?"

"After a good ten minutes of waiting and not even a hello, I said to him, 'Are you new around here? I've never seen you before.'"

"No, you didn't."

"Yes, I did, girl. It was a weak line, but it worked. He's new in town. Only been here for three weeks. His name is Khalil. He works construction."

That surprised Champagne because Alexis usually didn't go for blue-collar brothers. "Construction?"

"Yes, construction. Anyway, we talked a little more, and he asked me if I'd like to go out for dinner one night. So I said yes."

"You said yes?"

"I figure why not. I've been praying for God to send me the right mate, and I'm not saying he's it, but I know I need to be more open and stop carrying this list in my head on what the perfect man is."

"I know that's right, because your list was unrealistic." Champagne recalled Alexis and her pulling out a piece of paper with "the qualities of a good man" on it. It went something like this: Christian man, honest, hard-working, making sixty Gs a year, over six feet tall, in good physical condition, great lover, no kids, must be at least thirty.

After reading the list, Champagne told her, "I've already got the man."

"Don't brag."

"What are you willing to compromise on?" Champagne asked.

"Well, you know there's one thing I'm not comprising on, and that's him being a Christian."

"Is he?"

"Yes. I asked him what churches has he attended since he's been in town. He said that was the first thing he did, find some place to serve the Lord."

"Get out of here."

"I know, right. "

Champagne was glad for Alexis and told her so. "Make sure you call me, no matter what time it is, and let me know how things go."

"You know I will."

They shopped a little while longer and separated in the parking lot.

Champagne hoped this Khalil guy was the one for Alexis. She was tired of seeing her best friend single, and thought she deserved a man, some children, and the white picket fence with the big yard, all the things little girls dream of having when they picture their lives as women.

When Champagne was young she dreamed of being rich beyond her means, jet-setting from place to place, purchasing whatever she wanted, whenever she wanted it. A man was never in the picture. Don't get it twisted, Champagne didn't think she'd be lonely for life but her main concern was to make her life successful. She'd been in and out of relationships, mostly shortterm, dated occasionally, and had sex once in a while. Then she met Zyair and her life plan changed.

One evening Champagne and Zyair were out to dinner. Their relationship was just getting off the ground, and they were both in denial of their feelings toward each other. Of course, neither wanted to be the first to admit that they were falling in love. They were both afraid of jumping into a relationship headfirst, due to past romantic failures. They both tried to be nonchalant about what they had, not labeling it and just letting it be, although, neither could deny their feelings were growing stronger by the day.

While at dinner, Zyair asked, "What does a man represent to you?"

Thrown off, Champagne asked, "What kind of question is that?"

"Just a question." Zyair wanted to see where her head was. He was ready to make her "the one."

"I don't know how to answer that."

"Answer it honestly."

Shit, that was a question she'd never given any real thought to. She knew what a man was supposed to represent, security, peace, family, a sense of well-being, but up to this point she hadn't seen any evidence of that. To her; a man just represented companionship, a date, and sex. She didn't want to tell him that because thinking it made her feel a little apprehensive, so saying it out loud surely wouldn't be any better.

"Companionship," she told him, leaving the rest out. He was satisfied. "What's companion, to you?"

"Someone to talk to, someone to share your wishes, your dreams, and your securities with. Someone to cuddle with and make love to."

Zyair knew he could be those things.

***

Returning to the present moment, Champagne glanced at her Gucci watch, an extravagant gift from Zyair, and saw that time was ticking. Sometimes she felt like he spent way too much money on her. Not that she was complaining, because being spoiled was nice, she just wasn't used to it. She made well over seventy K a year and saved more than she spent, which was a good thing now that she thought about it, especially since it allowed her to start her own business.

Instead of going home, Champagne decided to go to the office to copy the clients' files she was interested in taking with her. She'd been glancing through them all week but not wanting to make it too obvious, decided to wait until the last possible moment to make copies. No one should be in the office other than the security guard, who she knew wouldn't say a word, because Jackson treated him with arrogance and disregard.

When Champagne arrived at the office she was surprised that Jimmy, the security guard, wasn't at his post. As she walked toward her office, she noticed that Jackson's door was slightly ajar and that a ray of light was shining through the crack. She could also hear soft music playing in the background.

Knowing she was wrong and nosy for what she was about to do, she moved closer to the door and peeked through the crack, only to see Camille dancing seductively in front of Jackson. The form-fitting skirt and jacket she wore to the office was on the floor, while she paraded in a red spaghetti-thin G-string panty, black thigh-highs, and a red lacy bra with her breasts flowing over the top.

Champagne looked at Camille and noticed that she appeared much thicker in the near-nude than fully dressed. It was a kind of thickness that would turn on any man, or woman if you went that way. It was definitely turning on Jackson, whose attention was razorsharp, watching every hip thrust and every pelvic movement.

When Camille's hand caressed her stomach and moved on to her breast, squeezing her nipples, his eyes followed. When her hands moved down between her legs, rubbing her pussy, his eyes followed. Champagne found her eyes following as well.

When Camille turned around, Champagne noticed that her eyes were closed. She bent over in front of Jackson, and he grabbed her ass and started massaging her buttocks. Champagne could feel her pussy walls opening and closing, and that could only mean one thing. The scene before her was turning her on. She didn't quite know how to react to this. On one hand she was disgusted with herself. On the other, she had to admit that curiosity was getting the better of her.

Common sense finally took over, and she turned away and hurried toward her office. Sitting behind her desk, she tried to catch her breath. There was no way she was going to stay here and make copies, after the episode she'd just witnessed.

Now, the challenge was getting out unnoticed and unheard. Grabbing the files she wanted from inside her desk, she walked softly into the hallway, careful not to make a sound. She made it down the hallway, past Jackson's office, and out the front door. Everything in her wanted to turn around and take one last look, but the fear of being caught was enough to make her leave the premises.

On the way home, Champagne stopped off at Kinko's to make the copies she needed. She knew Zyair wouldn't be home until late that night. There was a conference being held at his restaurant, and he liked to stay and make sure things ran at a smooth pace.

Pulling up into the driveway, Champagne had a brief flashback of Jackson and Camille. She shook the image out of her head but not before recalling the fullness of Camille's breasts. "What the hell is wrong with me?" she asked herself.

Chapter Six

"Caught In The Middle"

Will Smith

Zyair was looking across the floor at a group of people gathered near the bar and couldn't help but notice that one of the men in the group looked real familiar. At least, his profile did, because he hadn't yet turned around to give Zyair a full view of his face. Taking a step forward to get a closer look, Zyair turned quickly because, at that exact moment, the brother turned around. It was the last person on earth Zyair wanted to see, Ty'ron the dick sucker. It was a college memory Zyair wanted to erase from his mind altogether.

Ty'ron noticed Zyair the second he walked in the restaurant and was torn between leaving and staying. But leaving really wasn't an option, since he was one of the speakers. The conference was for Financial Advisors, and Ty'ron worked for one of the top Black owned companies in the United States. With the knowledge that he possessed, he was capable of making someone rich beyond their dreams.

When Ty'ron first entered the restaurant and saw Zyair, he didn't know whether to approach him and apologize, or knock the shit out of him. The college incident stayed in the back of his mind. He knew he was wrong for violating Zyair in his sleep. In a way he felt that he deserved what Zyair and his boy Thomas did, but then again, he would have preferred the ass whupping Zyair was going to lay on him.

Ty'ron couldn't help but wonder if he and Thomas were still in touch. *Damn, Zyair still looked good as hell.* He was always a handsome man. If given the chance I'd turn his ass out. Ty'ron knew he was dead wrong for these thoughts. Instead of focusing on Zyair, he needed to focus on his speech.

In the meantime, Zyair glanced at Ty'ron and wondered if he was gay. He had to be, the way he'd sucked his dick like a pro. From his appearance, you couldn't tell because he looked all man. In this day and age you could never tell a person's sexuality by their appearance. All you had to go on was their word.

Turning around, Zyair decided it was time to leave. All of a sudden he felt a headache coming on and was developing an upset stomach. Finding his hostess DaNeen, Zyair told her, "I'm leaving you in charge."

"You are?" DaNeen asked, surprised.

Zyair normally stayed to the end when something was going on in the restaurant. "Yes. Just make sure everything is cleaned and locked up."

"I will. You don't have to worry about a thing."

"All right, I'll see you tomorrow." On that note, Zyair walked out.

Once in the car Zyair pounded on the steering wheel. He yelled out loud, "Shit!" He'd put the incident so far in the back of his mind, and to have it standing there, staring into his face, was mind-blowing. Now was definitely the time for that vacation he and Champagne had discussed.

Which is just what Champagne suggested the second Zyair walked in. She didn't let him get in the door good. "Baby, let's take that vacation we talked about as soon as possible."

"Whoa, whoa. Where did this come from?"

"I'm just ready to go. Tomorrow is my resignation day, and before I start a new venture I'd like to spend some time with you," she said, following him into the living room.

"I hear you. Shit, I'm ready for that vacation just as much as you are. Where do you want to go?"

"I thought we discussed Hedonism?"

This surprised Zyair. When he'd first suggested it he didn't think she'd agree. "For real?"

"Yes, for real." Champagne was half-amused hearing the excitement in his tone. She also knew that his imagination was running wild and after witnessing Jackson and Camille, she knew she could do the voyeur thing. "Let's call the travel agency and leave this weekend."

Zyair almost said that was too soon that he needed to arrange things at the restaurant. Normally he'd make sure things were in order, doubled check the calendar, speak with his employees and give them a "watch everything and make sure nothing goes awry" speech. This time he wasn't going to do that. He knew it was time to trust them, to let go and enjoy life a little more.

Plus, after seeing Ty'ron, he needed the vacation just as much as Champagne and the sooner the better, the farther away the better. "Let's do it." Zyair said.

Pleased, Champagne kissed him on the cheek and suggested they go swimming.

"I don't feel up to it."

"But I have a surprise for you." Champagne was using her suggestive tone.

Zyair recognized it but the headache that started earlier was now pounding. He took her hand. "I'm sure you do, sweetie, but I have a terrible headache. I need to take some Advil and lay down."

Disappointed because her plan was to put it on him, Champagne said, "Oh, okay." She kissed him on the cheek and told him to get comfortable while she made him some chamomile tea to relax him.

***

The following day Champagne was standing in Jackson's office. Her heart was racing. Uncertain about how he would respond, she was anxiety ridden and fearful. "I'm resigning," she told him. "I'm giving you one month's notice, but I'm leaving for a one week vacation, so I won't be in next week and—"

"Whoa, whoa, hold up. Hold the fuck up. What the fuck are you talking about? What's this all about?"

Champagne was fed up, she was done, and no longer had to put with his attitude, and she wanted him to know it. "I know you need to stop talking to me like that."

Going on, Jackson said, "Do you really think you could just come in here and quit just like that? Like you haven't signed a contract? Like you're not obligated to several clients? And on top of everything else, you tell me, not ask me, but tell me you're taking a one week vacation."

"I'm not a child, Jackson. I'm not a child, and I'm not one of your bitches that need to ask your permission. As a matter-of-fact, I'm a grown-ass woman that hasn't signed a contract in over two years. Your ass forgot, and I didn't mention it. This is your business. That's the kind of shit you're supposed to keep tabs on, not me. I'm going on vacation. I have more than enough time saved up, and I've contacted my main clients and told them

I was resigning. I also informed them that your lover, Camille, would be taking over." That part slipped out but Champagne was on a roll. "Not only that, but—"

"But nothing, but nothing. You owe me. I made you!" Jackson said hysterically. He depended on Champagne more than he thought. She'd trained everyone that came in after her and made him tons of money. She'd convinced his best clients to stay with him when he acted like an asshole, and was always the middleman when there was conflict.

What the hell did she mean, she hasn't signed a contract in two years. Thinking about it, he realized she was right. She hadn't, and that possibly meant that some of the clients hadn't either. This wasn't something he felt like dealing with. Jackson knew that the right thing to do would be to sweet talk her, offer her a raise, maybe even a partnership but his anger got the better of him. "You know what? You can leave right now. I don't need any notice. Pack your shit and go."

Champagne looked him up and down and shook her head. "That's just what I wanted to hear." Then she turned around and strolled out of his office, leaving him with a stunned look on his face.

"She'll be back," Jackson said from behind the door, trying to convince himself.

When Champagne stepped into the hallway, some of the employees were smiling at her.

They'd overheard the exchange and gave her the thumbs-up. Most of them wanted to quit as well but just didn't have the heart to.

"You're doing the right thing," Talla, Jackson's secretary, told her. "I might be right behind you."

Smiling, Champagne decided to give her a life lesson, "Talla, you're a quick learner. You're smart and intelligent. Life has so much to offer, yet you take the abuse from Jackson on a daily basis. I know he pays you well, but you have to value yourself a little more, know your worth and—"

Jackson walked out of his office and glared at her. "I thought you were leaving?"

Champagne looked at him and rolled her eyes. She started walking away and felt proud of herself.She was on her way to bigger and better things, things she'd worked hard for and thoroughly deserved.

Chapter Seven

"Freaks Come Out At Night"

Whodini

The flight to Jamaica went smooth. That's the way it ought to be when you're traveling first-class. Champagne read a book, while Zyair napped.

When they finally landed, Champagne glanced around in awe as she always did whenever they traveled, each new place providing a new adventure, a different thrill. She loved traveling and seeing new cultures. She'd take in the sights, the sounds, the aromas, and the people.

Glancing around, she noticed that the majority of tourists were white. It always amazed her how white people would travel thousands of miles to be surrounded by Black people.

She and Zyair saw a group of women singing, "Welcome to Jamaica," and they stopped to listen for a brief moment.

"Come on, baby, we don't want to miss the shuttle."

Zyair pulled her along, past a group of young boys asking in a low tone if they wanted to purchase some ganja.

"No, thanks," Zyair quickly replied.

Together Champagne and Zyair carried with them four suitcases. They were seated on the shuttle bus, next to a white couple tonguing one another down. They looked at one another, kissed quickly and held hands, each attempting to prepare themselves for the all the stories they'd heard about Hedonism.

The white man came up for air and looked at Zyair. "What resort are you going to?"

"Hedonism."

Glancing down at their bags, the couple smiled and said, "First time, huh?"

"Is it that obvious?" Champagne asked. The couple laughed.

"Believe me," the man said, "you won't be needing all that luggage." Then he introduced himself as Joe, and his wife as Cassandra.

"I'm Zyair, and this is my wife, Champagne."

"What unusual yet beautiful names," Cassandra told them.

Champagne wondered if she was seeing things. *Did she just wink at me?*

"This is our third time visiting," Cassandra said.

"Wow, you must like it a lot," Champagne slumped back into her seat.

"You have no idea," Joe said.

"Is it everything they say, sexy, full of surprises, naked people everywhere, people having sex out in the open?"

"Yep. You definitely have to be open-minded."

Neither Champagne nor Zyair said anything because they thought they were open-minded, but were they really? Would they be able to handle all the nakedness?

As they drove through the streets of Jamaica, the sun was beaming in their faces and Champagne pulled out her shades, put them on, and glanced at the couple that sat beside them. *Freaks?* she wondered.

Zyair wondered if they were swingers, and after looking and listening he knew they were.

"How long before we get there?" Zyair asked the driver.

"About an hour and a half," he replied.

Champagne glanced at her watch and sighed. They'd only been in the van for fifteen minutes, and it seemed like an hour. She was hungry; tired, thirsty, and in need of a stretch.

Champagne was ready to get out of the van, stretch her legs, breathe, and make sure she was alive. First of all, the driver was speeding along with all the other drivers. In Jamaica they drove on the opposite side of the street, and every couple of miles, there was a sign that would read: OVER 200 PEOPLE KILLED ON THESE ROADS, DRIVE CAREFULLY.

After about the fifth sign, she tapped Zyair on his shoulder and asked him, "Do you see those signs? Can you believe it?"

The driver, overhearing this, said, "Don't worry, pretty lady. I take good care of you, make sure you get there safe."

Champagne smiled in response. She loved his strong, confident accent.

"Do you think we can stop and get something to drink?" Cassandra asked.

Everyone was in agreement.

"Sure," the driver replied. "There's a little spot coming up. We'll stop there, get food, drinks, and eat some conch."

"Conch?" Zyair asked. "What's that?"

"It's what the natives eat, especially the men. Makes them strong, virile, at attention."

Everyone laughed because they knew what he meant when he said at attention.

"I eat it every day, and I have six kids."

No one said a word. The last thing either couple wanted was six kids.

A few minutes later, they were pulling up in front of something that looked like a shack on the outside but was a full-fledged dining area on the inside. The ladies sat, while the men went to order their food.

While the men were away, Champagne wanted to hear more about Hedonism, so she asked Cassandra, "Do the people really have sex out in the open?"

"Yeah, girl, you see the more people drink and the later it gets, the more their inhibitions are down. What side are you and your husband staying on?"

"What do you mean what side?"

"The nude, prude, or optional side."

Champagne laughed. "You mean to tell me that's how they separate the people?"

"Yes, that way no one is insulted or offended, and they don't have to take part in something they don't feel comfortable with."

Before she could go on, Zyair and Joe appeared with platters of the spiciest aromatic foods.

Champagne could feel her mouth watering. "Where's our driver?" she asked, looking around.

Zyair nodded in the direction the driver was in. "Out back smoking weed with the owner."

"I don't know if I feel comfortable riding on these dangerous roads with someone that's getting high."

"They do this every day here," Joe informed her. "Don't worry about it. It's a part of their lifestyle, their culture. To them marijuana is a cigarette."

Zyair sat across from Champagne. "Joe was telling me to be aware of the people who try to befriend us in Hedonism."

Champagne addressed Joe and wondered if it's him and his wife they should be aware of. "Really? Why?"

"Well, first of all, you two are a very attractive couple, and that makes you swinger material."

"Swinger material?" There was no way in hell Champagne would be swinging with or from any-thing other than her man's dick.

"A lot of that goes down here. As a matter-of-fact, that's why a lot of people vacation here, to do things they normally wouldn't do."

"So what you're saying is people just approach you and be like, 'Let's fuck?'" Zyair asked.

"What they normally do is send the woman over. She'll try to befriend Champagne and maybe invite you out to dinner and for drinks."

Cassandra picked up from there. "Then she'll ask you if you want to dance, and that's when she'll make her move and try to test the waters, see how close she can get to you, feel you up. She'll say suggestive things, and the next thing you know, everybody is doing the wild thing."

Zyair was liking what he was hearing. Just the thought of another woman feeling Champagne up and she letting it happen was getting his dick hard. But her being with another man was a definite no-no. He wasn't trying to hear that.

"Oh, hell no!" Champagne declared, "I'm not with any of that."

Cassandra laughed. "Never say never, girl."

Just from her saying that, Champagne and Zyair knew they were with "the freakism."

Back in the van, after eating and having a couple of drinks, everyone fell asleep but not before Zyair whispered in Champagne's ear, "I can't wait to make love to you on the beach."

As they got closer to the resort, everyone took notice of the tight security at the gated resort. It was like being in a different world. One second they were in the ghetto, the next, in paradise.

They climbed out of the van, and someone came to grab their bags.

Champagne and Cassandra hugged, and Zyair and Joe shook hands.

"We'll see you around," Joe said as he and Cassandra walked away. "Maybe we can hook up later for drinks or something."

"That'll be cool," Zyair replied. There was no doubt about it. They were going to be on the nude side.

Zyair and Champagne found out they were on the optional side. As they were led to their rooms, many of the workers greeted them, telling them, "Enjoy your stay."

"Wow! Everyone is so nice and courteous here," Champagne commented.

"They have to be, if they expect everyone to be ass out."

Together they laughed and entered the room. "There's no TV." Zyair walked over to pull back the curtains and was caught off guard when he saw a dick swinging left and right and breasts bouncing. "Oh, shit!" he yelled out.

Champagne walked over to see what caused the alarm.

"You think we can do it?" Zyair asked.

"After a whole bottle of something."

Together they stood and continued looking out the window for a full five minutes.

"You tired?" Zyair asked.

"I'm too excited to be tired. Let's take a quick shower and walk around, see what this place has to offer."

They found out that it had a lot to offer; and it only took the first night. They met up with Joe and Cassandra, who were sitting with a group of people at the bar, where the women were topless and the men had towels around their waist.

Zyair and Champagne felt a little uneasy but got over it after a few drinks. Champagne wore booty shorts and a skimpy top, something she would never wear out in the open in the States, and Zyair wore swimming trunks. There was no way he was showing his shit.

Everyone was a little tipsy, and someone suggested they go over to the Jacuzzi. Champagne looked over at Zyair, who was drinking more than usual.

"I'm with it, if you are," he said.

So over to the Jacuzzi they went. There was nakedness everywhere. Zyair looked at Champagne to see if she was uncomfortable. He whispered, "It's up to you."

"I don't know." Champagne wasn't sure how she felt about Zyair being around all these naked women and wondered if Zyair was comparing dick sizes.

"Aw, come on, don't be scared," someone yelled out. "It's nothing. No one even cares. Look around you."

They did, and no one did care. People were just walking about, drinking, playing volleyball, all naked, like it was the most natural thing in the world.

"You know what? Fuck it. We're in another part of the world, we don't know anyone here, so why not?" Led by the liquor, Champagne slipped out of her shorts.

Zyair noticed she didn't have any panties on.

She then took her top off and climbed into the Jacuzzi.

Everyone started clapping.

A surprised Zyair followed her lead. While in the Jacuzzi, Zyair tried to take in the sights without making it too obvious.

Champagne caught on and told him, "It's okay. You can look."

The couple right next to them started kissing. There was nothing wrong with it. It just caught them off guard, but it became something when the woman straddled the man and rode him right in front of everyone.

Feeling more than a slight uneasiness, neither Zyair nor Champagne knew how to react. Do they watch? Do they turn away? Do they say something? They decided to do what everyone was doing—Ignore it, and act nonchalant, laid back, and indifferent, as if it didn't matter one way or the other.

They continued to drink and chat with a couple across from them. That didn't last too much longer because, right in the middle of their discussion, the man sat up on the edge of the Jacuzzi and his mate started sucking his dick.

Unable to control himself, Zyair told Champagne, "I'm ready to go to our room."

She couldn't agree more. Standing up and feeling overexposed once again, this time nipple protruding and sexual energy racing through her body, she started to climb over the edge.

Zyair pulled her down. "I need a few seconds."

She took that to mean, his dick is hard and he doesn't want everyone to see.

After a brief moment, they climbed out of the Jacuzzi and somehow made it to their room without attacking one another.

They never made it to the bed, though, because when they stepped through the door, Champagne told Zyair, "Fuck me." She'd been wanting to tell him that as soon as she saw that lady straddle her man.

Champagne let out a low and deep moan. She was close to an orgasm, a sensation she'd been wanting. Zyair didn't know that she had already begun playing with her pussy under the pressure of the water, so when he said he was ready to go, she was with it.

Taking his hand and leading him over to the dresser closest to the door, she leaned over, and took her fingers and spread her pussy wide open from behind.

Savoring the moment, Zyair stood with a gleam in his eyes. Loving her aggressiveness, he stepped closer, grabbed her ass cheeks, and entered her with force.

"Shit!" Champagne cried out. She wasn't expecting that. She thought he would try to tease her, but she enjoyed this just the same.

Slowly leaving the walls of her wetness, he pulled back and entered her with force again. "Ummmm . . . I like that."

He knew she would, but then he decided to take it down a notch and slide in and out a little at a time, driving her crazy.

"Didn't I tell you to fuck me?" She wanted it fast and furious. "Come on, Zyair, do it like you mean it."

Zyair gave her just what she wanted. A hard, intense fuck. He grabbed onto her waist and pulled her hips toward him, forcing himself deeper and deeper inside her with each thrust.

Either it was Champagne's imagination, or his dick was thicker, longer, and stronger. Her moans were growing louder and louder.

Zyair was covered in sweat, some of it dripping off his body. Normally this would have irritated the hell out of her, but not today.

"I want to cum with you inside me," she told him.

He knew she would start playing with her clitoris, and it would be a matter of minutes before she exploded.

Later that night after showering, they went out one last time for drinks and a burger at the midnight grill. They came back to their room and lay in bed discussing all they'd seen so far.

Champagne wondered if this experience would change them as individuals, if it would change their relationship and their sex life would become more exciting and fulfilling as a result.

Not getting that deep with it, Zyair was wondering how he could get Champagne to make love to a woman while they were there. He wanted to bring it up but was apprehensive about how she would react.

Then, suddenly unable to help himself, he blurted out, "Have you ever thought about sleeping with another woman?"

"What?"

"Have you ever thought about—"

"I heard you."

After a couple seconds of silence, Zyair said, "Well?"

"I'm thinking."

"Either you have, or you haven't."

It wasn't that simple because in all actuality it really wasn't something she'd given any thought to, aside from her experimenting when she was younger, and that was her secret.

"No, not really."

Disappointed, yet intrigued, he said, "Why not?"

"I don't know. I'm not against it or anything. It's just never been something I was interested in."

"Would you try it?"

Zyair tried to appear blasé with his questioning but Champagne knew better.

"Why are you asking? Do you want me to? Do you want to have a threesome or something? Is that what this is about? You want to fuck someone else?"

"No, no, I don't want anyone but you, but a brother ain't gonna lie, I'd like to see you with another woman."

Champagne looked over at him. "How long have you been thinking about this?"

"Since we've been together."

"Why bring this up now?"

"Because of where we're at. Because the opportunity may arise. Because we don't know a soul here." Champagne grew quiet. She was actually considering his words but fear kept her from voicing it. What came out instead was, "If I agreed to something like that, which I probably wouldn't, who would we get? I can't just be with anyone and I'm not trying to lick any girl's pussy. Plus, I don't even know what kind of woman I would be interested in. Then what if you're attracted to her? What if she wants to have sex with you? I wouldn't be able to handle that. And what if I get turned out."

"What do you mean, what if you get turned out?"

"You know, we both saw *Trois*."

"That's a movie."

"Nah, that shit happens in real life."

"It wouldn't happen to us." Zyair was secure in his spot, at least to the point where he didn't believe a woman could take his away.

Champagne looked at him and quoted Cassandra, "Never say never."

Chapter Eight

"Man Size Love"

Klymaxx

Champagne and Zyair were having the time of their lives. Even when surrounded by others they still enjoyed the comfort of one another. So far the Hedonism experience had been euphoric. It was like one big party, all day and night. They ran across a few other Black couples, although not too many. They were definitely outnumbered by White people.

But here it didn't make much of a difference, because when naked and all walls are down, people tended not to see color.

Their final night came around leaving them feeling gloomy and sulky. They didn't want to leave, but knew they had to. Having been gone for a week, they needed to get home and handle business.

Out for their last drink and far past tipsy, Zyair asked, "Can you believe this is our last night here?"

"I know. I am not looking forward to going home." Champagne had a lot on her plate. She had to find office space, hire an assistant, and get settled with clients. Shaking the thoughts out of her head, she said to Zyair, "Let's do something different and daring."

His ears perked up. "What?"

"Let's make love outside."

"For real?"

"Yeah."

He didn't need to be convinced. He stood up. "When? Now?"

Champagne stood up and laughed. "No, not now. Let's go dancing first."

As they left the area, they passed a table of women. One of them eyed Champagne down. Zyair had noticed her watching them the whole time they were there. He wanted to bring it to Champagne's attention but decided not to push the issue.

That night while they were on the dance floor, Champagne was pressing her ass up against Zyair when a few things happened all at once. She turned around to kiss him and suddenly felt hands on her hips and breast, pressing up against her back. Startled, she turned around to find an attractive woman dancing a hair's breadth away from her. She was so close, you could feel her body heat.

"I hope you don't mind," the woman said in a slightly husky voice, her lips full and seductive.

Champagne didn't know how to react, and there was an uneasiness in the pit of her stomach.

The woman placed her hands on Champagne's hips. "It's just a dance."

Tipsy and knowing that Zyair was getting turned on convinced Champagne to throw all caution to the wind. "I don't mind," she said.

The whole time Zyair had been holding his breath. This was the girl from the bar. The one that had been watching them. She was sexy as hell. It was obvious she was mixed with something other than Black. Her skin was bronze, and she had short, straight hair that was cut close. And though small-busted, she had the biggest nipples he'd ever seen. You could see right through her blouse.

While he was checking her out, Champagne was surprising herself, doing the same thing. She felt the girl's hands wandering from her waist up to her breasts. Champagne turned around to read Zyair, looked in his eyes to see if he was experiencing the same sensual emotions she was.

He noticed a little fear and leaned forward to kiss her. "Relax," he whispered in her ear. "You're just dancing. Think of it as foreplay."

She had to admit, she was turned on and her pussy was becoming lubricated. Champagne found herself sandwiched between them. She could feel the girl grinding on her ass. Looking around to see if anyone was paying them any attention, she wasn't surprised to find that no one was. This was something that happened a lot on this little island.

Closing her eyes and getting lost in the music, Champagne, Zyair, and the mysterious woman must have danced together for over a half an hour. Champagne was so turned on that her pussy hurt. It was throbbing uncontrollably.

"I'm ready to go," she told Zyair. Facing the woman, she told her, "Thanks."

The woman grabbed her hands and told her, "Anytime," and kissed her on the lips sensually.

It was a closed-mouth kiss, but the sensation it caused was on a whole other level. Champagne then took Zyair's hands and led him to their room in silence, where she retrieved a blanket.

Zyair was afraid to say a word, not wanting to break Champagne's spell. He could feel the sexual energy radiating off her body and knew tonight's lovemaking would be intense. Not just because of the dance but it was their last night in Jamaica.

They returned to the beach fully clothed and spread the blanket out. Zyair sat down first, and Champagne sat on his lap, straddling him.

"I love you, you know that, don't you?" Champagne kissed him on the lips.

"I love you too." Zyair grabbed her hips and pressed her into him.

"That was interesting on the dance floor," Champagne said as she ran her hands down Zyair's rippled back.

"Yes, it was. It was sexy. I was ready to take you on the dance floor."

Champagne pressed up against his hardness and smiled. "Yes, I could tell."

Zyair pushed her hips up and pulled up her dress.

He linked his fingers underneath her panties. "Let's take these off."

Champagne stood up and let him pull them down.

As she stood close to his face, he took in her scent. Placing his face on her pussy, he pushed her legs open and placed his finger inside her, moving it in a circular motion.

She pressed into his hand. "That feels good."

Zyair removed his finger from inside Champagne. Then he stood up and pulled the dress over Champagne's head. While doing so, he licked her stomach and moved up to her breast. He unsnapped the bra and bit down gently on her nipples.

Once her dress was off, he unzipped his shorts and revealed that he wasn't wearing any underwear. Then he took his shirt off.

Champagne reached out and massaged his dick, which was standing at attention. She got on her knees and started licking the head of his penis, covering the whole length of it with her mouth, running her tongue around it in circular motions.

He loved when she did that. He placed his hands on the back of her head and started moving in her mouth, and Champagne was taking it all in, trying not to let an inch of it out of her mouth. He knew she was trying to make him cum, but he wasn't ready for that yet. He pulled away.

"What are you doing? I'm not done yet."

"Let's lay down. I want to taste you."

Not one to turn that down, Champagne stretched out on the blanket.

Zyair pressed her legs open and sat between them.

He looked down at her beautiful body. "How did it feel to have your breast caressed by a woman?" He ran his hands down the length of her body, resting between her legs.

With fervor, Champagne took his hand and placed it on her pussy. "It felt soft. I was turned on."

That's what he wanted to hear. Zyair replaced his hand with his mouth and started licking her walls.

Champagne closed her eyes and concentrated on the pleasure that was seeping through her pores. When Zyair placed his tongue on her clitoris, she knew it would be a matter of minutes before she exploded.

Pushing her hips into his mouth and grabbing his head, she was startled to hear the voice from the disco say, "Can I join in?"

Zyair stopped what he was doing and looked up.

Champagne did also. They both saw her standing before them naked.

She looked at Champagne. "My name is Whisper, and I've watched you all day. I want you, not your husband."

Champagne sat up. "I'm not gay."

Whisper laughed and sat down next to them.

By now, Zyair was sitting up, praying silently in his mind that Champagne would say yes. He watched in silence as Champagne's eyes became consumed with desire.

"You don't have to be gay to let me make love to you. I want to taste what your man was tasting. You'll never see me again, I'll never see you again."

Champagne knew this was true. She also knew that Zyair wanted this. This Whisper person did say she wanted her and not him.

Champagne looked over at Zyair, whose eagerness was written all over his face. She decided to throw all caution to the wind. "Yes."

Before Whisper could change her mind, Champagne reached out to her and grazed her lips with her tongue.

Zyair moved over to the side. "I'll watch."

Whisper took Zyair's spot and placed her fingers inside Champagne and licked the juice off. "You taste as good as you look."

Champagne couldn't speak. Her body tingling from head to toe, she was almost shaking.

Whisper told her, "Relax. I'm not here to hurt you, only to please you." Whisper covered

Champagne's whole pussy with her mouth and flicked her tongue back and forth, tapping her clitoris.

Please her, she did.

Champagne experienced an orgasm that shook her to the core. It came from every cell in her body. She called out to Zyair, who leaned over and started kissing her in a fit of lust.

Placing her hand on Zyair, Whisper said, "Let me kiss her, let her see what she taste like."

Zyair moved and watched as Champagne devoured Whisper's mouth.

Caught up in the moment, Champagne found herself wanting to taste Whisper, wanting to see what a woman's pussy would feel like on her mouth. She opened her mouth to voice this curiosity but the words wouldn't come out. What did come out was, "Zyair, I want you inside me now."

Whisper nibbled on Champagne's ear and murmured, "Remember me always." She moved over to the side and looked at Zyair. "Can I watch?"

Zyair looked at Champagne, who nodded.

Climbing on top, he entered her with such heat and such passion that Whisper placed her hands on her own pussy and played with her clitoris, bringing herself to orgasm right along with him.

Chapter Nine

"Meeting In The Ladies Room"

Klymaxx

Champagne lay in the bed and replayed the experience of the night before. She felt like she wanted the one-time thing to happen again but told herself it was never to happen again. She was even nervous about facing Zyair the next morning.

Fatigued from the lovemaking, Champagne tried to climb out of bed without making a sound. She didn't want to wake Zyair. She headed to the bathroom to masturbate.

Little did she know, he was awake and had been for quite some time. He was replaying the scene over and over in his mind. It was like a movie to him, the way Champagne's body responded to Whisper's touch.

As Zyair watched, his dick got so hard, he thought it was going to explode. Realizing that she was trying to sneak out of the bed, he spoke up. "Good morning."

Startled, Champagne walked over to the bed and kissed him on the cheek. "Good morning, sweetie."

Zyair reached for her hand and pulled her back on the bed.

Relunctantly, she sat next to him. "We don't have time to make love again. You know we have to get up and pack."

Zyair sighed. "I know."

"It's back to the real world and away from fantasy island."

Zyair sat up. "Do you want to talk about last night?"

"No. At least not right now."

She needed time to process it, analyze it, and replay it over in her mind. She wondered if she was secretly gay, or if she was bisexual. She questioned her actions. Why didn't she push Whisper away? Why was she so turned on? Did she do it for Zyair? Was it the liquor, or was it something she wanted? Had she been in denial all her life? Was she gay as a youngster?

Champagne stood up. "Look, I'm going to take a shower and start packing. While I'm packing, you need to shower. That way we can save time and grab breakfast before we catch the shuttle to the airport."

"We can save more time by showering together," Zyair said, feeling a need to be close to Champagne.

"That's fine."

***

An hour later they were dressed, packed, and headed to the lounge area for breakfast when, out of the corner of her eye, Champagne caught sight of Whisper talking to one of the workers. Quickly, she averted her attention, but not before glancing her way again.

This time she was busted. Whisper looked at her, winked, and licked her lips.

Either she was crazy, or Champagne got moist.

She grabbed Zyair's hand and started pulling him along.

"Whoa! Whoa! Why are you pulling me? What's the hurry?"

"No hurry. I'm just starving."

The light was streaming through the window when they arrived at Newark Airport. The car service was waiting to take them home. Travel weary, they both slept on the way.

Back at home, they felt lost, displaced, and just plain old out of it. Filled with fever-pitch excitement and exhilaration, the Hedonism vacation was unlike any other they'd taken. Nothing could compare.

To return home to the restaurant and numerous messages on the answering machine from Jackson was anticlimactic and dissatisfying and, in an odd way, made the vacation seem surreal.

The first couple of days, they didn't return any phone calls but just sat around the house looking at one another. Then that got old and they started to get on with their daily routine.

It'd been a week since their return when Champagne decided to make an appearance at her old job. Damn, she couldn't believe that's what it was now, her old job. Even though she was going on to bigger and better things, change was hard and there was a somberness about the whole thing. After all, she was leaving seven years of her life behind, but she knew in her heart of hearts that she was doing the right thing by making a commitment to herself and her future.

She woke up rejuvenated, focused, and ready to conquer the world. She pulled back the blankets, climbed out of the bed, and stretched. Then she went to brush her teeth.

She glanced at the card taped to the mirror and read it out loud, "You can say 'Good morning, God,' or 'Good God, it's morning.'" She chose to say, "Good morning, God," and put her focus on making this a productive day. She was going to be the strong one, the one to bite the bullet, the bigger person, and try to draw some kind of truce with Jackson. She didn't want to leave with hatred and dislike on her heart. Life was too short for such bullshit. Plus, Jackson, asshole that he was, had still taught her a lot.

Before leaving the house, Champagne called Zyair for support at the restaurant, only to find he was in a meeting. She then called Alexis.

"Girl, I haven't seen you since you've been back," Alexis told her. "I miss you."

"I was only gone a week."

"Yeah, but a lot can happen in a week."

"Don't I know it."

Champagne thought of Whisper. She wondered whether she should tell Alexis about the escapade. Lord knows, she wanted to, but she didn't feel like being judged. She didn't want to be found out, or be told she was perverted, bisexual, or gay. She didn't want to be labeled or to hear something that would cause her to question herself or her sexuality. *Shit!* She was doing it enough to herself, and having someone else do it would've been a bit too much.

Sometimes she thought she was going overboard with the constant mind games she played with herself. She tried to just think of it as something that happened. She wanted to just let it be, let it go. Why was she making so much out of it? Why was she blowing it up? She tried convincing herself, "It's something that happened in the heat of the moment, that's all, nothing more, nothing less."

"Want to meet for lunch?" Champagne asked Alexis. She and Alexis agreed to meet at The Cheesecake Factory, one of their favorite places.

Not only for the dessert, which in itself was delectable but the food was just as delicious. Just thinking about it made her want to hurry up and get going with her day.

When Champagne walked into her former place of employment, all heads turned. She knew they'd heard she was leaving and wanted to jump up and ask her all kinds of questions, but the fear of Jackson and his wrath kept them seated.

"Hi, Champagne," Takia said. "He's in his office. Are you here to ask for your job back?"

Champagne looked at her like she'd lost her mind. "Now you know better than that."

"He's been lost without you, girl," she whispered. "I'm telling you, if you did, you could get whatever you wanted out of him."

"All I really wanted out of him is some respect, and I couldn't even get that."

"We all want that. You know how he—"

Before she could finish, Jackson's office door opened and he looked at Champagne, first with surprise then with contempt. "What are you doing here?"

"Can we step into your office?" Champagne asked, thinking now that this wasn't such a good idea.

Jackson walked into his office, and she followed, closing the door behind her. She waited for him to sit down, he didn't.

"Are you here for your job back?" He hoped so but of course, he didn't want to tell her that.

"No, I'm here for closure. I'm here to thank you. I'm here because I feel bad about walking out on you the way I did."

"You feel bad? You feel bad?" he asked, his voice getting louder and louder.

Champagne threw her hands up. "Listen, Jackson, I didn't come here for a confrontation. I'm here because I know that you've helped me in my career, because I learned a lot from you, and I thought maybe we could discuss where it—where we went wrong."

"Why do we have to discuss anything? You got too high and mighty. You started thinking you too good for this place."

"That's a lie, and you know it. I got tired of you coming on to me. I got tired of you disrespecting me as a woman. I got tired of you walking around here like king ding-a-ling." Champagne felt like she had nerves of steel, saying what had been in heart for quite some time.

"You never said, 'Hey, Champagne, nice job. Hey, Champagne, I appreciate all you do. No, you just took me for granted."

"You're not a damn child. Why do you want to be praised? This is a job. I'm not raising you or anyone that's up in this joint, and I am king ding-a-ling, as you say. This is my ship, and I run it the way I see fit."

"Running it the way you ran it made you lose your best employee, and believe me, I know that's what I was."

Jackson didn't say a word. He knew he was arrogant, and he knew he took advantage of his employees. He also knew what she said was true, but he is who he is. When he opened his office door and saw Champagne standing there, he seriously hoped she was there for her job back and was ready to offer it to her. Clients had been calling all week, telling him they weren't going to renew their contracts since they'd heard Champagne wasn't there anymore.

"Let me ask you this—How do some of the clients know you quit? Were you planning this all along, a takeover?"

"No, I wasn't planning, and am not planning a takeover. Look around. This is a small office, word gets around. You were yelling and screaming at me my last day here."

Feeling defeated, Jackson sat down. "If I offered you your job back, a partnership, and more money, would you consider it?"

Champagne knew the answer was, "No way in hell," but she told him instead, "I'd think about it. Give me at least a week and I'd get back to you."

"A week is too long."

"Well then, if I have to give you an answer right now, it's no."

Jackson waved her away. "Take a week then."

Champagne turned to leave the office but she knew she couldn't go out like that, that she shouldn't lead him on. "Jackson, I have to apologize again. I know I'm not coming back here. I'm ready to explore other possibilities, so there's no need to wait on my response."

Before he could say one word, she rushed out of the office and out of the building, with a smile on her face. Champagne felt like a load had been lifted.

Now she was on her way to her favorite place to see her best friend. It couldn't get any better.

When Champagne walked into The Cheesecake Factory, she was disappointed not to see Alexis waiting in front. She glanced around and spotted her. She wasn't sitting by herself but with a man, dressed in jeans and a T-shirt, muscles bulging in every direction. His arm was resting against the back of Alexis's chair. If she sat any closer to him, she would have been nestled in his arms.

That must be Khalil. Champagne was surprised to feel a pang of jealousy. She thought they were going to have lunch together, just the two of them, and didn't feel like sharing her friend with anyone.

Alexis was so engrossed into whatever this man was telling her that she didn't notice Champagne as she approached. Champagne stood behind her and cleared her throat. "Hello."

Alexis, recognizing the voice, jumped up out of her seat and hugged her. "Hey, girl." Pulling back, she checked her up and down. "You look good. You got a tan and everything. I missed you."

Champagne felt a little better and told her, "I missed you too." She then looked over at the uninvited guest. "Are you going to introduce us?"

Alexis giggled. "This is Khalil, my new man, and this is Champagne, my best friend."

Champagne was surprised to hear her say "my new man." Where did that come from? They'd just met, and she was talking relationship? Weren't things moving a bit fast? She couldn't wait to get Alexis alone. They had some serious talking to do.

Khalil stood up and pulled the chair out for Champagne, who did take note that, at least, he was a gentleman.

"It's nice meeting you," he said. "I've heard so much about you."

"In a week's time? Wow! I wish I knew more about you." Champagne didn't know what was wrong with her, but she just had to be bitchy.

Alexis noticed it right away and stood up. "I'm going to the ladies' room. Champagne, you care to join me?"

The way Alexis looked at her, Champagne knew she'd better join her.

When they walked inside, there were a couple of women washing their hands. Alexis waited until they walked out and tore into Champagne. "What the hell is that all about?"

Her tone threw Champagne off balance. "What are you talking about?"

"You know what I'm about. I'm talking about your rudeness and your scrutiny. I'm talking about you acting like you don't like Khalil and you don't even know him."

Champagne knew she was right. All she could do was apologize and be honest. "I'm sorry. I thought it would just be you and I meeting. I thought I'd have you all to myself."

Alexis pulled Champagne into her arms. "That's so sweet, and I know you mean well. But baby, I'm into this man, and I just wanted y'all to meet."

Champagne pulled away. "You really into him?"

"Yeah."

"You don't think this is moving a bit fast?"

"Maybe. But I'm tired of being by myself, of not having any companionship."

"Well, do you think it's wise to jump into a relationship just because you're tired of being lonely?"

Alexis rolled her eyes. "Why are you hating on a sister?"

"I'm not hating. I'm just saying, you don't want to hop into a relationship just because . . ."

"It's not just because. Listen, I appreciate your concern but you have a man. I've finally got one too. I enjoy his company, and he enjoys mine. You should be happy for me."

There was really nothing left for Champagne to say. Alexis was going to do what she wanted to do anyway. "Okay, let's do this," Champagne suggested. "Let's go back to the table and start all over. I promise, I won't be an asshole."

"You promise?"

Champagne took her hand, and together they walked out of the bathroom.

Chapter Ten

"Give It To Me Baby"

Rick James

Later that night Champagne waited for Zyair to come home. She couldn't wait to tell him about Khalil. She was hoping to convince Zyair to investigate him. She knew he did it with his employees, so why wouldn't he do it for her friend?

"Are you crazy?" he asked her. "What are you thinking of, invading someone's privacy like that?"

"Well, you do it for your employees."

"That's different. That's because they'll be working for me, handling my money."

"But she's my best friend. I'm worried about her."

"She's a grown-ass woman, Champagne." Champagne felt like he wasn't even trying to understand. She wanted him to get that the reason she was concerned is because Alexis just met this guy and for her to be calling him her man so soon just didn't sit right with Champagne. As a matter-of-fact, he didn't fit right to her either. There was something about him that just really bothered her.

She didn't know what it was, but whatever it was, she was going to find out one way or another, with or without Zyair's help.

"You don't think you're just jealous?" Zyair asked.

"Why the heck would I be jealous?"

"Because you think you're going to lose your best friend."

Champagne rolled her eyes.

"It was just a thought."

Champagne knew there was some truth to it, that there was more than a slight chance that he was right. After all, Alexis was her best friend and had always been available to her. Whenever she wanted to do something, or needed someone to talk to, all she had to do was pick up the phone and Alexis was there.

The more Champagne thought about it, the more messed up she felt. She now saw how much she benefited from her friend being single. How messed up was that? Champagne also recalled the many occasions Alexis wanted to spend time with her and she was unable to, because Zyair had made plans.

She recalled the saying that some people take comfort in another's misery. She hoped she wasn't that type of person. Champagne knew she should be happy for Alexis. It was about time she got involved with someone. She just didn't want things to change, and she knew they would. So before Khalil took Alexis away, Champagne was going to look into his background and make sure he was worthy of her.

She knew she was wrong, but she convinced herself that it would be worth it, should something pop up. If it didn't, that would be even better, because then they could do things together as couples.

Champagne told Zyair, "You know what, sweetie, it's not my business. I'm reading way more into this than I should. And not only that, who's to say that's it going to last?"

"Good. What you need to be doing, instead of thinking about Alexis and her new man, is focusing on your new business. You know you're about to start your interviewing process. Why don't you get together your list of questions?"

Champagne knew Zyair was right once again, and she planned on doing just that in the morning, after she was well rested and she could concentrate on what she was doing.

Later that night Champagne was awakened by Zyair's touch as he pressed up against her ass. She turned over and touched his face.

"What were you dreaming about?" he asked. "You were moaning and playing with yourself."

"Get out of here." Champagne recalled that she was having a sexy-ass dream, but there was no way in hell she was playing with herself.

"No, for real, you were."

Damn, she was busted. She was dreaming that she was making love to a woman. Was she that turned-on that it was affecting her sleep? Reality had set in. She realized that it wasn't only in her waking hours that she thought about her sexual escapade in Hedonism. She was consumed with it day and night. She tried to tell herself that what happened was a one-time thing, but she was slowly starting to think it went far deeper than that.

That night in Hedonism stirred something up in her.

Another person might say it brought out the freak in her. She didn't know what it meant. All she knew for certain was that she wanted to try it again.

Why? Why her? Other than the fact that the way Whisper caressed her, kissed her, and put her lips on her pussy made her feel good. Or was it the way Whisper was certain of herself and her skills? There was a tenderness about it, something she'd never experienced before.

Now, don't get her wrong, Champagne felt these things from Zyair but this was on another level. They say, women know what women want, when they want it, and how they want it. Well, it sure seemed like it, because the way Whisper made love to her pussy, devouring it like it was the best dessert she ever had, still had her thinking, wishing, and wanting.

They, whoever they are, also say that women have a deeper understanding of each other in and out of bed. Champagne couldn't verify any of that on a relationship level but she could on a friendship level because sometimes when she was going through it or having a moment and Zyair couldn't relate, she would call Alexis, who would know instantly what to say or what to do about it.

Damn, why was this consuming her? She wished she had someone she could talk to about it, spill her desires out to without being judged but there was no one. She definitely wasn't going to tell Alexis.

"So," Zyair said, interrupting her thoughts, "what were you dreaming about?"

Champagne decided to be honest. *What the heck! What is he going to do or say, other than have more questions or want details?* "I was dreaming about sex . . . sex with a woman."

Champagne could read the interest on Zyair's face as he moved closer to her. If he got any closer, he would have been inside her.

"Want to tell me about it?"

Champagne recalled the details but she just didn't want to give them up. What she was willing to give up, though, was the fact that she'd been having these thoughts a lot lately. "I don't really remember the details." Champagne saw the look of disappointment on Zyair's face. "Zyair?"

"Yes?" There was hope in his voice.

"I know that we're trying to better our relationship, and I also know that the only way to do that is with honesty."

On the honesty note, Zyair sat up again and braced himself. He was starting to get nervous. When someone started talking about honesty in a relationship, you couldn't help but wonder where they were going with this. He wanted to rush her along and make her get to whatever point she was trying to make, to say whatever she had to say, so he could deal with it.

"Go on."

Laying on her back, looking up at the ceiling, Champagne said, "I think I might want to try, I might want to, um . . ." Damn, how come she couldn't just say it? Why couldn't she just say she wanted to be with a woman again, and not while intoxicated? She wanted to be sure that she enjoyed it as much as she remembered.

Zyair seemed so interested in her dream that she hoped he'd be like, "Good. Let's do this," or maybe it was just something he wanted to see once more. Maybe this time around he would want to take part in it, and that wasn't something she felt she could handle. If he said yes, would it now be an open relationship? Was an open relationship something she wanted? What would it consist of? Would he be sleeping with other women? Would he go down on them?

After thinking it over, Champagne was pissed she even opened her mouth.

Growing more anxious by the moment, Zyair told her, "Go on and say it. Say what's on your mind. I love you no matter—"

Before he could finish, Champagne said, "I want to sleep with another woman." There she'd said it and couldn't take it back. Would she regret it? She didn't know why she even felt the need to tell him. Maybe she should have kept it to herself and did this on her own, but she didn't want to sneak.

"You want to what?" This is definitely not what he was expecting her to say.

Champagne covered her face. "You know what? Never mind. Forget I said anything."

The last thing Zyair wanted Champagne to do was close down. He removed her hands. "There's no need to take it back. I want whatever you want. I want for us to try new things. I want for us to be able to tell each other our fantasies. I don't want to have any secrets."

Champagne started to interrupt, but Zyair was on a roll.

"I want for us to be best friends again. Somehow we've lost that. How are we going to do that if we can't say what's on our mind? I want us to be able to say anything and everything to one another without the judgment. Like I said, I want what you want, even if that's to bring another woman in our bed for us."

Okay, okay, he was getting the wrong impression. She wasn't talking about bringing another woman into the relationship or into their bed for them but for herself. It sounded like that's what he thought she meant, so Champagne knew she had to clarify that right away. She sat up. "Hold up, hold up, hold up. I didn't say anything about bringing another female in our bed for us."

Confused and disappointed, Zyair thought he was going to have is cake and eat it too. He asked her, "Well, what did you mean?"

"I guess what I'm asking you is to do what we did in Jamaica but not under those conditions, not under the influence. I want to see if I enjoyed it as much as I did for myself, and not because of you."

"Would that be so bad, enjoying it because you were under the influence?" Zyair asked.

For a brief second a shot of insecurity swept through him. What the hell did that girl do to his woman? Did that Whisper put it down like that? Was she that good that Champagne was thinking about it a week later? Zyair knew his pussy-eating skills were up to par but was he building himself up? Nah, there was no way he was as good as he was only in his mind. No way in hell. After all these years, he knew that Champagne couldn't be faking her pleasure.

He couldn't help it. He just had to know. "What about it did you enjoy? Was she better than me? Did she make you cum harder?"

Champagne could tell immediately where these questions were coming from—his insecurity—and didn't want to take it there. She touched his arm. "Sweetie, it's not that serious. And if you're going to start doubting us and how you make love to me, then let's just forget I said anything."

Okay, he messed up and he knew it. He didn't want her to change her mind, because although he may have jumped to conclusions thinking she'd let him be a part of the next escapade, he was more than willing to watch once again.

"No, no, I don't doubt us. That's not it at all. It's just that we never talked about what happened. Whenever I brought it up, you nixed it off or changed the subject."

His statement was correct. She did want to pretend that none of it happened. That obviously didn't work because it was still on her mind. She now wanted to close the subject, and turn over and go back to sleep, but she knew that wouldn't happen now.

"Okay, well let's talk about it now. What do you want to know?"

Zyair looked her in the eyes. "Did it feel good?"

"Yes."

"Did it feel different from when I make love to you?"

"Different yes, better no. And if you recall, we made love immediately after, and it intensified our lovemaking."

"What was different about it?"

"About what? Us?"

"No. You and her."

"You know how they say a woman's touch is softer, gentler?"

"Yes."

"Well, it's sort of true. There was sensuality there that I hadn't experienced before, a sort of sexiness that only women have." Seeing the confused look on his face, she knew she had to stroke his ego. "It doesn't take away from what you and I have, though."

"What turned you on most about her?"

To this question Champagne smiled and answered, "Her breast." She touched her own as she said this, and Zyair took notice.

Champagne had discovered she was a breast girl. She found herself looking at women when she shouldn't be, her eyes almost always wandering to breast level. One thing she was certain of, the next time the occasion rose she was going to be a bit more aggressive. She was going to reach out and touch. Was she going to go down on a woman? That she couldn't attest to but one never knows.

"How did she eat your pussy?"

Champagne looked at him and wondered if she wanted to go there. *What the heck! I might as well. After all, I might get a treat afterward.*

"How did she eat my pussy? You want me to tell you or show you?"

Zyair immediately got hard. "How are you going to show me?"

"I'll instruct."

Zyair climbed out of the bed and pulled off his briefs, and Champagne slid out of her gown, which was all she was wearing.

Champagne was wet and ready. "Kiss me," she told him as she straddled him, his dick sliding in her. She wanted to be on top, so she could be in control. She also wanted to sit on his face. Yes, that's how she wanted him to eat her out.

Zyair placed his lips on hers and started to tease her with his tongue.

She pulled her mouth away from his and sat up straighter. She placed her hands on his chest, bent over slightly, raising her pussy up slowly to the tip of his dick, and slammed down. Champagne, feeling aggressive, did this a few more times. "You like it?" she asked.

All Zyair could do is moan. He tried to reach out and grab her hips but she pushed his hands back down and continued to ride him at a slow pace, torturing him.

"Go faster," he told her.

"No, let me do this my way." Champagne then pressed down as hard as she could and started rocking back and forth. "Damn, this feels good," she said, getting lost in her own world.

Zyair could feel his orgasm building up, but it was too soon for him. He wasn't ready to cum just yet. "Come on," he said, "let me eat that pussy."

Champagne slid off him and straddled his face. "Tell me how you want it," he told her.

On her knees over his face, Champagne spread her pussy lips open and told him, "Lick the walls. I want you to taste every inch."

Zyair grabbed her buttocks and pulled her to his mouth. Then he put his tongue in as far as it would go. Champagne started pressing into his mouth, trying to feel every movement, every inch of his tongue.

Eventually she had to bend over and balance herself on her hands, while he devoured her.

Zyair then placed his entire mouth over her pussy, and started moving his tongue back and forth against her clitoris.

"Yes, yes, that's it," Champagne said, feeling so close to cumming. "Put your finger inside me."

Zyair did as she requested and started moving his finger in and out real slow.

Champagne, lost in the pleasure, started to grind and grind. "Shit, you're going to make me cum too fast." She sat up straight, grabbed her titties, and started squeezing her nipples.

All the while, Zyair was watching her. It'd been a long time since he'd seen her so animated.

Right at this moment, Zyair felt like the mutha-fuckin' man, and when she screamed out and told him to taste her and he placed his tongue deep inside her walls, he knew that he was.

After she was done cumming, Champagne immediately wanted him inside her. She climbed on him again, this time her back facing him, and rode him at a fast pace while touching her clitoris. She wanted another orgasm and wanted Zyair to get his as well.

It didn't take long for Zyair to grab her hips and press up inside her. "Ahhhh," was all he could manage to say as he exploded inside her.

When he was at the end of his orgasm, Champagne had hers. She threw her head back and yelled out, "Shit!" She climbed off him and collapsed in his arms.

"I love you," he told her.

Kissing him, she told him she loved him as well and they both fell asleep.

***

The next morning, Zyair ruined the whole after sex mood, asking her, "If I agree to do this again, what will I get out of it?"

Champagne just looked at him like he was crazy and started to get out of the bed. After all, he was the one that started all this shit. "You know what, Zyair . . . let's just forget the whole thing."

Not understanding what he did wrong, he grabbed her arm and said, "Wait, wait. What's wrong?"

Champagne looked at him in disbelief. She just shook her head. How could he not know what's wrong?

"Champagne, talk to me," Zyair begged.

"You want to know what's wrong? I'll tell you what's wrong. What's wrong is the fact that this was your idea in the first place, the whole 'let me see you make love with a woman.' I did that shit for you and now, because I enjoyed it and want to try it again, you're tripping. You're trying to change shit all up."

What could he say? She was right. It was his idea. They'd never said it would be a one-time thing, but they'd never said they'd have a repeat session either.

They'd just jumped into it headfirst. "I apologize," he told her. "I didn't mean that the way it came out."

Champagne didn't want to hear any apologies. She put her hands on her hips. "And what do you mean, what do you get out of the deal? What do you want to get out the deal? More pussy? A new pussy? Is that it? Is that what you want?"

That's what you wanted, he thought to himself but didn't dare say it out loud. Zyair glanced at the clock. He realized he needed to get up and get dressed. Plus, he didn't feel like having this conversation. "Champagne, the only pussy I want is yours."

Champagne didn't know whether to believe him or not, knowing she wouldn't get a straight answer and not wanting to hear him say, "Yeah, I want some new pussy," she decided to end this conversation. "You know what, let's just forget the whole thing. You have to work, and I have things to do today. Let's just get dressed and get on with our day."

Zyair didn't want to start his day on a negative note. He didn't want to forget the whole thing, but he knew not to press the subject just yet. "Okay, how about we try this? Let's take a day and think about everything we've talked about and put together a list of rules. The rules will consist of things that are acceptable and things that aren't. That's the only way we're going to go through with this."

Champagne really didn't want to agree because she was afraid of what might be on his list. She wasn't sure if she could handle it, but she agreed to it anyway. At least this way, she'd know where his head was.

Chapter Eleven

"What's Going On"

Marvin Gaye

Zyair shot the ball through the hoops. He was out with his boys, and they were wrapping up a game of two on two.

"So, what's up?" Thomas asked him as they settled on the bench. "Are we going to catch a bite to eat or what?"

"Let me call Champagne and see if she's cooking today."

"See, man, you're lucky as hell. A home-cooked meal. Maybe I could come over for dinner."

Zyair didn't want to tell Thomas that there was no way Champagne was letting him come and eat her precious food, at least not today. She was still pissed off at him, and from experience, he knew she could hold a grudge.

Since the incident that put her in that space with Thomas had just happened a week ago, it would be at least another two weeks before she even allowed him to eat her food.

Zyair, Thomas, Harrison, and Judge went out to a strip club the week before, and Zyair had to admit, a good time was had by all. Champagne never asked where they were going or what they did. There seemed to be little concern on her part. Zyair felt like a lucky man. He'd re-earned her trust, or so he thought.

To Champagne, it just took up too much energy to wonder what he was doing when he was out with his boys. If she did that, it could and would drive her crazy. It did once before, and she didn't want to go that route again. She decided to let his past infidelity be just that, a thing of the past. After all it was years ago, and it had taken her quite some time to get to this point.

Shit, from experience she'd learned that if you search you will find, and that when you go looking, you had to be prepared for any and everything. That's how she'd found out he was cheating before, by snooping. What made it so bad was that this was the only time she'd followed him around.

She felt at the time that she had the right. Zyair wasn't being as attentive as he normally was. They were into year two of their relationship and had settled into a routine, sort of like their current circumstance. The phone calls every few hours had stopped. The "I'm just checking on you to see if you need anything" had stopped. The "I just want to spend time with you, and let's have lunch together" had stopped. Even the good night phone calls.

On top of all that, the sex was almost non-existent, and the oral had dwindled. He no longer took the time to feel her, to smell her, lick her and be one with the pussy. Instead he would go straight for the clit, plucking it like it was a chord, like he was thinking, *Okay, let me hurry up and make her cum so I can get mine.*

Now this stuff, she could have slipped by a little, because she knew and understood that relationships often went through its peaks and valleys, its highs and lows. She'd decided that's what was happening, and a little more work and a lot more conversation could turn it around.

What made Champagne doubt this concept and think a little more was going on than she wanted to admit was the constant phone calls from his friend Divine.

Zyair was hosting an event for her company, which was just starting up. She was calling him an awful lot, more so than any of his other clients. It seemed like 75 percent of the time when the phone rang it was her. Champagne was a little bothered by it, and she let him know. Of course, he told her she was imagining things.

But being a woman, Champagne knew she wasn't crazy. She felt it in her gut that this chick wanted her man, and once again when she brought it to Zyair's attention, he dismissed it.

Well, late one night Divine called. Champagne listened while Zyair talked to her. The conversation sounded more personal than business.

The second they got off the phone, Champagne asked, "What the hell was that about?"

"Oh, she's just going through some things right now and needed to discuss them with someone," he told her.

"Well, she need to discuss the shit with someone other than you. You're doing business with her, you're not her damn friend."

What Champagne didn't know was that Zyair and this Divine chick grew up together. For some reason he'd withheld this information from her, and you know when information is withheld there's always more to the story.

Champagne ended up finding out from Thomas. Yep, he was always involved in some shit. She'd overheard him and Zyair talking. They were sitting in the kitchen and Champagne had just walked in the room.

"Man, I saw Divine the other day. She's come a long way since college. She's looking good, man."

Champagne turned around in time to see Zyair giving Thomas a look. Of course, she couldn't let that go. "What's going on?"

Zyair had this real dumb look on his face. "What are you talking about?"

Champagne put her hands on her hips. "Thomas is talking like you both knew her in your past."

Zyair knew he was busted. He didn't know why he just didn't tell her from the gate that Divine was an old friend. He tried to play it off by sounding nonchalant. "Oh, I thought I told you we went to school together." Champagne politely asked Thomas to leave, before ripping Zyair a new asshole. That night he slept in the spare bedroom.

Over the next few weeks, Champagne found herself going through his pockets, looking at his calendar, doing things that were so out of character for her. But she couldn't help herself, she was out of control. She had to know if her gut instinct was right.

One night while Zyair was asleep, she got hold of his cell phone and figured out his password, which wasn't too hard, seeing most men used either their birth date or numbers from their social security number for their code. Well, she found the evidence she was looking for. On his voice mail was a message from Divine expressing how wonderful last night had been, even if it was a mistake. She expressed her feelings for him and asked him, didn't he know how good they could be together, in and out of bed, and to please give her a chance.

Unable to take anymore, Champagne went into the bedroom and woke Zyair up by pushing him off the bed.

"What the—"

"I knew it, I knew it," Champagne ranted and raved. She shoved the phone in his face. "You tried to play me. How could you do this to me?"

Of course, he tried to act like he didn't know what she was talking about.

"Please, Zyair, don't play dumb with me. You've played me enough. I heard your little love message."

Zyair took the phone out of her hand and retrieved the message. As he listened, Champagne grabbed her belongings and started to leave.

Jumping up out of the bed, he apologized and apologized. He begged her to stay, saying he could explain, that it only happened one time.

Well, once was enough. She left him.

Zyair did everything in his power to get her back. He begged, sent flowers, kept showing up at her office at her house, discontinued all business with Divine, and lost money because of it.

Eventually Champagne forgave him and returned.

Thomas knew about the affair, and even though his loyalty lay with Zyair, she couldn't help but feel like he should have stopped him. After all, she was the one that helped him get his endorsement deal, she was the one that, when he got into a bad accident, assisted Zyair in taking care of him. She was the one that cooked for him and thought of him like extended family. That had changed over the years, though, because whenever something went down, Thomas either knew about it, was around, or was a part of it.

The night when Zyair got ready to leave she actually asked him where they were going and he told her, "To a strip club."

She wanted to ask if she could go as well, but she knew better. One, he was going with his boys, and two, it would give away the fact that the conversation they had earlier that week, the whole sex-with-a-female thing, was still on her mind.

That night at the strip club, Zyair and his boys were drinking and taking in the scenery when two strippers approached them and asked if anyone wanted a lap dance. Normally this was something Zyair didn't do, but after one too many drinks and seeing that the other fellows were with it, he decided, what the hell. Simply put, Zyair got caught up in the moment.

The next day they were all at his house watching a game. Champagne was with a client at a premiere, so they had the house to themselves. Harrison started joking with Zyair, "Yo, man, you should have seen your face when that girl was all on you."

Thomas laughed. "See, that's just what a man needs, a lap dance at the end of the day."

Once again Champagne walked in when Thomas was opening his mouth. Everyone shut up immediately when she gave them all the evil eye.

"So, you didn't tell me you got a lap dance, Zyair."

That's right, Champagne was putting his ass on blast in front of all his boys.

"Um-um, Champagne," Thomas said, trying to break the tension, "it was his first time. We thought it would be a good joke."

Champagne gave him the look and said, "Oh, really?"

Two minutes later his boys were all leaving. Champagne went upstairs without saying a word, leaving Zyair sitting on the couch waiting for the dam to burst.

Champagne didn't know if she was angry, aggravated, or what. She took a quick shower and decided to confront him on the lap dance.

Zyair hadn't moved from the spot he was in. He was still watching the game.

"So you got a lap dance, huh? You let some stankass ho that's been dancin' all night, niggas been feelin' all up on her, lookin' in her pussy—she was probably all sweaty and shit—and you let her get on you?"

Damn! When she said it that way, Zyair felt disgusted with himself. There was no way he could deny it, because she'd heard what she heard.

He decided to just make her understand that it really wasn't that serious, that all the other fellas were doing it, and that the truth of the matter was that he really didn't derive any pleasure from it.

"You expect me to believe that?" she asked.

He knew she wouldn't but it was still halfway truthful. The excitement of a honey rubbing up against him was exciting for a second, but then after looking around and seeing that numerous other people were getting the same thing done, and wondering how many people she'd been up on put a damper on the mood for him. It didn't soften his hard-on now but mentally he wasn't there. So instead of saying another word, he decided to suck it up and take the cursing out. He was wrong and he knew it.

So here Zyair and Thomas sat, Thomas wanting to come over for dinner, that is, if Champagne was cooking, and Zyair knowing damn well that, even if she was, he wouldn't be welcome. As a matter-of-fact, he wouldn't be welcome for a hot moment.

Deciding to change the subject, Zyair looked around to make sure no one was within listening distance. "So, what do you think of open relationships?"

Thomas raised his eyebrows. "Why are you asking me that? I know you and Champagne ain't thinking about no shit like that." He thought Zyair would be out of his mind to even consider it. There was no way in the world, he would let another man get all up in his. No way in hell.

"Nah, man, I was just asking, trying to get your opinion."

"Why would you want my opinion on something like that?"

"Just trying to make conversation. Damn! I overheard two of my employees talking about it."

Thomas didn't believe a word Zyair was saying. For one, Zyair never talked about his employees. I mean, he didn't really befriend them like that, and Thomas was having a hard time believing Zyair would eavesdrop. He just wasn't that type of man.

Thomas knew something was up but if Zyair wanted to play the conversation this way, he'd let him. He knew Zyair too well to believe this was some hypothetical.

Damn, Thomas thought, *I never would've thought Champagne had the freak in her like that but shit, one never knows.* Zyair's a lucky man. He's got a lady in the streets and a freak in the sheets.

"Well, what do you think about it?"

"What specifically are you asking me?"

Ready to let it go, Zyair told him, "I'm asking you about open relationships—switching, swinging, threesomes."

Thomas nudged Zyair. "Come on, come clean with me. You and Champagne, y'all into that? Is that what this is about?"

Zyair didn't know how much he wanted to tell Thomas, because Thomas sometimes blurted things out. "I'm just curious."

"What? You ain't satisfied with Champagne?"

"That's not what I'm saying. It's just that after listening to my employees it got me to thinking."

"Boy, don't fuck up what you have. You know you almost lost her once and you damn near went out your mind."

"I ain't gonna mess up. Just humor me. Damn! You're getting all emotional over my issue."

After looking at Zyair for a second or two, Thomas said, "Man, I don't know. Even though you're just saying you're curious, I don't really see Champagne being down with something like that. I'll say this, though—If I had a woman and that was something I might could get away with, I would. I'm only talking about the three-some thing, the having two women—hell yeah. But the whole swinging aspect of it, letting another man get with mine, oh, hell no."

Zyair laughed. That's definitely not what he was talking about. After ending the conversation, Zyair called Champagne to see if she was cooking.

She was, and Thomas was not invited.

Chapter Twelve

"I'm Every Woman"

Chaka Khan

Champagne stood at the door of her new office and felt an overwhelming sense of pride, and fear. Pride because she was going out on her own and fulfilling a dream, making an idea a reality, fear because she had no idea how this would turn out. She knew she was more than capable of doing the job, or running her own business. She knew her skills were up to par and she also knew that if she didn't know what to do about something, she could figure it out. She knew she had the goods to deliver. It's not like she was a novice in her field, she was one of the best.

Unlocking the door and taking the first step was an emotional event. Personal Touch, Inc. was her very own place of business, and that's just what she planned on giving each and every one of her clients. She would treat each and every one of them like they were her only clients. She knew that's what everyone said, especially when they were starting a service-based business, and it often started that way, only to wear off. But she'd vowed to offer a service with integrity.

Because she had some money saved and Zyair had fronted her what was considered an investment, she would be able to hire a secretary/receptionist and an assistant. The secretary would be there to type letters, brochures, make appointments, things that could be done in-house. The assistant would be someone that could run errands and assist in the handling of clients, someone she could depend on.

Zyair asked her, "Are you looking for somebody with experience, or somebody new to this business?"

"I'm looking for someone new and hungry, someone eager to learn, someone willing to grow with me, not someone who thought they knew more than me."

When Zyair wrote out the check to her, she kept thanking him for the loan. Finally, after going back and forth about the money she decided to listen when he said, "Just take the damn money, girl. It's an investment in our future together."

After listening numerous times to Champagne talking about how she wanted to do this on her own, Alexis told her, "Girl, your man loves you. He worships the ground you walk on, and with him helping financially, you will have a leg up on other businesses just starting out. What you need to do is be thankful for his generosity and that you have a man that has the money to help you fund your dream. Shit, this will allow you to hire people and everything."

When Alexis, the one who never cursed said, "Shit," Champagne almost passed out. This was another sign of Khalil being a bad influence. Alexis had even started to dress sexier. Her clothes were getting a little tighter, and she even showed cleavage a little more now. Champagne knew that these changes had to do with him but that was neither here nor there. Now was not the time to concentrate and worry about what Alexis was doing. What she needed to do was get prepared for the interviews she had lined up.

There was a coffee shop right down stairs and the plan was to meet the prospective employees at the office and if she liked them, they would go downstairs and continue the interview. If the first impression was one she didn't like, she'd wrap it up and send them on their way.

Glancing at her watch, Champagne noticed she had about thirty minutes before her first interview. There would be four interviews. Zyair told her she was taking on a lot, but she knew that she could handle it. All she had to do was pace herself. Her first interview was scheduled for 10:00 a.m., and she had them scheduled an hour and a half apart, her last interview coming up at 2:30. Okay, maybe she did bite off more than she could chew.

Champagne walked into the office, which had three rooms to it, the reception area, a small office for her assistant, and a much larger office, her space. Her office faced the front of the building and when she looked out the window, she could see the goings-on on the street below.

Champagne couldn't wait to furnish her office. She'd already chosen her colors, different shades of blue. She even had one of her past artist clients coming to paint a mural of a sunset for her. Thankfully her career choice was a creative one, and it allowed her to not be stuffy or have a conservative work space.

Tomorrow she would go out and start looking for furniture. She'd concentrate on her office first because she anticipated it being her home away from home. For the reception and assistant areas she would get the basics. Maybe later down the road, when she was a little more established, she'd go splurge.

Today for the interviews she had two chairs facing one another and a table, where they could fill out a personality questionnaire. She wanted everyone that would be working with and for her to vibe. She wasn't sure if this personality test thing would work, but she was going to find out.

She'd already put the coffee shop on alert that she would be coming and going.

The interviewing in the coffee shop was Zyair's idea. He told her, "When you interview in a more relaxed and casual environment, people tend to let their guard down, and are more themselves."

Not one to doubt a man with a successful business, she decided to take his word and was glad that she did.

Shanese, her first interviewee, although a college graduate, was as hood as they come.

Champagne thought, *You can take the girl out the hood, but you can't take the hood out of the girl.*

Shanese twisted her neck and chewed gum when answering questions.

Not even ten minutes had gone by before Champagne made the decision to end the interview right then and there.

Shanese thanked her again before leaving.

None of the interviewees worked out. Either they didn't have the type of energy she was looking for, or they wanted too much money. After the last interview, Champagne decided she'd stop by Private Affairs and see what Zyair was up to, but not before going to this new furniture spot she'd heard about that was owned by two gay men. She'd overheard two women discussing how they could go broke in there, that the furniture was eclectic, yet natural.

She definitely didn't want to go broke, but she was prepared to spend a little money. Champagne wanted a different feel to her office. She didn't want the typical desk, chair, and loveseat but was aiming for comfort and relaxation. She wanted her clients to come in and feel at home, not feel like they were being interviewed or put on display. After all, her business dealt with personalities, and she wanted her surroundings to reflect that.

When Champagne pulled into the parking lot, she noticed Thomas standing by a Lexus convertible. He appeared to be in a heated conversation with some guy. She had to look twice because the guy looked very familiar, but she couldn't place him.

Climbing out of her car, she grabbed her purse and locked the door behind her. She wanted to get into the store without Thomas seeing her, but just as she was opening the door, she heard her name being called.

"Champagne, hold up!"

Damn! She turned around and saw Thomas walking her way.

"What are you doing on this side of town?"

"Shopping for my new office."

"Oh, congratulations! Zyair told me all about it. He's so proud of you."

"Thanks."

"So how's your friend, Alexis?"

Champagne tried her best not to roll her eyes.

Thomas was always asking about her. She'd already told him she wasn't hooking them up. Plus, he wasn't Alexis' type anyway. But now, with her dating Khalil, Champagne didn't know what or who she would be attracted to. "Thomas, you need to give that fantasy up. Alexis has a man now, and I think they're serious."

Thomas frowned. "She has a what?" His attraction to Alexis was serious. He wondered how he could convince Champagne that he was ready to let go of his doggish ways to be with Alexis. He wanted her to know that he was aware of the fact that Alexis was a dime and deserved to be treated as such. Now here Champagne stood, crushing his heart with the information that Alexis had a man. Oh, hell no, he needed to find out more information.

"A man. I didn't stutter." Champagne was amused by the look on Thomas' face. He looked as though his feelings were hurt for real.

"Who? What's his name?"

"Khalil."

"Who the hell is he? Where's he from?"

"He's new in town." Champagne was ready to wrap up this conversation. She glanced at her watch. "Other than that, I don't know much about him."

"What do you mean, you don't know much about him? That's your girl. You need to find out more information."

When he said that, Champagne knew she'd found the right one to look into Khalil's background, but would he do it without Zyair finding out? She needed to think on that one before saying anything to him.

"That's what I'm trying to do, Thomas." She glanced at her watch once more. "Listen, I've got to go, but we'll talk more later." She just turned and walked away without even waiting for him to say good-bye.

Thomas watched her as she swayed her way into the building. He couldn't help recalling the conversation he and Zyair had. "Uh-huh-huh," he said to himself, you just never know which ones are turned out."

Chapter Thirteen

"Freak Like Me"

Adina Howard

Champagne sat in Zyair's office as she waited for him to finish talking to his cook. After leaving the furniture store, she'd called him up and told him she felt like doing something, hanging out. He agreed. They hadn't made a decision where they would be going. The only thing they knew was that they would do something out of the ordinary, something different.

Champagne knew that they weren't really into the club scene but a dance or two might be nice. Shit, it'd been a while since she shook her ass but then again, after taking into consideration the way women danced now, especially in videos, ass popping, titties shaking, maybe that was a good thing.

"Do you have anything in particular you'd like to do?" she asked Zyair, before he left the office.

"Nothing comes to mind. You decide, and when I come back, let me know."

Well, he'd been gone now for a full fifteen minutes and she was getting anxious. Especially since
she'd made the decision where she wanted to go.
Boy, would he be surprised. How was she going
to tell him that she wanted to go to a strip club to
see some naked ass? He'd probably think, *Here
we go again*. How was she going to tell him that
even though she was pissed at him for getting a
lap dance? After thinking about it, not only did it
turn her on but now she found herself wanting one.
Champagne knew that sounded hypocritical but it
was what it was.

When Zyair finally returned, Champagne
blurted out, "Let's go to a strip club tonight."

Zyair hadn't even made it in his office good.
"Did you say a strip club?"

The look on Zyair's face caused Champagne to
laugh, "Why are you looking at me like that? We
both said we would try new things. Well, let's start
tonight." Champagne knew she wouldn't have to
wait long for Zyair's response, because, being a
man, this was one offer he couldn't pass up. She
wasn't one to bad-mouth strip clubs. She just
wondered why men frequented them. What was
the point? After a couple of hours, didn't they get
tired of seeing naked ass? Well, tonight she was
going to find out what the hoopla was about.

"You want to go now?"

"Well, I was thinking we'd go home and change
clothes first."

"Fine with me." Zyair couldn't get out the door fast enough.

On the way home, Champagne was tripping. She couldn't believe she was about to step in a strip club with Zyair. "What club are we going to go?" she asked him.

Zyair had to think about which one to take her to. He didn't know what would appeal to her. "It depends on what you're looking for."

"What do you mean by that?"

"Well, there are two types of strip clubs. You've got the ones in the hood, where any and everything goes and then—"

Champagne cut him off. "What do you mean, where any and everything goes?"

"Sex, drugs, and whatever else you can think of."

"What's the other type?"

"Upscale, hands off, more attractive. There are two kinds of strip clubs crunk/upscale. Believe it or not, most people have a better time at the crunk clubs as opposed to the upscale clubs because the dancers at the crunk club refuse to let a brother leave out the club with a nickel. They want all the money and they work for that money. Whereas, the other type of club, most of the women think that Spike Lee or some director is about to cast their asses."

Champagne looked at Zyair. "How do you know so much?"

Zyair laughed. "I'm quoting Thomas."

That, Champagne could believe. "Why don't we go to both."

"Are you sure?" Zyair was still in disbelief.

"I'm more than sure. We can stay maybe an hour or two at one, then go see another."

Zyair was feeling like the man. "Your wish is my command."

He couldn't believe any of this was happening. He was actually going to the strip club with his lady. He felt a little weird about it, knowing it wasn't going to be the same as if he was with his boys.

Then again, maybe it was a good thing, because then Champagne would see that when he's with Thomas and the crew, he's not the wild, off-the-chain guy that gropes on, proposes, and gets oral sex from a stripper. He hoped Champagne wasn't trying to set him up, see how he was going to be if they did this threesome thing. Maybe he needed to stop thinking about it so much.

They were definitely trying to take their relationship to the next level. Zyair wondered how he should act. Should he act calm and not look around? He definitely didn't want to appear uptight in any way. When he was with his boys, they just entered the club, found seats, and started passing out singles.

Zyair didn't feel like second-guessing his actions, so he told Champagne while they were getting dressed, "I have to be honest. I'm a little nervous about this."

"What are you nervous about?"

"I don't know what to expect. I don't know what's acceptable and what's not. Do I tip? Do I just sit there? Do we call people over?"

"How about this . . . why don't we just go with the flow. Do what you normally do, and if I approve, I just might let you get a lap dance."

Zyair looked at her like, *Yeah right.*

Once in the car, they decided to go to Bottoms Up first. Zyair had never been there but he'd heard a lot about it. He'd heard that the dancers were shapely and that for most of them anything goes. Heck, a man can hope, and his hopes were high.

Champagne glanced over at Zyair and wondered what he was thinking. If she wasn't mistaken, he had a little smirk on his face. She could just imagine. She had to admit, she was a little nervous as well. What if she got there and was disgusted? Then again, what if she got there, was turned on and lost her damn mind.

She pulled out her lipstick case; touched up her lips. Her heart was racing but she was determined to see this through. After all, it was her idea.

Zyair decided to start from the bottom and work his way up. He couldn't wait to hear what her opinion would be of the spots.

When they pulled into Bottoms Up parking lot, Zyair looked at Champagne. "Are you ready?"

She opened the door and replied, "As ready as I'll ever be."

When they entered the club, Champagne felt like she was on the set of a BET afterhours video. Not only were women walking around with nothing on but people were everywhere. She had to walk through a crowd and say excuse me numerous times just to get to where she was going.

Looking around, Champagne was surprised to see that there was an even number of men and women there. She told Zyair, "Damn, it's crowded as hell in here."

Zyair noticed as they walked through, men and women checking Champagne out. They paid no attention to him.

Some guy had the audacity to come up to Champagne and ask her, "What time are you dancing?"

Zyair looked at him and said, "She's not."

The dude looked Zyair up and down, decided he didn't want any trouble, and just walked away.

Zyair asked her, "Do you want to stay here?"

"I'm okay. Let's just stick together."

After squeezing their way through the crowd, Zyair spotted an empty corner of a couch. He took Champagne's hand and pulled her toward it.

The second they sat down a young lady dressed in the smallest and tightest dress either of them had ever seen asked them if they wanted a drink.

Champagne ordered an apple martini, and Zyair ordered a Corona. Before their drinks arrived two women came over to them and asked them if they wanted a table dance or to go into the VIP room.

Champagne looked them both up and down. They were total opposites, one was real short with at least size D titties. Champagne wondered how she got those big-ass breasts on that little body. Her hips were small, and her breasts were the only curves she had, average in the face, with "weave of life." Champagne knew she would not be the one.

The other girl was a little cuter but a bit too thick, borderline chubby. She also had the weave of life.

What's up with all this fake-ass hair? Champagne didn't really know what her type was but it definitely wasn't these two.

Zyair was watching Champagne, waiting to see how she would answer them.

"No, thank you."

They looked over at Zyair. "You heard the lady."

When the girls left, Champagne wanted to know what happens in the VIP room.

"Every and anything," Zyair informed her.

When the drinks were brought over, they sat back on the couch, sipped and watched the dancers.

Champagne couldn't believe all that she was seeing. If she wasn't mistaken one of the dancers appeared to be pregnant. Men were putting their hands inside women's panties that is if they were wearing them. The women were bending over, opening their pussies up wide. It was a hot mess.

"See anybody you want to tip?" Zyair asked.

There actually was one girl that had gotten Champagne's attention. Champagne heard someone call her Chocolate.

That she was. Chocolate-complexioned, medium height, probably about five-four, size C breasts, a small waist, and an ass for days. When she turned around, Champagne noticed the butterfly tattoo on her ass, a wing on each cheek. When she made her booty clap, the butterfly appeared to be flying.

Before Champagne could get a chance to call her over, someone else did.

"You want a lap dance?" Champagne asked Zyair.

Before he could give her an answer, Champagne calls someone over and tells her, "Give my man a lap dance."

Zyair looked at Champagne and asked her was she sure.

"Yes, I'm sure. I might get one after you."

That was something Zyair couldn't wait to see. "Maybe you should go first."

"No, you go first."

The next thing you know, it was on. Zyair was sitting straight up, real tight. He kept telling himself, "Don't get hard. Don't make it seem like you are enjoying it too much."

Champagne could tell what he was trying or more like trying not to do, so she grabbed his hands and told him, "Loosen up. We're here to have fun. You have my permission." She placed his hands on the dancer's breasts.

Champagne then summoned over another dancer and told her she wanted a lap dance as well.

Zyair was in complete shock. He was too focused on what was going on with Champagne to really get into his own lap dance.

Champagne was allowing this woman full access to her body. Her hands were everywhere. It wasn't until the girl tried to expose Champagne's breasts that she put an end to it.

Zyair was a little relieved because although turned on, for a second there he was getting a little jealous.

When the dancers walked away, Zyair saw Champagne look up at Chocolate, the girl with the butterfly on her ass.

Champagne pointed her out to Zyair. "I think she's sexy."

Little did she know, Zyair already noticed that Champagne had been peeping her.

The girl saw Champagne point her out and started coming in their direction.

On her way over to them, she was grabbed by another girl, who was just as sexy.

Zyair glanced at Champagne and thought to himself, *It's about to go down.*

They both stood in front of Champagne, all eyes on her.

"I saw you watching me."

"I was," Champagne admitted.

"I'm Chocolate. This is my girl, Cinnamon. You want a private show?"

Zyair wanted to yell out, "Hell yeah!"

"What does a private show entail?" Champagne asked, pleased that Zyair was letting her take the lead.

Zyair wasn't crazy. He knew what he was doing. He knew to let everything be Champagne's idea.

"Well, you can get a private lap dance, you and your man, or just you and he can watch. For one hundred dollars, you can watch us do each other, and for a hundred dollars apiece we'd do you both."

Zyair didn't open his mouth. His eyes said it all, "Just say yes to anything."

Before Chocolate could continue on with her proposition, there was a ruckus two tables over. Two men were arguing. Champagne couldn't make out what they were saying but she could make out that one of the dudes had a gun.

Zyair spotted it the second she did. He grabbed her hand, pulled her up, and along with others, they ran out of the club.

After making it to the car, Champagne and Zyair looked at one another and burst out laughing.

"Can you believe that?" Champagne asked. "We could have gotten killed while trying to get our freak on."

Zyair started the car up. "Where to next? Do you want to go home, or do you want to try the other place?"

"What's it called?"

"Fantasies."

"Is that where you and Thomas go?"

"I've never been, but I heard it was upscale and that the quality of women is definitely of a higher class."

"How much higher in class could they be if they're stripping?"

Zyair didn't have an answer.

"Let's go. I'm not ready to turn in yet." Champagne had to admit, she wanted to see more. She was also glad things happened the way they did, because she wasn't sure what answer she was going to give the Chocolate girl, but she knew it was a yes to something. When they arrived at Fantasies, Champagne noticed the difference immediately. One, it cost twenty dollars per person to enter, two, the clientele was predominantly white businessmen. The dancers were more attractive and had better bodies than the other women at Bottoms Up.

Another major difference was that someone seated you and gave you a menu with the prices of all the services they provided.

Although the atmosphere was more appealing, the prices were ridiculous when you compared them to Bottoms Up.

"Goddamn!" Champagne stated.

The same girly show that they could have witnessed at Bottoms Up for fifty dollars would cost them one fifty here, and the only thing that a single was good for was a peek at someone's titties. And a drink was ten dollars, with a two-drink minimum.

After being seated, they decided to at least get a lap dance, which was twenty dollars. After all, they'd paid their money to get in.

Champagne picked out a Spanish girl who called herself Shala. She promptly ran down the rules of the lap dance. By the time she was done with the rules, Champagne said exactly what Zyair was thinking, "Let's leave."

When they got to the car, Zyair asked Champagne what she would like to do now.

"Go home," Champagne said, ready to make love.

Zyair broke the speed limit all the way home. What would have normally been a forty-five-minute drive took thirty minutes.

Neither of them said a word. They just headed toward the bedroom.

When they stepped in, Champagne asked Zyair, "When I was getting my lap dance, did you like watching?"

"I always like watching." Zyair was referring to the strip club and Jamaica.

Champagne started to undress, and Zyair knew this meant for him to do the same.

In less than five minutes, Zyair was kneeling between Champagne's knees, his face deep in her pussy, and his hands on her breasts, squeezing her nipples. Champagne threw her head back and told him, "Lick it, lick my walls."

Zyair separated her lips to put his tongue in as far as he could. He pressed his chin on the lower part of her pussy and shoved his tongue in and out of her like it was a dick.

Champagne held his head tight against her and humped his tongue. "Suck my clit," she demanded. She was ready for an orgasm.

And Zyair was ready to give it to her. He was also ready to get deep inside her. This was his pussy, and he wanted her to know it. He wanted to hear her say it. He took both of his hands and pushed the skin back from her clitoris and flicked his tongue back and forth, then suckled it, flicked back and forth and suckled some more.

He knew she was about to explode when her body started quivering and bucking.

"Oh, Zyair, it's yours, baby," Champagne called out as she climaxed.

Zyair removed his mouth and climbed on top of her.

He gripped both cheeks of her ass and entered her real patient-like. He wanted to feel every inch of that pussy, and he wanted her to feel every inch of him.

He pulled out on a one, two, three count and slammed inside her. It was driving them both crazy.

It wasn't long before Zyair looked Champagne in the eyes and said, "I'm about to cum," and cum he did. Hard.

Chapter Fourteen

"My Girl"

Temptations

The next day Zyair, floating on cloud nine, met Thomas at the gym.

Thomas was spotting Zyair and could tell something was up. "All right, out with it."

"Out with what."

"What's got you so happy this morning?"

"You wouldn't believe me if I told you."

"Try me."

"Let me finish up these chest presses, then I'll tell you."

Thomas couldn't wait, so he refused to spot Zyair until he spit out whatever information he was about to share.

Zyair sat up on the bench, shook his head and said, "Man, you'll never believe what Champagne and I did this week."

"What?"

"Went to a strip club."

"Together?"

"Yep."

Thomas stood in front of Zyair. "You're straight lying."

Zyair lay back down on the bench. "Why would I lie about a thing like that?"

Thomas took the bar and placed it in Zyair's hand. "Because, man, I thought she hated you going to strip clubs."

"She hates me going with your ass."

Zyaid did a few press-ups, placed the weight back on the bar, sat down and said, "Guess what else?"

Thomas raised his eyebrows. "I don't know if I can take anything else."

Zyair needed to tell someone of their adventure for the weekend and there was no one he really trusted with issues of the heart other than Thomas. Patting his chest, like 'I'm the man' he told Thomas, "She suggested it. She also let me get a lap dance."

Thomas took a step back, looked at Zyair and told him, "You're lying," but the look on Zyair's face told him he was telling the truth. "You're one lucky man."

"Don't I know it."

"What's gotten into you two? First you go to Hedonism, then you go to the strip club together. What's next? Swinging?"

Zyair stood up. "Hell no!" He grabbed his towel and his bottled water off the floor. Together they headed toward the locker room.

Thomas couldn't let the conversation go. "Never say what you won't do because to me it seems like you two are on your way to a whole other level of freakiness."

Zyair just laughed. He knew Thomas wanted to hear more, and there was only so much information he was willing to give up. "Man, come on, let's go get something to eat."

In the meantime, Champagne was in her office. She had another interview set up today and Lord knows she hoped this one prospective employee was better than the others. She really needed to hire an assistant and fast. There were a couple of events coming up for her clients and her being the sole everything to every one wasn't working. Nor was her being picky.

Zyair had told her, "That's how it is sometimes, and it's better to be picky and take your time than to hire someone just because you're in a hurry. When you have your own business and you're doing all the hiring, you have a hard time choosing someone because your company is your business, your baby, and you don't know who to trust or who will take it as seriously as you."

She'd set up this interview downstairs in the cafe like she did the others.

Please let this be the one, please let this be the one, she thought over and over to herself. She needed to do business without having to worry about if something was going to get done or not.

Champagne told the person she was interviewing that she would be sitting at the table in the corner, closest to the kitchen. That way they wouldn't be looking around for one another.

After glancing at her watch, Champagne decided to leave fifteen minutes early and have a cup of coffee or tea so that she would be relaxed by the time the young lady arrived. She grabbed the folder with the resume in it, locked her office door and headed downstairs. When she got to the door, she looked at where they would be sitting and saw someone already there. She headed toward the table.

The young lady seated there stood up. "Champagne?"

"Candy?"

"Yes." She put out her hand for Champagne to shake.

Champagne felt a sense of relief. Candy was professionally dressed. She wore a black pants suit with a white tailored blouse, opened-toed heels, small silver hoop earrings, and had her hair pulled back. She was attractive in a don't-have-to-try-hard kind of way. Champagne was also impressed with the fact that she'd arrived early and wasn't chewing gum.

"I apologize if my being early is an inconvenience, but I figure it's better to be early than rushing or late."

Champagne sat down and told her, "That's okay."

She placed the folder with Candy's resume on the table. She waved her hands for Candy to sit as well.

Champagne sat back and crossed her legs, "So, tell me about yourself. Why do you want this position?"

Candy went on to tell her she'd always been interested in the entertainment business and after being a personal assistant for an executive at a law firm, she grew tired of the corporate world and made the decision to leave and look for something where she could combine her skills and something she loves.

"When I saw the position for this job in the paper, I decided to give it a try and send in my resume."

Champagne went on to ask her a number of questions about her past job and about her organizational skills.

At the end of the interview, Champagne didn't bother having her fill out the personality test. She knew she'd found the person.

"If I was to hire you, when would you be able to start?"

"I could start as soon as tomorrow."

Champagne stood up to signal that the interview was over.

Standing up, Candy asked her, "How soon before you make a decision?"

"In the next day or two. I'll give you a call either way."

They shook hands and went their separate ways. When Champagne got back to her office, she called Alexis and told her, "Girl, I think I've finally found an assistant."

"Good for you, girl."

Champagne could tell that Alexis was preoccupied. "What are you doing?"

"Nothing. Laying here with Khalil."

Champagne rolled her yes. "Why don't y'all come over for dinner?"

"When? Tonight?"

"How about tomorrow?"

"Hold on."

Champagne heard Alexis ask Khalil if he would mind going over Champagne's for dinner the next day. She couldn't hear his reply.

"We'll be there," Alexis told her. "What time?"

Off the top of her head, Champagne told her to be there by eight p.m.

They hung up the phone. Champagne called Zyair and told him about Candy and dinner.

Feeling good about the day, Champagne thought, *Why wait? I already know I'm going to hire her.* So she picked up the phone and called Candy.

"Hello?"

"Candy, this is Champagne."

"Oh, hi."

"I'm calling to say you've got the job. Can you come by the office Monday around one p.m., so we can talk more about what's required?"

"Sure, I can do that."

"Okay, I'll see you then."

"That you will."

Champagne hung up, pleased with herself. She found an employee, and she was going to give Khalil the opportunity to impress her.

Chapter Fifteen

"Superfreak"

Rick James

That evening while relaxing on the couch, with her legs thrown over Zyair's and her eyes closed, she laid her head and recalled the night of the strip club.

She had to admit that she had a good-ass time and was even thinking about going back.

She wished she could tell Alexis about it, but knew this was something she had to keep to herself. Alexis wouldn't understand at all. When she really gave it some thought it pissed her off because she wanted a best friend that she could share any and everything with.

When Champagne opened her eyes, Zyair was looking at her.

"What were you thinking about?"

"Nothing. I was relaxing."

"Nah, I could hear your mind working. Come on, give it up."

"You really want to know?"

"I wouldn't have asked if I didn't want to know."

"Okay." She sat up. "I was thinking about the strip club."

This got Zyair's attention. "Oh, really?"

"I came up with another idea."

"Oh, really?" he repeated.

"Let's go to a gay club."

"What?" Zyair stood up. "I don't know about all that."

Champagne started laughing.

"What's so funny?"

"Do you think I'm talking about a men's club?"

"If you're not, then what are you talking about?"

"An all-girls club."

Zyair sat back down. This was something he had to think about. Champagne seemed to be pressing this girl-girl issue. First she wanted to see some naked ass. Now she wanted to see women dancing with women.

On the one hand Zyair was excited about the turn of events but on the other, he couldn't help to think about all the horror stories he'd heard about men "coming out" and leaving their significant others.

Deep down in the back of his mind, he was a little apprehensive about going to the gay club. What if Champagne saw some girl, fell in love and left him. *Nonsense,* he thought to himself. Champagne likes dick too much. Plus, he knew he could throw down in the bedroom.

Nonetheless, Zyair was so nervous about agreeing to yet another adventure that he decided he would come up with some "gay club rules." Rule number one was Champagne must stay in Zyair's sight at all times, rule number two was Champagne must stay in Zyair's sight at all times, and rule number three was Champagne must stay in Zyair's sight at all times.

"Okay," he told her, "let's go."

"Cool."

"But I've got three rules," he told her.

"What kind of rules could you possibly have?"

He told her the three rules, and her reply was a kiss and an, "I love you too."

"Are you nervous?" Zyair asked Champagne as they got dressed.

"A little," Champagne confessed.

"I am too."

"Yeah, right. Your ass is probably excited."

"I'm not going to lie, I am excited, but at the same time I don't know what's going and what's not going to happen."

"Well," Champagne said, "what do you want to happen?"

"It's up to you."

Champagne looked in the mirror, she was wearing a pair of Seven Jeans and a fitted black tee with black stiletto shoes. She was going for the casual yet sexy look. "How do I look?"

Zyair, who wore jeans and a black T-shirt, told her, "Sexy."

It was just what she wanted to hear. "Okay, let's go."

After searching on the internet, they'd chosen a club in the city.

When they arrived in the city, Champagne suggested driving past the club so they could see the clientele. "Just to get a feel of it first," she told him.

Zyair knew that was part of the reason but he also knew the other part was to get her nerves up before entering.

The windows were dark, and the door was closed. Sitting on the outside of the door was a white female with a spiked haircut stamping people's hands as they went inside.

Damn, the stereotype is true, Champagne thought. "So is that your type?" Zyair joked.

Champagne didn't know if she had a type when it came to women. What she did know is that if she was to deal with one, she had to be very feminine, similar to herself.

They drove around the block one more time before looking for a parking garage.

As they walked toward the club, Zyair asked Champagne, "Are you ready?"

She took a deep breath. "I'm ready if you are."

"ID please," the girl at the door said.

Damn, this chick is bigger than me, Zyair thought to himself. It definitely wasn't the same girl that was sitting on the stoop when they initially drove by.

They pulled out their IDs and handed it to her.

She took a quick glance at Zyair and a lingering look at Champagne, looking her up and down. She even had the audacity to lick her lips and say, "Hope you find what you're looking for."

Neither of them answered her. They stepped into the club and looked around. On the entry level of the club there was a bar the length of the floor. All the seats at the bar were taken. There was also a pool table in the back of the room, and house music blared through the speakers.

"Let's walk around," Champagne suggested. As they walked around, Champagne noticed that there was no particular type in the club. The women didn't all look like men or dress like men, they didn't all have short haircuts, and they definitely weren't of one race. There were also as many men as there were women in attendance. She wondered if they were experimenting just like she and Zyair.

Women were hugged up on one another, holding hands and kissing.

"Do you want to sit at the bar, or do you want to go upstairs and dance?" Zyair could hear the house music playing and knew Champagne loved that type of sound to dance to.

"Let's just chill down here for a little while," Champagne said. When Zyair didn't respond, she looked up at him, only to find him staring at something to the right.

Her eyes followed his gaze and landed on two women in the corner kissing and embracing passionately. They appeared to be lost in one another. Against her will, Champagne found her pussy tingling. She was full of nervous energy and could feel every nerve in her body.

She and Zyair must have been staring real hard because when the women came up for air, they both looked their way and smiled, causing them to look away in embarrassment.

"Maybe we should go upstairs," Champagne suggested. Dancing would relax her. When they reached the top of the stairs, Champagne located the bar and grabbed Zyair's hand. "I need a drink to loosen up."

He followed her while looking around. Eventually they found a table in the corner and sat down.

As they ordered a drink, a woman approached Zyair. "Do you mind if I dance with your friend?"

She was quite attractive and reminded Champagne of Victoria Rowell from *The Young and the Restless,* a sexy, innocent look.

Zyair looked at Champagne, who nodded.

What the heck. Might as well make an adventure of it, she thought.

Not wanting to seem overly possessive, it took everything in Zyair's power not to get up and follow them to the dance floor but after about three songs and what seemed like twenty minutes later, he stood up to see what the hell was going on.

Before Zyair could spot Champagne, she appeared in front of him with a totally different girl.

"Zyair, this is Selena. Selena, this is my husband, Zyair."

Zyair was pleased Champagne introduced him as her husband because he was feeling somewhat left out and lonely and wanted some attention.

"Come dance with us," Selena said.

Zyair stood up and followed behind them. He couldn't help but notice that Selena had an ass like Deelishis from *Flavor of Love*.

Champagne stood in the middle of them as they danced.

Zyair would tell Selena things like, "Grab Champagne's ass. Kiss her on the neck. Rub against her titties."

It must have been the liquor because Selena's hands were all over Champagne.

Aw shit, this might be it, Champagne thought. We really might be able to set this up. Champagne gave Zyair a look to try convey what she was thinking but that thought went out the window the second Selena pulled out a cigarette.

"I'm going to have a smoke," she told them. "Care to join me?"

Reading one another's mind, they both said no.

The rest of the night was uneventful. Champagne danced a couple more dances, and Zyair drank a few more drinks.

Champagne noticed that Zyair may have had one too many drinks. "Baby, I think we should leave."

Zyair knew she was right. He also knew that he would not be the one driving home, that Champagne would.

As they walked toward the door, Champagne could feel someone staring at her. She turned around and saw that it was Candy; the girl she'd hired.

Damn! Should I speak?

Before she could make that decision, Candy turned away.

Relieved, Champagne told Zyair, "Wait near the door. "I'll get the car."

Zyair slept all the way home.

Champagne went to bed a little agitated because she wanted sex and Zyair was in no shape to give it to her.

Chapter Sixteen

"Fake"

Alexander O'Neal

Champagne chose not to spend the weekend focusing on the fact that she saw Candy at the club. She would have to decide whether to address the issue or leave it alone. Today wasn't the day to make that decision. She needed to clean the house and prepare dinner for Zyair and their company. How she would get through this day with the hangover she had, she still didn't know, but hope was alive and if she finished it early, she'd be able to lay down before the guests arrived.

As a matter-of-fact, she was going to have to lay down if she wanted to be a gracious host. The reason she extended the invitation was because she wanted to get to know this Khalil character a little better. After all, he was spending a lot of time with her best friend. Earlier that day, Zyair was on the phone and mentioned the dinner get-together to Thomas. "Is Alexis bringing that new nigga?"

Zyair didn't recall telling him. "How do you know she's with someone?"

"I saw your girl and she told me."

"Oh."

"Well, is she bringing him?"

"Yeah."

"Well, I'm coming too."

"No, you're not."

"Why not?

"Because I know you. You've got a thing for Alexis, and I can see you starting some shit."

"Man, please, I won't bust his ass. I just want to see the knucklehead. Plus, ain't nothing like a homecooked meal."

"I don't know, man. I don't think Champagne is going to like this."

Just then, Champagne walked into the kitchen. "You don't think I'm going to like what?"

Zyair didn't answer. He handed the phone to Champagne.

"Hello?"

"What's up, beautiful?"

"Quit brown-nosing and tell me what I'm not going to like."

Thomas, never one to bite his tongue, said, "I want to come over for dinner."

Normally, Champagne would have thought about it but this time, she didn't. They could both evaluate this Khalil character. "Okay, just don't come empty-handed. Bring some wine or something." She passed the phone back to Zyair, who was staring at her in disbelief.

She turned around to finish cooking. "What?"

When Zyair and Thomas finished talking, Zyair walked into the kitchen and stood in front of Champagne, his arms crossed. "Okay, out with it."

"Out with what?"

"You're up to something. I can feel it."

Champagne tried to walk around him but he kept blocking her path.

"I don't know what you're talking about."

Zyair placed his hands on her hips and held her in place. "Don't start any trouble."

Champagne kissed him on the lips. "I'm not."

Zyair released her, not believing a word she said. "Is he coming by himself, or is he bringing someone?"

"He's bringing someone."

"Okay."

That afternoon Champagne was able to take a nap.

When she woke up, she noticed Zyair had fixed the table and cleaned the kitchen.

"Thanks, sweetie," she told him.

"You're welcome."

A couple of hours later, they found themselves dressed and sitting in the living room watching television. Champagne heard someone pull into the driveway. She walked over to the window, opened the blinds and saw a Quicksilver Cadillac EXT. She watched as Khalil got out of the driver's side and went around to open the door for Alexis, who had a box in her hand. She quickly closed the blinds and opened the door.

She greeted Alexis with a hug and said hello to Khalil.

Before she could close the door, another car pulled into the driveway. Thomas climbed out of his black CLK 350 and noticed everyone standing in the doorway, looking his way. He glanced at the EXT and then at Khalil.

The young lady he was with was still sitting in the car.

"Are you going to open the door?" she asked him.

He walked over and let her out, as Alexis and Khalil went into the house and Champagne waited at the door.

Champagne hugged him and pulled away. "Thomas, who's your date?"

By now Zyair was at the door, looking at Champagne out of the corner of his eye.

"This is Diamond."

Champagne noticed that Diamond was stunning. "Hi, Diamond. Come on in."

Once everyone was in the same room together, introductions were made, and Champagne took the box from Alexis.

"It's dessert."

"Oh, shit," Thomas said, "I left the wine in the car. I'll be right back."

Zyair followed Champagne in the kitchen. "You need to tell me what's going on."

"Nothing. Why do you keep asking me that?"

"Because I know you."

Champagne started laughing. "Stop worrying so much. Let's just enjoy the evening with our friends and their dates."

When they walked back into the living room, Diamond was asking Khalil if she knew him from somewhere.

"No, I don't think so."

"You just look so familiar to me."

"Well, you know what they say, we all have a twin."

Thomas was looking Khalil up and down. It was so obvious that Zyair bumped up against him.

"What?" Thomas asked.

"Let me show you something."

Thomas wasn't stupid. He knew Zyair was trying to get him out of the room to lecture him.

"Nah, man, show me later."

"Come on, everyone, let's have a seat and get to know one another." Champagne pointed toward the seating area.

For the next hour, conversation flowed back and forth freely. They learned that Khalil was one of the partners for a construction company and that he grew up in Atlanta and moved to New Jersey to help one of his sisters, who was having problems with her husband, and ended up staying.

Champagne noticed that Diamond kept staring at Khalil like she knew something no one else did.

Thomas stood up to go into the kitchen to get some ice, and less than a second later, Champagne walked in behind him.

"So what do you think of this Khalil guy?" she asked him.

"I don't know. It's something about him I don't like."

That was just what Champagne wanted to hear. "I feel the same way."

They exchanged a look. They both knew that a more in-depth discussion had to take place later.

Dinner proceeded in an uneventful manner, and surprisingly everyone got along fine. Champagne still felt suspicious about Khalil and couldn't get past the instant dislike she felt for him. She had to admit to herself that she played it off pretty well.

When the time came for the party to end, Champagne said, "We should do this again."

They all agreed, and Zyair and Champagne walked everyone to the door.

Alexis asked Champagne, "What are you doing tomorrow?"

"One of my clients has a book signing."

"Oh, okay. Then call me when you get a chance."

Chapter Seventeen

"I Didn't Mean To Turn You On"

Cherelle

Champagne stood next to her client, Hunter Irby, whose self-help book, *Lovin' the Skin You're In,* was on numerous bestsellers lists. She noticed that Hunter was fading fast. This was the second signing that day, and they were both tired and hungry.

Champagne leaned over and whispered in Hunter's ear, "It's almost over. Put a little more pep in your step and then it's a wrap."

Hunter looked at her and plastered a smile on her face in readiness for the next reader.

This was part of Champagne's job, keeping the clients on their toes, making sure they presented themselves in the best light possible. Champagne didn't attend every event with her clients. There wasn't enough time but sometimes she liked to show them how important and valuable they were to her. Soon she would be attending events even less, once she was able to hire a couple of more people.

After two hours of shmoozing at this book signing, Champagne just wanted to go home and relax.

Hunter was getting out of her seat so they could pack up and leave, when a woman came running over. "Wait, wait," she said.

Champagne looked up. "You've got one more," she told Hunter.

Hunter already had the book signed when the lady reached the table. Her pen poised for the name, she asked, "Who do I make it out to?"

"Sharon Simmons."

Upon hearing the name, Hunter looked up and started laughing. She stood up and reached out to give Sharon a hug. "Oh my God, what are you doing here?"

"I heard you were doing a signing and had to come see you."

Champagne took Sharon in with her eyes. She didn't know what had gotten into her. She was checking women out a little too often now and was hoping it wasn't noticeable.

Facing Champagne, Hunter introduced them to one another. "Sharon's a childhood friend of mine."

Extending her hand out for a handshake, Champagne said, "Pleased to meet you."

Sharon started laughing. "Girl, I don't shake hands. I hug." She placed her arms around Champagne and pulled her close, adding a little squeeze. "So what are you ladies about to do?"

Champagne shrugged.

Hunter looked at Champagne. "Well, let's go to dinner," she volunteered. "My treat."

Champagne's plan was to go home and cook dinner but there was something about this female's energy that she was feeling. She found herself wanting to know a little bit more about her. "Now, you know I'm not one to turn down a free meal,"

"I know a nice spot. It's about twenty minutes from here. A friend of mine owns it. Is that too far?"

"What kind of friend?" Hunter asked. Sharon laughed and winked.

Champagne wished she was in on the joke.

"Let me give you ladies the directions, and we'll meet there," Sharon told them.

Twenty minutes later they stepped into the restaurant. Sharon asked the hostess to get the owner.

"May I ask your name?"

"Tell her it's Sharon."

Less than five minutes later, the owner appeared. "Sharon," she greeted her, and they kissed on the lips. Champagne noticed the owner's hands were almost touching Sharon's ass and that she'd also closed her eyes when they kissed.

"Hunter, Champagne, this is Barbara." Everyone said hello.

"Follow me," Barbara told them as she led them to a booth that seemed to be hidden away in the corner.

Once they were seated, Barbara told them she would send someone over to take their order. As she walked away she said, "Sharon, don't leave without saying good-bye."

"Oh, I definitely won't."

Over the course of dinner, Champagne learned that Sharon was gay, not bisexual, that she liked women only. She wondered if she was "her type." *Stop it. Stop thinking these thoughts.* It was thoughts like this that made her question herself. What if she was really gay and just in denial? *Nah, that's not it.* This was just a moment, a phase she was going through.

When dinner ended and they were walking to the car, Sharon pulled out a business card and handed it to Champagne. "It was a pleasure meeting you. Call me sometime."

Champagne told her, "I enjoyed meeting you too. I'll definitely give you a call." She gave Sharon her card and placed Sharon's card in her purse. She noticed Hunter watching them with an amused look on her face. Thank God, she didn't ask any questions.

"We'll be in touch," Hunter told Champagne when Sharon drove off.

"That, we will."

When Champagne arrived home, Zyair wasn't home, so she called Alexis up. There was no answer, so she did the next best thing and went to bed. The day had been exhausting, and it was a rare moment when she got to turn in early.

Monday finally arrived. Zyair and Champagne were standing in the kitchen, Champagne making an espresso and Zyair peeling open the eggs he'd just boiled.

Zyair knew Champagne had something on her mind. She'd been quieter than usual that morning. After slicing the eggs, he asked her, "What's on your mind?"

"Huh?" Champagne pretended she didn't hear him.

"Where's your head at? You seem lost in thought this morning."

She wasn't lost in thought, she was thinking about Sharon and wondering when and if she should call her. If she did, what would they talk about? Would they go out to lunch? Would she be the female she slept with? Of course, she wasn't going to tell Zyair any of this.

"I'm just trying to organize the day's activities in my head."

"What do you have planned?"

"My new person is starting today."

"That's exciting."

Champagne didn't find it exciting. If anything, her nerves were shot.

Once Champagne arrived at the office, she was relieved that she'd told Candy to arrive at one p.m., as opposed to nine a.m. Now she had a chance to think about how she would handle Candy seeing her and Zyair at the club. Maybe she should just act like it wasn't anything. Sometimes the best thing is to do nothing at all. Shaking her head, Champagne decided not to focus on that. What she needed to do was put together a list of duties that need to be completed by the end of the week. So far, Champagne had nine clients. Their professions ranged from writer to company CEO.

Each client needed something different, whether it was booking interviews, making flight arrangements, putting their calendar together, making sure they showed up when they were supposed to, and on and on it went. She definitely needed someone to start right now. Four employees including herself would be ideal but right now she'd settle for three—herself, Candy, and another.

The pickings were limited. Nobody she'd interviewed to date had what it took. Champagne was considering hiring an intern from college or someone straight out of college. The more she thought about it, the more it seemed like a good idea. If she did that, she would be able to mold the person. Initially, she'd wanted someone with experience, but she realized that it sometimes came with attitude.

After making several phone calls, typing up a to-do list and, working on her company's Web site, Champagne glanced at the clock. She couldn't believe it was twelve already. Only one hour left before Candy showed up. Maybe less because, during the interview, she'd mentioned being a stickler for time.

Champagne needed a break and decided to run downstairs to the cafe and grab a salad and something to drink.

Over the past couple of weeks, before going upstairs to her office, she'd made it a habit to grab a cup of tea and the newspaper. The owner of the cafe always spoke to her, and today was no exception.

Champagne was waiting on her salad when the owner walked over. She couldn't remember his name for the life of her.

"So how's business going?" he asked.

"It's going. I'm having a hard time finding another employee."

"What kind of position is it?"

"Administration, and assisting me."

"I just might know someone."

Champagne couldn't hold it in any longer. She had to tell him she forgot his name.

"That's okay. It's James."

"James, in case you forgot, I'm Champagne."

"I haven't forgotten."

Champagne could hear the flirt in his voice. As long as he didn't try to come on to her, it was all good. "So who is this person you have in mind?"

"My niece. She just moved here from Virginia, and she's looking for a job."

"What kind of experience does she have?"

"I'm not sure but she's smart and can type. I'm not just telling you that either. After all, you know where I work."

Champagne laughed. "Call her. I'll be more than willing to meet with her. I'll bring a card down later."

The girl behind the counter gave Champagne her order, and Champagne paid for it and went upstairs.

She glanced at the clock and saw that she was downstairs for twenty minutes. "Damn." She only had fifteen or so minutes to eat.

Champagne sat at her desk and ate a portion of her salad, still wondering once again what she was going to do about Candy seeing them. She was almost certain Candy wouldn't bring it up.

It was five to one when Candy knocked on Champagne's open office door. "Hello."

Champagne was startled. She was in the middle of filing and didn't hear Candy walk in. "Hey, how are you?"

"Excited about my first day."

Pulling the chair out from behind her desk, Champagne sat down and told Candy to have a seat. Before she could even sit down, she said, "On second thought, let's sit at the table. That way I can go over a few things with you."

Looking at Candy, Champagne knew that she wouldn't be able to move forward without bringing up and moving past the fact that they'd seen one another over the weekend. Crossing her arms and leaning back in the chair, Champagne cleared her throat. "There's something we need to discuss before we move on to my expectations."

Candy had an idea what she was talking about. Of course, she wasn't going to bring it up, but she was glad Champagne did. She was curious to know whether her boss was gay and who she was with. Was it her husband, a friend, a brother, a lover?

Candy was well aware of the fact that a lot of couples frequented gay clubs to add spice to their relationships. As a matter-of-fact, she'd taken part in a couple of these escapades. Is that what Champagne's outing was about?

"This weekend we saw one another out, and I want you to know that what's done outside of this office, on personal time, is just that-personal. If seeing me out is going to affect how we work together, you need to let me know right now."

Champagne chose her words carefully. The more she'd thought about it, the more she felt it unnecessary to justify or explain why she had been at Fantasies. It was her and Zyair's business, not anyone else's.

Damn, that's all she's going to say. "No, of course not. We're both adults, and it is what it is."

"Good." Champagne uncrossed her arms and slid the folder across the table. "Inside are some forms that need to be filled out. Once you're through with them, we'll go over your job description and what's expected."

Candy took the folder, opened it, and pulled a pen out of her purse.

Champagne stood up. "I'll be in my office. Let me know when you're done."

In less than fifteen minutes Candy knocked on the door. "I'm done."

For the next half an hour, Champagne filled Candy in on her expectations. She told her that over the next two weeks, she would be responsible for answering the telephone, taking detailed messages, and going through the files, and learning about the clients, amongst other things.

Candy was anxious to get started. The only part of the job description she wasn't feeling was the answering the phone part. She didn't take this job to be a receptionist.

Just as she was thinking it, Champagne told her, "You won't be answering the phone for long. I'm looking to hire another person."

Together they determined for the time being that Candy would work from twelve to five p.m. Champagne did explain to her that in this line of work she had to be flexible and that some evenings and some Saturdays were required.

"Don't worry, you'll know in advance when you're needed, and we'll work something out as far as the normal hours go," Champagne reassured her. She also gave Candy a tour of the office. "Until I hire someone, you'll sit up front. Hopefully, that won't be for long, then the office to the right is yours."

Candy looked to the right. *Damn, my own office space.* She was liking that.

By the time they finished talking and going over how Champagne liked things done, it was four p.m. Champagne was worn out from talking. "You can leave early today."

"Thanks." Candy put up the papers she was looking over and told Champagne she would see her tomorrow.

When Candy left the office, Champagne breathed a sigh of relief. It felt good to finally have someone else in the office. It made it feel like a real business and not a one-person show. She knew that running her own business was going to be a challenge, but she just didn't realize how much of a challenge it would be.

Champagne was starving. She never got a chance to finish her salad. *I bet you it's soggy now. I know I should have had them put the dressing on the side.*

She reached for the phone to call Zyair. The second her hand touched it, it rang. She pressed the speakerphone button. "Personal Touch, how may I help you?"

"Um, hello?" the voice on the other end said. Champagne picked up the phone and placed it between her ear and shoulder. "Hello?"

"May I speak with Champagne?"

"This is she."

"Hey, lady, it's Sharon."

Champagne was pleased to hear her voice. "Hey."

"Do you remember me?"

"Of course, I do. How are you?"

"Fine. I was sitting here in my office and came across your card. Since I hadn't heard from you, I thought I'd give you a call."

"Well, I'm glad you did."

Champagne held the phone up to her ear and started pacing the floor, feeling a little nervous, as if she was on the phone speaking with a man. Champagne recalled being attracted to her and had even thought about her a number of times. She just couldn't bring herself to call her.

"Are you up for dinner this evening?"

Champagne wanted to say yes right off the bat but she knew she should call Zyair first to see if he had anything planned. She didn't feel like going through the process, so she said, "I'm free tomorrow."

"I'm not for dinner, but I am for lunch. Is that good for you?

It would only be Candy's second day. Champagne wasn't sure if she wanted to leave her alone in the office so soon. Then again, she was a grown-ass woman, and it was only lunch. "Yes."

"Good. Listen, I've got to go, but I'm looking forward to seeing you tomorrow. We'll meet downtown at Cora's Kitchen. You know the place?"

Champagne told her, "I do. They have the best soul food in the area. What time?"

They agreed on one p.m. and hung up.

Champagne sat back in her chair, placed her hands in her lap, and closed her eyes. She pictured Sharon and the way sexiness oozed from her body. What if she'd seen her at Fantasies? Would they have danced together? Would she have taken her home?

Champagne wondered what they'd discuss at lunch.

Would they have idle chitchat? Would they talk about one another's sexuality? I could always bring it up in the conversation. The more Champagne thought about it the more she was like, *It's time to get the ball rolling. If I'm going to sleep with another woman, I need to go ahead and do it, instead of thinking about it.*

On that note, Champagne decided to call Zyair and see what he was up to, how his day was going. She was ready to broach the subject again.

Chapter Eighteen

"I Wanna Sex You Up"

Color Me Badd

Zyair wasn't in his office to answer Champagne's phone call. He'd been to the bank.

The second he entered his office, DaNeen followed behind him. "I don't mean to bother you, but there's something I need to talk to you about."

"Give me about fifteen minutes to get settled and then I'm all ears." Zyair didn't like being rushed. He needed a few minutes to get it together.

DaNeen wanted to talk now. "Fifteen minutes?" She'd been putting off resigning for quite some time. Now she was ready to let him know that she'd be moving on. She was going to start her own dessert business and was going to ask him to be her mentor.

"Yes. Then I'm all yours."

DaNeen stood there and looked at him like she wished he was all hers. "You promise?"

Zyair didn't answer her. He just smiled and watched her as she walked away. After all, he wasn't stupid. He knew that she was attracted to him, and he to her. He also knew not to act on that attraction. Anyway, it would only lead to heartbreak and death. Champagne would kill him.

Zyair thought about the time DaNeen decided she wanted to come onto him. Of course, he turned her down. Now if he wasn't with Champagne, he might have took her up on her offer. She had sexiness oozing off her. That was one of the reasons he'd hired her. He recalled when she came in for her interview.

When DaNeen had walked in, he almost jumped up and hugged her.

This is a natural beauty, he thought.

As he interviewed her, he found her to be intelligent, funny, and sassy. For a minute there, he wasn't sure if he should hire her because he was attracted to her, but he was desperate. His other hostess had to resign because of a family emergency. Hire her, he did, and he'd been pleased with his decision ever since.

Zyair noticed he'd left his cell phone on his desk. He clicked down to MISSED CALLS and saw that Champagne had called. He tried calling her back but it went straight to voice mail. "Hey, sweetie, just returning your call." He then retrieved his messages from his service. *I'll return phone calls later*.

Picking up the phone, Zyair paged the front desk.

"Send DaNeen in please."

Less than a minute later, she was walking into his office.

"Close the door," he told her.

She did.

"Have a seat."

When she sat down, Zyair couldn't help but notice the slit in her skirt revealed a lot of her toned thighs. The skirt definitely hugged every curve.

"What can I do for you?"

DaNeen crossed her hands and placed them in her lap. "I'm leaving," she blurted out.

Zyair frowned. He didn't understand what she was talking about. "Leaving? Where are you going?"

"I'm resigning. I've decided to start my own dessert business."

"Wow! Where did that come from?"

Zyair didn't know she baked, didn't know she wanted to start her own business. Hell, when he thought about it, he didn't know a lot about her.

"It's something I've always wanted to do. As a matter-of-fact, when you hired me, I recall mentioning to you that I bake."

"I know you did but that's not the same as saying, 'I want to bake for a living.'"

"At the time, it was just a dream. Between working here, watching how you run your business, and taking entrepreneur workshops, I've realized it's something I could do as a business."

"Do you have any potential clients?"

"Well, I've been baking for parties and weddings. I also have two mom-and-pop restaurants I bake for."

"Impressive."

"You see, my working here has taken up so much of my time. I could use that time to get clients, you know, target restaurants."

"How come you never approached me about stocking your desserts?"

"I don't know. I just didn't."

"The first lesson you need to learn about business is to take advantage of every opportunity."

As DaNeen stood up, Zyair noticed her curves once again. *I wonder if she would be down for a threesome.*

"The other thing is, I need a mentor and I wanted to know if you would be it."

Without a second thought, he told her, "Sure."

DaNeen came around the desk and threw her arms around him, kissing him on the cheek.

At that exact moment, Thomas came busting through the door. "Yo, man, you wouldn't—" He stopped midsentence and wondered what the hell was going on. "Oh, excuse me, I didn't mean to interrupt anything."

DaNeen stepped back. "I'm sorry," she told Zyair. "I just got carried away."

Thomas was taking it all in with a raised eyebrow. He sat down and followed Zyair with his eyes as he stood up to walk DaNeen to the door.

"Listen," Zyair told her, "you don't have to quit. We can work something out until you're up and running."

From where Thomas was sitting, it appeared as if DaNeen batted her eyes and pushed up her cleavage as she said, "Are you sure? I don't want to be an inconvenience or anything."

"I'm sure," Zyair reassured her, and closed the door behind her.

Thomas couldn't wait for her to leave the room.

"What's up with you and her?"

"Nothing, man. She's my employee."

"Are you sure she's not more than that?"

Zyair didn't bother answering the question. He just sat down behind his desk. "What's up?"

Thomas started to speak, "Listen, the—"

"Wait, before you even tell me. What I tell you about busting in my office without knocking?"

"I see why you feel that way now."

"Man . . . please. You know I'm as loyal as they come."

Thomas stood up. "Remember at dinner, my girl kept saying she knew that Khalil dude from somewhere?"

"Yeah."

"Well, you're not going to believe this shit."

The way Thomas was acting, Zyair could tell it was something big. "What?"

"That nigga is a freak. Listen to this—he fuckin' hangs out at that club, Free for All."

Zyair had no idea what he was talking about. "Free for All?"

"You know, the swingers club?"

"How does your girl know?"

"She's a freak too!"

Zyair laughed.

Thomas wasn't done yet. "Not only that but he's done porn too." Before Zyair could get a word in, Thomas added, "She's bringing me the tape tonight. You know we've got to tell Alexis, right."

Zyair started shaking his head. "Nah, man, that's something I'm not getting into."

"What do you mean, you're not getting into it. We're talking about my future wife, and your woman's best friend."

"And?"

"Do you care about Alexis?"

"Man, don't ask me no stupid shit like that. She's my girl's best friend. Of course, I care about her."

"Do you care about your boy?" Zyair just looked at him.

"Well, I love that girl."

"Yeah, okay."

"I'm going to marry her one day. As soon as I get all this fucking around out of me, she's going to be mine. I don't want this Khalil character to ruin her."

"She's a grown-ass woman."

"I know that, but I think you should at least tell Champagne."

"I'll think about it."

"Nah, man, action. We need some action."

"I told you I'll think about it."

"I don't want him destroying my goods."

"I heard you, man."

Thomas stood up. On his way to the door, he turned around. "Be careful."

"Of what?" Zyair had no idea what he was talking about.

"That fine honey you got working for you."

Zyair waved the comment off. "What is this, first grade? I'm a taken man."

Thomas wasn't fooled. He knew Zyair was bothered because what he'd said was true. Thomas looked at him real serious and said, "Yeah, and you need to remember that shit."

Chapter Nineteen

"Temporary Love Thing"

Full Force

Champagne was nervous as she got ready for lunch with Sharon. Was it just lunch, or would it be considered a date?

Maybe it was because she was going to lunch with a lesbian, or maybe it was the fact that she figured that Candy was either gay or bisexual.

Champagne had noticed how appealing Candy was when she'd interviewed her. And today, for some reason, she kept sneaking peeks. She knew if she didn't hurry up and handle this threesome thing with Zyair she was going to go crazy. It was consuming her. Maybe once they did it, it would be out of her system.

"I'll be back in two hours," Champagne told her after she'd given her a list of things to do and a few phone calls to make.

"If I have any questions, should I call your cell phone?"

"That would be fine."

Fifteen minutes later, Champagne was entering the restaurant. The second she put her foot through the door, she and Sharon spotted one another at the same time. Champagne could feel Sharon checking her out as she walked across the room. She found herself looking down at her outfit, hoping Sharon liked what she saw.

When Champagne reached the table, Sharon surprised her by standing up, walking around the table, and kissing her on the cheek.

"Thanks for coming," she said.

"No need to thank me. I wanted to."

Sharon licked her lips. "Did you now?"

Champagne caught it and figured it was just something she did when talking, that it wasn't a signal or a sign.

At that moment the waitress walked over and placed menus on the table. "Would you ladies like something to drink?"

Sharon looked at Champagne. "Diet coke, please."

"I'll take the same." The second the waitress walked away, Sharon said, "So tell me about yourself."

"What do you want to know?"

"Let's start with why you said yes to my invitation."

"I found you interesting," Champagne told her.

"Interesting how?"

All of a sudden Champagne felt shy but she wasn't going to let that get in her way.

"Maybe interesting is the wrong word. What I mean is, you know how you meet someone and you like their vibe immediately . . . when you feel like, that's a person you can kick it with?"

"Yeah, I know."

"Well, that's why I agreed. That and the fact that Hunter thinks you're cool as hell."

"The feeling is mutual. Hunter and I have known each other for ages."

"Do you want to know why I called you?" Sharon asked, breaking Champagne out of her thoughts.

"Because you think I'm cool as hell?"

"Cool, cute, and sexy."

The waitress came with their drinks. "Are you ready to order?"

They told her they needed another minute.

Champagne and Sharon quickly picked up their menus and started looking at the choices.

"I think I'll order the salmon dish," Champagne said.

"Yeah, that's a good idea. Plus, it's light." Sharon waved the waitress over and placed their order.

While she did that, Champagne decided to continue flirting with Sharon. Why sit here and pretend? She was on a mission. When the waitress walked away, Champagne said, "So you were saying?"

"I was saying that I think you're cute."

"Cute's for kids."

"How about, I think you're sexy as hell?"

"How do you know I won't get offended? How do you know if I'm even attracted to women?"

"I don't know. If you're offended, please tell me."

"I'm not."

"Good. Because when we met, I thought I was feeling an energy."

Champagne frowned. Was she that obvious? "What kind of energy?"

"And I'm checking you out on the 'quiet-tip' energy."

Champagne laughed. She did think it was on the quiet tip. "Damn!"

"Let me ask you this," Sharon said. "What's your sexual preference?"

"Confused."

Sharon leaned across the table, surprised that Champagne gave her such an honest answer. "Confused?"

Champagne spotted the waitress heading their way with their plates. She waited until she placed them down and walked away. Then she told Sharon, "Listen, I want to be clear, honest, and upfront."

"Damn, girl, didn't know this lunch date was going to be this serious."

"I didn't either, but I've got a feeling about you."

"What kind of feeling?"

As they ate and talked, Champagne talked about the Hedonism experience she and Zyair had. She hadn't told anyone else about it, and it felt so good to get it out.

"Ever since that experience, I've been thinking about doing it again. I want to see if I'll enjoy it as much sober, or if it was just a drunken experiment."

"What do you want it to be?"

"I'm not sure. I mean, what if I enjoy it the second time around and can't get enough? What if I get turned out?"

"How are you going about looking for this female? Don't tell me you and your man went to a strip bar or a gay club."

Champagne started laughing. "Why not?"

"You have, haven't you?"

"Yep."

Sharon just shook her head. "Don't you know that's what all couples do when they're trying to get it on? Why do they think it'll be that easy?"

"Believe me, we know it's not."

"Why don't you two use someone you know?"

"We don't know anyone that will be down."

"What exactly are you looking to make happen?"

Champagne couldn't help but wonder, *Was Sharon asking all these questions because she might be open to it, or was she just asking out of curiosity?*

"Well, Zyair can look, maybe touch. I'm not even sure about that."

"What else can he do?"

"What do you mean, what else can he do?"

"Is he going to be involved sexually?"

"As in intercourse?"

"What else?"

"No, this is really about me."

Sharon sat back in her seat. "What if I told you I was interested?"

Champagne sat back in her seat too. *Shit, she's just playing with me.* "I thought you didn't like men?"

"I never said that. I don't have anything against men, I just don't want one in my bed. Plus, you said he'd just watch."

Champagne felt her pussy get instantly wet. Could this really be happening? Had she actually found the person? What would Zyair say? What would he think of Sharon? After all, she is fine. Would he be attracted to her, not that it would matter, because she wouldn't be attracted to him.

"I don't know what to say."

Sharon reached across the table and took Champagne's hand. "Don't answer that right now. Go home, talk to Zyair about it. Let me know what he says."

Liking her touch, Champagne asked, "Why are you offering to be the one?"

"Because you look like you'll taste good."

There was nothing Champagne could say to that comment. She was sure Sharon could feel her hands sweating.

"Let's enjoy the rest of our meal," Sharon said.

All Champagne could do was agree.

On the way back to the office, Champagne imagined her and Sharon making love, Sharon's hands and mouth all over her body. She thought about Zyair sitting across the room or on the foot of the bed watching as Sharon played with her titties and licked her juices. She pictured him masturbating while watching.

Champagne knew her thoughts were racing out of control when she almost ran a red light. How she made it back to her office in one piece was a mystery to her.

Candy was sitting at the receptionist's desk, and on the telephone when Champagne walked in. In the sitting area on the couch sat a young lady reading a magazine.

"Hello," Champagne said.

"Please hold," Candy said to whomever she was speaking to on the telephone. She looked up at Champagne. "This is a potential client."

Champagne glanced at the young lady on the couch.

"Hi, I'm Shay," she said as she stood up. "I was down at my uncle's, and he told me you were looking to hire someone. I thought I'd drop my resume off."

The last thing Champagne felt like doing was speaking on the phone or interviewing someone. She needed to get her head together after the conversation she and Sharon just had. She also wanted to call Zyair, but she didn't want to be rude. She told Candy to take a very detailed message.

Champagne walked over to the desk and reached past Candy. "Excuse me." She couldn't help noticing how good she smelled. She pulled open a drawer and pulled out a piece of paper and gave it to Candy. "As a matter-of-fact, ask them these questions and tell them I will get back to them."

She looked at Shay and told her, "Give me five minutes and I'll speak with you."

"Thank you," Shay answered.

Champagne went into her office, closed the door behind her, and exhaled. She sat at her desk to clear her head and tried to focus on the business at hand.

Five minutes later, she opened her door and told Shay, "Come on in."

Champagne could see the nervousness on her face. "No need to be nervous. This isn't an official interview."

That didn't turn out to be true, because thirty minutes later, Shay was walking out the door with the job. "Thank you. Thank you so much," she told her as she was leaving.

Champagne smiled. She felt in her heart that she'd made the right call hiring this young lady. There was something about her, that "it" thing people talked about. She'd moved here on her own with money saved, found an apartment, and up until this moment was working various temp jobs.

After she was gone, Candy knocked on Champagne's door.

"Come in."

"So did you hire her?" Candy sure hoped so. She couldn't wait to do hands-on work, get involved with the stars, party plan, do the fun and exciting part of the job.

"I sure did. She's starting tomorrow."

"That's good."

Champagne told Candy to have a seat, and they talked about how her first day on the job went, if it was what she expected.

Champagne then told her that she was going to let her assist with planning a party for an up-and-coming actress.

Now that's what I'm talking about, Candy thought.

As Champagne stood up to leave, Candy stopped her, "Champagne?"

"Yes?"

"I just want to thank you again for this opportunity. I promise, I won't let you down."

Champagne nodded. "I know you won't."

"See you tomorrow," Candy told her.

"That you will."

Chapter Twenty

"Back And Forth"

Cameo

Over the next couple of days, Champagne kept wondering how she was going to tell Zyair she thought she'd found the one. The reason she had yet to tell him was because at first she thought maybe she'd do a "we just happened to run into one another, and oh, by the way, this is Sharon" routine. That idea came and went because she didn't think she'd be able to pull it off.

"Did you tell him about me yet?" Sharon asked, when they spoke earlier that day.

"No, not yet."

"Are you chickening out?"

"No."

"Aren't you ready for my tongue?"

Whenever they talked, Sharon was always messing with her this way, saying things to turn her on. Verbal foreplay is what she called it.

"I'm ready. I'm going to do it today."

***

Zyair had told her earlier that he would be home early and hinted that he'd love some of her home cooking. "I've missed you," he told her. "We haven't been spending enough time together since you started your business."

"You knew it was going to be that way."

"I know, and I'm not complaining. I want you to be as successful as you want to be. I just need some time with my lady."

The way Champagne decided to play it was to cook his favorite, yet simple meal of meatloaf, mashed potatoes, and broccoli. Then they'd make love, and when it was over, she'd bring up Sharon. She'd say something like, "I've befriended this girl."

Of course he'd ask who, and she'd tell him she was a gay girl. From there the tale would unfold.

Too bad that's not the way it went. The second Zyair entered the house, she knew it wouldn't wait past dinner. She was too hyped. "I found her," she blurted out.

"Found who?" Zyair had no idea what Champagne was talking about but he could tell from her body language that she was excited about it.

He followed her into the kitchen, where she started to pour them each some wine.

"What are you talking about? Who have you found?"

Champagne handed Zyair the drink. "You know . . . her."

Still a little confused, Zyair looked at Champagne, who started to move her eyebrows up and down.

"Oh, her?"

"Yes, her."

"Who is she? Where'd you find her? How did you meet her? Did she approach you, or did you approach her?" He had a ton of questions for Champagne.

Champagne told him how she and Sharon met. She told him about them going out to lunch and having a few casual conversations. "The next thing you know, she was telling me she was gay."

"So, she just came out of nowhere and told you that?"

Champagne wasn't sure how much she wanted to tell him and how much she wanted to leave out. "Well, I was talking about you and the fact that you own one of the top restaurants in the area, and she said her exgirlfriend owns a restaurant."

Zyair really hoped this wasn't someone he knew.

"Which restaurant?"

When Champagne told him, he felt a little relieved that he didn't know her personally. Of course, being in the business he'd heard of her. "Go on."

As Champagne went on with her story, Zyair had to admit to himself that he was feeling somewhat left out, the same way he felt at Fantasies. He thought they'd find someone together. He didn't think she'd initiate it on her own. However, the thought of another woman in his bed outweighed any minor fear.

"How did you ask her?"

"I didn't really ask. She sort of volunteered."

Oh, hell no.

Zyair wasn't stupid. That meant this chick was trying to get with Champagne anyway. She must have wanted her real bad to suggest it. He needed to know all the details before he made a decision.

"How did she volunteer?"

"We were talking about relationships and sex."

"Sex?"

"Women talk about sex all the time. She was telling me about Hedonism. She asked me if I'd been there. I told her what happened with us while we were there, and she asked me if I ever thought about doing it again. So I told her yes."

Zyair wasn't too sure if he really wanted to go through with it again. Plus, it sounded a bit too coincidental. Between going to the strip club and the gay bar, he was feeling like Champagne wanted this just a tad bit too much. He didn't tell her he was having second thoughts, though, and decided to just go along with it and hope that it didn't blow up in his face.

That night as they lay in bed, Zyair suggested to Champagne that they watch a porno movie, something they hadn't done in quite some time. Probably since they first got together.

"Why? I don't think we should watch one. We need to just go with the flow."

He didn't want to press her. *I'll just watch in the morning when she goes to work.* He thought to himself.

That night when they made love, Zyair was trying to go all out, over-caressing, over-kissing, and basically overdoing it.

"Sweetie, this is not a competition," Champagne told him. She could tell he was trying to prove a point. She could also tell that his excitement about the whole thing was wearing thin, so she decided to bring their lovemaking up a notch. While he was inside her, she closed her eyes, pressed him down inside her, and started to grind her hips in a circle, knowing he wouldn't last too long.

And he didn't.

Afterward as Champagne slept, Zyair had a difficult time falling asleep. In his gut, he felt concerned. Not wanting to feel like an outsider in his own house, in his own bed, he was telling himself he had to be in control of the situation at all times. What happened if this girl started giving it to his woman better than he could? How would he handle that? He didn't think about any of that when they were in Hedonism because that was a spur-of-the-moment situation. This one, however, was going to be planned.

He wondered what this Sharon girl would be open to. Would she let him touch her? Would she suck his dick, or was she one of those lesbians that would only let him watch? *Shit, was there levels of lesbianism?* he wondered.

Then there was the fact that she was a lesbian, and not a woman into men and women. Did that mean all he could do is touch? Would he even be allowed that much access? He wanted to join in, at least get his dick sucked by her.

It's official. He'd bitten off more than he could chew.

It was time to come up with some rules for real. Rules such as, anything sexual will only occur when both of us are present. He wasn't crazy. He'd heard stories about how people started sneaking off and seeing one another. Another rule, there'd be no "being the best of girlfriends." Hell nah, that wasn't happening. He was going to have to figure out how to handle that one because they were already talking on the phone and having lunch together.

Zyair felt Champagne stir. He shifted a little closer to her, hoping to wake her.

"Why are you still up?" she asked, interrupting his thoughts.

"I don't know."

Champagne didn't believe that. After all, she was right next to him and was feeling his energy and his restlessness. "Do you not want to do this? Have you changed your mind?"

Not wanting to change his mind and outright disappoint her, he needed to think on it for one more day. "No, I haven't changed my mind. I'm just a little disappointed that you went about this without me. I feel left out. After all, this was supposed to be an 'us' thing, not a 'you' thing."

Champagne didn't say a word. She knew what he was saying was true.

"What if I came home and said, 'I found her,' to you?"

Champagne answered honestly, "I wouldn't like it."

"I know you wouldn't."

They both remained silent for a minute.

"You know what," Zyair said, "I'm bugging, that's all. Let's go ahead and do this."

Champagne sat up. "I don't want you to do something you really don't want to do."

Zyair was ready to end this conversation. "I want to. Let's go to sleep and talk about it in the morning."

"All right." Champagne laid back down and cuddled up next to Zyair, her back to his chest.

Then she turned around and kissed him on the lips. "I love you."

"I love you too," Zyair told her.

The next morning when they awakened, neither brought up what they'd talked about the night before. Zyair had made up his mind that he was going to let it happen, and once it's done, that was going to be the end of it.

Champagne was ready for it to happen and wanted to ask him, "When?" but she decided to wait and speak with Sharon first.

Chapter Twenty-one

"I Wonder If I Take You Home"

Lisa Lisa

Alexis sat in Champagne's office with some serious news to share with her girl. As she waited on her to finish talking to the receptionist, she was growing impatient.

"I'm sorry," Champagne said when she entered the office and closed the door behind her. "It's been a hectic day."

That morning when Champagne arrived, both Shay and Candy were there. Champagne gave Candy a list of things to do. One of her actress clients was starting a foundation and some research needed to be done. If Candy did a good job, Champagne would consider letting her come with her out of town to meet the client.

Alexis stood up and gave Champagne a hug. "Girl, I've missed you."

They hadn't talked or seen one another since they had dinner at Champagne's.

"I missed you too," Champagne replied. "Between me and my business and you and your man, we haven't had the time to see one another."

When Alexis thrust her right hand out and started wiggling her fingers, Champagne couldn't help but notice a ring. "What is that?"

Alexis could barely contain herself. "I'm engaged, girl."

Champagne plopped down in her chair. "Did you hear me? I'm engaged."

Champagne thought Alexis had lost her mind or declared temporary insanity. "Engaged?"

Alexis could tell that Champagne wasn't happy about the news. "Aren't you happy for me?"

There was no way on God's green earth that Champagne would even pretend she was happy. If that made her a bad person, so be it. There was something about Khalil that rubbed her the wrong way, and she was going to find out what it was.

"You just met him."

"I knew you were going to say that. I know we haven't been seeing each other that long but you can't help who you fall in love with."

Champagne wanted to throw up. She couldn't believe Alexis was talking about being in love and she barely knew the man.

"In love? Girl, please . . ."

Alexis sat back in her chair and crossed her arms. "I don't even feel like sharing my good news with you. I come in here all excited, wanting to tell you about my engagement, thinking you'd be happy for me and support me, but no, you don't even congratulate me."

Damn, she sure knows how to make a girl feel bad. "I apologize, Alexis. If you're happy, I'm happy."

Alexis pouted. "You don't mean it."

Champagne stood up, walked over to Alexis, grabbed her hands, and looked her in the eyes. "I love you, girl, and I am happy for you. I'm just concerned and scared. What if—"

"Let's not do the what-ifs." Alexis pulled her hands away. "I could 'what if' my relationship to death. Hell, I could 'what if' our friendship, I could 'what if' life, and it'll get me nowhere."

Champagne threw up her hands. "Okay, you're right. I'm being an ass. I apologize. Let's start over." Champagne pulled Alexis out of the chair.

Alexis frowned. "What are you doing?"

"We're starting over. Go to the door and act like you just walked in."

"Are you serious?"

"Come on, please." Champagne wanted to make it right.

Alexis decided to play along. She stood up and walked to the door.

"Go ahead."

Alexis came running toward her. "Oh, girl, guess what?"

"What?"

Alexis stuck her hand in Champagne's face and wiggled her fingers. "I'm engaged."

Champagne threw her arms around Alexis. "I'm so happy for you. Let me see the ring again."

Knowing they sounded phony as hell, they both started laughing, and Alexis thanked Champagne for trying.

Alexis sat down and turned serious. "Listen, I know you love me and that you worry."

"I also think you deserve the best God has to offer."

"How do you know it's not Khalil?"

Champagne felt like rolling her eyes but didn't want to hurt Alexis' feelings again. "You know what, you're right. I don't know. He just may be the one intended for you."

Alexis gave Champagne a hug, stood up, and started walking toward the door.

"Where are you going?" Champagne asked. "You just got here."

"I love you, girl, but I've got to run. I just wanted to stop by and share my news with you."

Champagne told Alexis she loved her too and walked her to the door. The second she got back into her office, Champagne picked up the phone to call Zyair but he wasn't available.

She needed to speak to someone about this engagement and the only other person she knew that would care was Thomas. *Damn! Think, Champagne, what's his number?*

Champagne closed her eyes to try and recall the number. Snapping her fingers, she opened her eyes and dialed a number. Thomas picked up the phone.

Champagne didn't even say hello. "Can you believe he asked her to marry him?"

"Who the hell is this?" Thomas yelled into the phone.

"It's me, Champagne."

"Oh. What's up?"

"Alexis got engaged to that Khalil guy."

"Repeat what you just said."

"I said Alexis got engaged to that Khalil dude."

"What the hell are you talking about? You didn't tell her?"

"Tell her what?"

"About the porno and the swingers club."

"Thomas, I don't know what you're talking about. What porno, and what does it have to do with Alexis?"

"I told Zyair."

"Will you tell me what the hell you're talking about." Talking in circles was getting on Champagne's last nerve.

"The young lady I was with at your dinner party, remember she kept saying she thought she knew him from somewhere?"

"Yeah."

"Well, it turns out she knows him from this swingers club she goes to occasionally, and on top of that he used to be a porn star."

Champagne almost dropped the phone. "You told Zyair about this?"

"I told him to tell you."

"You know what, let me call you back." Champagne went to hang up the phone but she heard Thomas yell in the background, "Wait!"

"What?"

"Are you going to tell her?"

"You're damn right, I am."

"Let me ask you this, would you want to know without proof? And before you say yes, think about it. You know how you women are. You have to see it to believe it or have hard evidence."

"Shit, shit, shit, shit!" She hated that he was right. "So what are we going to do?"

"We're going to get evidence. My girl thought she had the movie he was in, but she doesn't. I'll try to locate it, and in the meantime, we can go to the swingers club."

Champagne pulled the phone away from her ear. "I know you're crazy. There is no way in hell I'm going to one of those places with you."

Thomas laughed.

"What the hell is so funny?"

"Girl, please . . . I'm not trying to have Zyair kill me.

"What I was thinking about is casing the joint, maybe even setting him up."

"How are we going to do that?"

"Diamond will help us."

"Are you sure?"

"I'm sure."

"Okay, then set something up with her. Call me and let me know what and I'll do whatever I have to do, short of going inside the swingers place."

"Cool."

"Thomas?"

"Yes?"

"Diamond was your date, right? Why would she help you?"

"Don't worry about that. She and I are good friends. Plus, she owes me one."

After hanging up, Champagne picked up the phone to call Zyair again. Before she could dial the number, there was a knock on the door.

"Come in."

It was Candy, "Didn't you say you wanted to meet with me today?"

"Yes, give me about twenty minutes. Bring with you the research information you did."

"Okay."

Champagne was unable to reach Zyair. What the hell is he up to? Is he that busy that he couldn't call me today? She was pissed off at him and needed him to know it. How dare he have information about Khalil and not share it with her? She could hear him now, "It's not our place, and it's not our business."

That's some bullshit. Her best friend is her business.

Chapter Twenty-two

"My Prerogative"

Bobby Brown

"Why haven't you answered my phone calls?" Champagne asked Zyair when she was finally able to reach him. "I've been trying to call you all day."

"Remember I told you I have a couple of meetings today? You know I'm trying to get financial backers." Champagne forgot all about it. She'd been so consumed with herself. She almost felt bad for not really listening to Zyair, but not so bad that she'd hold back her wrath. "How come you didn't tell me what Thomas told you about Khalil?"

"I didn't know whether I should or not."

"You didn't know?"

"That's what I said." Zyair wasn't digging the tone of Champagne's voice. He'd been dealing with assholes all day, begging for money, and to now be putting up with some bullshit wasn't going to fly with him. "Listen, I think you need to stay out of this whole AlexisKhalil affair."

Champagne couldn't believe he would say that, knowing how close they were. "So, you're telling me if you knew something about one of the women Thomas was messing with you wouldn't say anything?"

"Listen," Zyair said, "I've had a long day, and I'm really not in the mood for a confrontation."

Before Champagne could answer him, Shay buzzed in.

"Hold on," Champagne told Zyair. "Who is it?"

"It's someone named Sharon."

Champagne picked up the line Zyair was on and told him she'd call him back, that a client was on the other line. Why she lied, she didn't know, especially since she could have called Sharon back.

As soon as Champagne came back on the line, Sharon said, "What's up, sexy?"

"You." Where that reply came from, Champagne had no idea.

"So did you tell your man about me?"

"I did."

"And?"

"Honestly, I think he's having mixed feelings."

"Mixed or jealous feelings?"

"Both."

"So what's the final verdict?"

"Here's what I was thinking. Why don't you stop by his restaurant for a drink this weekend? That way you two can meet, and we'll take it from here."

"I can do that."

They continued to make small talk and hung up about fifteen minutes later.

What are you doing? Champagne asked herself. She needed to just drop this whole thing, but she was like a woman possessed.

She didn't know if she should bring it up again when she arrived home. She didn't want Zyair to let his imagination run too wild and start thinking she was going to do this with or without him. A part of her was thinking about doing just that but she didn't want to go behind his back. She preferred to be upfront about everything. She didn't like being secretive, and that's why she wanted to tell Alexis what she knew.

Champagne called into the intercom, "Candy!" She needed an outsider's opinion. "Come here please."

Ten seconds later, Candy was walking in the office.

"Yes?"

"Let me ask you a question. If you knew that your friend's mate did some things in the past that were just foul and may potentially be doing them now, would you tell them?"

Candy didn't need to think about it at all. "What I would do is get hardcore evidence. Or I'd let the person know what I know, and that if they don't tell, I will. I'll give that person the room to come clean."

"Okay, thanks."

Candy stood waiting. "Is there anything else?"

"Nope. Nothing else."

Champagne hoped Thomas would hurry up and call her back. She didn't want to walk around carrying this burden, withholding important information from a friend.

In his office, Zyair was agitated, and all Champagne did was agitate him even more. How did she know what Thomas told him? There was only one way and that's Thomas' ass. Zyair picked up his phone and dialed the number.

The answering service came on.

"Call me. I want to know what you told Champagne and when you told her."

As he was hanging up the telephone, DaNeen poked her head in the office. "You have a minute?"

"I do," he told her.

She stepped in. "When do you think we'll be able to sit down and go over my business plan?"

"We can do it tonight," Zyair said, not in a rush to get home just to be told off.

"Are you sure? I don't want to put you out or anything."

"Nah, I'm sure. What's your schedule for today?"

"I get off at seven."

"Well, come by my office then."

DaNeen said, "Thank you," and walked away.

Zyair found himself following her with his eyes. *What am I doing?*

Champagne was exhausted. The past couple of weeks were draining. She'd set up her office, got adjusted to her new environment, hired new employees, met a prospective lover, and found out her best friend was engaged to a man she couldn't stand and didn't know why.

She also entertained a couple of her former clients who stopped by, brought gifts, and expressed interest in becoming her client exclusively. They told her that they stayed with Jackson because of her. She just felt, though, that she needed to be careful and not take on too many clients. But, then again, what was "enough"? Champagne walked through the front door of her house, dropped her briefcase near the couch, and went straight to the kitchen. She kicked off her shoes and went over to the cabinet for a wineglass, placed it on the counter and went to the refrigerator and took out her bottle of Moscato, an inexpensive, but smooth wine.

Zyair sometimes got on her about drinking cheap wine but she just ignored him. She'd drink whatever she felt like drinking. After pouring a glass, she headed toward the living room. Suddenly, she turned around and grabbed the whole bottle.

Once in the living room, Champagne placed the bottle on the coffee table, stretched out on the chaise, and proceeded to sip her wine.

The next thing you know, she was being awakened by Zyair. "Hey, sleepy head." He kissed her on the forehead.

Champagne sat up and glanced at the time on the television. It read 1:32 a.m. "You're just now getting home?"

Zyair sat at the end of the chaise. "Yeah. I thought I would be home earlier, but two of my coworkers got into it in front of the customers and I had to intervene."

Champagne glanced at the empty bottle next to her.

No wonder she fell out.

Zyair followed her gaze. "I see you had a party by yourself."

"I was trying to unwind," Champagne said, pulling herself up off the couch. She grabbed the bottle and her empty glass and headed toward the kitchen, Zyair following right behind her. She placed the bottle and glass on the counter.

Zyair didn't feel like walking on eggshells. "Do you want to talk about this Alexis thing? I don't want it to blow out of proportion, and you hold on to being upset with me."

"No. I have to make up my own mind about how I want to handle this."

Relieved, Zyair turned to walk away.

"But," Champagne started, turning him back around, "I am still upset that you knew about it and didn't tell me."

"Well, how did you know I knew anything?"

Champagne went on to tell him about Alexis coming to the office and announcing her engagement.

Even he was surprised and thought it was too soon for that.

"So I had to call Thomas to tell him."

Zyair wasn't buying it. "You called him because you knew he would react."

Champagne didn't deny it. This bothered Zyair. She wasn't one to call up his boys, and for her to call Thomas over something like this, he knew she was up to no good.

"Don't go destroying friendships behind this mess."

Champagne whined, "I'm not."

"I hope not." Zyair turned to walk away then stopped. "Are you getting ready to go to bed?" He placed his hand on the small of her back.

From the low tone of his voice and from the way he was looking at her, Champagne knew he was in the mood. All she was in the mood for was a quickie. Not wanting to let him down, she asked him, "Are you making me a proposition?"

"Of course."

"Well"—Champagne placed her hands on the front of his pants and grabbed his penis—"I have a proposition for you." She could feel him getting excited.

"Yeah?"

"Why don't we do it right here, right now? All I have to do is pull my skirt up and bend over. How'd you like that?" Champagne started to unbutton his pants.

"I thought maybe I could take a shower first."

"Well, I think you can take a shower afterward. Come on, let's be spontaneous." She had his pants and underwear down, and Zyair stood at attention.

"Maybe that's not such a bad idea."

Champagne turned around, pulled up her wrinkled skirt, and pulled down her panties. "Do your thing, baby."

Zyair couldn't get into her fast enough. "How do you want it?"

"Fast and hard." Champagne started moving back into him.

Neither of them said a word, until Zyair exploded inside her. "Damn!" was all he could say as he pulled out.

Chapter Twenty-three

"Turn Off The Lights"

Teddy Pendergrass

The following morning at the breakfast table, Champagne decided, *To hell with it*. She said to Zyair, "Can I call Sharon and have her come by tonight?"

"Why tonight?" *Why is she asking me this now,* he wondered. *Why did tonight have to be the night? Didn't I put it down in the bedroom last night?*

"Honestly?"

"Yes, honestly."

"I keep thinking about it, and I want to move past it. I think the only way to do that is to do it."

Zyair realized that this was something that wasn't going to go away. There was no way out, and he too was ready to end this chapter, so he agreed.

"Are you sure?"

Zyair felt like he really didn't have a choice in the matter, so he told her he was positive.

Later that afternoon, Champagne called Sharon and told her, "Tonight's the night."

"He said it was okay?"

"Yes."

"Are we meeting at your house?"

"Yes."

"Champagne, are you sure about this? You think he's going to be able to handle it?"

"He handled it in Jamaica."

"Yeah, but this time is different. This time it's on the home front."

"I don't think he would have agreed to it if he couldn't handle it."

"All right, if you say so."

Champagne proceeded to give Sharon directions to her address, and the time she should arrive.

That day Champagne wasn't able to focus on anything at the office. Her mind kept drifting, imagining what was going to happen. Thank God, it was Friday, because had it been any other day, her clients would have been shit out of luck.

The day couldn't go by fast enough, and when the time came for it to go down, Champagne and Zyair were walking around the house in total silence and anticipation. He was dressed comfortably in sweats and a T-shirt, and she had on a shirt-dress, with nothing underneath.

"How do you think it's going to start?" she asked him.

"I don't know," Zyair told her. "Let just let whatever happens happen naturally."

Champagne agreed. From that point on, she started watching the clock, waiting for Sharon to arrive.

From the time Sharon walked through the door, Zyair felt like a third wheel. Sharon came bearing gifts for Champagne, handing her flowers and candy.

Zyair thought Champagne was a little too happy, and immediately became jealous. He offered Sharon a drink.

She declined then said, "Listen, we don't have to play the get-to-know-you game. We all know why I'm here. So where's the bedroom?"

Her aggressiveness threw Zyair off but turned Champagne on. Zyair wondered, *Should I follow them or wait until I was called?*

He didn't have to wonder much longer because Champagne told him, "Come on."

Zyair was a little bothered by the whole thing. One, it was moving too fast, and two it was obvious he was just there to observe.

Champagne entered the room first. It seemed like it only took a couple of strides for Sharon to be standing in front of Champagne, and Zyair sat in the corner watching, taking it all in.

Sharon reached out and ran her hand down Champagne's face. "I want you."

Scared, Champagne could feel the nervousness in her stomach. She wondered, *How would the sex start? What would Zyair do while me and Sharon made love? Would he stay the whole time? Would he leave the room? How long would it last? Would Zyair want Sharon to leave immediately, or would she stay the night?*

Champagne glanced over at Zyair, who nodded his approval, silently telling her, "Get the show on the road."

Champagne led Sharon to the bed. *Should I stand? Should I sit?* She decided to stand and leaned in to kiss Sharon. She'd been wanting to kiss her since the day they'd met.

Sharon pulled back. "Let me kiss you."

Champagne relaxed and waited, and Sharon leaned in and softly placed her lips on Champagne's. Sharon pushed open her mouth and slowly ran her tongue in it. Her kiss was passionate and unrushed.

Champagne could feel her pussy throbbing. She wanted to grab Sharon's hand and press it against her pussy. Sharon must have been reading her mind because she told her, "Don't rush it."

Zyair sat back and let them do their thing. He released a tight breath. It was going to happen again, and this time, he was filled, not with anticipation, but with apprehension. He wanted to yell out, "All right, get going," but he knew that would ruin the mood.

Sharon led Champagne to the bed and slowly unbuttoned Champagne's shirt-dress. She was surprised to find that Champagne wore nothing underneath. "So you're ready for me?"

"Yes."

"Lay on the bed."

Zyair sat in the comer and admitted to himself, he was turned on. He wanted to take his dick out and play with it but decided to wait. He just let his hands drop to his side.

Champagne lay back on the bed, her dress open, and Sharon leaned over and ran one of her hands down her torso. "You're so toned."

When her hands reached Champagne's pussy, she cupped it and pressed the top of her palm down.

Champagne moaned and arched her back.

Sharon then leaned over Champagne and ran her tongue across Champagne's nipple so gently, it felt like a breeze. She did this repeatedly. Then she squeezed both breasts together and bit down.

This caused Champagne to jump. It hurt, yet it felt good.

Sharon, seeing Champagne's response, did this a few more times. Then she made her way down to Champagne's pussy.

Once between Champagne's legs, she played with her pussy lips, pulling on them with her hands and teeth.

Zyair stirred in his seat.

Sharon looked up at him and told him, "You can come closer," and he did.

Sharon sniffed Champagne's pussy. "I hope you taste as good as you smell." She placed two fingers in Champagne's pussy and opened and closed them. She did this with one hand, while squeezing Champagne's nipples with the other. "I'm about to eat this pussy raw," she said. Then she slid her fingers out real slow and stuck her tongue as far up in Champagne's pussy as it would go.

Zyair watched, intrigued. Sharon's tongue was so far up Champagne's pussy, even he was impressed.

Sharon started to move her tongue in circles, then made it pointy and tongue-fucked Champagne.

Champagne reached down and grabbed Sharon's head.

Sharon took this as a sign to move to Champagne's clitoris. She didn't have to go searching for it because it was in her face, hard and ready to be sucked.

While Sharon sucked, licked, and nibbled on Champagne's clitoris, Zyair had his hands in his pants stroking his dick.

It wasn't long before Champagne called out, "Oh, shit, I'm about to cum."

Sharon wasn't ready for her to cum yet. She wanted this to last a little while longer, so she removed her mouth.

Champagne tried to pop up but Sharon pushed her back down.

"What are you doing?" Champagne asked.

Not answering her, Sharon placed one finger, then two, then three inside Champagne. Then she pulled them out and placed them in her mouth, sucking on them one at a time.

That shit turned Zyair on so much that he had to stroke his dick harder and faster than he wanted to.

"You like that?" Sharon asked Champagne. "Do you want to taste it?"

She dipped her fingers back in, pulled them out, and placed them in Champagne's mouth.

Tasting her own juices made Champagne want to taste Sharon's but before she could say anything, Sharon replaced her fingers with her mouth once again. This time it was obvious that she was ready to make Champagne explode.

Champagne closed her eyes and started grinding her hips against Sharon's mouth.

All the while, Zyair was playing with his dick. He wasn't doing it to cum. He was going to save that for Champagne.

Suddenly a sound escaped from Champagne. It sounded like it was coming from the essence of her being.

Sharon continued to suck and lick until Champagne's body stopped quivering.

Zyair stood up. He wanted to kiss Champagne. He needed to be a part of this.

"Let me watch you fuck her," Sharon told him.

Champagne looked at Zyair. She sat up, took her dress off, and turned over. "Fuck me from behind." She looked at Sharon and told her, "You lay on the bed. I want to see what you taste like," surprising both Zyair and Sharon.

"You don't have to," Sharon told her.

"I want to."

Sharon looked at Zyair.

"If that's what she wants."

Sharon got undressed, and Zyair couldn't help but notice how similar her body was to Champagne's.

Champagne watched Zyair watch Sharon. She wasn't jealous because she knew that Sharon wasn't into men.

When Sharon lay on the bed, Champagne looked at her. "Let me know if I'm not doing this right."

"I'm sure you'll do just fine. Just do to me what you like done to you."

Champagne looked at Zyair and told him, "Give me a minute."

He stepped back and took his shirt and pants off. He watched while Champagne massaged Sharon's breasts and played with her nipples.

Champagne then started kissing Sharon. Her heart was racing, she was anxious. She wondered if she would like the taste of pussy or if it would turn her off. She had to find out. Sliding down Sharon's legs, she pulled Sharon to the edge of the bed and got on her knees.

Zyair took this as a sign and knelt as well.

Champagne placed her head between Sharon's legs and ran her tongue on the inside of Sharon's walls. Then she covered Sharon's pussy with her mouth.

"Do to me what you like," Sharon said.

Champagne started imitating how Zyair ate her pussy. She found, to her surprise, that she liked the taste. "Come on," she told Zyair, "put your dick in me." He didn't have to be told twice. He entered her with such force. He wanted her to know that he was the master of that pussy.

Champagne started pushing back.

He took that as a sign to fuck her harder. The harder he fucked her, the more passionate she was in eating Sharon's pussy.

Sharon grabbed Champagne's head. "Shit, girl, are you sure you haven't done this before? You going to make me cum all over that face."

On that note, Zyair looked up. He watched Sharon's face as she came all over Champagne's mouth, which made him cum as well. He pushed his dick up as far as it would go in Champagne's pussy.

When he was done, he was surprised to find that he was still semihard.

Champagne felt like she was in another zone. She told Zyair, "Put it in my ass."

Still inside her, he asked, "Are you sure?"

"Come on, do it now before I change my mind."

He pulled out of her pussy, spread her cheeks apart, and slowly entered her ass, using her pussy juices as a lubricant. He was ecstatic, because she'd always told him, "The ass is a special treat."

They both closed their eyes.

Sharon climbed off the bed and sat on the floor. She was intrigued with what was going on as she watched Zyair move in and out of Champagne's ass real slow and steady. She placed her hands under Champagne and found her clitoris, and started pressing on it.

This made Champagne move along with Zyair, causing his dick to go in deeper.

"Awwww," Zyair kept repeating over and over, his eyes closed. "This feels so good."

Champagne couldn't speak. She was too busy enjoying the feel of Sharon's fingers and the pressure of Zyair's dick going in and out of her ass. They'd done this a couple of times before, but it was a while ago, and she'd forgotten how good it felt.

"I'm going to cum again," Zyair yelled.

"I am too. Press harder, Sharon," Champagne said. Sharon did as she was instructed.

Shortly after, Zyair and Champagne came together.

When it was done, he pulled out of Champagne real slow. "I'm going to the bathroom to get a rag. I'll be back."

When he left the room, Champagne lay and looked at Sharon, who was standing up. "You don't want to lay down?"

"No, I think I'm going to be leaving."

"You don't have to leave."

Sharon sat on the bed and rubbed Champagne's face. "Thank you."

"No, we should be thanking you." Sharon bent over to kiss Champagne.

They were so deep into the kiss that neither of them noticed when Zyair walked in the room. He stood there with the rag in his hand and watched them. When they pulled away from one another, he walked over and handed Champagne a warm rag.

He looked at Sharon. "Do you want to take a shower?"

"That would be nice."

After wiping and sitting up, Champagne said, "I'll show her where everything is."

That night after Sharon left, as Zyair and Champagne lay in bed, he asked her, "Did you enjoy it?"

"Yes, but I was concerned about you."

This surprised Zyair. He didn't think Champagne realized he was in the room half the time. "I'm glad to hear that because emotionally I was messed up. On one hand I wanted it to stop, then I didn't want it to stop. I wasn't sure how involved or uninvolved I should be."

"Well, whatever decision you made was the right one."

He moved closer to her and wrapped his arms around her, and together they spooned. "I have to tell you what made me feel better was when you allowed us to have anal sex in front of her. That made me feel like I was a priority."

As an afterthought, he added, "You know how rare it is when you give me the ass."

Champagne laughed. *I wonder if things will ever be the same between us.*

Zyair was thinking, *This shit will not happen again.*

Chapter Twenty-four

"Used To Be My Girl"

O'Jays

It had finally happened, and neither knew what to say to the other. A couple of days had gone by, and Champagne wondered if she should pretend like it meant nothing. She didn't know if that was something she could do. The lovemaking was good as hell between her and Sharon, and between her and Zyair afterward. She knew immediately that she was going to be looking for a female lover.

Does that make me gay? Champagne already asked herself that question a million times. In Jamaica, when they came back from Jamaica, while they were on the hunt, and now. Her answer was a definite no, but after watching an episode of Oprah that featured women who had been married for years and suddenly discovered they were gay, she wasn't too sure.

It's just a phase, that's all. Just a phase. She hoped she was right, and that's all it was.

She was in her office with the door closed when she heard Candy come in the front door. Truth be told, she was attracted to Candy, but it was an attraction that she had to keep under wraps.

"Candy, come into my office." Candy walked in.

"Yes?"

"Remember that business trip I told you about that I have to go on?'

"Yes."

"Well, I want you to go with me. After all, you did the majority of the research, and I believe it'll be good for you to actually meet the client and learn more about the foundation."

Candy liked that idea. She was ready to get away as well. She knew it was business, but being in Washington D.C. meant she just might get a chance to party.

"Is there anything you need me to do?" Candy asked.

"No. Just continue pricing the halls and hotels for Ms. Trina Houston."

Not only was Candy assisting Champagne in setting up a non-profit for one of her clients but she was also helping in the planning of Trina Houston's wedding.

Trina was one of Champagne's moneymaking clients. She was getting married and starting a non-profit organization. Balancing the two was becoming a challenge, and she needed Champagne's expertise.

Champagne watched Candy leave the office and shut the door. She couldn't stop herself from wondering how good Candy ate pussy. *Stop it, girl. You know better than that.* She was feeling out of control with this whole sexuality thing. A door had been opened and she just couldn't seem to shut it.

Shay buzzed Champagne's phone. "There's a Sharon on the line."

Smiling, Champagne picked up. "Hey there."

"What's up, sexy?"

"Nothing. What's up with you?"

"Just thinking about you."

Shit, shit, shit! Champagne wondered what she was supposed to say to that.

"Oh, and what were you thinking?"

"How good you taste."

Before Champagne could stop herself, she asked, "When do you want to taste me again?"

"Mmmmmm . . . is that an invitation?"

This is my chance to take it back. "I don't know. Maybe."

"With or without Zyair?"

Champagne knew the answer was without but would that mean she was cheating? Was it cheating when you slept with someone of the same sex?

"All you have to do is say the word," Sharon told her.

What the hell am I getting myself into? Before Champagne could answer, Shay poked her head in the door. "Your appointment is here."

"Listen, is it all right if I call you back? Someone's here to see me."

Sharon told her that was fine.

Champagne felt a little relieved to be hanging up the phone. She was also glad her client was there to take her mind off whether she was a lesbian or turning into one. This obsession was becoming ridiculous even to her.

The night after Sharon left, Zyair had barely said a word. If anything, he was more distant. Champagne felt like he was pulling away. Was he, or was it her imagination?

The following day Zyair was in his office thinking about what had transpired. He wasn't sure how he felt about it. On one hand, he was turned on, but on the other, he was glad it was over and definitely didn't want it to happen again. This incident with Sharon—that's what he was going to call it, an incident—just didn't sit right with him. Sharon seemed like she was into Champagne more than he would have liked. He had to admit, he felt threatened.

What happened in Hedonism was different because they were not on their home turf and it was spontaneous. The more Zyair thought about it, the more it seemed like Champagne had pressed the issue a bit too much. Did that say something about him as a man? Did that say something about his lovemaking?

After about half an hour he was ready for Sharon to get her ass out the house.

I mean, damn, how much kissing, tittie rubbing, and pussy licking can one do?

He hoped this let-me-see-if-I'll-enjoy-making-love-to-a-woman-sober shit Champagne pulled on him was done with. That question should have been answered.

Zyair glanced at the clock. He was meeting with DaNeen shortly to go over her business plan.

Knock, knock.

Zyair looked up to see DaNeen poking her head in the door.

"Is it all right if I come in?"

Zyair waved her in. "Come on." He couldn't help but notice how sexy she looked. He was noticing it more than usual. It wasn't just in what she wore but there was something else about her. Maybe it was the confidence she carried because she was trying to do her thing.

Champagne's doing her thing too, he thought to himself, trying not to notice how high the slit was in her skirt. When she sat down, he thought he could almost see her panties.

DaNeen caught him looking and positioned herself so that he could see even more.

She'd been wanting this man for quite some time now. Everything about him turned her on. His gentleness and the way he handled people, his generosity, the way he treated his lady when she was around.

DaNeen wanted all those things to herself, and she was tired of waiting. She'd been watching him for over a year, trying to get close to him but it just wasn't happening. Well, she was determined to make it happen, and not only one time.

Bringing his attention to her face, Zyair said, "Let me see what you've done so far."

"Can I come around there and show you?" Her plan was to stand as close as possible to him and rub up against him if she could.

"Sure."

DaNeen walked around the desk and bent over while opening her folder, her breast resting on his arms.

Zyair felt himself responding. This was unusual for him. Normally he could keep his desire under control. He was going to blame it on Champagne. She was the one who opened Pandora's Box.

He looked up at DaNeen. "You might want to back up some."

Placing her hand on the center of her breast, DaNeen said, "Oops, my bad."

For the next hour they went over her business plan, with Zyair suggesting some changes she might want to make. Throughout that hour, he noticed DaNeen's subtle touches. He knew she was doing it on purpose and was flattered by it. But being flattered and fucking around was a world apart. There was no way he was going to cheat on Champagne. He was just going to ignore her advances.

When DaNeen left the office, Zyair breathed a sigh of relief. He didn't know what was going on with him. He did know that it was dangerous. He needed someone to talk to. As usual, he called his boy Thomas.

"Yo, man, we need to talk," he said when Thomas answered the phone. "Stop by the office."

Thomas told him, "Okay."

The day progressed as usual, Zyair checking on the restaurant, mingling with the clientele, and watching DaNeen out of the corner of his eye. A couple of times when he looked up, he caught her looking his way.

A couple of hours later, Zyair was walking toward his office when he heard Thomas's voice. "Yo, man, wait up."

Zyair waited until he was beside him. They gave each other dap.

"So what's up? What do you want to talk about?"

"Wait until we get in my office, man."

When they stepped into the office, Zyair spilled the beans. "Man, it's DaNeen."

Thomas's eyes got real wide. "Don't tell me you fucked her."

"Nah, man, you know me better than that."

"Are you about to fuck her?"

"No."

"You want to fuck her?"

The look on Zyair's face gave Thomas his answer.

"I knew it, I knew it, I knew it."

Zyair knew it too. Thomas had warned him about her. He remembered him saying, "She wants you, man. Don't get yourself stuck in the wrong situation. That's what gets people in trouble, situations."

Sitting on the oversized chair, Thomas asked, "So what are you going to do about it?"

"I don't know."

"What do you mean, you don't know? Does that mean you're considering stepping out on your lady?"

"Nah."

"Then what you call me for? To share with me the fact that you think somebody is cute?"

Zyair started laughing. "I know, it's just that . . ." Zyair threw his hands up. "You know what, never mind. I'm tripping, that's all."

"You see, that's what your ass get for hiring somebody as fine as her. You want me to ask her out?"

Zyair, a dead-ass serious look on his face, sat next to Thomas. He leaned over and placed his elbows on his knees. "If I tell you something real personal, you better not tell any of the boys."

Thomas smacked his leg and jumped up. "I knew it. You did fuck her."

Growing frustrated, Zyair told him, "No."

"Then what the hell is it? You're getting on my damn nerves, acting all secretive and shit. Out with it."

"I let another woman eat Champagne's pussy."

Thomas sat down. "Repeat that."

"I let another woman—"

Thomas didn't let him finish. "You're lying."

"No, I'm not."

Thomas just wasn't believing him. "When?"

"Last night."

"Oh, shit!"

Zyair was expecting more of a reaction. "Oh, shit? That's it?"

"What more do you want me to say? I'm in shock. I didn't think Champagne would be down with something like that."

"This ain't the first time."

"What? And you're just now telling me?"

Zyair went on to tell him about Hedonism.

"I told you, you would turn into freaks going there."

Zyair wanted to tell him how he was feeling all crazy now, like maybe they'd done the wrong thing.

"Give me details."

"Hell no. So you can sit around and fantasize about my woman? You must be out of your mind."

Thomas all of a sudden got dreamy-eyed. "I wonder if Alexis is into women?"

Zyair playfully knocked Thomas upside the head.

That night, while Zyair and Champagne lay in the bed reading, Zyair decided he wanted to bring it up. He sat his book down.

"Champagne?"

She looked up from her book. "Yes?" From the look on Zyair's face, she could tell he was in serious mode. She didn't feel like talking. She just wanted to read her book.

"Will you put your book down? I need to talk to you about something."

Champagne turned the book over on her lap. "Go ahead."

"It's just that we haven't talked about what transpired the other night."

Shit, I knew this was going to happen. "What is there to talk about? It's done and over with."

"Is it?"

How can he possibly know? "Yes, Zyair, it is."

For some inexplicable reason, he didn't believe her. What was he to do about it? Nothing. All he could do was take her word and hope to hell she meant what she was saying.

"Did you enjoy it?"

"Yes, Zyair I did."

Zyair didn't like the tone of her voice. She was acting like he was bothering her. "Damn, Champagne, all I want to do is talk about it."

"We didn't do all this talking after it happened in Jamaica."

"That's another country. This is in-house."

"What difference does it make?"

"It makes a hell of a difference."

"Why?"

Zyair took Champagne's hand. "Listen, I'm going to keep it real with you. I'm feeling a little insecure. I didn't think it would affect me this way, but it has. And I need some reassurance that it was an 'us' thing and a onetime thing."

Champagne wanted to tell him it was. She wanted to mean it when she said it.

"I love you, Zyair, and nothing can change that."

They both wondered if she was being honest or trying to convince them both.

Chapter Twenty-five

"Keep On Movin'"

Soul II Soul

"You know I have to go away for four days, right?" Alexis said to Champagne as they sat in Alexis' living room. "I'll be away when you return. Khalil and I are going to Cancun."

Every time Alexis said his name, it irritated the hell out of her, especially with what she now knew. She wanted so bad to tell her, but she needed to get some hard evidence first.

"Really? Whose idea was that?"

"His."

If Alexis could smile any harder, Champagne thought she would throw up. On one hand she was glad for her friend but damn, why couldn't this joy come from someone else? Ashamed of the way she was feeling and ready to take action, Champagne told Alexis she had to leave.

Alexis wasn't fooled. "When I come back, we need to talk."

Champagne looked at her. "About what?"

"Us."

Champagne told her, "We'll do that."

The second Champagne got into her car, she picked up the phone to call Zyair.

She thought to herself, *Alexis has really lost her mind behind this Khalil fellow.* Then again, who was she to talk about someone losing their mind? She was thinking about sleeping with women.

When Champagne spoke to Zyair, all he had to say was, "You really need to stay out of this."

Do I really want to get involved? Should I mind my own business? Not only that but I know Zyair is going to be pissed that I got his friend involved.

She tried to convince herself that she was doing the right thing because her friend was in trouble, and it was her duty to step up to the plate and do what she had to do to help out.

After Thomas told her about Khalil being a porn star and going to swingers clubs, her concerns grew because she knew they were having sex. Alexis let that one slip out.

Freak it, I'm going to call Thomas, and we're going to get to the bottom of this.

When Champagne arrived at her office, she picked up the phone and dialed Thomas' number. It went straight to his answering service.

"Thomas, it's Champagne. Call me at my office. I wanted to speak with you about Alexis and the bad man." She laughed to herself when she said "the bad man." Champagne wondered why this was becoming a mission to her. The "save Alexis" mission.

Champagne stood up and walked over to the window and watched the people below. She wondered where they were going, what they did every day, if anyone of them were struggling in their personal lives, their sexual lives.

Champagne thought about when she and Alexis were younger and how they "played" with one another. Is that something all young girls did? Damn, she wished she had someone she could ask. She wondered, was it out of curiosity that they explored one another's body, or was her sexuality being formed? She wondered did they both turn out heterosexual because it's what they were supposed to do. She did remember that it felt good and that there were days when she couldn't wait for Alexis to come over so they could "do it."

It started when they were in the fourth grade and continued until they got to middle school. That's when life changed and boys became a big part of their life.

Damn, this is some deep shit. I might have been gay back then and due to life circumstances and wanting to be like everyone else, I went the other way.

Champagne realized she'd blocked this memory, or pushed it so far back in her mind. She wondered if Alexis had done the same. She couldn't even remember when they stopped or how they stopped. Was it discussed, or was it just over?

Maybe this is why I'm bugging out over this relationship with Khalil. Zyair said I was acting jealous. I think l am.

With this revelation, Champagne had to go back to her desk and sit down. She needed to think, was she in love with Alexis. *Nah, that's not it. I'm thinking too hard about this whole thing.*

On that note, her cell phone rang. It was Thomas. "Hello?"

"Hey, you," Thomas said. "I got your message. What's up?"

"I thought I left a message for you to call me at my office?"

"Does it really matter what phone I called you on?"

"You don't have to get smart."

"You know what, you're right. I apologize. I just have a lot on my mind today."

Champagne could understand that. "I know what you mean."

"So what's up?"

"I want to do what we talked about."

"What?"

Exasperated, Champagne said, "You know . . . follow Khalil."

"Really?"

"Yeah. Find out from your friend when he goes or if she can get any information, and we can get the ball rolling."

"I will but let me ask you this, do you have a plan? How are we going to do this? Are we going to go in the place, and if we see him what happens then? I'm sure we can't take cameras in there."

Champagne hadn't thought that deep into it. One thing she did know is that she wasn't too keen about going inside.

"Maybe we can sit outside and take pictures of him coming and going."

"That'll be an all-night thing. What if he's not even there?"

"Well, shit, Thomas, I don't know. Why don't you come up with something? You're the one who's always talking about Alexis is going to be your wife. Come up with something to save your wife."

Thomas was quiet. "Thomas, are you there?"

"Yeah, yeah, I'm thinking. Listen, give me an hour and I'll call you back."

"Okay."

After they hung up, Champagne asked herself, "Why? Why am I doing this?"

An hour later Thomas called back. "Okay, here's what we're going to do. I called my girl, and she said they have friends in common, so she's going to make a couple of phone calls and get some information."

"Does she know why we're doing this? Would she be doing it if she knew you wanted Alexis?"

"Don't worry about all that. I got this."

Champagne hung up and wondered how they were going to pull it off. *Okay, I'm not going to think about it. I'm going to just focus on work.*

Pressing the intercom button, she called Candy into the office.

"Yes?"

"Are you packed and ready?"

Candy started laughing. "The truth? I always wait until the last minute to pack. If I try to pack earlier, I have too many options and end up getting frustrated."

"You know we only have a couple more days until we leave."

"Yeah, I know."

Champagne told her, "Listen, I'm stepping out for a moment. Hold down the fort."

"As always," Candy said, wondering where she was going.

Before Champagne could say another word, her cell phone started ringing. She glanced at the ID. It was Thomas. She pressed the ACCEPT button. "Damn, didn't we just get off the phone?"

"Check it, we can do this tonight."

Moving the phone from her mouth, Champagne told Candy, "That's all." She waited until Candy left the office to say, "You mean, go to the swingers club?"

"Yeah, I was told he'll be there tonight."

"You're lying." Champagne couldn't believe it was happening this fast. There was no way in the world the same day they came up with the plan that they could see it through. Shit just wasn't this easy.

"Listen, do you want to do this or not? You need to let me know so I can plan accordingly."

"How? What exactly is the plan?"

"Let's figure that out when we get together later."

They made arrangements to meet at eleven that night at her office. Champagne had to come up with something to tell Zyair. For her to up and leave in the middle of the night would definitely cause some suspicion. Hopefully, this would be one of those nights he stayed at the restaurant real late. If not, she'd tell him one of her clients was having a party in the city and she had to attend.

"Well, this is certainly last minute," Zyair responded when she told him the lie.

"I know. Initially I wasn't going to attend but she practically begged me." Champagne told him that one of her former clients was considering switching to her company and wanted to speak with her after a dinner party she was having. There was no way in the world she could tell him what she and Thomas were up to, and she'd told Thomas not to say anything either.

He wasn't too keen on lying to his boy, but Champagne convinced him that if he didn't even mention it, he wouldn't be lying.

It worked out anyway, because Zyair was staying at the restaurant late.

That night while getting ready, Champagne changed clothes numerous times, all the while wondering, how Thomas knew beyond a shadow of a doubt that Khalil was going to be there.

All he would tell her is, "I've got connections."

Well, so be it. As long they got the evidence they needed she could care less.

The plan was as follows. Thomas and Champagne would meet up at her office. From there, she would get in his car, and they would go to the spot.

Champagne's stomach was in her chest. Her instincts told her, "Don't do this," but she couldn't stop herself. It's like a force was pulling her to do the unthinkable.

When they arrived at the club, they would walk in together as a couple. There was a rule there that no man could go in alone. He had to be accompanied by a woman.

Walking in unfamiliar surroundings with nakedness everywhere, this was the part that scared her.

She knew she wouldn't feel comfortable walking in a place with her man's best friend and people all around making love or doing whatever it is they do. She expressed this to Thomas, who told her not to worry about it, they could go their separate ways.

Of course he had his reasons. He wanted to see what he could come back and get into without it being awkward. Two, she was his best friend's girl, and as it stood, they were going behind his back.

"We'll do a walk-through and see if we spot him," Thomas told her.

"What will we do if we see him? We can't just walk up on him and yell out, 'Busted.'"

"No, we can't but what I can do is make sure he sees me. Then when you have another dinner party, and he sees me again, I'll handle the rest."

The rest of the evening flew by.

As agreed upon, they met at Champagne's office. He called her from around the corner and she met him outside.

Climbing into his car, she asked him, "Are we sure we want to do this?"

"There's no turning back now," he told her. He glanced at what she wore and thought to himself that Zyair was a lucky man. "You look nice."

Champagne smiled and thanked him. She closed the door, relaxed in her seat, and placed her head on the headrest.

Thomas pulled off slowly and asked her, "Why are we doing this again?"

"I keep asking myself the same thing. All I'm coming up with is, there's something about him that doesn't sit right. It's just an instinct, and I only want what's best for my girl and I don't think it's him."

"Isn't this the kind of thing that breaks up friendships, when people butt in?"

Champagne looked at him and crossed her arms. "Well, you're butting in. Why are you butting in?"

"Because I love her."

If it was any other time, Champagne would have laughed but there was a seriousness to his tone.

When she didn't make a crack, Thomas asked her, "You don't have anything to say?"

Champagne shook her head. "You know, we all do things, feel things, and say things we can't explain sometimes. They are just what they are. Who am I to judge?"

Thomas knew she was speaking about other things but he didn't feel it was his place to pry. But he did have something else he needed to know. "Let me ask you something."

"Go ahead."

"What is it about me you don't like? I want you to be honest with me too, because I know whatever you say is probably what Alexis is thinking."

"It's not that I don't like you. I don't want you to think that. I care for you a lot, Thomas. You're like a brother to Zyair. Therefore, you're like a brother to me."

"Then why do I feel that way? Sometimes when I come over I feel unwanted. I don't know what I'm stepping into when I see you, if you're going to be in one of your happy, welcome-to-my-house or one of your get-out moods."

Champagne didn't realize she behaved that way. Okay, yes, sometimes he pissed her off with some of his sexist remarks and comments he made about women, but she didn't not like him, and she wanted him to know that, especially with what he was doing for her today.

She positioned herself so that she could face him. "Thomas, please hear this. I do like you. It's just that sometimes when the fellows are around, I get insecure."

"But why take it out on me?"

"I don't mean to take it out on you. You're one of the connections to Zyair's player past, and sometimes when I hear you two talking you make it sound like he's missing out on something. That's the last thing I want him to think."

Thomas was real quiet as he contemplated on his response. Did he tell her how much he admired what she and Zyair shared, that he wanted the same thing for himself? Did he tell her that sometimes he didn't feel worthy and that he wondered if he would be able to be the type of man a woman wanted and needed? He chose not to say those things. Instead he said, "Listen, Zyair loves you, and nothing I say out of ignorance or out of anything else will change that. If anything, he's the one that's telling me what I'm missing, that I need to settle down and find the one. I envy what you guys have. I would never jeopardize that. Although, my bringing you here to the house of swingers just might do that."

It was then that Champagne realized they were in the parking garage.

"You do know he'd kick my ass, right?" Thomas turned off the car.

Champagne didn't want to answer that.

Thomas wasn't done yet. "Let me ask you this, does Alexis have any idea how much I want her?"

Champagne didn't have the heart to tell him that although Alexis had made comments about how good looking he is, she thought he was a straight-up dog. "She does but if you want her to take you serious, you need to be more serious and stop acting a male whore."

Thomas knew what she was saying was true. He was getting tired of playing the game and was also ready to step it up and step up to Alexis.

Climbing out of the car, he told Champagne, "Come on, let's go catch this chump."

Champagne walked behind him. She could feel her body shaking in anticipation of what she might witness. "We are going our separate ways, right?"

"Yes, Champagne. We've gone over this a few times already."

"I know, but I'm trying to be sure of what we planned."

"If you see him, you're going make sure he sees you and then I'm going to have a dinner party and you're going to say something to him that'll make him stop seeing Alexis. But if I see him first, do you think I should approach him?"

Thomas removed her hand and placed his hands on her shoulders. "Get it together. Breathe or something."

Champagne started laughing because she realized she was having a meltdown.

This worried Thomas. "Maybe you need to sit in the car and let me handle this by myself." ·

Champagne didn't want that to happen. She had to admit, she was curious about what was going on inside. She'd heard so many tales about swingers; and now she wanted to see for herself. Maybe if she thought of it like Hedonism, it wouldn't be so bad. After all, they'd sat next to people having sex, and once you got over the initial shock, it become almost natural.

She grabbed his hand. "Come on, let's do this."

When they stepped up to the door, there stood two of the biggest men Champagne had ever seen. They had to both be over six feet five inches and 300 pounds.

Goddamn, she thought.

The men frisked Thomas and looked Champagne over. She felt like they were looking inside her. The men allowed them to pass, and once inside, they showed their IDs and paid one hundred dollars to enter.

One hundred dollars, Champagne thought. Not a lot to pay for a night of sex with anyone and in any way.

Once they walked inside, there was a long hall-way with numerous rooms on either side.

Thomas looked at her and asked, "Are you ready to go our separate ways?"'

"Not yet." She took his hand, and together they went toward the first room.

The first room must have been the "get acquainted" room. There was a lot of touching, laughing, and kissing. Basically people were sizing one another up. One of the things that surprised Champagne was that most of the people there looked like they could be your neighbor or coworker. A couple of them looked like they could be your parents.

Champagne laughed to herself. It was obvious kinkiness didn't discriminate.

"Are you ready to separate?" Thomas asked.

"Yep, I'm thinking I can handle it."

Little did she know, in the next room two women were laying side by side, caressing one another. They were lost in their own world, with their tongues meeting, eyes closed. Champagne found them to be attractive. Both had athlete bodies. One was Puerto Rican and the other Black. Champagne always associated these places with white folks. Boy, was she wrong.

Glancing around the room, she counted three others, two men and another female. The others were drinking and observing. She watched as one of the men walked over and knelt down beside the women. They opened their eyes and pulled him in. The Black woman caught Champagne's eyes and beckoned her over.

There was no way in the world Champagne was going over there. Instead she averted her eyes, and when she felt the woman look away, she looked at them again.

The man was placing himself between the Puerto Rican's legs. He cupped her ass and pulled her up to meet his dick, which was already covered with a condom.

At least they come prepared. Champagne couldn't pull away, and when he plunged into the woman, she instantly became moist.

A man whispered in Champagne's ear, "Why don't you take off your dress?" and ran his hand across her ass.

Champagne took that as a sign to leave the room. She was about to turn the corner when someone grabbed her and threw her up against the wall.

"So this is what you do?"

Champagne was staring in Jackson's face. She couldn't help but look down and notice the outline of a hard dick on his briefs. She looked up at him and the smirk on his face. This shit is going from bad to worse. "Take your hands off me."

Jackson pressed up against her and pushed her body into the wall. "You could come here, but you can't give me any pussy." He looked around. "Where's your man?"

Champagne was getting ready to panic. Then she saw someone's fingers reach around Jackson's neck and pull him off her.

It was Thomas, and he looked ready to tear Jackson's ass apart. "Get your hands off her now."

Jackson landed against the wall across from where they stood.

Thomas looked at Champagne. "You all right?"

Champagne nodded.

"I always knew you were a whore." Jackson looked like he was ready to charge Thomas.

Thomas turned to face him. "Don't even think about it."

Why is this happening? This is what I get for even being here. Champagne grabbed Thomas by the arm. "Let's get out of here."

By this time, security had arrived and told everyone they needed to leave the premises.

Jackson had to get his final words in. "Don't think this will be the last time you see me."

Thomas stood in his face. "Are you fucking threatening her?"

Jackson wasn't backing down. "You don't look like that Zyair fellow to me."

Champagne pulled Thomas. "Come on, ignore him. Let's go."

Security escorted them to the door.

Once they were outside, Thomas asked Champagne, "Who was that asshole?"

"That was my old boss."

Thomas tilted his head and frowned. "Your boss?"

"Yeah. Now you see why I quit? He was always throwing himself on me, and it just got to be too much."

"Does Zyair know about this?"

"No. I was able to handle it."

In exasperation, Thomas asked, "Why do women do that?"

"Do what?"

"Not tell their men when someone is harassing them? Why do you ladies think it's your job to handle it?"

"I don't speak for all women. I speak only for myself. It's not that I think it's my job to handle anything. If I can, I will, and if I can't, then I'll hand it over."

As they were walking toward the garage, they heard a car slam on brakes. Looking up, neither could make out the person inside the car. It was DaNeen.

What the hell? DaNeen was on her way home from hanging out with her girls in the city. She was driving by the garage when she spotted Thomas and Champagne. Of course, she knew who they were. She knew who anyone was that played an important part in Zyair's life.

She glanced around to see if Zyair was on the premises. Then she remembered, he was staying at the restaurant late that night, and if she recalled correctly; she thought she'd overheard him saying to someone that Champagne had a dinner date with a client. His best friend certainly didn't look like a client to her.

She was definitely going to use this bit of information to her own advantage.

DaNeen couldn't help wondering what his woman and his best friend were doing out in the middle of the night, and why would Champagne lie about her whereabouts?

On the drive to her office, Thomas told her he didn't see Khalil. He didn't tell her that he would probably be going back there.

Champagne was disappointed that they didn't get anything on him, and pissed that she'd worked herself up into a frenzy over the whole thing.

"Maybe something else will come up," Thomas offered as a way to console her.

"Maybe this is God's way of telling us to let things fall however they may. If Khalil is really who we think he is, it'll eventually come out."

"You think so?"

"I don't know. It just sounded good saying it." Thomas laughed.

When Champagne went to climb out of his car, he placed his hand on top of hers. "Thanks, Champagne."

"For what?"

"For clearing up my misunderstanding."

"What misunderstanding?"

"You know, the fact that I thought you didn't like me."

Champagne kissed him on the cheek. "You're welcome. I know you're a decent man, Thomas. You just need to let others know it."

When Champagne arrived home, Zyair was laying in the bed. "How did it go? Do you have a new client?"'

"I believe I do." Champagne started to undress. She wanted to tell Zyair about the night's events.

It was on the tip of her tongue but she decided to wait. She and Thomas would tell him together.

She went into the bathroom to shower and brush her teeth. She was horny and wanted to do something about it.

Zyair called from the bed, "Are you about to take a shower?"

"Yes, and when I get out, it's on."

For a second there, he was curious about this impromptu shower but after hearing that it was for a session of lovemaking, that curiosity faded.

While in the shower Champagne thought about the swingers club and what she'd witnessed. It surprised her that not everyone was naked, and that there were just as many people there observing as there were participating.

She thought about the two women and the man that were making love, and found her fingers making way to her pussy. She fondled with her hairs and looked up at the shower head. *I wonder if I can make myself cum with that*. Yes, she and Zyair were going to make love but there was nothing wrong with an extra orgasm.

She took the shower head down with her right hand and spread her legs just a little wider. She took her left hand and separated the skin just above her clitoris. Champagne closed her eyes and leaned back against the shower wall. She positioned the shower head so that the water would hit the top of her clitoris and immediately she felt her legs buckle. Champagne felt a moan coming on and tried to keep it low. She didn't want Zyair to hear her. She brought the shower head closer to her clitoris so the water could hit it harder. Her pussy walls pulsated, and it wasn't long before the buildup erupted and her orgasm hit hard, buckling her knees. She pressed her lips together and looked up at the ceiling. "Oh, shit," she whispered.

After her orgasm, she completed her shower and stepped out. She dried off and went into the bedroom, where Zyair was laying back with his hands behind his head and his eyes closed.

Champagne, on her hands and knees, straddled him and kissed him on the lips. "Open your eyes," she told him.

He obliged.

She met his mouth with her tongue and licked his lips.

Zyair reached up for her but she grabbed his hands and held them down to his side.

"I want to do all the work," she said. Being the man he was, Zyair didn't object.

Champagne nibbled his neck and caressed his chest. Then she moved her hands down between his legs, cupping his balls.

"You're feisty tonight," he said. "What kind of dinner party was that?"

Champagne shushed him as her mouth made its way to his navel, where she dipped her tongue.

She knew she would be going away, she knew that she was wrong for lying to him and she knew she was wrong for her sexual thoughts that did not include him. She was going to make it up to him.

She then ran her tongue from his navel and stopped when she reached his dick. She looked at it and decided she wanted to devour it. She placed it in her mouth and covered the whole length of it. She felt it hit the back of her throat and slowly brought her mouth up and licked it with her tongue.

Zyair grabbed the back of her head and tried to push her back down.

She pushed his hands back into the bed. Looking up at him, she told him, "Let me do this my way." She licked all around his dick and pushed it straight up so that she could lick and suck on his balls. She went back and forth, from the left testicle to the right, and then tried to put both in her mouth while stroking his dick. She let her tongue fall under his balls and ran it from his balls to his ass and back up over and over again.

Zyair was squirming and moaning.

Champagne wanted him to do more. She went back up to his dick and placed it in her mouth, licking and sucking, sucking and licking. She licked the top half and stroked the bottom half, kissed around it and started sucking again.

"Oh, girl, you're going to make me cum." Zyair grabbed her head again and tried to push his dick down her throat.

Champagne wasn't having it. She moved his hands and climbed on top of him. She straddled him and held herself up on her feet. She sat on his dick and started moving real slow up and down, squeezing her walls when she got up top and loosening them when she slammed their bodies together.

After doing this for a couple of minutes, she pressed down on him as hard as she could and started to grind. She knew that by doing this, not only she would cum but he would as well.

And that's what they both did. They ended the night with a kiss and a cuddle.

Chapter Twenty-six

"All Around The World"

Lisa Stansfield

It was now the day before the trip, and Candy was excited to be going to Chocolate City, especially since a couple of her friends lived there. Their plane was scheduled to leave Newark Airport at 5:30 p.m., and Candy was looking forward to the short first-class flight. She was also happy because her friend Elsie would be in town, and she would be able to set up some time to meet with her, perhaps for dinner.

Candy wasn't too sure what she should pack. She picked up the phone and called Champagne on her cell.

"Hello?"

"Hey, it's Candy."

"Are you packed yet?"

"That's why I was calling. I don't know what to pack."

"Well, you know we'll be gone for four days. Thursday, we have a meeting with Trina, Friday is the banquet, Saturday morning and early afternoon we'll be busy meeting with her wedding planner, and Sunday is a free day. So bring business casual, something dressy for the banquet, and whatever else you want to bring."

When they hung up, Candy went through her closet and picked out what she deemed proper. The one issue she encountered was the "something dressy" for the banquet. Instead of driving herself crazy over it, she decided to wait until she arrived in D.C. and hit the stores there. After all, she shopped well under pressure.

While on this adventure, she hoped to get to know Champagne better. In the office, everything was so tight and so business-like. She wanted to get to know the woman she saw at Ladies First, the lady that was dancing, laughing, and having a good time.

Candy knew the reason she and Zyair were there. It was the same reason most couples came to female gay clubs, to get their freak on or for foreplay. She also had a feeling that the person named Sharon who called the office often was more than an acquaintance. It was apparent in Champagne's behavior when they were on the phone together.

Champagne had finished her packing so she could have some time with Zyair before she left.

That night they were out to dinner. Zyair was sitting across from Champagne, taking her in with his eyes. Sometimes it amazed him that she still looked as good as the day they met. The intense attraction he had for her was still there, and he wondered if it would always be. He'd heard that it comes in spurts, the attraction and the love.

I love this girl so much. Why are we putting off the inevitable? It's time to set a date. "Champagne?"

"Yes?" Champagne looked up from her dessert menu.

"When are we going to set a date?"

"A date for what?"

"For us to get married."

This is not what I want to discuss the day before I leave. "Why are you asking me that now?"

"It's something I've been thinking about for a while now, and I'm ready."

Now you're ready, just when I've just started exploring sexually. "I thought we were going to wait a couple of years."

Zyair tilted his head and frowned. He felt as though Champagne was fighting him on this. Leaning across the table, he asked her, "What? You don't want to get married now?"

"I didn't say all that."

"Then what are you saying? Why put it off, if it's what we both want? I don't get it."

"There's nothing to get or not to get, Zyair. I just hadn't given it any thought. The last time we even discussed this, we both agreed that we would wait a couple more years, after your new restaurant was open, and I decided what I wanted to do business wise."

Zyair had to admit, she was right. That was what they'd agreed upon. But a person was entitled to change his mind, and he told her this.

"Zyair, can we talk about this when I get back?"

"Why can't we talk about it now?"

"Because . . ."

"Because? Now you and I both know that is not a good answer. What? You don't want to marry me now?"

"Why are you jumping to conclusions?"

Zyair didn't understand what the hell was going on. He felt like he was begging her to marry him. *A woman is the one that should want to get married. She should be the one anxious to set a date. She should be the one asking him, are they going to continue on like this forever.*

Interrupting his thoughts, Champagne said, "Zyair, it's not that I don't want to get married. You just need to understand that I've gotten comfortable in our relationship the way we are, and yes, I admit, maybe that's not a good thing. It's just that when you look at relationships now, marriage isn't really a big deal. People live together, create futures, and have kids without a ring.

Even though she didn't exactly say it, what Zyair heard was, "I don't want to marry you."

"You know what"—Zyair signaled for the waiter to come over—"let's just drop it. If you don't want to set a date, you don't have to. You just need to know that I'm ready to get married, and I'm ready to set a date."

Champagne wondered if this meant that he would be willing to leave her if she wasn't ready. It's not that she wasn't ready. If he'd said something about setting a date a couple of months ago, she just may have done that. She didn't even know why she was so resistant.

"Okay, when I get back, we'll start thinking about a date," she said, wanting to change the subject.

The waiter approached the table. "Are you ready for dessert?"

Champagne was but she could tell that Zyair was ready to leave.

"No, thank you. Just bring us the check." They rode home in silence.

Every time Champagne tried to make conversation, Zyair would speak in short sentences, which only left her frustrated. It was a relief when her cell phone rang.

Zyair glanced over at her when she picked it up. Without looking at the caller ID, Champagne answered, "Hello."

"What's up, sexy?" Sharon greeted.

Champagne snuck a quick glance at Zyair who was pretending he wasn't listening.

"Nothing. Do you mind if I call you back?" Champagne was trying not to sound too personal.

"Are you busy?"

"Yes."

After a short pause, Sharon told her, "Sure, call me when you're alone."

The second Champagne hung up the phone, Zyair asked her, "Who was that?"

This threw her off because he never asked her who she was talking to. "It was a client," she lied, knowing he would be upset if she said it was Sharon.

"Did I hear a client say, 'Hey, sexy'?"

Oh, shit, he heard that? "That's not what you heard. What they said was, 'Hey, Champagne.'"

Zyair wasn't crazy. He was almost certain that's what's he heard, but he didn't want to argue about it because there was a slight chance he could be wrong. After all, the phone wasn't up to his ear and he was trying to listen a bit too hard. This wasn't something he normally did, but things had changed once again between them and he was concerned.

"You don't have to believe me. I know who was on the phone, and I know what was said."

"Whatever you say, Champagne."

This wasn't the energy Champagne wanted to leave Zyair with. She knew she needed to reset the tone once they arrived home, but looking over at Zyair she knew that it wasn't going to be easy bringing him out from where he was mentally. Sex was almost always the answer but she just wasn't up to it tonight.

When they pulled into the garage, they both climbed out of the car without saying a word and went into the house. Zyair headed for his office, and Champagne for the bedroom. He just needed some space, and she was going to finish packing.

The following morning when she woke up, she was surprised to find that Zyair didn't sleep in the bed with her. She knew for sure that he would come to his senses when he realized she was leaving the next day and would make up with her. If not that, at least come cuddle.

No such luck.

When she walked into the kitchen he was cooking breakfast for two.

Before she could get a word out, he walked over to her and pulled her into him. "I love you, and I apologize for acting like an ass last night."

This caught her off guard. All of a sudden she was overcome with emotion.

Zyair pulled away. "Why are you crying?"

"I don't know. I've just been feeling so overwhelmed lately, and then last night I couldn't find the right words to say to—"

Zyair cut her off. "Let's not talk about that now. Let's just enjoy breakfast and each other's company. When you get back, we'll deal with other things."

Champagne wondered how many things they would have to deal with. She hoped this business trip would give her an opportunity to think about what direction she was headed in, with the thoughts she'd been having. On second thought, maybe she needed to spend a weekend in a spa. That way she'd be more relaxed and be able to clear her head.

Chapter Twenty-seven

"Rumors"

Timex Social Club

When Candy arrived at the airport, it was a little after 4:00 p.m. Champagne was already there and noticed Candy as soon as she walked up.

"Hey, lady." Champagne patted the seat next to her.

Candy placed her small luggage on the floor and sat down. "Girl, this airport traveling and getting settled thing is a pain in the ass."

"I know that's right."

Candy wasn't one to chat when on the plane. She liked to be left alone to read, sleep, or listen to her music. She decided to see what kind of traveler Champagne was. "Okay, we need to get this out the way."

Champagne looked at her. "What?"

"Do you like to talk and have conversation when you're traveling, or do you want to be left alone?"

Champagne started laughing. "I know where you're going. Girl, I'm one of those leave-me-alone-and-let me-be people as well. You don't have to worry about me talking you to death."

Candy placed her hand on her chest and said, "Whew! You don't know how relieved I am."

"Do you want to discuss our itinerary before we get on the plane?"

"Yeah, we can do that."

Champagne bent over and picked up her briefcase. She pulled out two pieces of paper and handed one to Candy.

For the next hour or so, they went over their plans for the weekend. This way Candy would know what was expected of her and when she was required to be around.

Candy was glad they did that, because she didn't want this to be the one and only business trip she was allowed to go on.

The plane ride was uneventful and short. When they landed, they headed to the hotel and agreed to have drinks together that night. After drinks Candy was going to meet up with Elsie, and Champagne was going to have dinner with her client.

In her hotel room, Champagne picked up the phone to call Alexis. There was no answer. She then called Zyair, and when he didn't answer, she decided to go downtown and shop. After all, she had a couple of hours to kill before she and Candy met up for a drink.

Zyair was sitting at a table in his restaurant with Thomas. They were discussing Champagne and Alexis. DaNeen was across the room, watching and trying to read their lips because whatever they were talking about had them both looking intense. Ever since she'd seen Champagne and Thomas out that night, she wanted to tell Zyair but the time just never seemed right. She wanted them to be alone, and for him to be so devastated that he fell into her arms. What would be ideal was for her to make this happen while Champagne was away. She tried to read Zyair's lips as he told Thomas, "I asked her when we were going to set a date, and she all but said we weren't."

Although Zyair pretended that everything was kosher with Champagne prior to her leaving, it really wasn't. He was having serious doubts about where they stood. He thought things were getting better between them, that them going to Jamaica and experimenting was going to bring them closer together.

"Did she say those words to you?"

"No, she didn't have to. I could feel it."

"Man, that's some bullshit. Sometimes what we think a person means is not what they mean at all. I would not go on a feeling. When she comes back, you and her need to sit down and really talk, figure out what's going on."

"I feel like it's my entire fault for allowing some-one else into our bedroom. Between that and Hedonism, we fucked up."

Thomas didn't have anything to say on that sub-ject. He himself wished he could set up something like that with someone.

"Nah, you don't need a drink. It's just that." He hesitated. "You know I've got feelings for Alexis, right?"

"That's what you've been telling me for years."

"Well, I'm ready to make my move."

"What are you talking about, man? Why are you coming to me with this?"

"Because you're my boy, and I don't know who else to go to."

Zyair didn't respond.

Thomas went on, "I'm ready to settle down and change my ways. I'm ready to have what you and Champagne have."

"You mean had."

"No, have. No matter what you think is going on, you and Champagne belong together. I want to belong to someone like that, and I believe that person is Alexis."

"You're serious, aren't you?"

"As a heart attack."

"Well, why haven't you asked her out before now?"

"I wasn't ready."

"What makes you . . ." Zyair's voice trailed off along with his eyes.

Thomas followed his gaze and noticed Champagne's ex-boss, Jackson, and an attractive female walking toward them. *Fuck! Fuck! Fuck! I hope he doesn't say anything about seeing me and Champagne at the spot.*

Jackson put out his hand for Zyair to shake. "Zyair."

Zyair never really liked Jackson. He believed there was something underhanded and slimy about him. Not wanting to be an asshole, he shook his hand.

Then Jackson turned toward Thomas. "Funny seeing you here."

Zyair looked at Thomas. "You two know each other?"

Aw shit, here it comes. Thomas wasn't stupid. He knew to be prepared for anything.

"Your woman knows him too."

Zyair looked confused. "Of course she knows him. He's my boy."

Jackson knew immediately that Zyair wasn't up on the fact that "his boy" and Champagne were at a swingers club together the other night.

"Yo, man, why don't you step?" Thomas said.

Turning toward his date, Jackson told her, "Go have a seat. I'll be right with you in a minute."

By now Thomas had stood up. "I asked you to step."

Zyair stood up as well. "What the hell is going on?"

"Oh, your boy didn't tell you he and your girl were out together the other night?"

Zyair looked at Thomas and could see guilt written all over his face. "What the hell is he talking about, Thomas?"

Thomas, caught between a rock and a hard place, felt like he had no choice, but to tell Zyair what he and Champagne were up to.

Jackson was amused by what was going on, "Oh, so your boy didn't tell you they were at a swingers club?"

Zyair frowned. "Man, what the hell is he talking about?" He looked at Jackson. "Word is bond—You need to get up out of my restaurant and stop with the bullshit."

"You think I'm bullshitting? Ask your boy. No, as a matter-of-fact, where was your girl Friday night?"

Thomas couldn't even punch Jackson in the mouth because he spoke the truth, and looking at Zyair, he could tell he was counting back the days.

Jackson laughed. "Let me leave you two alone."

Zyair signaled for security. Without taking his eyes off Thomas, he nodded toward Jackson and told them to escort him out.

Jackson followed them out with a smirk on his face. "Don't hate the player," he said. "You just got caught up in the game."

Zyair faced Thomas with fire in his eyes. "You need to tell me what he's talking about."

"It's not what you think, man."

Raising his voice, Zyair asked, "What do you mean, it's not what I think? What the fuck are you talking about?" He started pacing the floor. "Please tell me you were not at a swingers club with my woman. Please tell me she didn't lie to me about where she was goin'."

The look on Thomas' face told him all he needed to know. If he was going to speak, he needed to speak fast. "It's not what you think, man. We went looking for Khalil. Diamond told me that he hung out there, and that's where she knew him from."

Before Thomas could even finish, Zyair's fist came out of nowhere and punched him in the mouth. All Thomas could do was stand there with his hand over his mouth.

Zyair's stance was one of "I'm about to kick your whole ass, muthafucka."

Security was right back on spot, with DaNeen following close behind.

Thomas threw his arms up. "I'm out, I'm out." He started to walk away but then turned around to face Zyair. "Man, you really need to hear me out. I would never do anything to hurt you. You need to believe that."

"Just get out my face before I fuck you up."

Thomas knew the best thing to do was leave and deal with the situation later. He also knew he needed to call Champagne as soon as possible and let her know what was up.

Chapter Twenty-eight

"Secret Lovers"

Atlantic Starr

It was their last night in D.C. and Candy and Champagne were ordering drinks at the bar. Champagne's phone rang, and she looked at the caller ID, THOMAS. *I wonder what he wants.*

"Excuse me," she told Candy. "I have to take this call." Champagne stood up and went toward the ladies' room. "Hello?"

"It's Thomas. What's up?"

"Nothing."

Not one to beat around the bush, Thomas came out with it. "Zyair knows about us going to the swingers club."

"What?" Champagne knew he didn't just say what she thought he did.

"Jackson came into the restaurant and caused a scene, and Zyair punched me in the mouth."

"Hold up, hold up. What do you mean, Jackson came into the restaurant? Did you tell him why we were there? Did you try to explain?" She was panicking, wondering what Zyair could be thinking right now. Should she call him, or should she wait until she arrived home to talk to him? *Shit! Shit! Shit!*

"What was I supposed to say Champagne? I tried to tell him what Diamond told me about Khalil, but he wasn't trying to hear a word of it and I can't say I blame him. Shit! I knew we shouldn't have went there together. This is fucked up. I may have lost my boy over this bullshit."

Champagne couldn't think of a word to say. She was trying to figure out what she was going to say to Zyair. What was there to say? All she could do was tell the truth. After all, she really didn't do anything wrong, but she knew he wouldn't understand. He'd already warned her to mind her business. Fuck it, it's going to be what it's going to be.

"Do you think I should call him or wait until I get home?"

"Yeah, I think you should, Champagne. You also need to know that he thinks you don't want to marry him."

Champagne didn't have to ask what gave him that impression. She already knew she was to blame. Damn it, what the hell was wrong with her? She'd been losing her mind lately. Was it really worth it? Was it worth losing Zyair?

"Thomas, thanks for giving me a heads-up. I'll call him and try to set things straight, although I don't think it's going to happen over the phone."

"Well, let me know if you need me."

As Champagne walked toward the table, Candy studied her facial expression.

Champagne sat down. She called the bartender over and ordered a shot of Patrón.

"Damn, you ain't playing," Candy told her.

Champagne didn't respond.

"What's up? Is everything okay?"

Needing to talk it out with someone, Champagne said, "I think I fucked up."

"Fucked up what? What happened?"

Champagne went on to tell Candy about how she didn't trust her best friend's boyfriend. She told her how, unbeknownst to Zyair, she and Thomas went to a swingers club to catch him fucking up and ran into her ex-boss.

In the process of telling this story, Champagne had a couple more shots of Patrón and was feeling quite nice. "Anyway, Zyair found out because Jackson came into his restaurant and caused a scene. This whole thing has become a mess, and I don't know what to do about it."

While Champagne was in a talking mood, Candy decided to ask her about the time she and Zyair were in Ladies First. "So what's up with you and Zyair coming to the 'ladies bar'?"

Champagne figured, *To hell with it*. "We were looking to do something different."

"Something like what?"

"Why are you so curious?"

"I just am. I know that most couples go to the clubs looking to get into something."

Champagne didn't bother answering. She stood up and said, "Maybe I should go to my room and call Zyair."

Candy stood up also. "I don't know if it's a good idea for you to call him when you're in this condition."

Champagne felt herself tilt a little to the left. "You know what, maybe you're right. Maybe I should wait until the liquor wears off. I think I'll go to my room and lay down."

"How about I walk you to your room? I don't think you're going to make it on your own."

Champagne looked Candy in the eyes. "That just might be a good idea."

Chapter Twenty-nine

"It's Ecstasy When You Lay Down Next To Me"

Barry White

Zyair was in his office, his head in his hands, when DaNeen approached him.

"Are you okay?"

Looking up, he told her, "As okay as I can be."

DaNeen walked around his desk and started massaging his shoulders. "Do you want to talk about it?"

Everything in Zyair knew he should ask her to leave, but he didn't feel like being alone. Plus, her hands felt good. "I don't know, DaNeen. Maybe I've been a fool all this time. Maybe I was living a lie with Champagne. How could I have been so stupid?" He looked up at her. "Nah, I refuse to believe that. There has to be a logical explanation. But then again, what would be a logical explanation for your boy and your woman to be at a swingers club? Can you think of one?"

DaNeen told him she couldn't, and added, "I would've never done anything like that to you. You don't need anyone like that." She turned his chair around to face her. "You need someone like me, Zyair, someone that wouldn't go behind your back with your best friend."

Zyair could feel that this was going in the wrong direction but he needed comfort, needed to feel appreciated, something he hadn't been feeling lately. As a matter-of-fact, Champagne had been neglecting him. He felt like the love was one-sided, like he was the one carrying the relationship, the one using up all the energy to keep her happy and satisfied. He was tired of being taken for granted. "Even if what Thomas said is true, what the hell were they thinking?"

DaNeen didn't know what Thomas said, and she really didn't care. "I don't know, Zyair, but what I do know is, women tend to forget what they have and how good they may have it. If you were my man, I would shower you with love and affection."

Zyair liked what he was hearing. He wanted to be showered with love and affection. He didn't want to be treated as an afterthought. "Damn, girl, that sounds good."

"I have something that will feel just as good." DaNeen didn't wait for an answer. She bent down and placed her lips on his. She waited for him to respond, and when he did, she sat on his lap.

In the back of his mind, Zyair was telling himself to stop, but the hurt in his heart was urging him on. He turned her around so that she was straddling him.

"Is the door locked?" he asked her.

DaNeen stood up and went to check. It wasn't, so she locked it.

Zyair stood up, and together they moved toward the chaise. Zyair sat down, and DaNeen stood in front of him and slid her skirt down.

Zyair was surprised to find that all she wore underneath was stockings and a garter belt.

She leaned over and unbuckled his belt.

He stood up, and together they pulled his pants down.

DaNeen lay back on the chaise, and Zyair climbed on top of her. There was no foreplay, no kissing, no caressing.

They looked each other in the eyes, and DaNeen, still seeing the hurt on his face, told him, "It's okay. I've been wanting this for a long time."

Zyair placed his hands under her ass and pulled her into him real hard. He did this a couple of times, until he heard her wince. After realizing that it wasn't DaNeen's fault that he was hurt, he decided to slow down his pace.

She understood what he was doing and allowed him to have his way with her. However he wanted her, she'd give herself to him. If he wanted to fuck her hard, she'd let him. If he wanted to make slow, passionate love to her, she'd let him.

Zyair was in a daze. He was well aware of what he was doing and knew he was in the wrong. He thought doing this would make him feel better but it didn't. As a matter-of-fact, it made him feel worse because he wasn't that kind of man and he was operating outside himself. He was operating off his emotions.

Deep down, he knew Thomas and Champagne wouldn't mess around with one another behind his back. He also knew that Champagne had been bugging over the whole Khalil and Alexis relationship. He could see her doing something as stupid as going to a swingers club to get evidence. He was just pissed off by the deception and being left out of the loop. Especially Thomas' role.

He wondered what they saw when they were there. To him there was something intimate about that excursion.

As Zyair felt himself about to cum, he realized he didn't have a condom on and pulled out of DaNeen. As he came in his hand, he wondered what Champagne was doing at that very moment.

Chapter Thirty

"Say Yes"

The Whispers

Candy wanted so bad to make love to Champagne. She was laying behind her in the bed, spooning, rubbing her hair as she cried and talked.

"How could I have been so stupid?" Champagne asked. "I might have destroyed the best thing in my life by being foolish."

The Patrón had Champagne telling it all. She told Candy all about Hedonism and about Sharon. "I don't know what's gotten into me. When we went to Hedonism, I had no intentions on being with a woman, but once it happened, it seemed like that's all I could think about. I used the excuse of trying it again sober to see if I liked it, and I found I did." She turned over and faced Candy. "What do you think it means? Do you think it means that I'm gay?"

Candy could see how vulnerable Champagne was feeling and wanted to take advantage of her so bad but she knew to do that would jeopardize her job. "No, I don't think that. I think you were curious and wanted to experiment, like you said. Sometimes we need to try things more than once to see if it's what we like. You found out that you did, and I personally think it's okay to like more than one thing."

Champagne wanted to believe her. "You really think so?"

"I speak only the truth."

"Kiss me."

Although this is what Candy wanted, she was caught off guard. "Huh?"

"I said kiss me."

Candy pushed Champagne on her back and lay on top of her. "Is this you talking, or is it the liquor talking?"

"It's me talking."

"I work for you."

"I know."

"Are you going to be able to handle it?"

"All I'm asking for is a kiss."

"Nothing else?"

"Why? Do you want something else?"

Candy didn't respond with words. She responded by planting soft kisses on Champagne's lips. "Listen," she said, "if we go on with this, I want you to know I don't expect anything from you. I just want to make you feel better."

Champagne placed her hands on each side of Candy's face and said, "Stop talking and make love to me."

As Candy kissed her, she thought about Candy and Sharon, and the fact that if it had been another time and the circumstances were different, they could have seen where this would go, but because things were the way they were they couldn't. Champagne knew this was going to be it, her last time making love with a woman, and that her choice was to be with Zyair.

"Let's get undressed," she told Candy.

Candy climbed out of the bed and headed toward the bathroom. "Come, follow me."

Champagne stood up and followed behind Candy to the bathroom.

Candy took two rags off the rack and told Champagne, "Let me wash you."

No one had ever offered to do that to Champagne before, and it kind of turned her on. She undressed as Candy watched and stood in front of her naked.

By now Candy had wet the rag and was on her knees. She pushed Champagne's legs apart and placed the rag on her pussy; pressing down on it. She looked up at Champagne, who was looking down at her.

"Open your legs some more," Candy told her. Champagne did as she was instructed.

Candy then spread Champagne's lips apart and washed between her lips. She then pushed the skin back over her clitoris and wiped it gently. She replaced the rag with her tongue, sucking on it gently.

Champagne's knees buckled, and she grabbed Candy's head and pressed it against her pussy.

Candy pulled away. "I'm not done washing you yet." Candy then took the rag and wiped from Champagne's pussy to her ass. "I'm going to lick every inch of you."

When she was done wiping Champagne, Candy went to wipe herself.

"Let me do you," Champagne offered.

"No, this is about you," Candy told her. She then took Champagne's hand and led her to the bed.

"Lay down."

Champagne did just that. "Spread your legs wide." Champagne did that as well.

Candy placed her knees between Champagne's legs and kneeled over her. She kissed her on the mouth. "After tonight, we're going to go back to work and pretend like this never happened."

Champagne hoped she could do that. Even if she couldn't, at this moment she would have agreed to any and everything.

Knowing that this was going to be her last girl-on-girl encounter, she pulled Candy up to her and said, "I want to taste you while you're tasting me."

"No, this is all about you," Candy told her again.

"This is your boss talking. Do what I say."

Candy laughed. "Yes, ma'am. How do you want to do this?"

Champagne said, "Sixty-nine."

"Me on top and you on the bottom?"

"However you want to do it is fine with me."

The following morning they decided to not pretend that nothing happened.

Before Candy left to go to her room, Champagne told her, "I wasn't so drunk that I don't know what happened last night."

This pleased Candy. "Good."

"Thank you."

"Anytime."

"Really?"

Candy looked Champagne straight in the eye. "Really." When Candy left the room, Champagne knew she had to do what she'd been putting off, and that's call Zyair. She retrieved her cell phone out of her purse and dialed his cell number.

Zyair was laying in the bed when he heard his phone ring. He knew it was Champagne, but he felt too guilty about what had transpired between him and DaNeen to answer the phone.

Later than night when he arrived home, he called up Thomas and told him to stop by the following morning. He needed to hear Thomas out before Champagne arrived and before they spoke.

Whatever Thomas said was going to dictate how he approached this whole situation with Champagne.

A couple hours later when Thomas arrived, they were sitting in the den, and Thomas was explaining how he and Champagne ended up at the swingers club. "Man, I know I was wrong for not telling you, but I promised her. And I know you wouldn't want her going into a place like that by herself."

Zyair was having mixed emotions about the whole thing. On one hand he wanted to fuck Thomas up again, on the other; he respected what his boy had done for him.

Thomas went on to add, "I would never do anything to jeopardize our friendship, you must know that. But like I was telling you, I'm in love with Alexis. Why? I can't even explain it, but I kid you not, man. I really think she's the one. And when I met Khalil, and after talking to Champagne and hearing her doubts about him, I too got caught up in the moment."

By the time Thomas finished apologizing and trying to set the record straight, Zyair had made the decision to do a background check on Khalil. He just wanted to nip all this shit in the bud and move on. He also knew that in order to move on, he and Champagne were going to have to come to some sort of understanding about their relationship. Limbo wasn't working for him anymore.

He also knew he was going to have to talk to DaNeen. He didn't want to lead her on. He knew she had feelings for him, and he wasn't the type to play on someone's emotions.

He glanced at the clock. *Yep, that's what I'll do,* he thought to himself. I'll handle this whole situation with DaNeen, and then I'll speak with Champagne.

Chapter Thirty-one

"Smooth Operator"

Sade

DaNeen was sitting in Zyair's office, listening to him apologize for the night before.

"Why are you apologizing? You didn't do anything wrong."

"I'm not apologizing for the sex. I'm apologizing for the circumstances in which the sex occurred. DaNeen, I've known for quite some time that you've had feelings for me and I have to be honest with you. I've looked forward to coming to work and feeling your energy. It boosted my ego. I shouldn't have let the other night go as far as it did, but it happened, and we have to move on."

"What the hell do you mean, we have to move on? I thought we were going to take this to the next level. Your girl and your best friend deceived you."

"Yes, they may have but that's not a reason to start a new relationship."

DaNeen was real quiet, which made Zyair nervous. He didn't know if she was plotting something or accepting what he was saying to her.

She stood up. "You know what, Zyair, you're right. I wouldn't want you under these circumstances anyway. If there was going to be an us, I would need a whole you. I'm a big girl, and I took you any way I could have gotten you the other night and I too could have stopped it."

Zyair was impressed with the way DaNeen was handling the whole thing. "Under different circumstances, I know we could have been together."

DaNeen knew that the words coming out of his mouth were true because Zyair didn't speak nonsense and untruths. He was a stand-up kind of guy. She couldn't leave the room without telling him something she'd been keeping from him, especially if it meant there was a possibility of them getting together ever.

"Zyair, I need to tell you this. I saw Thomas and Champagne leaving the swingers club."

"What?"

"Let me finish. My brother is a bouncer there, and he told me that Champagne and Thomas were put out because they caused a disturbance. It appeared as if they were busting in and out of rooms."

Zyair just shook his head. "Thanks for telling me."

Then DaNeen added, "I'm giving you a verbal two weeks notice."

"I understand."

As DaNeen was leaving Zyair's office, she spotted Champagne "ear hustling."

Stopping in front of her, she told Champagne, "Don't fuck up. I'm watching you."

Champagne didn't respond. She'd caught an earlier flight home to make a new start. Before she left Zyair's office a wedding date would be set, and no one was going to impede her plan.

Although she'd overheard Zyair and DaNeen's entire conversation, she chose not to address it or make an issue of it. She'd created this situation, and she'd realized that in order for them to go forward, she had to leave the past in the past.

Champagne startled Zyair when she entered his office. His phone was in his hand.

He immediately hung up. "I was just going to call you. What are you doing home so soon?"

"I needed to see you. There's something I have to tell you."

"Is it about you and Thomas going to the swingers club?"

Champagne was all ready to plead her case when Zyair stopped her.

"I know what happened, and I know why. I know how crazy you are about your girl and that you would do anything to look after her, and that includes enlisting Thomas."

Champagne looked down at the floor, feeling guilty. "I manipulated Thomas. I used the fact that he's in love, or thinks he's in love, with Alexis to confirm my suspicions about Khalil."

"Why are you so against this Khalil fellow?"

"I don't know, Zyair. I wish I could explain it. Maybe, it's woman's intuition."

"Well, your intuition was right."

"Huh?"

"I did a background check."

"Huh?"

"Not only is he a porno star, but he's been arrested numerous times for operating a prostitution ring."

"What?"

"He's a pimp."

"I knew it! I knew he was sheisty. That muthafucka. We need to call her right now. Oh my God, we can't."

"Why not?"

"She's in Cancun with him. They won't be back until tomorrow."

"Well, I guess we'll have to wait until tomorrow."

Champagne sat down and told him, "Have a seat. Zyair, I apologize for all I've been putting you through. I hope it's not too late for us."

"It's never too late but you need to know we can't continue this way. Our relationship has been damaged, and I need to know that in our darkest hour we will fight, that you will fight for us."

"I will, Zyair. I will fight for us, and to prove it to you." Champagne reached inside her purse and pulled out a small box.

"What the hell is that?" Zyair asked, jumping up. "Sit down. You're ruining my moment."

"Uh-uh, you will not do this." Zyair went over to his desk, opened the top drawer, and pulled out a small box. "I'm the man. It's my duty to wax that booty."

They both laughed.

"Seriously though," Zyair said as he got down on one knee, "will you marry me?"

Champagne kissed him on the lips. "Yes, Zyair, I will."

Chapter Thirty-two

"End Of The Road"

Boys II Men

Champagne and Thomas were waiting at the airport for Alexis and Khalil to arrive. Zyair had already told them he wouldn't be far behind them, something he needed to check up on.

"I'm telling you," Thomas said to Champagne, "you should let me handle this."

Champagne nudged him. "Man, we ain't trying to go to jail."

Thomas poked his chest out. "I'll go to jail for my woman."

Champagne started laughing. "Calm your ass down. This is your opportunity to be there for her."

Thirty minutes later, Alexis and Khalil were walking down the vestibule. Both parties spotted each other at the same time.

Alexis hugged Champagne. "What are you doing here?"

"Don't I get a hug?" Thomas asked.

Alexis smiled and gave him a "church hug."

"It's like that?" Thomas put his hands on his chest, feigning heartache.

"You're lucky you got that," Khalil said.

It took everything in Thomas' power not to lash out.

Champagne pulled Alexis to the side. "I need to talk to you about something."

"Well, can't it wait?"

"No, it can't."

"Whatever you have to say, you can say it in front of Khalil."

Growing impatient, Thomas exploded, "Your man is a pimp! And we got proof."

Alexis looked at Thomas and then Champagne. "You think I don't know that? That's in his past. He's saved now."

Khalil had a smug look on his face. "We ain't got no secrets. I tell my baby everything." He grabbed Alexis' hand.

"But did you tell her this?" Zyair asked as he approached with a white woman and stood behind Khalil.

Khalil turned around, and when he saw the woman, he dropped Alexis' hand.

The woman said, "I thought you were on a business trip?"

Alexis asked Khalil, "Who is this?"

"I'm his wife and the mother of his two children."

"What is she talking about, Khalil?"

Khalil ignored the question.

"Are you going to answer me?"

Busted, Khalil said, "What is there to say?"

Right then Thomas punched him in the face and sent him staggering back.

Devastated, Alexis turned to walk away, and Thomas followed close behind.

Champagne looked at Zyair. "Should I go with them?"

Zyair said, "Thomas got it."

Chapter Thirty-three

People only do what you allow them to.

As Alexis Olivia walked through West North National Airport to her car, so many thoughts were running through her head. How could she not have known Khalil was married? When she really thought about it, the signs that he wasn't all he pretended to be were there. She should have seen them because they were what every television, every book, and every woman that's probably been burned say to look out for.

There were times when he didn't answer the phone or call her back until hours later with half-ass excuses about what he was doing. There was the smell of a lady's perfume in his car, which she ignored. There was him coming to her house all the time and her never going to his. All these signs and more she ignored because when they were together he made her feel like a queen. He made her feel like she was all that mattered. He made her feel safe and he made her feel desired in a way that no other man had.

"Alexis . . . Alexis, wait!" Thomas yelled.

Alexis kept walking; she didn't want to wait. She was embarrassed because she felt like she had been played yet again and one would think that after receiving a master's degree in Psychology and being a therapist at West Park High, she would know better. She thought about her college days and how she was in love with Brother. She thought he was the best thing since sliced bread. He was saved, studying to be a minister and even had her turning her back against her friends because they weren't Christian enough. Only to find out he was cheating on her with a woman from the church; a woman who counseled her and had Bible study with her. She thought about her high school sweetheart John and how he cheated, and now here she was in her early thirties and being made a fool of by another man. She'd already made up her mind that this would be the last time it happened and if there was anything she meant, anything she was going to keep her word on—this was it.

No one would ever use her again. No one would ever make her feel like she didn't matter.

Alexis would not give her soul, spirit, her love or body to another living being without getting something in return.

At this point and with the way she was feeling, the something she wanted would have to be material and substantial. If she became dubbed as a gold digger and as a user, she could care less. Alexis was going to be a woman on a mission.

If people considered her new plan as one that would make her a whore, she didn't care about that either. There was a time when that's all she cared about, her reputation and what people thought of her. Well, no more.

The only thing she cared about from this point on was getting what was hers and what she felt was owed by all the men out there that had wronged a sister, namely her. Alexis was not taking the bullshit anymore. She would accept nothing less than the best. She was going to start looking out for number one; herself.

It was time for her to become someone else. No more Miss Goody Two Shoes, as she was known from middle school, high school, and college. She tried her best to live according to the Bible. She tried her best not to stray, not to fornicate, although sometimes she fell short. She didn't swear, she rarely drank and she tried her best to submit when it came to her relationships. Well, change had come and it was time for her man, or should she say men, because she planned on having more than one, to do whatever it took to please her.

"Alexis, wait up," Thomas yelled.

Alexis turned to see him jogging toward her. All she wanted to do was get to her car. She turned back around and sped up. She wondered if everyone in the airport was looking her way. Did they know that she'd been bombarded by people she cared about? Her best friend, Champagne, Champagne's husband, Zyair, and his best friend who she knew had been lusting after her for years, Thomas Hughes. Did they know that they had destroyed her reality?

All she wanted to do was return from Cancun with her man and get on with their life together. They were supposed to be gone for four days and ended up extending their vacation to six days and seven nights because they were so into each other. When they arrived at the airport, the last thing she expected to see was Thomas and Champagne standing there.

Initially, Alexis was irritated that they were in the airport waiting on her like she was a child and aggravated when Champagne told her they needed to talk. She thought about the pleasure on Champagne's face when Thomas revealed that Khalil was a pimp. Why would her best friend take pleasure in hurting her?

Then Zyair appears out of nowhere with Khalil's wife. Initially she didn't believe him, but when Alexis looked at him and saw the look on Khalil's face, she knew it was true.

To keep from breaking down, Alexis walked away, leaving Khalil, who Thomas punched in the face; Khalil's so-called wife cursing him out; Champagne, who looked smug and Zyair who looked like he was wondering what he got himself into.

"Please Alexis, wait up," she heard Thomas say again.

Alexis decided that she would stop and see what he could possibly have to say to her. "What, Thomas? What do you want?" She knew she sounded like a bitch but you would sound like one too, if you'd just found out the man you just got engaged to already had a wife. Again, Alexis wondered how was it that she allowed Khalil to play her.

Thomas stopped a few inches from Alexis. He was standing so close to her that she could almost reach out and touch him. She could see that he wanted to by the way he was rubbing his hands together. But the look on her face must have said, keep your distance because he just stood there and said, "I just wanted to make sure you were okay."

Alexis started laughing and it wasn't a laugh where one found something funny. It was a laugh of a person who had been through it, a laugh of someone that was mentally drained and a laugh of someone who was almost to the point of not giving a damn anymore.

"Do I look okay to you, Thomas?"

Before he could respond, Alexis placed her palm on the side of his face, looked him straight in the eyes and caressed his cheek. "I know you're concerned about me, but I just need to be alone right now. Can you respect that?" She dropped her hand and started to walk away, but something stopped her. Perhaps it was the new person she'd decided to be. The more aggressive person. *Maybe I'll start the new me right now.*

"If you need—"

Before Thomas could finish what he wanted to say, Alexis turned back around and stepped to him. She placed her lips on his. She kept her eyes open so she could see what his response would be, which was to part his lips and let her do whatever she wanted to.

Alexis let her tongue slide into his mouth. She ran her tongue around his slowly, then pulled his tongue into her mouth and slowly sucked on it as though it were a flavor. She put her body a little closer to his and could feel Thomas' dick getting hard. She wanted with every fiber in her being for him to pull her close. She wondered what she was doing to him, what she was making him feel on the inside and not just on the outside physically. She moved her body even closer and pressed into him, to the point where they could have been one. She gave him a look that said, *don't hold back*. She could tell that he got the message because he grabbed her ass and pressed his dick into her and moved his hips slightly.

Alexis couldn't believe she was letting Thomas rub up against her in plain view of people. This was so out of character but she couldn't help herself. She was hoping Khalil was watching because she wanted him to be as hurt as she was. Maybe he'd even wonder if something was going on with Thomas the whole time they were together. That thought alone made Alexis wrap her arms around Thomas' neck. She continued to dip her tongue in and out his mouth. She kissed him with such passion she wasn't giving Thomas a chance to think about or comprehend what it meant, if anything.

This is not me Alexis said to herself. She knew she should pull away because here she was playing with this man's attraction to her.

"Wow," Thomas said when she stepped back.

Alexis looked down at his dick and could still see the imprint. He followed her eyes and told her, "I apologize. I just got carried away by the kiss."

Alexis shut him up and placed two fingers on his lips. "Don't apologize. I'm the one that initiated it."

Thomas started to say something else but Alexis shushed him. "I have to go. I need to be alone."

Thomas grabbed her hands and asked her not to leave.

Alexis finally looked around and noticed that people were looking their way. She didn't see

Khalil, but she did see Champagne and Zyair staring at them with a look of bewilderment.

"Am I supposed to stand here in the airport?" she asked him.

"How are you going to get home?"

"My car is in long-term parking."

Still holding onto her hand Thomas said, "Alexis, I'm really sorry it came out like this. It's just that—"

Alexis pulled her hand away and told him, "Don't say another word. I need time and space." And on that note, she turned and walked away. She knew he was watching her walk, so she not only added a sway to her hips, but she turned and told him, "Call me."

Standing not too far behind, watching the whole episode, was Champagne who felt a little guilty about what transpired. She knew she could have and should have addressed it in another way, but she couldn't help it.

Zyair looked at her. "What the hell was that about?"

Champagne knew he was talking about the kiss. She was wondering the same thing, so all she had to offer by way of explanation was a shrug of her shoulders and a "your guess is as good as mine but believe me, I will find out."

Zyair couldn't let it go at that. "I thought she couldn't stand Thomas." He'd heard Alexis say it numerous times. She had called Thomas every possible adjective that could describe a male whore.

"Well, maybe she changed her mind."

Zyair didn't say a word. He just watched Thomas watch Alexis and hoped some shit wasn't about to go down. His gut instinct told him it was and he wondered if there was anything he would be able to do about it. From the look on Thomas' face, he doubted it very seriously. He knew Khalil's type. He wasn't about to let this go without repercussions. They all would have to watch their backs.

That evening alone in her bedroom Alexis lay in her bed and stared at the walls. She looked at the paintings she'd collected that depicted black love. A painting of a man and woman embracing; a painting of the man carrying the woman in what looked like a garden; and her favorite, the one of man, woman, and child being embraced by a black Jesus. Normally when she glanced at them, she would feel warmth. This time she felt disgusted, with herself that is. Was she really that desperate to have love in her life that she hung paintings up in her bedroom? She knew she would be taking those down tomorrow. Her eyes then fell on the picture of Khalil that was on her dresser, in a frame no less. She got up out of the bed, walked over to the dresser, snatched the picture off it, walked into the adjoining bathroom, took the picture out of the frame, ripped it up and threw it in the small waste basket under the sink. She placed the frame on the sink, looked in the mirror and wondered why she couldn't bring herself to tears. *Maybe once I cry I'll feel better.*

She so desperately wanted to cry, to have some sort of release. She was confused in her emotions. A part of her wanted to call Khalil and ask him how he could do this to her, how could he declare his love and be married. *I should have known better, we were only together for a couple of months.* But Alexis wanted to believe in him. She wanted to believe that someone could fall for her so quickly, someone who appeared to have it all together, someone that said they wanted a monogamous relationship. *What a joke; all he wanted was my pussy.*

She walked back into her bedroom and opened her armoire. Inside were movies that she liked to watch over and over. Since the tears she wanted to fall never did, she pulled out one of her old-time favorite films, *She's Gotta Have It*. She put in the DVD, grabbed her remote, laid back on the bed, and pressed play.

After the movie was over, Alexis felt so empowered she declared out loud, "Fuck it, I'm going to be like Nola Darling. Men will be for my pleasure only and any type of relationship I have with them will be on my terms."

Later that night Alexis lay in her bed with her eyes closed. For a moment her thoughts kept drifting to Khalil and all the promises he made to her. What he would do for her and what they would mean to each other. She thought about the way he made her body feel so alive. She thought about the first time they met at the Laundromat. She thought it must be fate that her dryer stopped working that day. She recalled how when he walked in, she couldn't help, but notice how strong he looked. His muscular physique was evident in the T-shirt and jeans he wore. He was definitely her physical type.

That day Alexis did something that was out of character for her. She approached him and asked him was he from the area. He told her he was new in town and that his name was Khalil Simmons. It wasn't until they went out to dinner that she learned he was in construction. Well, that's what he told her but by then she was smitten. Heck, he even claimed to be a Christian. How could she not have known the truth? Alexis opened her eyes and tried to get him out of her head.

Think of something else, think of someone else, she told herself. Her thoughts started drifting to Thomas. *Imagine him making love to you . . . let your body take over your mind.*

Alexis, not one to really masturbate, decided to do just that.

She closed her eyes and imagined Thomas' tongue circling around her clitoris, stroking it, and dipping inside. From the thought alone she could feel a warmth travel up through her thighs. She squeezed them together and tried to suppress the pleasure but then decided to go with the feeling, to allow the emotions that were going to come. She had on a thin nightgown and placed both palms over each nipple as she ran her palms over her nipples in circles and started pinching them.

Damn, that feels good.

Alexis allowed her hands to go lower as she pushed her hips up off the bed and pulled her gown up over her waist. She stroked her pussy through her panties gently at first, but wanting to feel the pressure from her own hand she pressed harder using mostly the bottom of her palm.

Realizing the pleasure she could give herself, she pushed her panties to the side and ran the fingers of her right hand between her pussy lips. She didn't want to put them inside just yet. She was enjoying teasing herself more than she thought she would and she wanted to make this moment last. With her left hand she played with both nipples.

At this point, Alexis wasn't pretending or trying to imagine that it was Thomas or any other person trying to please her. She was pleasing herself and thinking, *Shit, this can become a habit. I don't need a man. All I need are my two hands.*

Masturbation wasn't something she participated in, but she'd heard women say all they needed were their fingers and she was about to find out how true it was.

She then took one of her fingers and dipped it into her pussy. She dipped it in and out, pumping her hips up and down, loving every moment of it. She'd keep her fingers deep inside her for a couple of seconds and move them in circles.

Alexis could feel her heart beating and her breath coming quicker and quicker. So she pulled her fingers out to catch her breath and start all over again. This time, she used both hands, one to move the skin from around her clitoris and the other to touch it. The first touch caused her to jump.

Relax, Alexis, relax.

She relaxed her body and tried it again. She thought about how Khalil would touch her there with his tongue, moving it in circles, so she copied the movement with her finger. She wondered if that's why she fell so hard so fast. Was it because of his oral skills? When he made love to her, she experienced her first real orgasm; the kind that made her body shake, quiver and jerk—the kind that made her call out. She couldn't believe that she'd missed out on that. Heck, she'd been having sex since her last year of high school. Just thinking about it made her feel a rush in her stomach and that caused her to move her hand away. She took another deep breath.

Just go with it.

She tried it again, but first she put her finger in her mouth to make it moist and put it back on her clitoris. Whenever she felt her clitoris becoming dry she'd put her finger back in her mouth, wet it and back on her clitoris. She was ready to cum. She was ready to feel the explosion that would take over her body and leave her exhausted.

Her heart was racing, her nipples were stinging, and she could feel an energy building up from her feet to her thighs, to her back and finally to her pussy.

Alexis surprised herself by screaming out loud as she arched her body and put two fingers inside her to feel the moistness that was dripping from deep inside. She felt her body relax and sink into the bed as she left her hand cupping her pussy. She closed her eyes and sighed. *Oh my God, I can't believe this. I can't believe I actually made myself cum. I'll never judge another person that say they masturbate. This may have been my first time doing so, but it won't be my last.*

Alexis felt the need to call someone up and tell them about this experience. The orgasm made her feel as though a weight had been lifted, even if it was temporary. Guilt? Did she feel any? Not at all. *Damn, does that mean I'm going against God?* She hoped not and if it did, she knew that He would forgive her.

When Alexis moved her hand the tears finally fell, and with the tears came feelings of hopelessness. She wondered if she would ever get it right with men. What was she doing that was wrong? Why couldn't a man stay faithful to her? Was she not good enough? Did she wear a sign on her forehead that read, I'M A FOOL, YOU CAN TAKE ADVANTAGE OF ME?

Alexis shook her head and tried to erase these thoughts. "I will not go there, I will not go there, I will not go there," she repeated over and over until she fell asleep.

Chapter Thirty-four

Change is challenging, yet necessary.

The second Alexis entered The Red Oak, which was the new hot spot in town; she saw that it was crowded. Normally she wasn't into crowds, but since this was the new her, she'd have to deal with it, accept it, and make the most out of it. As she excused her way through the crowd she took in the cream and gold decorum. The tables were set with what appeared to be satin material, candles, and a slim vase with one lily, which gave the appearance of an upscale club. The lighting was dim and the music was old-school R&B, which suited the twenty-five and over crowd just fine.

Alexis glanced around and was relieved when she spotted Champagne who already had two Martini glasses in front of her.

"What's up girl?" Alexis greeted as she bent over to give Champagne a kiss on the cheek.

"Nothing. I ordered us each a Watermelon Martini."

"Thanks girl," Alexis said as she sat down.

Champagne was glad to see Alexis and surprised to see her in a formfitting dress, when normally she dressed conservatively. They hadn't talked in over two weeks and after what took place at the airport, she had started wondering if it was because Alexis was through with her. She wondered if she had crossed the line.

Champagne tried calling Alexis numerous times and either Alexis didn't answer the phone or when she did she told her she was busy. Champagne knew that meant to back off. She was going to give Alexis one more week and then she was going to knock on her door and make her converse.

Not one to beat around the bush, Champagne asked as she sipped her Martini, "So, what was up with that kiss you gave Thomas at the airport?"

Of course she was concerned about her friend's well-being, but ever since the kiss, Champagne had wanted to ask her that question. She surely couldn't leave it on the answering machine. After all, she knew Alexis was going through it emotionally. Who could blame her? She was obviously hurt and needed time to process the damage done to her heart. The pain was noticeable because of her behavior and her not reaching out.

By not calling Champagne or really taking her calls it was understandable that Alexis was feeling dejected, despondent, and distant. Who wouldn't want to be left alone at a time like this? Being best friends and not communicating like they normally do left Champagne concerned about their friendship and Alexis' state of mind. But instead of hounding Alexis like she wanted to, she chose to let Alexis work through it.

Not that she had any choice because Alexis wasn't ready to open up and after hearing Alexis tell her when she was ready to discuss it with her, she would, Champagne decided, leave well enough alone. So, Champagne let it go and moved on. She made the decision to just be there the best way she could for Alexis, in spirit. The way she figured it, when Alexis was ready for her support, an ear or a shoulder, she would be just a phone call away.

So when Alexis finally called her, Champagne was pleased. She missed her friend and wanted to talk about what transpired and when Alexis suggested they meet for drinks, Champagne was surprised. She asked Alexis was she sure she wanted to meet for drinks or should they meet for dinner.

"What? A sister can't go out for a drink?" Alexis asked her.

It wasn't that a sister couldn't go out for a drink. It's just that Alexis wasn't one to drink unless it was a special occasion.

So Champagne told her yes and they agreed to meet at The Red Oak.

Seeing Alexis sit across from her, Champagne realized just how much she missed her and how worried she was. She wanted to find out what the hell was going on with her friend and she wanted to catch her up on her and Zyair. They had finally set an "almost" date for the wedding.

"So," Champagne asked, "what's up with you not returning a sister's phone call, cutting me short when you did and making me stress out? I was worried about your ass and again what was up with that kiss you gave Thomas?"

Alexis didn't answer right away. She continued to sip on her drink and glance around the room. After surveying their surroundings, she told Champagne, "Girl, I don't know what came over me. I think I temporarily lost my mind."

Champagne didn't get it. "So, you tongue someone down because you're losing your mind?"

Alexis didn't like her tone. "Are you judging me? Is that what I'm hearing?"

"No, no. I'm not judging you. You know that's not my style. Shit, we all have our stuff with us." Champagne still hadn't told Alexis about her bisexuality. Yep, that's what she had labeled herself and the reason she hadn't told her was because like Alexis, she didn't want to be judged.

"I'm just surprised that's all," Champagne told her.

Alexis didn't respond right away because her attention was elsewhere.

"Oh, girl, look at all the men up in here," Alexis said, "especially that one over there."

Champagne looked around and was not impressed with the abundance of men. Just like Alexis she wasn't a club attendee because being in her thirties she felt like she was too old. She felt that people went to clubs to pick up potential bed mates and that was not something she was interested in. After all, she had the pick of the litter when it came to men.

Champagne turned around to see what or who had Alexis' attention and noticed him right away. Even she had to admit, the man Alexis was staring at was a looker. He was well over six feet and cocoa complexioned; with the most immaculate goatee Champagne had ever seen. You could tell beneath what appeared to be a shirt made for his physique that he went to the gym on the regular and when he laughed, which he was doing wholeheartedly, his dimples showed across the room.

Now a man that fine has to have a whole bunch of issues with him. There has to be some kind of drama in his life.

"He's definitely fine," Champagne remarked.

The next thing Champagne knew was Alexis had placed her glass on the table and stood up.

"Where are you going?"

"I'm going to introduce myself. Where do you think I'm going?"

Champagne sat stunned as she watched Alexis head toward Mr. Handsome.

I can't believe she's doing this. It's so unlike her to be so aggressive. Champagne watched as Alexis approached him and tapped him on his shoulder. Then again, maybe she shouldn't have been surprised because Alexis told her that when she first met Khalil, she went up to him.

Oh my God, she's actually interrupting his conversation. Alexis is really showing her ass tonight. Please do not let this man disrespect her. I really don't feel like dealing with any bullshit tonight. Please do not let him disrespect her.

Champagne continued to watch to see how it would all play out. She saw him turn around and watched as they exchanged a few words. She noticed Alexis laughing.

Okay, good, he must like her.

A few seconds later, Alexis came walking back in Champagne's direction.

Before Alexis even had a chance to sit down, Champagne said, "Girl, I can't believe you did that."

"Did what?" Alexis asked with a sly look on her face. "All I did was introduce myself."

"Yeah, that's what I'm talking about. When did you become so bold?"

Alexis laughed. "Girl, this is a new me. I've made the decision not to allow men to lead me. It's time for me to be the leader, to take the first step, it's time for . . ."

Alexis stopped midsentence and was looking over Champagne's shoulder. The frown on her face made Champagne turn around. Alexis was staring at Khalil, who was dressed in a casual but tailored suit that looked expensive, even from a distance. Champagne looked around to see if his wife was in the vicinity. She didn't spot her. He was actually standing by himself with a drink in his hand perusing the area. Although Champagne could see why Alexis was attracted to him, she still couldn't stand him. It was obvious he hadn't noticed them yet, because if he had, she was sure he'd come over and Champagne did not want that to happen.

"It's time to go," Champagne said. The look on Alexis' face told a tale of a woman scorned and she didn't want a scene.

Alexis shook her head, breaking her trance. "We don't have to leave. I came out to have a good time and a good time I will have."

"Are you sure?"

"As sure as ever. I refuse to let him ruin my night. Plus, we're about to have company." Alexis nodded her head to the right.

Champagne turned again to see who she was talking about. Heading toward their table, making their way through the crowd was Mr. Handsome and a friend.

Alexis couldn't help but to sneak another glance Khalil's way. She wanted to confront him, but knew she wouldn't. So, it was a relief that company was heading their way, although unpleasant and unexpected.

"I invited them to sit with us," Alexis told Champagne.

This invitation threw Champagne for a loop. "You know you're wrong for this. You should have asked me first. I thought this was our night out together." She couldn't care less if they heard her or not.

What Champagne wanted to do was walk away but she wouldn't do that to her girl. One, she wouldn't want it done to her and two, with the way Alexis was acting, she didn't think it would be a good idea.

"Hey ladies," Alexis' new friend greeted.

Champagne looked at him and his friend, who was just as handsome. She did have to admit to herself that if she were on the market, he definitely would have been her physical type.

"I'm Shamel and this is my boy, True." He was looking at Champagne when he said it.

Alexis moved closer to Shamel staking her claim.

"What's up, sexy?" True asked Champagne as he swallowed her with his eyes.

Champagne decided to play nice, make conversation but not lead him on. She was here with Alexis and she might as well make the most of it. There was no sense in adding to the myth that black women are bitches.

"Come on," Shamel said, "let's go upstairs to the VIP room."

Shamel led the way, followed by Alexis, Champagne and then True. Champagne could feel True staring at her ass the whole way up. She thanked God that she wore pants. She hoped that this man did not become disrespectful because she would have no problem putting him in his place. However, her intuition, sixth sense or her third eye as she sometimes called it, was telling her, she was going to have to let him know that this was not that kind of party.

When they reached the top of the steps, the bouncer gave Shamel daps and let them right in.

When they walked in Champagne glanced around. She appreciated the color scheme which was purple and gold; royalty colors.

Shamel led them to a table and pulled out a chair for Alexis as True pulled out a chair for Champagne.

Once everyone was seated, Shamel asked, "So what are you ladies doing after you leave here tonight?"

"What are you doing?" Alexis asked, with a seductive undertone.

What the hell? Champagne looked at Alexis, who purposely would not look her way. Champagne knew Alexis could feel her staring at her. The old Alexis would never have behaved this way, walking up to a strange man, inviting him over to their table, and basically throwing herself at him.

"Maybe you ladies would like to join us?" True suggested, getting straight to the point.

"I have to get home to my man," Champagne said, hoping to squash any ideas he may have had about them getting together. "I do have a man, you know."

Alexis gave Champagne a "why you gotta blow up the spot" look.

She looked like she wanted to go off on her but instead she told Champagne, "Damn, girl, loosen up. We're just trying to kick it."

"That's right sexy," True said. "You've got a man and I've got a woman. What's the big deal?"

Before anyone could say another word, Champagne heard a familiar voice asking, "So? What do we have here?"

It was Thomas and not too far behind him staring in their direction was Khalil. She hoped they had not spotted one another.

Chapter Thirty-five

Think about what you really want before you go making demands.

When Thomas entered the VIP room, it seemed like the first person he spotted was Champagne. She was with two men and if his eyes weren't deceiving him, there was Alexis, who was wearing a dress that hugged every curve on her body even with her sitting down. She appeared to be laughing and touching on the man that sat next to her.

"What the fuck?" Thomas swore. This was the last thing he needed to see especially after learning that Louis Johnson, one of Rutgers University's top basketball players had decided to sign with another sports agent. He'd been trying to win him over for months with dinners and the promise of more money than he could spend, only to have his rival James Giovanni sign him.

"What? What's wrong?" the young lady he came upstairs with asked.

Playing it off he said, "What the hell is my boy's lady doing sitting with those knuckleheads?"

Although his initial reaction was because of Alexis touching a man that was not him, he was also curious why Champagne was out and sitting with these two men.

Where the hell was Zyair? Was he in Atlanta? Did he know that while he was in Atlanta checking on his restaurant that Champagne was out with another man? This shit was not cool and Thomas was going to let them all know it. He was definitely going to inform them of his presence.

Thomas looked at Alexis and wondered if this was why she hadn't returned any of his phone calls? Was it because she'd found someone to replace Khalil so soon. What happened to her heartache over Khalil? Not that he wanted her to be heartbroken over what another man did or how another man treated her. He didn't want that at all. What he did want, he had to admit even to himself is to be her knight in shining armor, the one who came to her rescue.

"I'll be right back," he told the young lady he was with.

"Where are you going?" she asked.

He looked in Champagne and Alexis' direction. "Over there."

Of course the young lady he was with didn't like it one bit but she really didn't have much of a choice.

"For what?"

"They're good friends of mine and I want to make sure everything is okay."

She looked in Champagne and Alexis' direction and told Thomas, "They look fine to me."

Not wanting to disrespect her because Thomas was trying to change his ways, he told her, "Well, looks can be deceiving. I'll be right back."

"Why don't I go with you?" She was persistent. Thomas had to give her that.

"Listen . . ." he couldn't say her name because he couldn't think of it and he hoped she didn't catch it, but she did.

"My name is Luscious," she told him with her hands on her hips, pissed that he would even forget.

"Listen Luscious, why don't you wait for me by the bar and I'll be right back. Get whatever you want."

Luscious was pissed. She placed her hands on her hips again and told him, "Well, don't think I'm going to wait too long."

Thomas, who wasn't in the mood for attitude, especially after seeing who he hoped would one day be his future wife up in another man's face, told her, "Do what you have to, we're not a couple," and walked away.

He thought about the day after the airport incident when he told Zyair that he was going to end up marrying Alexis. He had laughed and asked him didn't he think he was jumping to conclusions. He told him he was being prophetic.

The second Thomas was up on the table, he asked, "So, what do we have here?"

When Champagne heard his voice, she jumped out of her seat so fast that it appeared as if she'd either been busted or was waiting on him to come over.

"Thomas, hey." She hugged him and whispered in his ear, "I am not having a good time. Alexis has lost all her mind. Get me out of here."

Not knowing if it was because she was caught in the company of another man or if these, what he assumed to be knuckleheads were bothering her, he told her, "Your man just called me," loud enough for all to hear.

On that note Alexis stood up, "Excuse me, fellas." She looked at Champagne and asked, "Do you mind if I steal Thomas for a second?"

Champagne moved to the side as Alexis grabbed Thomas' arm and pulled him a short distance away.

"What are you doing?" Alexis asked him with much attitude and with her hands on her hips and neck snapping.

Thomas started laughing.

"What the hell is so funny?"

"You," Thomas told her.

"What's so funny about me?"

Thomas, who was a bit amused, asked her, "What's up with the street attitude? You know damn well that's not you."

"What do you mean it's not me? You don't know me." Alexis knew she was just acting out.

"I know enough about you to know that you're not street and that you're a lady. I also know enough to know that you might have had one too many drinks."

Alexis rolled her eyes.

Thomas started laughing again.

This time Alexis stomped her right foot. "Why are you still laughing?"

Thomas didn't bother responding. He looked over toward Champagne who looked bored by whatever the two men were talking about. "I think your girl is ready to leave."

"No, she's not." Alexis looked at Champagne and saw her unease. "We're having a good time."

"Maybe you are but she's not and I think you should let her leave. As a matter of fact I think you both should leave."

Alexis looked at Thomas like, *how dare you.*

"And I think you should leave with me."

Alexis looked in Thomas' face, only to see that he was dead serious. "First you come and interrupt my good time and now you're trying to steal me away."

"Exactly." Thomas wasn't beating around the bush. "Come home with me."

"For what? Sex? I'm not fucking you."

Thomas was surprised that Alexis used the word fucking. He had never heard her use profanity before and it must have shown on his face.

"That's right, I'm not fucking you."

Before Thomas could respond, Luscious was up on them. "So, who's your friend?"

Thomas turned around and said, "I thought I asked you to wait by the bar."

"You did and I told you I wasn't going to wait forever." She was eyeing Alexis the whole time.

Alexis stepped back and told Thomas, "I see you have your hands full. I'll leave you two alone."

When she turned to walk back toward Shamel, Thomas took her arm and told her, "No, you stay right here."

"Oh," Luscious said, "you're just going to disrespect me like that."

Thomas let go of Alexis and told her, "You know what. We didn't come here together, so there's really no need to act like we did. You're up here in VIP where you wanted to be, so go do your thing."

"You know you are so right. I just used you to get in here anyway. There are other men that have it going on in more ways than you."

Thomas didn't bother responding. He wasn't with that ghetto shit.

Luscious looked around and recognized several ball players and celebrities. The same ones Champagne noticed when she walked into VIP and the few new ones that had arrived. She faced Thomas, "Shit, there are better looking men in here than you, with more money anyway," and walked off.

Alexis was still standing there when Thomas faced her.

"So that's your type?"

"No, you're my type," he told her as he wondered how he was going to get her to spend the rest of the evening with him.

Chapter Thirty-six

Watch your back and your front; you never know who's eyeing you.

Off to the side, Khalil was watching everything and he could feel his pressure rising. What he wanted to do was go and knock Thomas the fuck out for ruining what he had with Alexis. He knew that he handled the situation at the airport wrong. He was thrown off guard. He would have never thought that Alexis' crew would dig into his past and pull out his wife. Yes, he was married, but he was also in the process of leaving her. He regretted not telling Alexis, but he knew that she had morals and beliefs and one of those was married men were off limits. He knew this because she told him that during one of their conversations. He wasn't playing with her mind. He'd fallen in love with her, with her innocence, with her vulnerability, and with her sense of right and wrong. It was something he missed in women. It was something he missed in his wife. He wanted an opportunity to speak with Alexis to explain his side. To apologize.

Khalil looked over at their table and every fiber in his being wanted to knock Thomas the fuck out. However, he knew that wouldn't do anything but soothe his ego and piss Alexis off. Now was not the time, it would have to wait. He also knew from the first time he met Thomas over Champagne and Zyair's house that this Thomas character was feeling Alexis. It was all in the way he looked at Alexis and sneered at him.

Khalil needed to come up with something that would destroy Thomas but he knew that would take some time and time was all he had.

Khalil had spotted Alexis and Champagne the second they walked through the door. He chose not to approach them just yet because he wasn't sure what he wanted to say. He watched them as they headed upstairs to the VIP section and made the decision to follow them. His boy who was working the entryway let him in.

His first thought when he looked at Alexis was, *She is looking fine as hell.* His second was, *Why the hell did she have on that tight-ass outfit?* He knew Alexis, hell he loved Alexis and when they were together tight clothes was not her style. He wondered if she was looking for trouble and his third thought was, *Would she want me back if she knew I was physically separated from my wife?*

Yes, he never told her he was married. He would have eventually changed that, all he needed was time and because of Thomas, his time had run out.

He watched Alexis approach Shamel. He watched Shamel and his friend take them up to VIP and he followed them. He stayed just a few people behind.

The plan was to approach Alexis the second he had a chance. Like all women did, he knew that eventually she would have to go to the ladies room and that's when he would make his move. The thing of it was, it appeared like it was never going to happen. Right when he'd just about made up his mind to just walk over there, who approached her but Thomas?

I'm a man just like he's a man. I'm stepping up. Khalil made the decision to approach the both of them, Alexis and Thomas. Whatever the hell went down was just going to go down.

"No, you're my type." Khalil heard Thomas say.

"Alexis," Khalil said.

Alexis looked past Thomas, who turned around with swiftness.

"Oh, hell no! You need to step the fuck back!" Thomas said as Khalil stepped up. He was two seconds away from punching him in the face once again but Alexis placed her hand on his arm.

Khalil ignored Thomas and looked directly at Alexis. "Can I talk to you?"

Alexis was in shock. Her heart was pounding and she felt like she was about to start hyperventilating. *This cannot be happening . . . This cannot be happening.*

At the exact same time, Champagne just happened to look in their direction. When she saw what was taking place she stood and headed over in their direction to protect her girl.

Shamel and True also stood. Shamel was wondering what was going on and if he should intercept.

"Please, I just want to apologize. I want to explain."

Thomas, who was two seconds off Khalil's ass told him, "I'm going to say it one more time—step . . . the . . . fuck . . . back."

By this time Shamel, True, and Champagne were up on them. "Is everything okay, Alexis?" Shamel asked.

Alexis placed her hand on Thomas' shoulder. "It's okay."

Thomas didn't think it was okay and he didn't want to let it go.

"Is there a problem?" Shamel asked Thomas.

"I don't know. Is there?" Thomas had not taken his eyes off Khalil.

"All right y'all, this shit is getting out of hand. Khalil, you need to leave," Champagne said.

"Please, will everyone let me speak?" Alexis asked.

No one said a word, they just looked at her.

"Khalil, there is absolutely nothing you can say to me to justify what you did or how you hurt me, so please just leave, please."

The tone in her voice sounded wounded and Khalil could hear it.

"Please," she begged. "Please just go, I don't want any trouble."

Khalil took a step toward her but Shamel and Thomas took a step toward him.

Khalil looked at Shamel, "Who the hell are you supposed to be?"

"A friend," Shamel answered.

Thomas looked at Shamel as well. "Man, I got this."

Shamel didn't move. He stood his ground. "I'll step off when Alexis tells me to step off."

"Khalil, please just go," Alexis said.

Khalil looked at them and knew to leave well enough alone for now. He didn't say a word; he just turned around and walked away. It would be the one and only time he'd ever done that or planned on doing it.

Alexis then turned to Shamel, "Shamel, it was a pleasure meeting you—"

Shamel cut her off, "Are you dismissing me? I thought we were going to get to know one another."

"I'm not dismissing you or telling you I don't want to get to know you. I'm just letting you know that this night is over for me and I'll call you."

"Damn, man. She ain't worth it," True said.

"Man, shut up," Shamel told him and looked over at Thomas, who looked familiar. Shamel had never had this happen to him before. He'd never been dismissed and he contemplated making a scene but what would be the point. It was evident Alexis didn't like drama. He'd just look like an ass. Plus, he and Alexis had just met. So he told her, "You make sure you do that," and walked away with True behind him talking shit.

"Come on girl, let's go." Champagne took Alexis' hand and tried to pull her along.

"No. I'm going to stay here and talk to Thomas."

"Huh?" Thomas and Champagne said at the same time.

Alexis looked at Thomas, "We'll be back."

Alexis started walking away with Champagne following behind her. They were headed toward the ladies' room.

"What's up?" Champagne asked the second they walked through the door.

Alexis looked at Champagne, she opened her mouth to speak, but the next thing she knew, she was crying.

Champagne knew there was no reason to ask why she was crying, it was obviously because of all the drama that just took place. The only thing she could think of to do was pull her friend close to her and tell her, "Let it all out, it's all right, that's what I'm here for."

A short while later Alexis pulled away. "I'm sorry, it's just that seeing Khalil made me realize there was never any closure and maybe I should talk to him. Maybe I need to find out why he wasn't honest with me."

"What! Are you crazy? You need to leave well enough alone, you need to just let his ass go and move on."

"It's not that easy Champagne. I was in love with him."

"I understand all that, but what I don't understand is why you're staying here with Thomas."

"Maybe it's to spite Khalil. Maybe it's because Thomas obviously cares for me and I feel like I owe him an explanation for the kiss. Maybe it's because you've been ready to leave for quite some time and I'm not."

Champagne didn't say a word. She realized there was nothing she could say. This was Alexis' moment and she was going to let her have it; even if it meant biting her tongue.

"I'll be all right. I'm with Thomas. I'm sure he won't let anything happen to me."

Champagne gave Alexis a tight hug. "I'm sure he won't. Just be careful. I love you and I know you lost someone you cared about because of our actions and I apologize. I'm sorry if I'm being insensitive. It's just that I want what's best for you. That's why I did what I did; searched his background and shit. Please forgive me."

Alexis hugged her back, but she couldn't forgive her just yet. She still felt it could have been handled better. "I love you too, sweetie."

They stepped away from one another. Champagne wanted to know, "So, are you ready to leave?"

Alexis laughed. "I told you, I'm going to stay here and hang out with Thomas for a little while."

"Are you sure?"

"Yes, I'm sure. I never got a chance to thank him for trying to be there for me." Alexis couldn't help but notice the worried look on Champagne's face. "I'll be all right. I'm a big girl."

"Well, I just want you and him to know that if he does anything stupid, I will kick his ass."

Alexis laughed. "I'm sure you will."

Chapter Thirty-seven

Sometimes you want what you think you can't have, but the reality is you probably could if you just asked nicely.

As Champagne was leaving the bar, she felt her phone vibrating. *Who the hell? I'll look at it when I get to my car.*

Champagne waited in front of the club for the valet to bring her car around. She decided to check and see if maybe it was Zyair. She opened her purse, pulled out her phone and noticed that there was a text message. It was from Candy, her old employee and lover.

Hey, beautiful. I was just wondering how you were. I'm going to be in town next week and would love to get together. Let me know what's up.

Champagne was about to text her back but decided to wait and think about if she really wanted to do that because it'd been over a month since she last saw Candy and that was in a motel room and it wasn't just for a visit. Champagne thought back to that moment. A few weeks prior to their last sexual encounter, Candy informed Champagne that she was giving her a few weeks' notice. This surprised Champagne because she thought they had a good working relationship. She hired Candy when she first started the Agency. She was thinking of training her to be a publicist when she gave her notice.

"What? You don't like working here anymore? You have a new job?" Champagne asked her.

"Oh, no, it's nothing like that. It's just that I'm going to support a friend. He has AIDS and well, he needs me."

What could Champagne possibly say about that? If it were her she'd probably be doing the same thing.

"Are you sure you don't just want to take a leave of absence? I can hire a temp and hold your position for you."

"I don't want to tell you yes, because I don't know how long I'll be away or even how I'm going to feel after this is over with."

Champagne could hear Candy getting choked up. She reached out and tenderly took Candy's hands in hers. "You do know if there is anything and I mean anything you need, I'm there for you."

"All I want is you," Candy told her, "but I know that's not possible because of your man."

"This is true," Champagne pointed out.

"And I know that what happened on our business trip to DC was supposed to be a onetime thing. But I would love to make love to you again Champagne as a way of saying good-bye."

Pretending that she didn't hear what Candy said, Champagne looked toward the filing cabinet and started moving in that direction.

"If you can get someone in here right away, it would give me the opportunity to train them," Candy told her knowing Champagne wasn't going to respond to what she just said.

Business was business and Champagne had hers to run so she got on it. She appreciated the fact that Candy gave her so much notice in the first place.

Champagne went through the resumes that flowed in consistently from experienced people to students who wanted to intern. She was seriously considering going the intern route because it would save her money.

Within a week's time she and Candy interviewed over fifteen people. It was exhausting but they finally hired Shana.

Candy did an excellent job on training her before leaving.

Candy's last week of employment had finally arrived. Champagne asked her if she wanted to spend Friday together, since she wasn't leaving until Sunday.

"Friday after work?" Candy asked.

"I've decided to close the office Friday. I don't have any appointments and since you're leaving, I was thinking we could spend the day together, go to a spa and have lunch."

Champagne knew Candy wasn't a spa type girl but since she was leaving soon and because Champagne was paying for it, she figured Candy would be more than happy to go and experience something new. They both needed a day of relaxation and pampering. If Champagne had to, she would force Candy to sit or lie back and enjoy the occasion.

How they ended up at a hotel afterward Champagne couldn't figure out but they did. Perhaps it was the being pampered, getting massages, manicures, pedicures, and then going out for lunch and having drinks afterward that did it. They were so relaxed and had enjoyed each other's company so much that Candy brought up the subject of their tryst.

"How come we don't talk about what happened on the business trip?"

"What are we supposed to say about it?" It wasn't a topic Champagne felt needed to be discussed.

"Did you enjoy it?" Candy wasn't letting it go.

"Of course."

"Would you do it again?" Candy boldly asked.

"With you?"

"Who else would I be asking about?"

Champagne looked at Candy and felt her pussy get moist. She closed her legs tight and tried to change the subject. "So what are you going to do while you're in DC other than be with your friend?"

Candy knew what she was doing. "Don't change the topic. Don't you want to feel my tongue on your pussy and in your pussy?"

Champagne wondered if those drinks Candy had were getting to her or if she was just saying how she felt. "Come on Candy, don't do this to me."

"Do what? Tell you how good you tasted to me? Tell you I would love to be with you one more time before I leave?"

"That's exactly want I'm asking you not to do to me."

"Let me make love to you again Champagne. Let me remind you how good I can make you feel. I'm leaving town after this and it could be my thank you and my good-bye."

Champagne did not recall saying yes but less than an hour later they were walking through the doors of Paradise, an upscale hotel. Champagne was lying on the bed with Candy lying on top of her looking into her eyes. She knew she should

*have felt guilty about being there, but she didn't
and she wondered what that meant.*

"Tell me what you want me to do" Candy stated.

*"Whatever you want to do to me," Champagne
told her.*

"You want my tongue deep inside your pussy?"

"Yes."

"You want my tongue inside your ass?"

"Yes."

"Tell me what else you want."

*"I want your fingers inside me. I want my liq-
uids to go down your throat."*

*Candy moaned from deep within her throat
and put her mouth on top of Champagne's and
pushed her lips apart with her tongue. She ran
her tongue inside her mouth and Champagne
kissed her back.*

*Champagne tried to wrap her arms around
Candy, but Candy knocked her hands down and
held them to her sides.*

*She looked her in the eyes again and told her,
"Keep your hands to your sides. I'm in charge."*

*What was there for Champagne to say other
than okay?*

*Candy unbuttoned Champagne's shirt and
caressed her breasts through her bra. She pulled
Champagne's bra straps down and pulled the bra
beneath her breasts and licked her nipples from
one to the other and then bit down on them gently.*

"Let me take my clothes off."

Candy ignored her and moved down below her belly with feathery, light kisses. When she got to Champagne's pants, she unbuttoned, unzipped, and pulled them down just past her hips.

Again, Champagne said, "Let me take off my clothes."

Again, Candy ignored her. She pulled Champagne's pants down to her thighs and placed her mouth on top of her panties over her pussy.

Champagne tried to push her body up so she could see, but Candy pushed her back down. "Relax sweetie, let me do this the way I want to."

Champagne listened and laid back.

Candy pushed the panties to the side and started licking and sucking on Champagne's pussy lips.

"You're not wasting any time?" Champagne asked not expecting an answer.

Candy continued to lick and suck, tasting the juices that were beginning to flow. She placed her hands on Champagne's thighs and pushed them open a little more and stuck her tongue as far up in Champagne as she could and then gently pulled her clitoris from its hidden spot with her teeth.

Champagne moaned and bit down on her lip to keep from screaming. Candy's lips then encircled her clitoris, drawing on it deeper and deeper, pulling, tugging, and sucking gently.

The next thing she knew, Champagne's body heaved into the air from the orgasm that was flowing like a river. She opened her legs wider and held Candy's head in place. She didn't let her up for air, until she felt that Candy had sucked and licked every bit of juice she could.

A few hours later when they departed from one another, Champagne felt like Candy was in her system. It was a relief to know that she was leaving town. Champagne was afraid of what she would do. She was afraid that she would not be able to keep the promise she made to herself and to Zyair about leaving the whole bisexual thing alone.

Coming back to reality and present time, Champagne shook her head and looked at her cell phone again. To receive a text from Candy threw her for a loop. *I'm going to have to think about whether I want to see her or not. I don't want to be tempted.* Champagne knew she would. Lately, sex with a woman had been on her mind. And yes, she was trying to push it back, push it deep down into the crevices of her mind, but it wasn't working. She needed something to distract her.

What I need to do is go home and sex the hell out of my man and call Candy back tomorrow.

Chapter Thirty-eight

Sometimes you have to take a risk to know what your chances are.

This was Alexis' first time coming to Thomas' house and when she walked through the door, she had to admit that she was surprised that he had such good taste.

Champagne had told Alexis on numerous occasions that she had to see Thomas' house. What she failed to mention was that Thomas didn't just live in any kind of house. He lived on an estate.

"You live here by yourself?" Alexis asked.

This was a question Thomas was used to being asked by women whenever he invited one up to his place. By the look on some of their faces, he could tell they were making plans to try and snatch him up and move in. That was something he was not going to let happen.

Thomas was a "hit it and quit it" kind of man but that was growing old. He found himself wanting to settle down and maybe even start a family. All this playing the field, not knowing who wanted him for himself or his money was not the way he wanted to continue to live.

The thing of it was, as a child he never thought he would be the one living this way, financially successful and never having to worry about money again. His background and his upbringing until he became a teenager would have never predicted this outcome. If it wasn't for Ms. Dominique or Ms. D as he liked to call her, he didn't know where he would be.

He still thought about that day she changed his life. The day she offered him a chance of a lifetime. The day he was put on the right track.

Thomas was laying in his room with his eyes closed and his arm thrown over his forehead, when his social worker walked in. It was one of the few times he had the room he shared with two others to himself and he was enjoying the peace of it.

"Thomas, I may have some good news for you."

Thomas sat up and threw his legs over the edge of the bed. "What type of good news?" He'd already come to believe at his young age that good news was hard to come by.

"I believe I have a family for you."

For a second there Thomas thought he'd misheard her. "Huh?"

"I think I have a family for you."

He did hear her right. Thomas stood up and looked her in the eyes. "I thought you said this was it for me. That I was going to be here at this group home until I could do independent living. Why would somebody want me now anyway? I'm almost a man, unless they're just in it for the money."

Ms. Dominique sighed. "Listen Thomas, I know what I told you but things have changed. This family isn't in it just for the money. They're in it to make a difference in someone's life. They're in it to change a life."

"Yeah right, I've heard that before." And he had. He'd heard that and so much more. He'd heard that all he's good for is the money, that he'll never amount to a damn thing, that he was worthless and was even told don't get too comfortable.

So to hear that someone wanted to make a difference, it didn't faze him one bit. "That's what they all say initially, until I walk through the door and you leave."

"All I can tell you right now is that this family is different, but if you don't want to give it one last try that's fine with me. I'll find someone else for them. Someone that would love this opportunity."

When Thomas heard those words, he had to admit to himself that he didn't want her to give this chance to another kid. What if this time, this one time, the people were being honest? He wanted it, but he was scared. He was scared of it not working out and scared of being let down. If he got his hopes up and those hopes were destroyed once again, it would devastate him. But the look on Ms. D's face reassured him that wouldn't happen.

"Listen, I know you're scared," she told him.

"What! Ain't nobody scared."

"It's okay to be scared Thomas. I can't say I blame you, but I think you should give it one more try."

"Do they know how old I am? Are they prepared for a teenager? Did they specifically ask for a teenager?"

"Yes, they do, yes, they are and yes, they did."

"Did they say why they wanted an older kid?" He hoped they weren't going to try and slave him. Have him keeping house and working the death out of him.

"This couple has another son your age. They work with at-risk kids and they're looking to give a teen a chance for a normal life, a chance to experience a family."

"Why me?" Thomas wanted to know. "You have other clients you could have picked for this family Ms. D. Why me?"

At this point, Ms. D was getting exasperated and Thomas could see it on her face and feel it in her energy.

"Listen," she told him, "If you don't want this, you need to let me know by tomorrow. That way, if I have to I can pick someone else."

The truth was she didn't want to pick anyone else. There was something about Thomas that stood out from the other kids. He was smart. He had manners and although he had been abandoned, he didn't allow his heart and soul to harden like some of the other kids had. There was still hope.

"But I have to say this to you," Ms. D went on, "I would be very disappointed if you didn't take this opportunity. Because that's what it is Thomas, an opportunity for growth. I also think you would be a good match for this family. You have the potential to be so much more than you think."

The thing of it was, Thomas did want another chance. He did want to be with a family. Just like any other human being on the face of this earth, all he wanted to do was be loved. "I don't have to think about it, Ms. D. I'll do it. I'll go."

Five days later he was on his way to what might be his new foster parents' home. He was scheduled to stay the weekend and if they vibed, he would move in. On the way there, he was quiet, in his own world, deep in thought. He was trying to get past the nervousness he was feeling.

As they turned into the subdivision, Thomas was immediately impressed. The houses were larger than any he'd ever seen. The lawns were man-icured and kids were actually playing in their

yards. He noticed quite a few white kids and real-
ized he'd never asked if the family was white or
black. Well, it was too late now because they were
pulling into a cul-de-sac and as they pulled up into
a driveway Thomas was relieved to see a black
teenage boy sitting on the porch with headphones
on. He appeared to be writing in a notebook.

"We're here," Ms. D told him as they pulled into
the driveway.

That day changed Thomas' life. He walked in
the door with an attitude of *"I'm going to make the*
best of this situation and I will make this work."
And make it work he did. Along with the Turners'
assistance, encouragement and participation, they
got along great. Not only did he excel in school,
he ended up getting a scholarship for college
and money for college from the system. After he
graduated from college, he tried to reach out to Ms.
D. He knew how proud she would be of him, but
she'd left the agency and there was no forwarding
address. Thomas sometimes thought of her and
wondered how she was doing. Then again, maybe
it was best to leave the past just where it was and
that's behind him.

The way Thomas figured it, had it not been
for the Turners, had they not been there for him,
pushing him and telling him he could do it, he

would not be the responsible, grown-ass man he is now and that's why once he began making money, he'd send them some sporadically. If he tried to do it any other way, they wouldn't accept.

So to go from having no place to really call home, to being able to purchase the home of his dreams was an accomplishment. To go from a place of poverty to a place of prosperity was an even bigger accomplishment, that of owning his own sports agency in which he was extremely successful.

Thomas looked at Alexis who was walking around taking in the art on his walls. She noticed that most of the paintings were by an artist named Antonio Pierre Hunter.

"So you're a collector?" She asked.

Thomas stood next to her and looked at the painting she was standing in front of. "I wouldn't say all that. I just like what I like."

Alexis turned to face Thomas, "You're a sports agent right?" She already knew the answer to that. She'd heard Champagne and Zyair talk about Thomas' famous clients numerous times.

"Yes, and you're a counselor or a therapist, right?"

"Yeah, yeah, yeah." Alexis tried to blow off the rest of his inquiry. The last thing she wanted to discuss was the fact that she counseled some bad-ass, fast-ass teens. Teens, that when she tried to guide them and show them a better way gave her their asses to kiss. "Instead of discussing what we do for a living, why don't you show me your bedroom?"

"Huh?" That wasn't what Thomas expected to hear.

"Show me your bedroom. I want to see where the magic happens," Alexis joked.

Thomas was thrown off by her bluntness. This was definitely not the Alexis he knew. But he was a man and like any other man he was more than ready and willing to take the hint, if that's what she was throwing.

"Are you sure?"

Alexis smirked at Thomas' obvious discomfort. "Yes, I'm sure."

Thomas led the way upstairs. As they passed several rooms Alexis peeked inside and was surprised at how orderly everything was.

"Do you have a maid?" Alexis asked as they stepped in his bedroom.

"What, a brother can't be neat without any help?" Thomas joked.

"Not when they're as busy as you probably are."

"Actually, I do have someone that comes in twice a week, but I do cook my own meals."

When they entered his bedroom, Alexis was impressed. For some reason she imagined his room to be extremely masculine, everything in it being black, dark, glass or brass. She thought he'd have a big-ass television and a stereo system in it but there was neither. Instead the bedroom had a calming effect. The color on the wall was a soft pale blue and the bedroom set reminded her of the ocean. The carpet on the floor looked plush enough to sink her feet into. To her surprise, on the nightstand next to the bed were several books. The top of his dresser was covered in colognes and there was a little lounge area in the corner.

"You don't watch television or listen to music in your bedroom?"

"No, I use it to relax, sleep, and for extra-curricular activities."

Alexis laughed. She could imagine what those activities were.

She looked at his oversized bed and walked over to it. She stood in front of it and turned toward Thomas who stood behind her watching every move she made.

"You think your bed is big enough?"

"I sleep wild," he told her.

Alexis sat on the bed and asked, "Do you do everything wild?"

Thomas hoped he wasn't mistaken or was being misled. He could hear the flirtatious tone in her voice. He'd wanted this moment to happen for so long. After all, Alexis was his dream girl and he'd fantasized about making love to her many times. After taking a long look at her, he took her hands and kissed them. He looked into her eyes and asked, "Are you drunk?" If she was he would not go through with this. He wanted her to be clearheaded and mindful of all he was going to do to her. Thomas didn't want any regrets.

"I'm as sober as you are," she reassured him. Although the two drinks she had were making her feel a little tipsy.

"I just wanted to make sure before I kissed you," Thomas told her.

Alexis didn't want to waste any more time. She placed her hands on each side of his face, pulled him down on top of her and lay back on the bed.

"Are you sure about this?" he asked.

Alexis was more than sure, she decided that this was going to be the night for Thomas to finally get his wish. In all her past relationships, the men had dictated the when, what, and the how. No more, she was going to do this on her terms.

Plus, she was tired of waiting for Thomas to make his move. For some reason he was acting like a Mr. Goodie Two Shoes, all gentleman like. He wasn't being his usual aggressive self.

Alexis looked up at him, "Let's take a shower together."

Thomas was not expecting this at all. "Okay," was all that he could utter.

"Well, you need to get up," Alexis told him.

He stood up and told her, "After you."

Alexis got off the bed and started taking her clothes off, leaving behind a trail of clothing.

Thomas, after the shock wore off, looked to the heavens and stated, "Thank you, Jesus," and darted into the bathroom after Alexis.

Once in the bathroom, he followed Alexis' lead and took his clothes off while eyeing her body. He noticed that her body was flawless, almost creamy like a light coffee.

She turned the shower on. "Let's give it a few minutes to warm up."

Alexis could tell that Thomas liked what he saw. She immediately seized control by pulling Thomas close to her by his dick and started passionately kissing him.

Thomas' mind was blown. He never in a million years imagined that Alexis got down like this.

"Let's get in the shower," Alexis said.

After the kiss Alexis instructed Thomas to bathe her. She did this purposely so that he could enjoy every inch of her without fully experiencing her. Thomas quickly did as she requested and Alexis returned the favor.

Alexis turned the shower off and Thomas followed her out and into the bedroom. Alexis lay on the bed and opened her legs wide and gently ran her fingers up and down her pussy. She told Thomas to stay where he was and just watch. She continued to play with her pussy for a little while longer then asked Thomas to come over to the bed.

Like an obedient puppy he complied. He was rewarded by Alexis sitting up and covering the head of his penis with her warm mouth.

"Damn, damn, damn," was all Thomas could manage to say. Alexis was licking and sucking the head. She was teasing the hell out of him and she knew it. She wanted her to put the whole thing in her mouth, but instead she told him to lie on the bed and open his legs as wide as he could.

Thomas quickly assumed the position and Alexis went straight for the sides of his balls. All Thomas could do was squirm and moan.

Alexis continued to lick and suck Thomas' balls with expert precision. She then decided to try something she heard about on a cable sex show. The hostess said if you suck the area beneath the balls, and right before his asshole that he will turn straight bitch.

She did it on Thomas and found that statement to be true. The second Alexis' mouth touched that area Thomas' body lost all control.

Alexis looked up and said, "You better not cum yet."

Thomas did not hear a word she was saying. He was in a place that only a few men experienced and he was loving every minute of it.

Alexis decided to run her finger gently over his asshole. When she did this Thomas jumped and arched his body up. He looked at Alexis and said, "Who are you?"

Alexis laughed and told him, "The girl of your dreams. Now lie back down."

"I will," Thomas told her, "but I felt that finger on my asshole, and I just want to let you know that there ain't no gay shit going on around here. I'm a secure brotha."

Thomas wondered if Alexis made love like this to everyone. He hoped not, but if so he wanted to be the last. *Shit, I wish this had happened a long time ago.* Normally when a female gave it up so fast he wouldn't think twice about them but this situation was different. He knew Alexis was a different kind of woman. He knew she'd only had a few lovers. He knew this through Champagne because whenever he'd talk about he and Alexis getting together, Champagne would knock his fantasy down by telling him Alexis wasn't that experienced and was picky with the men she chose.

Well, tonight she chose him and he felt privileged.

Alexis started to masterfully work the head of his penis with her tongue. She slowly worked her way down to his balls, then onto his ass.

Thomas was wide open. He barely heard Alexis ask him to put his dick inside of her. She repeated herself as she climbed onto the bed and Thomas was more than happy to oblige her.

The best feeling in the world to Thomas was the moment the head of his dick first entered Alexis. He tried to delay the inevitable.

"What are you doing? What are you waiting for? Give it to me Thomas," Alexis demanded.

Thomas began to pound inside her.

"Yes, yes!" Alexis screamed out.

Thomas was trying to be cool with it and make it last. But when he felt Alexis' pussy flexing, he didn't know how much longer he would be able to hold on. It's wasn't too much longer because before he knew it, he was yelling, "I'm about to cum."

"Not inside me," Alexis told him, realizing they didn't use a condom.

He pulled out of her and moved his hand to jerk the cum out. Instead, Alexis pushed his hand away and firmly grabbed his dick, jerked, and pulled out every ounce of cum.

Thomas was done, amazed, and in love.

Alexis looked at Thomas. "Now I need you to eat my pussy. Do you think you can handle that? And I know you have condoms right, because we are not done."

All Thomas could do was look up at the ceiling again and mouth, "Thank you, Jesus."

Chapter Thirty-nine

Don't worry about others when you have a full plate.

The day after the drama at The Red Oak, Zyair hung up the phone and turned over to see if Champagne was still asleep. She was but this was something he couldn't hold in, so he nudged her. Champagne didn't budge. He nudged her again and this time harder.

"What?" Champagne whined.

"You won't believe this." Zyair was like a kid with a secret.

"Zyair, come on now, you know I'm trying to sleep late. I'm tired."

"That's what you get for trying to hang out all night."

"I was with Alexis."

"And?"

Champagne turned over and tried to read the expression on his face. "Did you wake me up because you're upset with me for hanging out?"

Zyair didn't mean for her to interpret his words that way. He wasn't upset about that at all. Hell, he

was supposed to be out of town, although it was
a surprise to come home and not find his woman
there.

Champagne really wasn't one to go out and not
call him and let him know she wouldn't be home.
This time she did just that and it pissed him off
just a little bit. It was called a matter of respect and
respect was something they tried to have for each
other in every way.

He did have to admit to himself that for a brief
second, when he realized she wasn't home and
hadn't left a message he panicked. *What if she's
with another woman—that Sharon chick? Hadn't
they let that moment go?* Thankfully, before he
could get any further into those thoughts the door
opened and in walked Champagne.

He didn't like her tone, so he looked at her and
wondered if she was still tired and horny. When
she arrived home last night, she was ready to make
wild passionate love but Zyair told her he was
exhausted.

*She gave him the look as though she didn't
believe him. After all, when is a man too exhausted
to accept the pussy? Of course, she tried to entice
him by taking a shower and coming out with just
a pair of lace panties on but he just couldn't get his
energy up.*

"Zyair, come on, I want to make love."

"I'm tired baby. I was at meetings all day and I don't think I'd be able to perform."

"Well, why don't we try to find out?" She wasn't giving up that easily.

Zyair really didn't want to turn her down but not being able to perform sexually was one of his biggest fears.

"How about I just eat your pussy?" he asked her.

She surprised him by saying, "I would love that and I promise not to hold back. I'll cum as fast as you make me."

Zyair was relieved. As much as he might have wanted to do more, he knew his dick and it just wasn't going to happen. Zyair knew this happened to other men because his boys discussed it from time to time. It came with age and activity.

After Champagne came, they both feel asleep.

Early the next morning when Zyair hung up the phone, he had news to share so he woke her up.

"I have to tell you something," Zyair told her.

"Whatever it is, it'd better be good, because you're interrupting my beauty sleep."

"Snappy, aren't we?" Zyair said. He didn't know what her problem was. Shit, she got what she wanted last night, an orgasm, even with his ass being dead tired.

"I think Alexis stayed the night with Thomas."

He had Champagne's full attention on that note. She sat right up. "What makes you say that?"

"Because I just called his house and I could have sworn I heard her in the background."

Champagne lay back down.

Zyair nudged her again, "Don't you have anything to say?"

"That voice you heard could have been anybody's."

"Call her," Zyair said.

Champagne looked at Zyair and wanted to ask him why he was so concerned with whose voice he heard in the background. She already knew the answer. It wasn't concern. It was nosiness and she had to admit she was right there with him.

"All right, pass me the phone."

Zyair grabbed the cordless phone and watched as Champagne sat up and dialed Alexis' number.

Champagne placed her hand over the receiver and told Zyair, "It went straight to voice mail."

Zyair raised his eyebrow and said, "That's because they're fucking."

Champagne rolled her eyes and left a message for Alexis to call her. She looked over at Zyair who was smiling from ear to ear.

"What are you cheesing about?"

"He finally got that ass," Zyair said with pride. He felt good for his boy, after years of talking about her, he finally sealed the deal.

"Zyair, don't disrespect my girl like that."

Laughing, Zyair told Champagne, "I'm not trying to disrespect her. I'm just saying—"

"What are you saying?"

"That my boy finally got that ass."

Champagne rolled her eyes, turned over and tried to go back to sleep but it wasn't working because now all she could do was wonder if the voice Zyair heard was Alexis'.

Chapter Forty

Never say never because you just might be right.

Two days later Alexis looked at the phone and wanted to call Thomas but hesitated. *What if he thinks I'm sweating him? What if he doesn't want to talk? What if in his mind, he finally got what he's wanted from me for so long, that now he wants nothing else to do with me?*

Even as Alexis had these thoughts, she knew it couldn't be anything further from the truth. She knew that Thomas was crazy about her and had been for quite some time. Let Champagne tell it, he wanted her the second they met. That was over five years ago when he moved back to town and opened his office. What he felt was obvious in the way he made love to her.

The first time she was in charge. The second time, he explored her body with his hands and his tongue for her satisfaction and her satisfaction only. The third time was for his satisfaction. He took her with a gentle roughness. Afterward, every cell in her body was tingling and every muscle was sore. It was just what she needed.

I'll call him later, she decided. Alexis glanced at the clock and knew that what she needed to be doing was getting ready for work. Today was going to be a long day. Being a therapist at West Park was sometimes tiring. She could tell today was going to be one of those days.

Alexis stood looking in the closet trying to decide what to wear. Normally she took her clothes out the night before but laziness had set in. She already knew in the back of her mind that she was going to wear one of her pants suits. It was just a matter of deciding which color. She chose the cream colored one she ordered from the Victoria's Secret catalog, with a brown camisole and some brown open-toed Nine West heels.

In the past Alexis' style was more conservative but because she was changing as a woman she would also change her style. Her appearance had never been an issue for her. She knew men found her attractive, but like most women there was always something she'd like to change. She was short in stature, five feet three, but she wore three-inch heels most of the time. She was small in frame and wore a size five or seven. It depended on the quality and designer of the clothes. If she could change anything, she'd probably give herself bigger breasts and slice about an inch off her thighs. But those were things she could live with or without.

After laying her clothes on the bed, she glanced at the phone one more time. *I can wait to call him,* she reminded herself and went into the bathroom to take her shower. As she turned the shower on, she thought about her lovemaking session with Thomas and how just for that moment, she didn't think once about Khalil. Even if she wanted to, she couldn't have because what Thomas did to her body made her stay right there in the moment. Perhaps that would be what she has to do. Stay in the moment to forget about him.

Fifteen minutes later as she was drying off, she heard her phone ring. She wrapped the towel around her waist and ran in the bedroom. She snatched up the phone.

"Hello?"

"Hey, sexy." It was Thomas.

Alexis almost breathed a sigh of relief. She had to admit that she was pleased to hear his voice and double pleased that he called her first.

"Good morning," she responded.

"I'm sorry I'm just now calling. I've been caught up with some legal things for one of my clients."

"That's okay," she told him, although it really wasn't.

"No, it's not. I don't want you to think I just used you."

Alexis didn't respond. She didn't know what to say.

"Are you on your way out the door?"

"I'm just getting dressed. I have to meet with some of my students' parents today."

"Would you like to have dinner tonight?"

The word yes almost came out her mouth but she stopped it. She didn't want to appear too anxious. "How about I call you later and let you know."

"You make sure you do that," he told her.

After a brief pause, each of them looking for words to say, Alexis ended the phone call. "I don't mean to rush off the phone but . . ."

"I know. You have to go."

When they hung up Alexis felt a little lighter. Why is that? She did not want to get worked up over a man. She promised herself that she wouldn't set herself up for heartbreak. That will not happen. So his answer to dinner would be no, at least not tonight, maybe another night. She was not ready to rush into things. Yes, they'd made wild passionate love but that did not make them a couple.

Although she planned on doing her thing and playing the field, Alexis didn't want to play games or mess with someone's emotions. That wasn't her style, but her concern right now was herself and her heart. Any man she came across that expressed curiosity about her, that interest would be reciprocated. But she was also going to let them know up front what kind of party it was. So if that meant putting Thomas off for a little while because he thought this was the beginning of them, so be it.

By the time Alexis arrived at West Park High School, she was running late. Lateness was a quality in others she disliked but somehow time got away from her. Maybe it was because of the phone call, but then again, maybe it was because of her thoughts, which somehow slowed her down. Whatever it was, she knew she had to get it together and fast.

She also felt a little nervous because it seemed like a car was following her. Every turn she took, they took. Maybe they were just heading in the same direction she tried to tell herself, but still her gut told her otherwise.

She went into her office and shut the door. She turned on the light and proceeded to pull out the files of her students.

Alexis sat down and looked through the files. She placed them in the order in which the parents were scheduled to appear. That was if more than half of them showed up. Sometimes she asked herself why didn't she choose a school in Newburg, the area in Jersey she lived in. It was nice and peaceful there and most of the families came from money, or the parents either cared or pretended to care. Instead, she chose to work in West Park, where some of the kids and most of the parents simply didn't give a damn. In her heart of hearts she knew why, it was because she wanted to make a difference.

There was a knock on her office door.

"Come in."

Ms. Maya McMillan stuck her head in. "Can I speak with you for a minute?"

Ms. McMillan was one of the few teachers she socialized with outside of school. Alexis preferred to keep her relationships at work in the workplace only.

Alexis closed the file she had open and asked Maya, "What's up?"

"I have someone I want you to meet," Maya told her.

"Huh?"

"I have someone I want you to meet," Maya told her again.

"Are you talking about as in a hook up?" Alexis didn't know how open she was to having a casual associate set her up.

"Yes."

Alexis had to ask, even though she knew this was not a situation she was open to at all. "Who?"

"My half brother."

Alexis wondered why Maya would consider her when it came to setting her brother up with someone. They didn't know one another that well.

Yes, they had lunch together a couple of times but best friends, she and Maya were not.

"Why me?"

"Why you what?"

"Don't you have any other friends you could play matchmaker with?"

She did but Maya's brother, Gavin, was over to her house a couple of days ago and he was looking through the yearbook.

"Are there any fine teachers teaching at your school?" he jokingly asked when he came across Alexis' picture.

"Who is that?" he wanted to know.

Standing over his shoulder and noticing who he was looking at, Maya told him, "That's Alexis. She's one of the counselors."

"I'd like to meet her."

"I don't know about that. She and I aren't really that tight."

Gavin laughed. "What's that got to do with me? I don't care if you're best friends or not. I think this may be my future wife."

Now that was something that made Maya laugh. "You know you're bugging right."

"I might be but just ask her. See if she'd be willing to meet me."

"I'm going to have to think about it," Maya told him and think about it she did.

She thought about her observations of Alexis and had to admit there was nothing that stood out that indicated she wouldn't be decent enough for Gavin. Not that he was the best thing since sliced bread, but he was her younger brother and he had a lot going for himself, a nice car, his own home, and his own business.

Maya knew that Alexis was recently in a relationship that didn't work out. She also knew that last she heard, Alexis was a church going, God-fearing woman. Was that something she should warn her brother about? After all, he was an ex-hustler. Or did it even matter since that was no longer his profession and since Alexis wasn't one to go around preaching the Word to people.

Heck, the more Maya thought about it, this matchmaking between Gavin and Alexis might just be a good thing. She just hoped Alexis didn't ask how old he was. Therefore, when Alexis asked Maya didn't she have any other female friends she could hook her brother up with Maya told her, "I do, but he wants to meet you."

"How does he even know who I am?"

Maya told her the yearbook story.

And just to think, I hated that picture. That wasn't anything new. Alexis disliked most pictures she took.

"Tell me a little bit about him," Alexis requested.

"Well, he's an entrepreneur. He owns several car detailing shops, property, and—"

That meant he had money. Alexis wasn't slow in what Maya was conveying so she cut her off. "Does he have any children?" She was more concerned about that.

"Yes." That wasn't something Maya could cover up. Plus, she loved her nephew. "And he takes good care of my nephew when he has him. He's a hands-on father."

Alexis wasn't keen on dating a man with children. But she also knew to find a man in his thirties that was childless, well, that would be short of a miracle. Thomas was one of the few exceptions.

"How old?"

"Six."

That wasn't so bad, Alexis thought.

"Okay, that's fine. Just let me know and I'll have him stop by here one day, that way there's no pressure."

After Maya left Alexis' office, Alexis prepared herself for her first parent conference. Why she set up her conferences on a Monday, she didn't know. All she did know is that this was not a good way to start a week off.

The first conference was for a student named Rena Pugh.

She looked at her appointment book and saw that Rena Pugh's mother was scheduled to come in. She mentally prepared to speak with Rena's mother. So far, every time she came in she had to be escorted out by security. This was not going to be an easy Monday.

Later that day Alexis was sitting in the teachers' lounge sipping on a cup of tea when Maya walked in.

"You look stressed."

"Girl, these parents are a trip."

"You ain't telling me something I don't already know."

"I mean, don't get me wrong, there are some that genuinely care and are concerned but sometimes it seems like they are few and far in between."

Maya didn't respond as she poured herself a cup of tea.

"You know, I've been thinking . . ." Alexis decided that it wouldn't do any harm meeting Maya's brother, maybe for lunch or after work for coffee or something. However they met, it would be some place casual. "I'm open to meeting your brother."

"Cool," Maya responded. "I don't normally do this . . . Hook people up because if it doesn't work out, I don't want to be the blame."

"I can understand that."

"Instead of me inviting him to the school, why don't you come by my house Saturday? My book club is getting together and I'll tell him to stop by."

Alexis' plan was for something more casual but hey, a book club was something new. There was a time she was thinking about joining one. At least this way, she'd get to see what it was all about.

"Can I bring a friend?" Alexis asked. She was thinking about Champagne.

"A female friend?"

"Of course."

"That's fine with me." Maya turned to walk out but stopped in her tracks. "In case you want to pick up the book we're reading, it's called *Sister Girls 2* by Angel M. Hunter.

"I just might do that," Alexis told her.

When Alexis returned to her office, she called Thomas like she said she would. She wanted to let him know that they would have to do dinner another night. She was glad to catch his voice mail because she really didn't feel like making up an excuse. She then called Champagne and left her a message to meet her at "their new spot" for an early cocktail. This was a new thing for her, having a cocktail after work. She didn't think it was out of hand because she only had one or two.

Throughout the day, Champagne had left numerous messages on her cell and office phone and she sounded anxious to speak with her. Before meeting up, Alexis wanted to hit the gym and run a few errands. She wasn't looking forward to it, but the sooner she got them done the better.

Looking at her cell phone, Alexis noticed a text from Champagne as well. *I wonder what that's about?*

Chapter Forty-one

Some things are best kept to yourself; just figure out which ones.

Champagne and Alexis were seated at a table in The Red Oak sipping on Martinis once again.

"So," Champagne started, "what's up with you not returning a sister's phone call, making me stress out? I was worried about your ass."

Alexis didn't answer right away, she continued to sip on her drink and glance around the room.

"What's up? You keep looking around? Are you looking for anyone in particular?"

Alexis turned to focus on Champagne. "I'm sorry. It's just that while I was running my errands today, I just had this weird ass vibe. Like someone was following me. And, it's not the first time."

"For real? Who?"

"That's just it. I don't know." Alexis shook her head. "You know what, maybe I'm bugging. Maybe I'm just on edge."

"Girl, you need to go with your instinct. If you think someone is stalking you—"

Alexis threw up her hands, "Whoa . . . I didn't say all that." The thought of a stalker was scary to her. She did not want to put that in the universe.

"Well, that's what someone following you means."

"You know what," Alexis requested, "let's change the topic."

"All right, how about giving me the dirt." Champagne was ready to find out if it was Alexis' voice Zyair heard.

"The dirt on what?"

"You know, you and Thomas."

"There's nothing to tell."

Champagne could tell that Alexis was holding back. They'd known each other long enough to be able to read tone, mannerisms, and inflections. Honestly, it kind of pissed her off that Alexis wasn't sharing.

Normally, they told one another everything, but ever since the incident with Khalil, it seemed like their friendship was changing. Alexis still hadn't said anything about the apology she made to her. Champagne wondered if that meant she didn't forgive her. That she was holding onto the hurt. They weren't communicating as much as they used to and she really needed to talk out this whole bisexuality issue. She would have preferred to do it with her best friend, but if that couldn't happen, she'd talk to Sharon.

Champagne and Alexis being distant with one another had happened before. This time it felt different. They were definitely going to have to talk it out.

Champagne knew they were grown women and that life often took over but she still felt somewhat abandoned. Especially since she thought that the whole fiasco with Khalil was going to leave Alexis in need of her best friend. Well, it was obvious she guessed wrong.

"There's really nothing to tell. We hung out, I stayed the night, and we're friends."

Champagne caught the "I stayed the night" part immediately. "Excuse me? Did you just say you stayed the night?"

Alexis kept a straight face, not wanting to give anything away. "Yes."

"Stayed the night as in slept over? Slept in the same bed and didn't leave until the morning?" Champagne couldn't believe what she was hearing. Alexis having a one night stand, those words didn't even sound right in a sentence. She wondered if her mouth was wide open from the shock.

"Yes."

"So, did y'all do the do?"

Alexis started laughing. "Listen to you." She mocked Champagne. "Did y'all do the do?"

"Well, did you?"

Alexis smirked and if Champagne wasn't mistaken, it even looked like she blushed when she replied, "That we did."

"Get out of here. You did not. I don't know what to say." Champagne was at a complete loss of words. She just knew Zyair was wrong when he said it was Alexis' voice.

Alexis motioned for the waiter to come back over. "There is nothing to say."

"How was it?" Champagne asked. On several occasions Champagne would overhear Thomas brag on his sexual skills and Champagne had to admit she wondered if it was just words or if he could back it up.

Alexis leaned across the table. "Girl, it was so good. I couldn't believe it myself."

"Get out of here."

"I'm telling you, Thomas put it down and quite well."

"Details girl, you know I want details."

Alexis' gaze looked like she was taking herself back to the moment and she was.

She was thinking about the way he turned her over and ran his hands over her ass. She thought about the way she spread her legs wider and waited for him to enter her. What he did instead took her by surprise.

He licked her down her back slowly all the way down to the crack of her ass and to her pussy, opening it from behind and entering her with his tongue. She moved her hips back and forth and wondered if she was smothering him.

She thought about how he stood up and put the head of his dick on her pussy and ran it on the inside of her lips and finally just when she thought she couldn't take it anymore, slammed inside of her so hard that she yelled.

"Do you want me to stop?" he asked her.

All Alexis could do was shake her head. She didn't want him to stop. She wanted more.

He pulled out slowly and slammed inside her once again.

She looked between her legs and could see his balls. She reached for them and started massaging while he grinded inside of her.

"Deeper," she told him. "Deeper."

Deep inside her, he pressed harder and pulled out slow and slammed back in. She wondered if he could feel her body trembling.

"Cum Thomas, I want you to cum." At this point, she wondered if it was even possible, he'd already had an orgasm.

She looked behind her and saw that he had closed his eyes and was starting to slide in and out of her real slow.

"That's right baby, concentrate, focus."

Before she knew it, his body got stiff and he pushed deep inside of her and exploded into the condom.

"Come on, girl, details." Champagne could tell by the look on Alexis' face that whatever took place was beyond words.

"Girl, he was gentle and rough at the same time. It's like he wanted me to remember every touch and every inch of him." She shook her head, "and his coochie eating skills were out of this world. I came so hard, I thought I was going to have a heart attack."

Champagne laughed and asked, "So what does this mean?"

"What does what mean?"

"Is this the beginning of something serious for you and him?"

"Girl, please no. I'm just having fun right now. As a matter of fact, remember Shamel?"

"The guy we met at the club?"

"Yes, the one and only. We're having a late dinner together Friday night."

Champagne didn't know what to say. She just wasn't used to Alexis acting this way. She also didn't know if she should say anything at all because Alexis was grown and she could do what she wanted to do.

"Really?" Champagne asked, not really sure what else to say.

"Yes, really." Alexis looked Champagne in the eyes and could tell she was holding something back. "Why are you looking like that?"

"Like what?" Champagne didn't think she was looking any kind of way. Yes, she was holding her tongue, but she didn't think that was being relayed on her face.

"Tight."

"I apologize, girl. It's just that I'm surprised that's all. I just want you to be careful. I mean you don't know this man at all."

"The only way I can get to know him is to go out with him."

"I know, I know."

"What else is on your mind?" Alexis asked.

Might as well come out with it, Champagne thought. "Our friendship."

"What about our friendship?"

"I feel like its changing. I feel like you haven't forgiven me for interfering in your love life."

Champagne watched as Alexis took a deep breath before speaking. She watched as Alexis reached her hand across the table and placed it on top of hers.

"It's not that I haven't forgiven you. It's just that I don't understand why Khalil's betrayal had to come out the way it did, at the airport around a ton of people. I don't understand why you would want to humiliate me that way."

"I'm so sorry about that Alexis. I wasn't thinking. I just knew that I didn't want you to be made a fool out of and I would do anything to keep that from happening. I do wish I would have handled it different and if I could go back and do it again, I would. I just hope that this doesn't put a strain on our friendship. You mean so much to me."

"You mean a lot to me as well and it won't affect our friendship. You're still my sister in spirit. I just needed time."

They both stood up and hugged one another and told each other, "I love you."

When they sat down, Alexis looked at her watch and said, "You know I can't stay too long. I've got to go shopping for my date Friday night."

Alexis brought her attention back to Champagne, "Enough about me, let's talk about you and the wedding we need to start planning."

Now, that was a topic Champagne had been procrastinating on for quite some time. Yes, she wanted to marry Zyair and yes, she knew they had set a tentative date six months away but something was holding her back.

"What's up with the look?" Alexis asked.

"What look?"

"The tight-faced look," Alexis observed.

Champagne hadn't realized she was tight faced as Alexis so eloquently put it, but she told her, "Girl, I'm scared."

"Of what?" Suddenly, it hit Alexis, "Are you scared to get married? You and Zyair have been together forever and I thought this is what you wanted. Shit at one time, you were stressed the hell out because you didn't think it was ever going to happen."

"I know, right?" Champagne shook her head. "I don't know what's up with me and this fear I have all of a sudden."

"Don't tell me you're having second thoughts."

Was this the time to tell Alexis what went down with her and Sharon? Was this the time to tell Alexis that she believed she was bisexual?

Champagne wanted to tell someone and who better than Alexis? She was keeping a secret from her best friend and wanted to share it. She needed to talk about the mixture of emotions. Her only fear was what Alexis would think. She recalled that at one time Alexis thought homosexuality was a sin, but that was when she was an avid churchgoer. She also knew that although she thought this, Alexis had become more tolerant since learning that a couple of the teachers in her school were gay and even a few church members.

"I have something to tell you and I'm nervous about telling you. I'm afraid of your reaction."

"What could you possibly have to tell me that would make you nervous?"

Champagne opened her mouth to say the words and closed it. She wasn't sure whether to blurt it out or build up to it.

"Girl, now you're making me nervous, just say whatever the hell it is you have to say."

Champagne took a deep breath. "Remember when Zyair and I went to Hedonism, the all nude resort in Jamaica a few months ago?"

"Yes."

"And prior to me leaving, we joked about me and Zyair hooking up with other people?"

Alexis hoped Champagne wasn't going where she thought she was going with this. "What? You got with another man and now you want to leave Zyair?"

"That's not it."

"Then what is it?"

"I slept with a woman in Hedonism and I've been with someone since I've been home and I think I'm bisexual."

Alexis almost choked on her drink. "What the . . . What the hell are you talking about?"

"I've slept with a couple of women."

"I heard that part, I'm talking about the bisexual part. You need to explain that part to me!"

"What's there to explain? I'm attracted to women and men."

Alexis didn't know how she was supposed to react. This was not something she expected to hear. Hell, Champagne was her best friend and she would have thought that if Champagne had been feeling this way, she would have told her a long time ago.

Curious to know, Alexis asked, "How did this all happen? Are you sure you haven't just been experimenting?"

"Girl, you know I'm in my thirties. I'm too old to experiment."

"What about Zyair? Does he know about the women?"

"Yes."

Alexis' eyes opened wide, "He does?"

"He does."

"Wow." Alexis looked at Champagne stunned. "I don't know what to say. I don't even know if I should ask you any questions."

Champagne didn't say a word. She figured Alexis needed a second or two to adjust to what she just told her.

"Is this something new? How long have you been feeling this way?"

"I don't know girl. I'm wondering if it was always in me." Champagne paused. She was about to bring up something and she had no idea how Alexis would react. "Remember when we were younger and we used to mess around with each other?"

It was a memory Alexis tried to forget as she got older. So she said nothing, she just listened.

"Well, maybe I was bisexual back then."

Alexis had to laugh at that one. "All kids experiment, it doesn't mean anything."

"How do you know?" Champagne asked.

"You don't see me interested in women, do you?"

Champagne laughed also. "I guess not."

"Is that why you haven't started planning the wedding?" Alexis asked.

"I don't know." Champagne was ready to get married but she also wanted to do her thing, see where this whole being with women could go. She didn't feel like she was done with it and she didn't want to go behind Zyair's back and sleep around, but it was starting to look like she had no choice.

Champagne thought about Sharon, the woman she felt most connected to and how she would call her every now and then to invite her to lunch. Champagne kept putting it off until Sharon called her out on it.

"What's the deal? Why won't you meet me for lunch?"

"I've just been busy," Champagne lied.

Always one to be blunt, Sharon told her, "Don't lie. I think you're afraid of me."

"Afraid? Why would I be afraid?"

"You're afraid of your feelings, your desires, your wants, and maybe even your needs."

Sharon was right so Champagne kept silent.

"You see, your silence is my answer. I know I'm right."

"If you know you're right and if you know what I'm afraid of, then why keep calling."

"Because I like you Champagne. Not just as a lover, but as a friend and I was hoping that if we couldn't be anything else, then at least we could be friends."

"I think maybe you're having some kind of mid-life crisis. My psychology books say sometimes it happens earlier than expected. Maybe you and Zyair need to take another vacation. Perhaps have a weekend getaway and talk about the whole marriage thing," Alexis offered in the form of advice.

"You think so?" Champagne asked.

"Yeah, I do."

"I just might take that suggestion," Champagne said knowing she was telling a bold-faced lie.

They both sat silent consumed in their thoughts, then they looked at one another and started to laugh.

"Girl, we're both a mess," Champagne said.

They continued to sit and talk for a while about nothing in particular until Alexis stood up. "I need to go shop before the stores close."

Champagne stood up too. "Call me."

"I'll do that." Alexis leaned over and kissed her on the cheek. "You make sure you talk to Zyair about what's on your mind. Shit or better yet, see that counselor you used to see, maybe she can help you sort things out."

"We'll see."

***

An hour and a half later after shopping Alexis was driving home. She reached over to get her cell phone out of her purse, when she felt someone hit the back of her car. She pressed on her brakes and looked out of her rearview mirror only to find that someone had run into the back of her.

"What the hell?" She turned her car off and opened her door. Before she could even climb out of her seat, the driver of the other car was standing by her door. He scared the mess out of her. *What if he's the one following me?* She instantly regretted opening her car door.

"I'm so sorry miss, are you okay?"

"I will be the second you back up and give me some space," she snapped.

"Is that really necessary?" he asked as he took a step back.

Alexis looked up to see who the hell this man was talking to. After all, he was the one that ran into her.

"How did you run into me? The light was red."

The man didn't answer. He just stood there staring at her through his sunglasses.

Alexis got out of her car and waved her hands in front of his face. "Hello, I'm talking to you. I asked you a question."

"Did you attend Seashore High?"

Alexis looked at him and tried to place the face. She was hesitant in answering yes.

"Alexis?"

She took one step back and looked him up and down. Whoever he was, he was handsome but this wasn't the time to be checking someone out. She needed to see if there was any damage done to her car.

She stepped past him and walked to the back of her car, which was a black BMW M3.

"It's just a little scratch," he told her, "I'll take care of it."

I bet you will, Alexis thought to herself. She looked at him again and tried to place the face. Behind the shades he looked handsome. *But even handsome men are crazy.*

"You do look familiar," she told him, "but you know it's been over fifteen years since I've been in high school."

"Maybe this will refresh your memory," he told her as he took off his shades.

The second she saw his grey eyes, she knew who he was.

"Finn?"

"The one and only."

Alexis was more than surprised to see him. Hell, she'd heard he went to prison right out of high school. Not only was he an ex-convict who went to jail for armed robbery, but he was also her childhood crush. Alexis reached out to give him a hug and he hugged her back and held on to her a second too long.

After she pulled away, she looked him up and down. He was still in shape. *Probably from the jailhouse workout,* and he was dressed in a suit.

"You know this doesn't excuse the fact that you just ran into me?" she told him.

"I didn't expect it to, but like I said I'll take care of it."

Alexis looked at her car and saw that there was a small scratch and a tiny dent.

A second later Finn was standing beside her. "Give me your contact information and I'll call you. We can get that fixed this week."

Alexis couldn't even be mad because she believed he would do just that.

"Let me give you my card," she told him, "and you give me your contact information and we'll go from there."

After exchanging information, he told her he'd call her that evening. She told him she wouldn't be around.

He then asked her if he could take her to dinner. *I don't think I can handle seeing another man right now.* She had sex with Thomas, now she had a date with Shamel and was going to meeting Maya's brother. "We'll see," she told him and walked back to the front of her car and climbed inside.

The second he pulled away, Alexis pulled out her cell phone and called Champagne. She got the answering service.

"Girl, you won't believe who just ran into me, literally. I'm talking about ran into the back of my car. Finn, girl! You remember fine-ass Finn with the pretty eyes? Anyway, I'll call you later. Oh, and don't worry, I'm fine. Love you."

Alexis hung up and continued to drive home while reminiscing about her first real tongue kiss and it just happened to be with Finn.

About an hour later when Alexis returned home, she was surprised to see flowers on her porch. Thinking they were from Thomas, she smiled, walked over to them, bent over, pulled the card out, and read it. "I'm watching you closely."

I'm watching you? What the hell does that mean? Alexis looked around to see if she saw anyone in the vicinity. Her heart was racing a mile a minute. Maybe her instinct was right and maybe what Champagne said was true, that she was being stalked. Again, she looked around. There was no one. She picked up the flowers and unlocked her door.

Alexis sat the flowers down on the table near the door and went into the kitchen to call Thomas. She placed her purse on the counter and dialed his number.

"Hello?"

"Hey, Thomas. It's Alexis."

"What's up baby?"

"Did you send me some flowers?"

Thomas hesitated in answering because he had not, and that meant some other man was trying to get her attention. "No. It wasn't me."

When Thomas told her no and said it wasn't him, it scared Alexis. For one, she didn't play that secret admirer shit and two; it scared the hell out of her. Just knowing that her intuition was right, that someone was following her and knew where she lived made her anxious.

"Hello?" Thomas said. "You still there?"

"I'm still here."

Thomas could hear something in her voice and whatever it was, he didn't like it. "What's wrong? What's going on?"

"I don't know."

"What do you mean you don't know?"

"Well, lately I've felt like someone's been following me."

"What! Who?"

"I don't know, and then when I arrived home there were some flowers on my porch with a card that said, 'you are being watched' and there was no signature."

Thomas didn't like this at all. "What! I'm on my way over." Zyair had mentioned to him where she lived before and for this he was grateful.

Alexis liked the fact that Thomas was ready to jump up and come to her rescue. But what was he going to do, come look at the card and wonder who left it like she did? There was no name or any information to indicate who sent it.

"That's okay. You don't have to do that."

"I know I don't have to, I want to."

"There's nothing you can do."

"I can look around."

Alexis could see that Thomas wasn't going to let up and she didn't want him to come all the way to her house for nothing.

"I said you don't have to do that." She made sure her tone implied that she was serious.

"Well, if you change your mind, just let me know."

"I will," she assured him.

"I got your message about dinner, how about Friday? Would you like to have dinner Friday?"

"I can't," she told him.

"You sure, I heard of this new restaurant and—"

Tired from the day and feeling thrown off because of the flowers, she told him, "Thomas, I'm not going to be home Friday night."

He didn't want to ask, he knew it wasn't his business, but he couldn't stop himself. "May I ask you where you're going?" *Please don't let her say on a date.*

"I'm going out with a friend."

"A male friend?" Thomas knew he was acting like a pussy and he also knew that he wouldn't care if this was someone else, but it wasn't someone else, it was Alexis.

No sense in lying. "Yes," Alexis told him.

"Is that why you won't go out to dinner with me, because you're seeing someone else?"

Alexis told him that wasn't the reason. She couldn't go out with him tonight because she was exhausted and that during the week it was just a challenge, period, but that she did want to see him again.

"Well, you make sure you call me tomorrow so we can figure out what to do about us getting together." Thomas hoped he didn't sound as heart-broken as he felt. *Damn it. What is this girl doing to me?*

"I promise. I will."

The sincerity in Alexis' voice made Thomas feel a little better.

When they hung up the phone, Alexis sat down and thought about Thomas and her feelings for him.

She had to admit she was feeling him. The little time they spent together showed her who he really was and that was the opposite of what she thought.

Truth be told, Alexis could actually see the two of them together as a couple but she wasn't ready for that just yet. Khalil had ruined it for other men. *Is that who's watching me? Is it Khalil?*

Alexis shook her head to get the thought out of it.

Chapter Forty-two

Keep your eyes open at all times, you never know who you might run into.

Friday finally arrived and as Alexis prepared for her date with Shamel, she admitted to herself she was a little nervous about going out with someone she just met. Hanging with and being around Thomas was one thing because he was part of her circle via Champagne but Shamel, well, that was another story.

What would they talk about over dinner? Would they click? Would she be comfortable around him? Was he going to try and get her to his house? Would she go? There were a million questions running through Alexis' head.

Get it together, girl. Don't worry about it, it's just a date. Enjoy yourself, make small talk and ask him questions about himself; men love that.

Alexis looked in her closet and pulled out the red wrap dress then her red stiletto boots that she'd purchased not too long ago. She showered, rubbed her body down with a vanilla body cream and got dressed. She wore her hair pulled back to show her face. She'd decided to let it grow down her back. Right now it was just a few inches past her shoulders when pressed. Alexis preferred to wear her hair natural. *Thank God it's naturally curly,* she thought as she looked in the mirror. Wearing her hair back also showed her cheekbones which were sharp like Angela Bassett's. Alexis liked to say they were from the same tribe. She then put on the diamond studs she'd just bought herself as well.

After she finished dressing, she looked in the mirror, liked what she saw and said, "The lady in red, that's what I am tonight, hot, on fire, and ready to take on the world." Yes, she was trying to psych herself up and looking good was one way to do it.

Alexis and Shamel were going to meet at this new lounge/restaurant that just opened up downtown called, "Lovers Lane." To Alexis that was an odd name to call a lounge but hey, whatever worked for the owner worked for her.

It was almost eight o'clock and she had to be there by nine. She was on her way and she would be on time, the question was would he be prompt as well.

As Alexis approached Lovers Lane she saw that they had valet parking. That suited her fine because it meant she wouldn't have to drive around looking for a place to park. She pulled up in front of the building and a young man walked up and pulled open the door.

The young man seemed surprised to see her, "Ms. Olivia?"

She recognized his face and recalled that this would be his first year in college. She glanced at his name tag.

"Michael, how's college treating you?"

"It's all good. I probably would not have made it out of high school had it not been for you."

Hearing something like that is what made her job worth going to. That's why she did the type of work she did. She wanted to make a difference. Most times she didn't think that she was, but hearing Michael's words told her she thought wrong.

"Thanks, sweetie but all the credit goes to you."

She stepped out of the way so he could park her car and walked into the lounge.

From first glance it appeared to be full to capacity but not to the point where the service might lack. There was a band playing that sounded like old school R&B in the back of the club on a small stage. A small number of people were dancing which was all that would be able to fit on the dance floor anyway. Even though the kitchen was upstairs along with seating for those who wanted dinner, Alexis could still smell the aroma of barbeque in the air.

Alexis glanced around and her eyes fell on Shamel at the bar. He was looking her way and smiled when she located him.

Am I going to have to walk up to him or is he going to come to me? Alexis' question was answered when he started walking her way.

She could tell he was taking her in from head to toe as she was him.

"You look dapper," she told him. The off-white linen slacks and shirt he wore made him look very put together.

"And you," he took her hand and kissed it, "you look beautiful." He released her hand. "Come on, let's go to our seat."

As they were moving from the front door, Alexis felt someone tap her on the shoulder. She turned around and saw that of all people, it was Thomas.

Did I tell him where I was going when I spoke with him earlier? She knew she didn't and she was certain he didn't follow her because from the time she hung up and got dressed there was no way he could have made it her house, so a coincidence this was.

"Thomas?"

Shamel turned around as well. They recognized one another immediately.

Shamel put out his hand. "Well, well, we just keep running into one another, us three."

Thomas, not wanting to seem like a jealous asshole, shook it. "Thomas," he said by way of introduction.

"Shamel."

Alexis just stood there looking from one to the other.

"Can I speak with you for a minute?" Thomas asked.

"She's on a date," Shamel told him.

"I'll let her come back."

Alexis frowned when she heard the word *let*. "You won't let me do anything. I'm a grown-ass woman and . . ." Before she went on, she looked at Shamel. "Please, just give me a minute." *Is he following me?* She hoped not. Thomas didn't strike her as that kind of man but she was going to find out.

Shamel frowned. "This is the second time you've done this to me. Are we going to make this a habit?"

Alexis stood on her toes and kissed him gently on the lips, "Of course not. Please, just give us a minute."

Shamel decided to give her just that, especially after the kiss.

"One minute." He tapped his watch to let her know he meant it and took a couple of steps back.

Alexis turned toward Thomas, "Just what in the hell do you think you're doing?"

"You look sexy," Thomas told her.

"Are you the one following me?"

Thomas just looked at her.

"Well, are you?" she pressed.

"You'd really stand there and ask me that, when I was the one who offered to come rushing to your house because you thought you saw someone earlier?"

"It's just odd that I'm here meeting with Shamel and you're here as well."

"How many spots are there in this area for us?"

Alexis knew that "us" meant African Americans. "Well, I guess you're right."

"What's up with you kissing him, didn't y'all just meet?"

Alexis sighed and didn't bother answering. "You said you needed to talk. What Thomas? What do you need to talk to me about?"

He had to think of something quick. "About the flowers and the note that came to your house and about us."

"And you have to talk to me about that now and here?"

Thomas didn't answer. Alexis knew what he was doing. "You just don't like me being out with another man."

Thomas didn't even try to deny it. "You're right, I don't."

"But you do know you have no control over that."

"I know." Thomas looked over Alexis' shoulder and saw Shamel heading their way.

"Come home with me."

Alexis laughed gently. "We're not going there again."

Before Thomas could respond Shamel was up on them.

"Your minute is up," Shamel informed Alexis.

"Listen, you just be careful, okay, and promise to call me so I know you got home safe." Thomas told Alexis.

That was not a promise she was going to make. "How about I call you tomorrow instead?" Alexis responded.

"I'll be waiting," he told her before he walked away.

Shamel followed him with his eyes. "Do you and him have a thing going on?"

"No, we're just friends."

"Is it something I need to be concerned about?"

Alexis looked up at Shamel and asked, "Now why would you be concerned? After all, this is our first real date. "

Shamel placed his hands around her waist and pulled her to him. "And I hope it won't be the last."

Alexis looked him in the eyes. "I'm sure it won't."

Shamel was still holding onto her when she told him, "You can release me now."

"Did you make reservations?" Shamel asked as he let her go.

Shit! Alexis knew she forgot to do something. "Oh my God, do you know I forgot."

"I'll see how long the wait will be."

Shamel walked away and when he returned a brief moment later he told her, "Forty-five minutes."

"Damn," Alexis said. "I apologize for forgetting."

"Listen, let's leave this place and go to my spot. I can order something for us to eat and have it delivered there."

"Are you sure?" Alexis asked.

"Yeah." Shamel nodded toward the right. "Plus, your boy can't seem to stop looking our way and I'm two seconds from stepping to him."

Alexis definitely didn't want that to happen. "What's your spot?"

"Dreams."

The only Dreams Alexis heard of was the strip club in North Jersey. "Are you talking about the strip club?"

"Yes."

Alexis took a step back and stared at him.

"Why are you staring at me like that?"

"You don't look like the type of brother that would own a strip club."

Shamel just laughed because he'd heard this before. "And what does that type of brother look like?" He knew that most people expected black men that own strip clubs to look like thugs or shifty characters but no, not him. He liked to keep his goatee tight at all times, have his hair cut low, almost bald, and he stayed dressed in designer clothes. He liked for his style to speak volumes and money.

They were walking toward the door. "I don't know but not like you. You look more like a . . . a . . . Actually, I don't know what you look like."

"I don't know whether I should be insulted or not."

"I'm definitely not insulting you."

They were outside and Michael approached them.

"Ms. Houston, you're leaving so soon?"

"That I am."

"I'll get your car."

When he walked away, Shamel looked at her. "You know him?"

"Yes, he was one of my students." During one of their prior conversations, she'd told him her profession. "Shamel, is your club a dive?"

"Sweetie, do you really think I would own or associate myself with some bullshit?"

"That's just it, I don't know. Plus, I've never been to a strip club before."

"Don't worry. Dreams is classy and I have only the best looking girls there with the best bodies."

"Do they show their coochies?"

"Not on the dance floor they don't. I have a rule and that's if the women choose to be nude, it's their choice but there's where it stops. There's no opening of the pussy or doing tricks with bottles and all the other shit that brought the riff raff in." What Shamel didn't tell her was whatever goes on in the back rooms was another thing altogether. What's done behind closed doors, stayed behind closed doors.

It was at that moment Michael drove up with her car and another young man was behind him in Shamel's car, which was a Mercedes G-class truck.

"Don't drive too fast," Alexis told him.

"Don't worry, I won't."

Less than a half hour later, they pulled up to Dreams. Every parking spot on the street was full as was the lot across the street. The only spots that were open were the two directly in front of the club. It was obvious that those two spots were for them. Shamel waved her into the first spot and then pulled in behind her. Before she could even turn off her engine, one of the bouncers was at her door assisting her out of the car.

Shamel was getting out of his car at the same time.

"What's up, boss?" the bouncer greeted.

"How's business?" Shamel asked.

"Busy as usual. A couple of troublemakers got out of hand but you know it was handled."

Shamel took Alexis' hand and together they walked in.

Alexis didn't know what to do when they first walked through the door. She didn't know where to look first. There were people everywhere. Near the bar, on the floor standing and sitting at the tables throughout the club. A couple of men were getting lap dances and there were two dancers on the stage.

On one hand she wanted to sit down and take it all in. On the other hand she felt like she wanted to place her hands over her eyes. She felt like she was somewhere she wasn't supposed to be, and seeing things she wasn't supposed to see. But that's how a good Christian lived. *Wow, I've really sheltered myself.*

Shamel was watching her look around. He wondered what she was thinking. Was she turned on, was she turned off or did it not bother her one way or the other? He couldn't tell from the look on her face.

"Come on. Let's go to the bar and get a drink. Then we'll go to my office and I'll have something delivered to eat."

Eating was the furthest thing from Alexis' mind. She started to tell him this when she thought she saw someone that looked familiar getting on the stage.

Alexis hoped what she was seeing was not real. She knew something was going on with Shay, but she would have never thought it was this. Shay was one of her students that seemed to be going through some changes. Alexis had summed it all up to hormones. Okay, maybe she was mistaken, after all there is someone that looks like everyone and hopefully this was the case.

"Alexis, you okay?" she heard Shamel ask.

She didn't answer. She took another look at the girl. *She looks just like her, I'm going to have to get closer to the stage and see if my eyes are fooling me.*

Alexis started to take a step away from Shamel. He stopped her by taking hold of her arm. "What's up? I'm trying to order you a drink and you're not paying me any mind. Again, are you okay?"

"I don't know."

"What do you mean you don't know?"

"I just see someone that's looks familiar."

"Really? Where?" Shamel glanced around the club to see who she could possibly know.

"The girl on stage." In her heart of hearts Alexis knew it was Shay but wanted to be in denial. She took in with her eyes what Shay was wearing and that's barely anything. All she had on was a white sheer G-string and a stringy looking bra that barely covered her nipples. She also had on tons of makeup to obviously make herself look older. Alexis watched as she moved her hips in a circular motion that suggested and hinted at a good time, maybe even the best time of a man's life.

"Who? Diamond?"

Alexis looked at him, "Is that what she calls herself?"

"Yeah, why? She's one of our best dancers," he told her.

"I also think she's one of my students."

Shamel put down the drink he was holding and told the bartender, "Pour it out, I'll be back."

He took Alexis' hand. "Let's go in the back."

Alexis looked at the stage once again before following Shamel into the back where his office was located.

Once inside he closed the door. "Have a seat."

Alexis looked around and saw that he had four midsized screens on the wall. Showing on the screens was the stage; the front door and what looked like two rooms inside the club. "You always know what's going on, huh?"

"Sweetie, you have to in this line of business. You never know when someone is going to try to get out of hand. I don't want any trouble and I don't take any bullshit." He pulled open his desk drawer and pressed a button, the screen with the view of the stage got closer.

"Is that your girl?" Shamel asked.

Alexis looked at the screen and saw that her eyes weren't playing tricks on her, it was Shay. "Yes, yes, it is."

Shamel shook his head. "Damn." He picked up his phone and told someone to have Diamond come into his office when she left the stage. "I didn't know she was underage," he told Alexis.

Alexis looked at the screen again and seeing Shay up there naked and gyrating, she could see why Shamel would have no idea she was underage. The way these teenagers looked today was a damn shame. Sometimes there was no way to tell their age unless you asked for identification.

"Have a seat," Shamel told her as he sat behind his desk.

Alexis sat in the chair across from him. She felt like she was being interviewed with the way he was looking at her.

"Why are you looking at me like that?"

"Because you are a beautiful woman."

Just like any other female, Alexis appreciated the comment. "Thank you."

Relaxing back in his seat, Shamel asked her, "So, tell me, how come a lady like you doesn't have a man?"

What was she supposed to say? Should she tell him the last one she had ended up being married, a pimp, and dishonest. "I just recently got out of a relationship."

"What happened?"

Before Alexis could respond there was a knock on the door.

Alexis could feel her heart racing; she figured it was going to be Shay.

"Come in," Shamel said as he looked toward the door.

Alexis didn't turn around and face the door. As much as she wanted to, she figured her face shouldn't be the first one Shay saw.

The door opened and in walked Shay wearing a robe. "You wanted to see me?" Shay glanced at the back of the woman's head that was facing Shamel.

"Yes, as a matter of fact I did."

Shay was standing between the door and Alexis. "Yes?"

Not one to beat around the bush, Shamel asked her, "How old are you?"

"Huh?" That was the last thing Shay expected to be asked.

"I asked how old are you?"

"I'm twenty," Shay replied with a straight face.

On that note Alexis turned around.

The look on Shay's face when she saw who was sitting in the chair could only be described as shocked, embarrassed, and busted. "Ms. . . . Ms. . . ." Shay couldn't even get it out.

Alexis stood up and with disappointment in her voice. "Shay, what are you doing?" Shay tried to get her emotions together. Alexis asked again, "What are you doing?"

Shamel wasn't saying a word. He was just sitting back letting the scene play out.

Shay looked from Shamel to Alexis. What was there to say, she knew she was busted. She knew she could not lie about her age with her school counselor sitting right there, but what she felt she could do was act indignant.

"It's none of your business what I'm doing here. What I do outside of school is my personal business. You don't run my life. I do what I have to do."

Alexis knew Shay was acting ignorant because there was nothing else she could do, so she let her have her moment. Shamel was just the opposite, he wasn't hearing it.

"Well, it is my business," he told Shay/Diamond, "and you've jeopardized it by being here. What I think you need to do is leave, bounce, get your shit, and go."

"Please Shamel. You know I need this job." If Alexis wasn't sitting there, Shay would have been willing to give him her body for exchange. Yes, she could go be a stripper somewhere else, but she would not be treated the same. Here at Dreams the girls were treated with respect by the clientele, if not, they were thrown out.

"You know damn well, I don't play that underage shit in my club. As a matter of fact, if any of the other girls are underage, you need to let them know, I will find out over the next couple of days. I am not trying to have the cops run all up in my shit."

Shay looked at Alexis with so much hatred that it threw Alexis off. She couldn't understand where that look was coming from. All she'd done in the past was try to help her, to be there for her, to offer advice from time to time. When she did, it appeared that it was appreciated. Alexis wondered again what was going on in Shay's life, if there was something in the family that was disrupting everything. Even though the look made her pause, what the look didn't do was stop her from standing up and walking toward Shay.

"What's going on Shay? Why do you need this job so bad?"

Alexis noticed that Shay was tearing up. This was a sure sign that something was definitely not right in Shay's life. Shay wasn't one of those students that showed emotion. If anything she was one of the girls that walked around with attitude all on her face, one of the girls who appeared to be frowning even when they weren't.

"I ain't telling you my business," Shay told her but didn't move. After all, she felt that Alexis should know what's up. They'd had enough counseling sessions in the past.

Shamel was looking at both of them. He decided he should leave them alone but not before giving Shay a look that Alexis caught. *What was that look about?*

He stood up. "You know what? I'll be right back."

They watched him leave the room. Once he closed the door behind him. Alexis turned toward Shay and asked her, "So, do you want to tell me what's going on? Why you need to work in a place like this?"

"Again, it's not any of your business." Shay turned her back toward Alexis but again didn't leave the room.

"Obviously you need someone to talk to or you would have left the room by now."

Shay said nothing.

"Listen," Alexis stepped in front of her so that they were face to face. "We can talk now or we can talk later."

Shay brushed past her and walked out.

Alexis turned and sat back down. She looked at one of the screens and noticed Shamel talking to Shay who appeared to be pleading. *Why would she plead to be a stripper?* Alexis wondered. She knew she wasn't going to be able to let this go and that was because she knew that Shay had potential. If a student stayed in school nowadays it was because they wanted to at least try, even if it was halfheartedly. At least that's what Alexis wanted to believe.

When Shamel returned, Alexis asked him, "What did she say?"

"It's not important. What's important is that she's leaving the premises."

"But I'm worried about her."

Shamel stood in front of Alexis and pulled her up and into him. She didn't fight it. "This is our night. Let's focus on getting to know one another and then tomorrow when we aren't together you can focus on Diamond, Shay or whatever her name is."

Feeling the closeness and the heat that was flowing from Shamel, Alexis could only agree. After all, she was out to have a good time and this was her first night in a strip club and she wanted to make the most of it.

"Do you want to get something to eat?"

The last thing that was on Alexis' mind was eating. What she wanted to do was go out and explore the club. "Not really, I want a tour of the club. I want to see what's behind those closed doors I saw when we came to your office."

What was behind those doors were private parties and private lap dances. "I can show you on the screen, but you have to keep it between you and me," Shamel told her.

"Of course but let's go out on the floor first. I want to check out the dancers up close."

"Come on," he told her and she followed him out the door.

"Where do you want to sit, at a table, the bar or a booth?"

Alexis looked around. Most of the tables and seats surrounding the bar were full, so she chose a booth. They not only looked comfortable, but they also were located on the side of the stage where she could see mostly everything.

Shamel waited for Alexis to sit down and he slid in next to her. "I might leave you here a time or two. There are a couple of things I have to take care of. Is that okay? Would you mind?"

"Not at all," she told him.

"The dancer that's coming up next, her name is Blue. At least I know she's old enough to work here."

"After Shay, how can you be so sure?"

"Because she's one of my boys' wife."

"Get the hell out of here. He doesn't have a problem with his wife being a stripper?"

"When they met she was a stripper. Of course he tried to change her mind but she wasn't hearing it. She loves what she does."

Alexis looked at the stage and the second Blue walked on the stage, Alexis felt herself get moist. *Oh, hell no, this is not happening.* Alexis could feel her heart racing. This shit had never happened to her before. The little incidents Champagne reminded her of; not that she'd ever forgotten, she just chose to push them so deep and so far away from her mind that it didn't mean anything—didn't count. Why the hell was her pussy getting wet over a female? Was it because of what Champagne had told her? Was it because she told herself that she was now a new woman ready to make changes? Well, hell that change didn't include being attracted to women.

Okay, okay, just because she was sitting here getting wet, didn't mean she was ready to sex down a female. It just meant her libido was up. At least that's what she wanted it to mean. Because now she was thinking about something she hadn't thought about in years. As a matter of fact, decades. She tried to put it out of her mind the times she and Champagne used to play around with each other. After all they were in their preteens and early teens. She didn't think it really counted. She did wonder what would have happened had they been caught playing. By that she meant touching each other, lying on top of each other hunching, and fingering each other. It was their secret then and it was their secret now and a secret it would stay.

Alexis watched Blue as she bent over while wearing a thong and noticed that on each of her ass cheeks were butterfly wings. She was entranced as Blue made them clap and made it appear as if the butterflies were flying. She watched as Blue stood up, faced their direction and placed her hands on her breasts. Alexis found herself wanting to reach out and touch. Hell, she wanted to experience a lap dance. However, wanting something and getting it were two different things. She wasn't ready for that.

Alexis turned to face Shamel only to find him watching her intently.

"Why are you looking at me like that?"

"You like Blue?"

"What?"

"You were so intense when you were watching her."

Damn, Alexis didn't think she was going to be that easy to read. "I think she's sexy." Those words were not supposed to come out of her mouth.

"Want me to call her over here?"

She wanted to say yes but was afraid to. What would happen if he did call her over? Would everyone look their way?

"You can always go into one of the rooms."

She really wanted to experience this moment to the fullest, but she just couldn't bring herself to admit it out loud. At least not here while she was supposed to be on a date.

"No, you don't have to do that. As a matter of fact, I'm ready for the tour of the club."

Shamel stood and helped her up. "Come on, I'll show you around."

Before they got far, Alexis heard someone say her name. She and Shamel turned around. It was Finn.

"Finn, hi." Alexis gave him a hug.

"Wow, I didn't expect to see you here," he told her.

Shamel cleared his throat.

Alexis turned to face Shamel. "Oh, I'm sorry. Shamel, this is Finn, an old friend."

Shamel knew who Finn was; he'd thrown him out a time or two. As a matter of fact, Shamel wondered what he was doing there now, he was told not to come back there.

They gave one another the head nod.

"I haven't heard from you about your car. I told you I'd get it fixed for you."

"I know. I planned on calling you this week actually. I've just been so busy." Actually she hadn't been thinking about it at all. She was going to take care of it herself. She didn't feel like dealing with him asking her out and her having to turn him down. Two and possibly three men were enough. There was that, plus the armed robbery charge that scared the mess out of her.

Shamel placed his hand on the small of Alexis' back and it did not go unnoticed by Finn. "You ready?"

"I'll call you this week, okay."

Finn looked at Shamel who was shooting daggers. He wasn't stupid; he knew that meant to get the hell out the spot. "Make sure you do that. I always pay my debts."

"I will." Alexis turned to walk away but stopped when Finn said her name again. "Yes."

He couldn't help himself, so he asked her, "Can I get another hug?"

Shamel stepped in front of Alexis, "Get the fuck out of here."

Finn started laughing, turned, and left.

"Damn Shamel, was it that serious?" Alexis asked.

"How well do you know him?"

She had to admit not well, she hadn't seen him in quite some time.

"Well, I don't think you should get to know him any better. He's trouble and I've had to deal with him on a number of occasions."

Alexis thought about what Champagne said when she told her to be careful and that there are some crazy men out there.

"What debt is he talking about?" Shamel asked.

"He hit my car the other day and he's going to get it fixed."

"I have someone that can do that for you."

Alexis didn't bother responding to that. It was something she was going to have to think about.

Although she'd told herself she was going to "get what was hers," she was well aware that to men, when they did something for you that required their finances it became something else. It was almost like you owed them and she needed to figure out a way to get it and not feel obligated. So she told him instead that she was ready for her tour of the club.

Take her around he did. Dreams was bigger than it appeared and it was obviously upscale and done in good taste. There were several rooms and only a few were empty. There was a room where people were just sitting and having conversation. There was a cigar room, a room where what appeared to be a bachelor party was going on but she wanted to see more. Alexis was shocking herself because all of a sudden she felt like a voyeur.

Alexis turned to Shamel, "Let's go back in your office. I want to see what's going on in one of the rooms where the door is closed."

"You sure about that?" Shamel asked. She'd already told him this was her first time at a strip club and he didn't want to run her off.

"I'm sure," Alexis told him.

"Okay, but I have to tell you, it be some shit going down in those rooms."

"I understand that."

"And you also need to understand that whatever you see stays here."

"I understand that also."

Shamel didn't normally do this, let someone look at what was for his eyes only. Only a few knew that he had cameras everywhere except the bathrooms and those who knew wouldn't say a word because they feared him. The reason he was doing it now was because he was hoping it would lead to them being physical.

There was something about Alexis that turned him on the first day they met. Normally, if a female walked away from him to talk to another man, he would have embarrassed her ass and his, but this time he didn't. He let it slide because he wanted to see her again.

Later that night his boy even called him out on it. "Man, you let that girl play you. That ain't you, what's going on?"

"Ain't shit going on, there's something about her, something different about her."

Of course True wasn't trying to hear that. "Ain't nothing different about no pussy. Pussy is pussy. The end."

Normally that would have been true but for the first time in his life, he was feeling like he wanted more with a woman and not just to fuck her. Don't get it twisted, he did want sex, but he also wanted more.

Oh, shit, does that mean I'm ready to settle down? Shamel wondered. In a way he thought he was. After all, he was in his midthirties. He was ready to have kids and when he looked at Alexis, not only was she so fine that he knew their babies would come out pretty, but she also had a head on her shoulders. There was also a quiet innocence about her. He'd been around enough women to know a thing or two. He was more than capable of reading them and summing them up.

Once they were in his office, he closed and locked the door. Alexis sat down and waited anxiously with her heart racing.

Shamel walked behind his desk, turned on the screen, opened a drawer, and pressed some buttons. All four screens came on. One obviously was on the main floor. Another showed a man getting a lap dance. One showed a group of women in a room together with a couple of dancers. The last room was one of a stripper sitting across from a male patron. They appeared to be talking and she appeared to be rubbing his dick through his pants. Alexis didn't know what to focus on.

"I'll be right back," Shamel told her.

Alexis just nodded as she watched the screen with the woman and man. She wanted to see how far it would go. She wanted to ask Shamel if he had sound so that she could hear what they were saying, but she held back.

"Want me to turn it up?" Shamel asked.

Damn, is he reading my mind? "Yes." *I wonder what's he's thinking? Is he thinking I'm a freak?*

"Which screen?" He already knew which one because she couldn't take her eyes off it. It was the one with Jada and one of her regulars. Shamel knew that some of his girls did extras for the patrons but that was their choice. It wasn't something he asked them to do, they did it because they wanted to and those extras included anything from masturbating, to touching and sucking. There were even a couple of the girls who let the men eat them out. Jada was one of the girls that had a special talent when it came to her mouth. He knew because he'd experienced it a time or two.

"The one with the woman and man." Alexis continued to watch as the woman stood up and started circling him.

"That's Jada," Shamel told Alexis as he walked out of the office.

Jada was now behind the man and she asked him, "What do you want me to do?"

"You know what I want you to do," he told her and he started to unzip his pants.

Jada placed one of her hands on top of his. "Not so fast. What's the hurry?"

"Come on girl, stop playing."

She stepped in front of him.

"You want me to suck your dick," she told him. "That's all you ever want me to do."

"That's because you do it so well." The man reached for his zipper again and Jada pushed his hands away.

"Let me do it." She got on her knees and started to unzip his pants as she licked her lips.

Alexis was all into it, she had forgotten about the other screens.

Jada unzipped his pants, reached inside and pulled his dick out. She then got on her knees.

"Damn! I always forget how big you are."

Alexis noticed it too.

"And thick," Jada said as she licked the head like a lollipop.

"Let me pull my pants down some," the man said.

"No. I want your dick only. Not your balls but this right here," Jada told him as she gripped his dick and took the whole thing in her mouth.

Alexis couldn't believe what she was seeing as Jada's mouth went down the whole length and width of him and came back up. Alexis wanted to put her hands on her pussy so bad but she knew she couldn't because Shamel could come back into the office any minute. *Am I really sitting here watching this and getting turned on?* Alexis was shocking herself. Watching other people have sex was not something she was into and it definitely wasn't something she'd thought she'd ever be into, but now she knew not to say ever or never. In the past, she'd never even considered watching porn, now she might give it a second thought.

Alexis watched as Jada slowly licked the man's dick, taking it all in. She watched as Jada licked and sucked on the head of it as the man closed his eyes. She watched as he threw his head back and tried to push Jada's head down.

Jada pulled his pants down farther and told the man to spread his legs. "I changed my mind," she said as she started licking his balls and placing both of them in her mouth.

Alexis watched as the man raised his ass up off the chair and she could feel her mouth water from the excitement.

Alexis was so busy watching Jada that she didn't hear Shamel enter the room.

"She's good isn't she?" he asked causing Alexis to almost fall out of her chair.

She turned around, looked at him and almost choked out the words, "Yes, yes, she is."

"Have you ever watched someone do this before?"

"No, this is my first time."

"Well, you might want to turn back around and watch her make him cum."

Alexis didn't want to continue watching in front of him but she couldn't help herself, she was drawn in. She turned back around and watched as Jada moved her head up and down the length of his penis. When she got to the top she'd lick around the head of it and go back down. The man started moving his hips up and down. It looked like he was trying to push his dick down her throat.

"I'm going to cum," he told her.

Alexis wondered what Jada was going to do. She didn't have to wonder long because suddenly Jada replaced her mouth with one of her hands and cupped the other to catch the semen as it flowed out.

Shamel was standing behind Alexis rubbing on her shoulders. Alexis was trying to catch her breath. Shamel was giving her time.

When she got up the nerves to, she turned and looked at him. "I can't believe I just watched that. I'm embarrassed."

Shamel stood in front of her and she let him pull her up. "Ain't nothing to be embarrassed about."

They were standing so close to each other, Alexis could feel the need for sex radiating off their bodies. *I'm a whore . . . I'm a whore,* Alexis couldn't help but think to herself. *Okay, I know I'm being ridiculous but it's like all of a sudden my libido is out of whack.* Alexis wondered if making love with Thomas had opened up a whole new world for her. Or had she always been a freak in disguise?

"How do you deal with seeing this every day? Does it excite you or are you immune to it?"

"It depends on the moment."

"What do you mean?"

Shamel placed his hands on Alexis' waist and pulled her into him. She could feel that he was hard. "I mean like now, watching you watch them and get excited turned me on."

It was at this point that Alexis asked herself how far she wanted to go and the truth was she didn't know.

Alexis cleared her throat and took a small step back.

"Am I making you uncomfortable?"

Alexis looked up at him and he could see that a kiss was coming.

Shamel normally didn't kiss, it wasn't his thing. He always thought kissing was for wifey, only this time he did. He bent his face down to meet hers, while pulling her back into him and placing his mouth on hers. He let her lead the kiss and was surprised at how much he enjoyed it.

When they finally broke apart, Alexis looked at him and told him, "I should go."

"Why?"

"Because I might do something I'll regret."

"Why would you regret it? I'm grown. You're grown. We can do what we want to do."

Alexis hesitated before answering. "This is true but it can wait. We can wait."

To Shamel that meant she had already made up her mind to let him make love to her. It was a known fact that a woman knows almost immediately if she's going to allow a man inside her and it appeared Alexis was.

"I understand," he told her, "but you don't have to leave."

Alexis shook her head, "No, I think I'd better leave."

Shamel looked at one of the screens and spotted Shay still in the club. "All right, I understand. Let me walk you out."

Alexis stepped back and let him lead the way while thinking, *What the hell am I getting myself into?*

Chapter Forty-three

Let the haters Hate. They're just mad because they know your power.

Saturday finally arrived and Alexis was exhausted. Between seeing Thomas the week before and then hanging out with Shamel at Dreams the day before, she'd had a busy two weeks. And, it wasn't slowing down. This was the night she was going to Maya's for the book club meeting and Maya's brother was supposed to show up. Truth be told, Alexis didn't feel up to dealing with another man. Two were enough.

She had an hour left before her day was over. She wanted to hit the gym for an hour and call the contact numbers for Shay. She wasn't calling to reveal what she'd learned about Shay. She was going to say she was calling because Shay had not come to school with the hopes of speaking to her. Alexis needed to find out what was going on and if there was anything she could do.

Alexis picked up the phone and dialed the main number that was on file. It said it was the house phone. She wasn't surprised when there wasn't a ring and she heard the operator saying the number was disconnected. She hung up and tried the other number, which said it was the number of an uncle. That number was also disconnected.

Alexis now had to make a decision. Was she going to take the next step and drive to the address that was in the files or was she going to let it go? Before she could make up her mind there was a knock on the door.

"Come in," Alexis called out.

In walked Victoria, one of her favorite students. Victoria was on the honor roll for the first time that school year. She was a sophomore trying her hardest to get a scholarship. So when she walked through the door with a long face, Alexis was concerned.

"Hey sweetie, what's wrong?"

Victoria plopped down in the chair in front of her desk. "My mom is driving me crazy."

This was nothing new to Alexis. Most mothers drove their teenage daughters crazy. "Why, what's going on?"

"I don't know. She's been talking about killing herself and killing this man she used to see."

"She actually said that, those were her exact words?" As a therapist whenever Alexis heard the word suicide or whenever someone hinted around about it, she knew to be alarmed and she knew it was a call for help.

"Yes, and I don't know what to do about it."

"Do you know what man she's talking about?"

"I have an idea but she won't really say. All I know is she's scaring me and I need you to go speak with her."

"Me?" What the hell was Alexis going to say to a grown-ass woman? All she could do was give Victoria a number for her mother to call and a card of a woman who would actually come to their house.

"Please Ms. Houston . . . Please will you talk to my mother?"

"That's not what I do, Victoria. I don't counsel parents, I counsel teenagers. I can refer you to someone else."

"So you're just going let my mother kill herself."

Alexis wasn't stupid. She knew what Victoria was trying to do. She was trying to guilt her but that wasn't going to happen. "No, what I am going to do is call a friend of mine that specializes in this kind of thing and have her call you."

"But I'm asking for your help."

Shit, this was the kind of thing that came with the job. She knew that she would come across parents who had less sense than their kids but that wasn't her fight. Her fight was for the kids.

Alexis opened her desk and pulled out a card, she handed it to Victoria. "Call her and tell her what's going on with your mother. She can help you."

Victoria didn't even bother to answer. She just snatched the card out of her hand and marched out of the office, slamming the door behind her.

Five minutes later, there was another knock on the door interrupting her thoughts. Alexis did not have the energy for another dramatic scene.

"Come in," she called out bracing herself and was relieved when she saw that it was Maya.

"Girl, what the hell is wrong with Victoria? She's in the hall calling you all kind of bitches."

Alexis just shook her head and waved her hand as if to say, *girl please*. Plus it wasn't her place to tell the business of students. "You know these kids when you don't do something they want you to do."

"Don't I know it. Just the other day, my student Tina—"

Alexis interrupted her midsentence. She didn't feel like hearing it. "Is the book club meeting still on?"

"Yeah, I came to give you my address." Maya placed a piece of paper on Alexis' desk. "Call me if you have any trouble finding my house."

"That's what MapQuest is for," Alexis told her.

"I know that's right." Maya turned to leave but stopped. "Don't forget my brother is going to stop by."

"I won't forget." Alexis really didn't feel like doing this but she made a promise. She was so glad she invited Champagne.

It was finally time to leave work. Alexis had just enough time to hit the gym for an hour, go home, shower, and call her father.

As a matter-of-fact, right now the person Alexis most wanted to see was her daddy. He'd called her the other night and sounded kind of down. When she asked him what was wrong, he told her nothing, but she didn't believe him; she could hear something in his voice. After all, she was his "baby girl" as he liked to call her and she was his only child.

Alexis' parents divorced once she graduated from college. That was something she didn't understand, why wait until then. If you were unhappy prior, you should have divorced sooner.

She spoke to her mother who lived in Georgia about once every week, but she spoke to her dad who resided in Florida more often. That wasn't anything new because even as a youngster, she went to her dad about most things. They were close and she loved it. Sometimes she even thought her mom was a bit jealous.

Alexis picked up the phone to call him then hung up. She decided to wait until she had some real time to talk. She didn't want to rush through a phone call with her daddy. Actually, a phone call wasn't good enough. She was going to make plans to go see him.

***

An hour later Alexis was at the gym. She'd just left the locker room after changing and was headed toward the tread-mill. She planned on doing twenty-five minutes on the treadmill, elliptical, and stair master, and then she was out.

The second she stepped on the treadmill, she felt someone tap her on the shoulder. Alexis turned around only to find Khalil staring in her face. The last time she saw him was the week before at the club.

"Go away," she told him as her heart raced.

"I need to talk to you."

The last thing Alexis felt like doing was talking to or seeing Khalil's face. She was not in the mood. "Khalil, there is nothing for us to talk about."

He wasn't going to give up that easily. "Please, just ten minutes, that's all I'm asking."

Alexis didn't know what to do. She could tell him to go away again and if he didn't she could always cause a scene. But what would that do other than embarrass herself. She could leave the gym or she could hear him out to try and get some closure.

She chose the closure. "Ten minutes," she told him with her hands on her hips.

"Well, can we at least leave the floor and go in the café?"

"No." Alexis looked at her watch. "The clock is ticking."

Khalil saw that he had no choice, but to say what he had to standing right there and he had no problem doing that. After all, he really cared for Alexis when they were together. His intent wasn't to hurt her or play her. Actually, he didn't know what his intent was. When he first met Alexis, he was seriously feeling her. His wife Suzette had left him and was begging to come back home. At first he was on the prowl, then he started considering it, then he realized he didn't want to be with her anymore anyway.

According to Suzette, she went to find herself. To him, that meant it was over. No, they hadn't divorced but in his mind they weren't together. Shit, his whole marriage was a sham. He met Suzette at a damn swingers club. Her family came from money, she was willing to share it and she gave good head. What was he to do other than take advantage of the opportunity? Hell, she proposed to him, it wasn't the other way around.

Khalil knew he was wrong for proposing to Alexis while legally he was still married, but he wanted her to himself. That was the only way he figured he could guarantee it. When he and Alexis came back from their trip to Cancun, his plan was to hunt Suzette down and divorce her ass. That Thomas motherfucker got to her first and ruined everything by revealing the marriage before he had a chance to.

Eventually Khalil was going to make sure that Zyair and Thomas got theirs. He wasn't stupid. He knew they were boys and he knew Thomas was into Alexis. He knew that even though Zyair was the one who brought Suzette to the airport that Thomas was behind it. However, for now, he wanted to try and make Alexis understand and maybe even forgive him.

"I'm waiting," Alexis said, interrupting his thoughts.

"All right, all right," Khalil said. "First off I want to apologize for hurting you. I didn't mean to. I was in the process of getting divorced when we met."

"And you couldn't tell me that," Alexis said.

"I was afraid you wouldn't want to date me."

"Were you afraid I wouldn't date you or were you unsure as whether or not I was going to give you the ass?"

Khalil was taken aback by what she said.

"You know Khalil; you hurt me, plain and simple. You weren't man enough to be honest with me then, why should I think you're being honest with me now?"

Khalil reached for her arm but she snatched it back. "All I'm saying is I apologize and that I want to make it up to you. You never gave me a chance to explain my situation. You wouldn't take my calls—"

Alexis cut him off. "Answer me one question."

"Anything."

"Are you still married?"

Khalil hesitated a second too long because Alexis placed her hands on his chest and pushed him back. "That's what I thought."

She walked away and this time Khalil didn't bother stopping her because he knew it wouldn't make a difference. However, he was not going to give up that easily.

"I will get her ass back, one way or the other," he said out loud.

Chapter Forty-four

Obsession and love are not that far apart.

Thomas and Zyair were sitting in Thomas' office. They were going out to shoot pool with the boys but there were a couple of things Thomas had to settle. One of his clients had gotten themselves arrested on a DUI.

Into the phone, Thomas said, "I'm not even going to ask you if you were drinking and driving, because I already know the answer." It was going to be one of the two answers they almost always gave; "I only had one or two drinks" or "I don't know why they pulled me over." It was always one excuse after the other. Well at least this one didn't do what another one of his clients did a few months back; try to switch seats with his passenger real quick. There is no "real quick" in climbing over someone when you're damn near seven feet tall.

"Tomorrow you're going to issue a statement I'm putting together, donate some money to a charity, and we're going to move on from there."

Thomas listened to what his client had to say, which must not have been much because a few seconds later he'd hung up the phone.

Zyair just shook his head. "I don't know how you do it."

"I do it for the money," he half joked. Thomas loved his job. He loved anything sports related. He loved being able to help young men make it and of course he loved the financial rewards that came with it.

"And that makes your job much easier, huh?"

"And you know this." Thomas shut down his computer. "Let's get out of here."

"Man, aren't you going to loosen up some? You all in a tie and shit. We're going to play pool remember."

"Yeah, I remember. What? You think I'm senile? I'll be right back." Thomas always kept a couple of sets of clothing at his office in the closet. His office also consisted of a private bathroom, a conference room, a small kitchen, and a seating area. He also had two people that worked for him, a receptionist and an assistant.

When they stepped outside, Thomas noticed that Zyair was following him. "Where did you park?" he asked Zyair.

"I had my driver drop me off. I figured we could ride together," Zyair told him.

"How do you know I didn't have plans afterward?" Thomas had tried earlier to reach Alexis with no luck.

Zyair stopped in his tracks. "Oh, shit, my bad, I didn't even think about that. I'll call my driver."

Thomas bumped Zyair's shoulder with his. "Man, I'm just playing with your ass. You don't have to call your 'driver'."

"Did you think this would be us?" Zyair asked.

Thomas had no idea what he was talking about. "That what would be us?"

"That we would be two successful black men."

Thomas looked at Zyair and smiled. "Hell yeah, I knew it. Shit, I didn't know how it was going to happen or when it was going to happen, but I knew it."

"Really?" Zyair wasn't asking in disbelief. He was asking because even though Thomas had confidence oozing out of his pores when they were in college, it seemed like when they were first starting their businesses everything was a struggle for them both. To make one another feel better they would quote to each other Frederick Douglass who said, "Without struggle there is no progress."

"Yep, that's why I tried so hard. I knew eventually it would pay off."

"I hear that," Zyair said. Zyair knew of Thomas' meager beginnings. After all, he was his best friend; therefore he knew that Thomas beat the odds.

As they were putting on their seat belts, Thomas said, "But you know what?"

"What?"

"There was a time when as long as I had money, as long as I could buy whatever I wanted and whoever I wanted, I was happy, but that's getting old man. I'm ready to settle down and be with one woman and share what I have with one woman."

"And you want that woman to be Alexis?"

"I do, man. I sure do."

"What is it about her man? You've been feeling her for a couple of years. She never gave you the time of the day, yet, that didn't deter you. I'm trying to figure out what kind of voodoo she put on your ass."

Thomas laughed. "Nah man, there's just something about her that gets me going."

Zyair didn't respond, because although Alexis was fine, he knew that in the past Thomas' women were finer, sexier, and more experienced.

They drove the rest of the way to the pool hall in silence, each consumed with their own thoughts.

Zyair was thinking about what transpired the night before, when Champagne's cell phone was going off. *She was in the bathroom taking a shower and normally he would just let it buzz. But for some reason, a reason he still couldn't put his finger on, he picked it up and saw missed call. He knew he should have just put the phone back down, but he couldn't stop himself. He pressed the button to see who it was. On received calls Sharon's name showed up over four times.*

Why the hell is she calling my woman so much? Champagne told me they rarely speak and here she's called her four times in one day.

Zyair couldn't decide if he wanted to bring it up and ask her what the deal was because then she'd know he'd been snooping.

When Champagne came out of the bathroom, she didn't even bother to look at her phone. She was looking so sexy in one of his T-shirts that he decided to leave it alone, at least until after they made love. And, the way he was going to make love to her, if she even had an inkling of wanting another woman, it wouldn't be for long. Sometimes he regretted sharing the fantasy of seeing her with another woman because seeing how much she enjoyed it brought up some insecurities he wasn't even aware of.

"Come here," he told her.

Champagne was able to tell by his voice that it was about to be on. "Why?" *she teased.*

"I want to taste you."

Zyair didn't have to say another word, because the next thing you know, Champagne was lying on the bed, legs spread and ready to go.

Zyair laughed. "Aren't you eager?"

"I've been thinking about this all day actually."

I wonder why? Is it because of Sharon? *Zyair wondered as he pushed Champagne's legs apart and bent his head down between her thighs to take in her scent.*

Champagne grabbed his head as she tried to force his face into her pussy, but Zyair resisted. He continued to kiss and nibble on her thighs.

"Stop playing," Champagne told him.

Zyair snickered and placed his tongue on the inside of her labia, running his tongue up and down. He then pressed his chin on the bottom of her pussy, applying pressure. He knew that drove her crazy sometimes. Then he put his tongue as deep inside her pussy as he could.

Champagne's hips started shaking and he knew that his tongue had hit one of her spots. He pressed on the spot with his tongue and then bought the tip of his tongue to her clitoris. Zyair knew that the clitoris had hundreds of nerves so he licked her clitoris from underneath to the tip and back underneath.

Champagne tried to grab his head and pull his mouth off her. *"I don't want to cum yet."*

Zyair wasn't listening. He was in control and he planned on staying in control. He grabbed ahold of her wrist and held on tight until he felt her body begin to buckle. He knew the time was near, so he placed one of his fingers inside her just barely. He moved it in and out and continued to lick.

"I'm about to cum!" Champagne moaned.

Zyair waited until he could feel her juices flowing down his chin. When she finished quivering he looked up at her, smiled and thought to himself, Ain't no need for a woman. Shit, I am the man.

Chapter Forty-five

Follow your gut instinct; you never know where it may lead you. It might take you right where you need to be.

When they pulled into the neighborhood, Alexis couldn't help but wonder how Maya could afford to live in an upscale area on a teacher's salary. Baldwin Estates homes started at three hundred thousand dollars. Alexis looked around and noticed that most of the driveways were empty. She wondered if everyone was out running errands on a Saturday afternoon. Normally that's what she did, especially when it was warm outside. Fall was here and winter was just around the corner. Alexis quickly wondered if she'd have someone to cuddle up with in the winter.

"Damn, your girl must have it going on," Champagne said.

"I know right. I wonder how she does it?"

"Shit, ask her."

"Now you know I don't be all up in people's business like that."

Champagne was looking at the house numbers. "There it is right there." She was pointing straight ahead toward a brick home that from the outside if one had to guess was over 2,500 square feet.

"Damn, her shit looks better than mine," Alexis noted as she parked the car.

"You sure this girl is cool?" Champagne wanted to know, "because you know how women are, especially when they don't know you."

"Girl, don't start with that. That's the problem right there with us women. We talk about one another instead of to one another. We're suspicious on each other instead of being—"

"Oh, Lord, there you go on with your sisterhood, can't we all just get along speech."

Alexis laughed and opened her car door, "Girl, come on."

As they walked up the walkway, Champagne asked her if she'd talked to Thomas lately.

"Yes, we talk briefly almost every other day."

"And?"

"And nothing, we're just friends."

"Well, according to Zyair, he wants to be more."

Changing the subject, Alexis told Champagne what transpired between her and Khalil at the gym.

"He's such an asshole. Don't get caught up in his web again girl."

That was something Alexis didn't have an intention on doing.

It was at that moment that the front door opened. Standing before them was one of the finest, yet thuggish men Alexis had seen in a long time. He was over six feet tall and had on a white T-shirt that fit so you could see every muscle, every cut and some of the packs on his stomach. His hair was in cornrows and his face hairless. His complexion was like chocolate and just as smooth.

"And there she is," he greeted them. "Just the lady I wanted to meet."

He pulled Alexis into him giving her a hug, which caught her by surprise. In the meantime, Champagne was standing there wondering what the hell was going on and who was this fine specimen standing before them.

"And you," he pulled Champagne into his arms giving her a hug as well. "I won't leave you out."

After he finished giving out hugs, he ushered them in.

"I take it you're the brother," Alexis said.

"Gavin," he told her.

"Champagne", Champagne said, "and it's obvious you know that this is Alexis."

Alexis nudged Champagne.

"They're having the meeting in the living room. It's straight ahead. Alexis, I'll speak with you afterward."

Alexis and Champagne watched him walk off. All Champagne could say was, "Wow."

When they entered the living room, all the women looked up. Alexis did a quick count of twelve and that included Maya who was walking up to them. "Everyone this is my coworker, Alexis and . . ." She looked at Champagne, who told them her name. "Alexis and Champagne, this is everyone. Y'all can introduce yourselves."

Everyone went around the room and introduced themselves. Maya noticed a couple of women from work but there were several she didn't know.

Alexis and Champagne listened as Maya proceeded to give a rundown on the procedures for the meeting. She asked Alexis if she had a chance to read the book, *Sister Girls 2* by Angel M. Hunter. The truth was she hadn't had a chance to finish it, with her busy schedule and all.

"I started it but didn't get an opportunity to finish."

"I read all of it," Champagne told them.

Alexis looked at Champagne, "You didn't tell me you finished it."

"Was I supposed to?" Champagne joked.

"When did you have time?"

"I didn't have to make that much time. It was a quick read. I read it in like two days."

"Good, then let's get started," Maya said.

***

An hour and a half later, when they were wrapping up, Alexis was surprised how much she enjoyed the meeting.

It was also obvious that Champagne had enjoyed herself as well because she was standing with a few women on the other side of the room deep in conversation.

Just as Alexis was about to walk up to them, she felt someone tap her on the shoulder.

"Hey beautiful." It was Gavin, Maya's brother. "Come in the kitchen and talk to me."

Alexis looked in Champagne's direction. She wasn't paying her any mind and so Alexis followed Gavin into the kitchen. At first glance he reminded her of Morris Chestnut, chocolate, muscular and intense looking with a pretty-ass smile.

Once inside, he poured himself some orange juice and asked Alexis if she wanted something to drink.

"No, thank you."

"So, my sister told you I wanted to meet you?"

"Yes."

"And you decided to come."

"Yes." *Damn, why is that all I'm saying?*

"Why?"

"Why what?"

"Why did you decide to come?"

What kind of question is that? "Because I had nothing better to do," she told him with a smirk.

"Damn, it's like that?"

"Well, don't ask a question you might not want the answer to."

"Duly noted."

They sat there for a few seconds looking at one another.

"How old are you?" Alexis asked breaking the silence.

"Old enough."

"No, for real."

"Does it matter?"

"Yeah, it matters."

"I'm twenty-nine."

Had Alexis been drinking she would have choked. She turned to walk away.

"Where are you going?"

"I can't go out with you. You're too young for me."

"You're in your thirties right?

"Yeah." She was thirty-two.

"Then what's the big deal? Age ain't nothing but a number and I can do just as much if not more for you than a man twice my age."

"Oh, really?" Alexis was feeling his boldness. She didn't know about this dating a younger man thing. Even though it was only by a few years, she still wasn't feeling it. She felt like younger men had to be tolerated a little more and she didn't have the energy to do that. However, he was so good-looking she was willing to hear him out.

"Let me take you out one time and if you don't enjoy my company then you don't ever have to see me again."

"Oh, there you are." Champagne walked in the kitchen. "You ready?"

Gavin didn't let her answer. "So what's it going to be?"

"Let me get your number and I'll think about it."

He reached in his pocket and pulled out a card. He opened one of the drawers in the kitchen, got a pen and wrote down a number on the back. He handed the card to Alexis. "This is my personal number. Call me with your decision sooner rather than later. I'm not a man that waits around."

"I'll do that."

Once Champagne and Alexis were in the car, Champagne asked what was up with Gavin.

"Nothing. He saw a picture of me and asked Maya to introduce us."

"Damn girl, look at you. Thomas, Shamel, and now Gavin. You're on a roll."

Alexis didn't respond, she was too busy asking herself what the hell was she doing. This wasn't her. Although she was trying to be this bad bitch, did she really want to be that person?

"Just be careful sweetie, because there are some crazy-ass men out there," Champagne told her as she'd told her a time or two before.

"You ain't said nothing but a word."

Chapter Forty-six

A day with someone special can make up for a week of hell.

It was Sunday and Alexis didn't have any plans. All she wanted to do was relax. Maybe finish reading *Sister Girls 2* and go to the movies. It was going to be a day just for her. The past couple of weeks had been hectic. She'd had a few dates, busted one of her students working as a stripper and had to deal with an irate student. She deserved a day of doing nothing.

After grabbing her book and cell phone off the kitchen table, Alexis went and sat on her porch, in her rocking chair. Just as she was getting comfortable, her cell phone rang.

She looked at the caller ID. It was Thomas.

"Hey there."

"What's up beautiful?" Thomas asked.

"Nothing. Just sitting on the porch reading."

"Are you doing anything today?"

"Nope, and I don't plan on doing anything. Today is my day for me."

"Well, you have to eat, let me take you to lunch."

Alexis hesitated because she really didn't intend to leave the house at all. She wondered if he sensed this.

"How about I bring you lunch instead?"

That suggestion perked Alexis right up. "Now that sounds like a good idea," she told him.

"What would you like?"

Alexis had no idea what she wanted so she told him to surprise her.

"What's a good time to come by?"

Yes, today was supposed to be a day by herself but like Thomas said, she had to eat. Alexis looked at her watch. It was just eleven o'clock. "Come around one." That would give her enough time to read a couple of chapters and take a shower.

After hanging up, Alexis gave herself one hour to read. That was hard to do considering her mind kept drifting to Shay. She'd made the decision to go by her apartment. The thing is she didn't want to go alone. Shay lived in "The Grove," which was a bad neighborhood and you just never knew what could happen. The drive to get there was around thirty minutes.

I'll wait and see if she comes to school Monday and if not, I'll have Champagne or someone go with me.

A few chapters and a shower later, Thomas knocked on the screen door.

When Alexis went to let him in, she saw that he was carrying a picnic basket.

"What's this?" she asked as she led him to the kitchen. "We're having a picnic?"

"Yes, right in your kitchen," he told her as he placed the basket on the counter.

"So what's inside?" Alexis was starving.

"Can I have a hug first?"

She gave him one and took in his scent. "You smell good," she complimented. "What is that?"

"It's an oil I bought from some Muslim guy. It's called Blue Nile."

"I like it."

"I'll pick you up some." Thomas opened the basket and pulled out a bottle of Moscato wine.

"I love that wine."

"I know." He knew because he called Champagne and asked her what type of food and wines Alexis liked. He then pulled out some containers.

"Can I look inside?" Alexis asked.

"Of course."

When Alexis opened them, she saw that he'd brought a cucumber, tomato, and cheese salad, with what smelled like sun-dried tomato dressing, some sort of quiche and there were a couple of slices of cake. She took a sniff and could tell immediately that it was her favorite kind, lemon.

"Okay, you need to tell me how you knew that Moscato is my favorite wine along with lemon cake and quiche."

"I have contacts," he told her.

"And do those contacts include someone named Champagne and Zyair?"

Thomas threw up his hands. "You got me."

Alexis was touched that he put this much effort into their lunch date and impressed that he did it in under two hours. She walked around the table and gave him a quick kiss on the lips.

"What was that for?" Thomas asked, pleased that he'd scored some points.

"It's for being thoughtful. You sit down while I set the table."

Thomas looked around and told her, "Your kitchen is so . . . so—"

"So white?" Alexis finished the thought for him. It's something most people commented on when they came over. Her cabinets were white, her floor was white, her refrigerator was white and her accessories were white.

"That and clean. It's so crisp looking, I'd be afraid to cook in here."

Alexis laughed, "Oh, believe me, I cook. Maybe not often enough but when it's just you, there's really no need to, especially when you can just pick stuff up and throw it in the microwave or go out and eat."

"I know just what you mean, I eat out often and I have to tell you, I'd love a home-cooked-meal every now and then, by someone other than myself."

"I'll take that into consideration," Alexis teased. "Sit down," she told him again.

Thomas did just that. He sat and watched as Alexis set the table and made their plates. They made small talk while eating but Thomas could tell something was on Alexis' mind.

"So, what's going on?" Thomas asked.

"Nothing."

"Are you sure?" Thomas wasn't easily fooled.

"Well, actually there is something going on but not with me. It's with two of my students."

"You care to share?"

"Well, one of my students came into my office and asked me to talk to her mom because she believes she's suicidal over a man and the other I found out is a stripper."

"Wow. How did you find out about the one that's a stripper."

Did Alexis really want to tell him about her going with Shamel? She didn't think so. "It doesn't matter, what does matter is that she is and when I confronted her, she walked out on me and hasn't been to school since. I'm concerned. I'm almost thinking about going to her house to see what's up."

"You don't think that's a bit much? The way these teenagers are today, you can't tell them shit, they know more than us."

"I know, but I still feel like I need to do something. The only thing is where she lives is not a welcoming area. It's the hood of all hoods."

"Where does she live?"

"In The Grove."

"Oh, hell no, you will not be going into that neighborhood by yourself. Should you decide to go, I'm going with you."

That was all Alexis needed to hear. "All right, then let's go."

"Today?"

"Why not?" Although the plan was to do nothing, she might as well do something productive and meaningful.

Before Thomas could respond, his cell phone went off. "Excuse me," he told her as he unhooked it from his belt.

"I'll be right back," Alexis told him and walked out of the kitchen to go to the bathroom.

When she was reentering the kitchen, she heard Thomas saying, "I asked you not to call me anymore and I mean that shit," then he hung up.

"Someone stalking you?" Alexis asked.

"It's this female I used to see. She'll call, then she'll stop calling for a while and then it starts up all over again."

"Block her number from your phone," Alexis told him.

Thomas looked at her and frowned.

"What?"

"I don't know why I didn't think of that shit."

"That's what we women are for, to give you men the answers."

Thomas stepped toward Alexis and pulled her into him. "I can't believe I'm finally spending time with you."

"Well, believe it," she told him.

"Can I kiss you?"

"Yes, you can do more than that if you want to."

Thomas stepped back and looked at her.

"Just not today," she teased.

"Girl, don't play with me like that. Shit, I was ready."

"I bet you were. Let me go get my bag and put some shoes on so we can go."

"Go where?"

"The Grove."

Thomas looked at his watch. He didn't think she really meant doing it today. He'd made plans with his boys to play basketball around four

"What? You have other plans?" Alexis asked.

"I did, but I can postpone for you."

"You don't have to do that."

"I want to."

"Damn, you're racking up the points today."

Thomas hoped so. He was trying his damnest to be sensitive, caring, and attentive. This was a new experience for him but hell, he'd do whatever it took to win Alexis over.

Thomas called Zyair and told him to let the others know that either he'd be late getting to the gym or he wasn't going to make it.

"It's going that good?" Zyair asked him. They'd spoken earlier that day when Thomas called to find out what types of food Alexis liked.

"I'm going to run an errand with her."

Zyair thought this was the funniest thing he'd heard in a long time. He could not stop laughing.

"What's so funny?"

"You man, being all domestic and shit."

"Whatever," Thomas told him, and hung up.

A half an hour later they parked in front of the building Alexis had on record for Shay. The appearance of the outside had not changed much. It still looked dingy and worn. The graffiti or tags as some called it were still everywhere.

"You sure you want to get this involved?" Thomas asked.

Alexis' answer was to start walking toward the building. Thomas followed behind her while making sure he was aware of all that was around him. What that consisted of was young wannabe thugs hanging on the corners and on the bench that was in front of the building. It was obvious some of them were drug dealers.

Little did either of them know that right across the street was one of Shamel's boys. He recognized Alexis from when she came to Dreams. Alexis and Thomas were now in the building, looking for apartment 3B. When they found it, Thomas stood close behind her as she knocked on the door.

"Who the fuck is it?" someone on the other side of the door yelled.

Alexis looked at Thomas, who said to her, "What's the girl's name?"

"Shay."

"I said who the fuck is it?" the person yelled again.

"We're looking for Shay," Thomas yelled back.

The door swung open and standing before them was a woman that was drunk as hell. You could smell the liquor coming out of her pores.

"Don't no Shay live here."

"Are you sure?" Alexis asked.

"What the fuck? You think I don't know who lives in my damn house."

"This is the address I have for her miss."

"Well, it's the wrong fucking address," she told them and slammed the door in their faces.

Alexis looked up at Thomas who took her hand. "Come on. Let's get the hell out of here."

When they were walking out of the building, Shamel's boy watched their every movement and he made sure to snap a picture with his cell phone.

When they pulled off, he called Shamel and all he got was a voice mail. He left a message telling him the honey he was with at the strip club was in The Grove with some other dude.

Chapter Forty-seven

People are not who they seem all the time, but they are always who they tell and show you they are.

Shamel was sitting a few houses down from Alexis'. It didn't take much to find out where she lived. He had Michael, the guy who set up the computers in his establishment search her name on the Internet. Not only did Michael find out where she lived but he found out her credit score, her history, who her parents were, and a whole bunch of other shit.

This was not Shamel's style, to be stalking a female. To him, he wasn't stalking her. To stalk a woman was to scare her, to leave her notes, to threaten her. He wasn't doing any of that, he was just staking his claim and trying to find out as much about her as he could. *Was he becoming obsessed with her?* he wondered. Maybe but he had set it in his mind to make her his and for her to be the mother of his children. He'd even dreamed it and as a believer that dreams often had a meaning, he'd decided to put it into action.

A couple of days ago, his boy called him and told him that he saw Alexis in The Grove. Later he showed him a picture that he snapped. When he saw the picture of the dude she was with, he recognized him as that Thomas character.

This motherfucker was getting on his last nerve popping up everywhere. Not only that but Shamel wanted to know what the hell was she doing at The Grove. That used to be his old stomping ground when everything he did was illegal, but since he was now on the up and up, it was his boys' spot.

Shamel also found out some information on Thomas; found out he was a well-known sports agent and not a fuck-up like he was hoping. He was going to have to come up with some sort of plan to get him out of the picture. Shamel wanted Alexis to himself. He was not one to share.

Because he'd been watching her for a few days he learned her schedule and knew that she would be home shortly. He had one of his boys farther down the block waiting for her car to turn the corner and when she was close by, the plan was for him to go set flowers, candy, and a teddy bear on the porch. He would be walking away when she pulled up.

His cell phone beeped, there was a text message from his boy, Now, now, go now. Shamel got out of his car with gifts in hand and placed them on the stairs. He could hear her car pull up into the driveway. He wondered what she was thinking when he turned around and they were looking at one another through the windshield.

What she was thinking was, *What the hell?* Alexis didn't recall telling him where she lived, but just because she didn't recall it doesn't mean she didn't do it.

The thing is she didn't like him showing up uninvited. Something about that didn't sit right with her. Her inner alarm was going off especially since she sensed someone following her. *Should I call the police?* she wondered. But what would they do, she had no evidence that it was Shamel, Thomas or anyone else. All she had was her intuition. Alexis looked at Shamel and noticed he was smiling. He didn't look threatening or like he'd come to do her harm. So she made the decision to trust him and turned off the engine, grabbed her purse off the floor, and climbed out of the car.

Shamel noticed that she did not look happy to see him.

"What are you doing here?" she asked him.

"I thought I'd bring you a gift." He moved to the right and she noticed the flowers, candy, and teddy bear on the porch.

Alexis would not have taken Shamel to do something so sweet and she almost swooned, but first she needed to let him know that she didn't like pop-up visits.

Before she could say a word Shamel told her, "Listen, I apologize for showing up unannounced. I just wanted to surprise you. When we talked the other day you sounded stressed."

Well, he wasn't lying about that, she was stressed. Shay still hadn't come to school. Alexis was starting to feel like she was missing and that concerned her. Victoria also came by her office again asking for her help.

"I have been," she told him as she walked around him to pick up the flowers. Like almost every woman on the face of this earth, she loved receiving flowers. She placed them up to her face and took a sniff. "Although I don't like when people just pop up, because you came bearing gifts, I'm going to allow you to come in."

"Let me." Shamel took the flowers out of her hand, picked up the candy, and the bear while she opened the door and followed her inside.

"How did you find my house? I don't remember telling you."

"You did during one of our conversations," Shamel lied.

Alexis accepted it as the truth because she just might have.

"Have a seat. I'm going to go throw on something more comfortable."

Shamel sat down in the living room and waited for her to return while looking around. He noticed that she liked neutral colors and didn't like clutter. On the coffee table were numerous books that appeared unread. One in particular caught his eye. The title was *The Art of Seduction*. He glanced through it and before he knew it Alexis had returned wearing leggings and a T-shirt.

"You have a nice place here," he told her.

"Thanks. Do you want anything to drink?"

"Like what?"

"Well, I have some wine and cognac."

"Cognac? What are you doing with cognac?" Shamel wondered if it belonged to that Thomas fellow, if he was the one she originally bought it for.

"It's my dad's."

He was glad to hear that, although he hoped it wasn't a lie. "I'll take some cognac."

"I'll be right back," she told him and returned shortly with a glass of wine for her and cognac on ice for him.

She sat next to him.

Shamel picked up *The Art of Seduction*. "Interesting read," he acknowledged.

"I just bought it, I haven't had a chance to read it yet. Actually, I just bought all those books." She handed him his drink.

"So you like to read?"

"I just joined a book club. I'm trying to catch up with them."

Shamel took a sip of his drink, draped his arm around her, and turned to face her. "So, tell me what has you so stressed?"

"Shay."

"Diamond?"

"The one and only. Since that night I busted her at your club, she hasn't been to school."

"I'm still bugging over that fact that she's in high school," Shamel said.

"I even went to her house to talk to her."

"You did? Where does she live?"

"In The Grove."

So that explains why she was there. "Did you go alone?"

"No, a good friend went with me."

He already knew who that good friend was but knew not to push.

"Have you seen her? Has she come back to the club?" Alexis asked.

Actually, she came back the next day and pleaded with him to give her another chance. There was no way in hell he could do that, especially now with Alexis being in his life. "No, I haven't seen her since that night either." Shamel had other uses for Shay. Alexis didn't need to know that. The only person that needed to know was Shay and he let her know that prior to her leaving the club the night after the confrontation.

"I'm really thinking about calling the police and reporting her missing. The apartment I went to, 3B, the drunk-ass woman who answered the door all but cursed me out and said she doesn't live there. I don't know if I believe her."

He was going to remember that number, "3B" and have someone check it out.

Alexis was surprised to see that she had drunk her whole glass of wine. *Damn, did I gulp it?* "I'm going to get another glass of wine. As a matter-of-fact I'll bring the bottle in here."

She wasn't acting like she wanted him to leave and that pleased him. When she came back in the room she was carrying the wine and the cognac. To him, this meant make yourself comfortable.

After she put the bottles down, she picked up the remote control and sat down, while turning the television on.

"So Mr. Shamel, tell me about yourself."

"Haven't I done that already?" After all, they have spoken on the phone numerous times.

"You told me surface stuff. I want to go deeper."

"Let's do this, you ask me a question and I'll ask you one." Shamel wasn't one to tell all his business.

"So, you're into games?" Alexis teased.

With seduction in his voice, he told her, "It depends on what kind of game you're talking about."

"Have you ever been in love?" was her first question.

The only time Shamel could remember being in love was when he was around seventeen. The girl's name was Melena. They broke up when she got pregnant and went against his wishes and aborted the baby. For the first few weeks before she'd made the decision to abort, Shamel thought he was being attentive, but she told him he was smothering her. Smothering her? He asked her how could she say such a thing, after all, he just wanted her to take care of her and the baby. That's not what Melena felt he was doing; she felt that he was crowding her; that he was being controlling. When she woke up, he wanted her to call him. If she didn't by nine o'clock, he'd call her, and then proceed to call her every three to four hours. If he didn't reach her, he'd just pop up. Her parents started to become concerned about him and questioned her. When she revealed that she was pregnant, it was her father who pointed out that if he was acting like he owned her now, how did she think he would act once she had the baby?

When Melena tried to talk to Shamel about it, he lost control and grabbed her and yoked her up. It's when she felt that he could become violent that she decided she could not have the baby. Of course, she didn't tell him of her decision. It's when her mother took her to the clinic that he found out. Little did she know, one of his homeboys was following her. When he figured out where she was going, he called Shamel who barged into the clinic and caused a scene that was so frightening to the other young women that were there, they called the police. Afraid of what he would do to her, Melena's parents placed a restraining order on him and she tried to stay as far away from him as possible.

There was also one other time a few years ago when he was in deep like and lust and what he thought was love with this chick named Lavonne. Now years later he knew that it was the sex that had him bugging out. She put it on him and did things with and to him that no other girl had done up to that point. She licked his ass, swallowed his cum like it was water, and even let him have her anally whenever he wanted to. He was strung out and thought she was too because she was so open to him sexually. It wasn't until she told him that she wanted to see other people that he lost his mind. He beat her so bad that she ended up in the hospital. Because by then, he'd been in trouble with the law and was not about to go to jail, he told her if she told anyone it was him who put her there, he would ruin not only her life, but her brother's, who was a drug runner for him. Of course she didn't tell and after she got out of the hospital she moved and convinced her brother to move with her.

That was an incident he put out of his mind and it was also one he was not going to share.

"Yes," he answered, "I was in love once when I was a teenager."

"What happened?"

"We were young. She got pregnant and had an abortion when I begged her not to."

"So you broke up with her because of that."

"That and other reasons." This was not something Shamel felt comfortable talking about, so he asked her, "What about you, have you ever been in love?"

Alexis was on her third glass of wine. She knew she needed to slow down, but she was not only stressed the hell out but tense as well. She rolled her shoulders and placed her hand on her neck and started to rub.

"Let me do that for you," Shamel volunteered.

Not one to turn down a massage, she did just that.

Shamel stood up, went behind the couch and started rubbing on her shoulders. "So have you?"

For a second there Alexis forgot the question. She really didn't want to go into the whole Khalil thing, but because Shamel was working magic with his hands, she found herself telling him about how they were engaged and she found out he was already married. "Remember the night we first met?" she asked him.

"How could I forget?"

"Well, he was in the club that night."

"Not that Thomas character?"

"No, the other guy."

Shamel recalled all that had happened that night and knew who she was talking about because he'd seen him in his club after that incident.

The longer he massaged her neck and shoulders and the more wine she drank, the more Alexis found herself getting relaxed.

"How come you don't have any kids now?" She'd asked him that question during one of their phone conversations. She was surprised to hear him say no.

"I don't know. After my high school sweetheart got pregnant, it just never happened again." There was an alleged pregnancy but once the baby was born, he had a blood test done only to find out that it wasn't his.

"Let's talk about something else," he told her as he moved his hands down her back.

Alexis closed her eyes, "Well, what do you want to talk about?"

"Let's talk about how you like to be made love to."

She kept her eyes closed and asked him, "Why should I tell you?"

"I'd think you'd want me to know."

"Why is that?"

"Because when we make love, I'll already know your likes and dislikes."

Alexis still had her eyes closed. "So, you think we're going to do it?" she joked.

"Honestly?" Shamel asked growing serious.

Alexis opened her eyes, "Yes, honestly."

"Yes, I do."

Alexis moved his hands off her shoulder and looked up at him. She knew he was right and was considering letting it happen today.

For some reason, she was getting turned on. Was it the wine? Was it his hands? Or was it the situation and his bluntness? Her body was screaming, *Yes, make love to me now,* but her mind was saying, *Slow down, you're getting out of hand.*

In the past her mind would have won out, but the past was no more, this was the new aggressive Alexis. The Alexis that wanted to do what the hell she wanted to and not be afraid. The Alexis who if she wanted to sleep with one, two or three men, she could do so. She didn't give a damn what or how anyone else thought, said or felt.

"Come sit next to me," Alexis told him. She'd made up her mind about sleeping with him, but she wanted to be as honest with him as possible. She didn't want him to think that their getting physical meant she was his exclusively. She didn't want to mislead anyone.

"What's up?" Shamel was aware that her mood had shifted slightly.

"If we decide to make love, it doesn't mean we are a couple." Alexis decided to be blunt with it, to keep it as real as possible.

That's what you think, Shamel thought to himself but said out loud, "I'm not a young kid. I know sex does not equal a relationship." After his experience with Lavonne, with other women and with him being thirty-five, he wasn't slow. He was intelligent enough to know this but it wasn't going to stop him from pursuing Alexis.

"I'm just letting you know because I'm not ready to be in anything serious. I want to date, I want to be free to be me and do me. I don't want to have to answer to anyone and you really need to know that."

Shamel put his finger against her lips. "Shhhh, we're not kids. I think we can handle whatever comes our way."

He moved in closer and waited for her to move closer before he initiated a kiss.

"Do you have any condoms with you?" Alexis asked.

"They're in my wallet in the car. Don't move, I'll go get them and I'll be right back."

"I'll go freshen up while you run out."

Shamel stood up, "Don't change your mind," he said it as though he were joking, but he wasn't, he was serious as hell.

Once Alexis heard the door close, she ran to her room and picked up the phone. She dialed Champagne's number. She wanted someone to talk some sense into her because she knew she was out of control, but she wasn't having any luck with this phone call.

She put the phone back down and went into her bathroom. She stood in front of the mirror and stared at herself. Do you really know what you're doing? Do you really know what you're getting yourself into?" she wondered out loud. "Well, it's too late to back out now."

"Alexis?" Shamel called out. He'd just walked back in the house.

"I'll be out in a second," she called out.

"How about I come to you?"

For a reason that she couldn't explain even to herself, she didn't want to invite him into her bedroom, which was odd because she was inviting him into her body. "No, I'll be right out. Make yourself comfortable."

He was doing just that. He took off his shoes and relaxed onto the couch, but not before he poured himself a shot of cognac and downed it.

"Hey there," Alexis said as she walked into the room this time wearing short-shorts and a camisole.

To have sex this time of day was different for Shamel. It was early evening and sexually he was a night man. When he went out to his car to get the condoms, he popped one of his "just in case" pills. The pill that promised to keep your dick hard longer than usual. Not that he needed it, but for Alexis he wanted to put it down and let her know he was a man of stamina.

Shamel patted his lap and Alexis took the hint and sat there. She must have had a look on her face because he asked her, "What's wrong, are you nervous?"

She was just that because getting with someone new was always nerve wrecking. "Shut up and kiss me," she told him.

He was more than happy to oblige. Alexis turned to straddle him, her breasts touching his chest. He had his hands on her ass and pulled her pelvis into him, so she could feel how hard he was.

Alexis knew she needed to slow this whole process down, but she couldn't. She was too turned on. She started to grind up against him as they kissed deeper. Shamel moved his hands from her ass to her breasts. He started sucking on her nipples through her shirt.

"Take it off me," she told him.

Once it was off, he placed his mouth on her nipples again and nibbled, a little too hard. She pulled away, stood up and pulled off her shorts. He stood up, took the condoms out of his pocket, pulled his shirt over his head and his pants down as Alexis watched.

She couldn't help but notice the thickness of his dick and the slight curve. It wasn't long but the way it was shaped, she knew that if he knew how to work it, pleasure wasn't too far behind.

"Sit back down," she told him as she waited for him to put the condom on.

He did as she demanded and waited for her to straddle him. She held her pussy lips open with her hands as she lowered herself onto him, taking it all in. Alexis was shocked when Thomas' face flashed before her. She shook her head from side to side to get the image of him out.

Stay in the moment, she told herself. *Stay in the moment.*

Once he was deep inside her, he placed his hands on her hips and told her, "Don't move, stay right there." He started moving his hips in circles, going deeper and deeper inside her, so deep that she pulled back.

"Where are you going?" he asked, holding her steady.

Finally he moved his hands and let her control the movement. He filled her up as she moved up and down and rocked back and forth while touching her clitoris.

"I want to cum with you inside me," she told him and cum she did at the same time as Shamel.

***

It was close to midnight when Shamel left Alexis' house. While they were making love, her cell phone had rung a number of times and she'd ignored it. It was now time to see just who was trying so hard to reach her.

Alexis climbed out of the guest bed, where they ended up making love and walked into the living room. Her cell phone was on the floor next to the lounger, which was odd because she could have sworn she'd left it in the kitchen. Then again, she did drink a whole bottle of wine by herself.

Alexis looked at the caller ID and saw that Champagne and an unknown caller had phoned numerous times.

"A shower, I need a shower," she said out loud. On her way to the bathroom, she thought about Shamel and his lovemaking skills. As far as fore-play was concerned he definitely wasn't Thomas, but he didn't lack in the pleasure department either.

Champagne left a couple of messages saying, "Call me back. I saw that you had called. Where are you? What's going on? Okay now I'm starting to worry."

Alexis dialed Champagne's number. The phone was picked up on the first ring.

"Girl, it's after midnight and you're just now calling me back. Where the hell have you been?"

Alexis almost told her but for some reason stopped. "I was out and about, doing what I do."

"What does that mean?"

Alexis laughed. "Girl, I don't know, it's something kids say all the time. I went and ran some errands and then came home and fell asleep. I didn't mean to make you worry."

"Well, you did."

"I apologize."

Alexis heard Champagne yawn. "You go back to bed. Let's talk tomorrow."

Not one to argue, Champagne said, "Okay."

Zyair, whose back was facing Champagne, turned over and asked, "Is everything all right?"

"Yeah, it was Alexis."

"Oh, okay."

"Something is going on with her," Champagne said.

"Oh, here you go with that shit again."

Champagne nudged him, "What shit?"

She didn't even have to ask, because she knew what shit he was talking about. He was talking about her being up in Alexis' business but shit, if she wasn't she'd still be with that married asshole Khalil.

Zyair gave her a look that said, "do you really have to ask." He then turned back over. "Let that girl live her life how she sees fit, Champagne, you can't keep interfering."

"I'm not interfering. I'm being concerned."

If she wanted to mistake the whole thing about her investigating Khalil with being concerned instead of interfering, he'd let her, so he didn't say a word because he knew better.

Chapter Forty-eight

Everyone that comes to your door should not be welcomed in.

Thomas was sitting across from his secretary, Lisa, giving her instructions on what needed to be done for the gathering he was having. It was something he did every year for his clients to show his appreciation and for morale.

"Please make sure the caterer is there on time."

"I know, I know," Lisa told him. They went through this every year. He'd repeat himself over and over and Lisa would just sit and nod her head or say I know, I know.

"Oh, and close the door behind you. I'm not to be disturbed for a couple of hours." Thomas had some contracts he needed to review before discussing them with his clients. Prior to him getting settled, he wanted to call Alexis and see what was up with her. Before he even had a chance to do that, Lisa came running into his office.

"Didn't I tell you I don't want to be disturbed?"

"You did Thomas but the car attendant called and said someone damaged your car."

Thomas was out of his seat in less than a second. His car was his baby and one of his favorite vehicles. It was a midnight-black Jaguar and it was one of his pride and joys. He spent a great deal of money on getting it suped-up.

Thomas brushed past Lisa who decided to follow behind him to see what was going on. He was so focused that he didn't say a word. Once in the hallway, Thomas hit the elevator button and didn't give it any time to hit his floor. He decided to take the stairs. It was only six flights and with the shape he was in he'd get there sooner. That's where Lisa drew the line though. She and stairs did not get along.

Once Thomas entered the parking garage, he could hear his car alarm going off. *What the fuck happened?*

When he finally reached his car, all he could do was stand there with his hands on his head, like it was about to explode. He looked around to spot the attendant, Jimmy, who was nowhere in sight. Instead some young boy who didn't look over twenty was standing there watching him, looking scared as hell in an attendant's shirt.

"Who the fuck are you?" Thomas was so angry he was trembling.

"I'm Sean the new attendant?" The boy answered with fear in his eyes and fake bravado.

"How old are you?" Thomas couldn't believe the garage was hiring kids to look after his shit.

"Eighteen."

"Where the fuck is Jimmy?" Thomas asked, looking around.

"He's on vacation."

Thomas started pacing. "Vacation? Vacation? I don't believe this shit. You didn't see this happen?"

The boy opened his mouth to speak but Thomas cut him off. "You didn't see this shit happening? Where were you when it was happening?"

By now Thomas was up in the boy's face, who kept backing up.

"I . . . I . . . I–"

"You what? Do you know how much this car cost?"

Thomas walked around the car touching it. The windows were broken out and there were several dents on each side of the car as though someone kept hitting it with a bat.

"Where were you?"

Sean felt Thomas' anger and knew there was no way he could tell this man where he was and that he was getting his dick sucked.

Sean was sitting in the booth, chilling and thanking God for this easy-ass job. He'd just gotten fired from a fast food joint because he cursed out one of the customers. He had his music playing, his feet up and was considering smoking some weed, wondering if he could get away with it when this cherry red Benz with tinted windows pulled up. The driver rolled the window down and it was the finest female Sean had seen in a long time. He was ready to spit his best game.

"What's up beautiful?" he asked as he tried to see who was on the passenger's side. He didn't have to try too hard because the other female who was just as fine as the first leaned over and said, "Hey handsome, can we park in here for a little while?"

"It's twenty-five dollars."

"What if we don't have it?"

Everything in him wanted to just tell them to go ahead but he didn't want to lose this job as well.

"Listen," the driver said, "I have to run inside this building for a brief meeting. If you let us park for free my girl here will take care of you.

Sean could not believe what he was hearing, shit like this never happened to him. There had to be a catch to it but he couldn't stop himself from wondering just what would she be willing to do.

"How about give you the best head in town."

The next thing Sean knew the girl was climbing out the car. Not only was she fine, but she had some big ass titties too.

"Come on, let's go in your booth."

Sean led the way and the driver pulled off.

They went inside the booth where Sean sat down on the chair and the girl got on her knees.

"You're really going to do this?" Sean could not believe his luck, his boys would not believe this shit.

"Yes, now shut up."

Sean prayed in his head that no one would show up to park.

She pulled his pants down and knowing that she wasn't going to have that much time because they came there to do a favor for a friend, she immediately started sucking his dick. She moved her tongue back and forth over the head of it and she went up and down his shaft. She placed her right hand on the base and as she moved her hand up she squeezed and she did the same thing as she moved down, while making sure her mouth was moist.

She could tell he was enjoying it because he grabbed the back of her head and kept saying over and over, "I don't believe this shit, I don't believe this shit. I'm going to cum soon. I'm going to come soon."

It was a good thing to, because less than a second later she heard a car alarm going off and she knew her job was just about done.

She started sucking faster and squeezing harder and right when she could tell that he was going to explode she moved her mouth and grabbed the towel she saw on the counter to catch his cum.

By the time he caught his breath and got himself together the car was pulling up.

"Somebody's alarm is going off," the female who was driving said as the other one got in the car and waved.

Before he could get a number or say anything more they drove off.

It was after they pulled off that he went to check on the car to see whose parking spot it was. When he saw how busted up it was and while he waited for Thomas and the police, he knew his ass was fired from yet another job.

"Where were you?" Thomas asked again.

"I was in the bathroom."

Thomas looked him up and down and noticed his zipper was down.

"Zip up your fucking pants and call the cops."

Sean zipped up his pants and told him, "The police are already on their way."

While Thomas waited for the police to arrive, he called Zyair up to tell him what happened.

"And you mean to tell me the attendant didn't see a thing or see anyone come in and out?" Zyair wanted to know.

"He claims he was in the bathroom."

"What about cameras?"

Thomas hadn't thought about that but you best believe he was going to do his own investigating. If he had to go around and ask every street hustler he knew that's what he was going to do. Between him, the cops, a private investigator, and the street, he would find out who did this shit.

Chapter Forty-nine

Charity can come in many forms;
two of them are time and money.

How she put herself in this position, she didn't know. Maybe it was because Victoria kept coming to her. Maybe it was because she was cutting classes and when Alexis asked her why, she told her she had to go home and check on her mother. Or maybe it was in the plan all along and she just wasn't listening. Nonetheless, here she was a week later pulling up in front of Victoria's house with her in the passenger's seat.

Neither of them said a word. What was there to say? Alexis couldn't make any promises. She couldn't say I'm going to save your mother's life and she couldn't make a guarantee to Victoria that everything would be all right.

Once the car was parked and the engine off, Victoria reached over and took Alexis' hand. "You don't know how much I appreciate this. It means a lot to me."

Alexis moved her hand. "That's okay sweetie."

"And I'm sorry I called you a bitch."

Alexis looked at her. "You should be."

When they got to the porch, Victoria took out her key and unlocked the door. She peeked inside first to see if the house was a mess. It wasn't, so she opened the door wider and stepped through with Alexis following behind her.

"Ma!" she called out.

She didn't get any response. "Ma!" she called out again with panic setting in.

"Girl, what the hell are you yelling for? I was in my room."

The woman walking toward them didn't look suicidal to Alexis. As a matter-of-fact she looked saner than Alexis felt sometimes. Her hair was cut short; almost pixie style and she looked to be in her twenties, although Alexis knew they were around the same age. Alexis also noticed that she was very attractive. Her skin was flawless, her breasts had to be a D-cup, and she had ass for days.

Victoria was standing in front of her mother with her mouth wide open. She was expecting her mother to look unkempt.

Her mother placed her hand under her chin. "Close your damn mouth girl, and who is this?" She nodded toward Alexis.

"I'm Alexis, the school therapist."

"I'm Shondell, Vicky's mom." She looked at Victoria. "What the hell have you done?"

"Actually Ma, I brought her here for you."

"For me? Girl, ain't nothing wrong with me. I was just going through a little something and now I'm over it. Shit, I'm past that motherfucker. Well, I'll be past him when I fuck up his life and take all his money when he finds out I'm having his baby. When he realizes that this good ass. . . ."

The more Shondell spoke, the more Alexis realized that her initial impression of sanity may have been incorrect.

"Maybe I should leave," Alexis said.

Shondell grabbed her arm. "You don't have to leave. I haven't had company in weeks. It'll be nice to have some company."

Alexis looked at Victoria who was mouthing the word, "Please."

"Come on. Let me get you something to drink."

Alexis followed her into the kitchen.

Victoria wasn't far behind. As they walked down the hall, she noticed that her mom must have been cleaning all day. When she left for school that day, the house was a mess. But now, nothing was out of place, the floors had been swept and even had the appearance of being waxed or mopped. No dishes were anywhere, not even in the dish strainer. There was even the smell of Pinesol about the house. Maybe she was getting better. Normally when Victoria came home, she'd have to put some order to the house.

When they stepped in the kitchen, Alexis noticed pictures on the table ripped up. Shondell walked over to the refrigerator and took out a gallon of water.

"You know, I loved that man with all my heart, with my everything and he just used me. Fucked me all he wanted to and then all of a sudden he's telling me he don't want me no more. Me!" Shondell put the gallon of water on the counter. "Okay, maybe just maybe, I should have listened when he told me he wasn't ready for a relationship, but he sure acted like he was."

Alexis looked over at Victoria who was just sitting there taking it all in with a look of pity.

Shondell went on. "You see that's what men do, use you and I got tired of being used. I was like, is this it? Is this what I have to live for? I was ready to go hurt that motherfucker but then this morning after my baby. . . ." She stood up and walked over to Victoria and kissed her on the cheek. "This morning when my precious baby left for school, it hit me. I have her to live for and I have this baby inside of me to live for and you best believe that motherfucker will pay some child support."

Shondell walked over to the table, forgetting all about the water she was supposed to be pouring. She picked up one of the pictures that wasn't cut yet. "Yeah, and it's going to be a pretty baby too."

When Shondell flashed the picture in front of Alexis she could have sworn . . . *No, it couldn't be.*

Alexis put her hand out. "Can I see the picture?"

Shondell handed it to her. When Alexis looked at the picture she couldn't believe it. The motherfucker this crazy-ass woman was talking about was Thomas. He was looking good as usual. He was standing by himself, distracted, as though he was unaware that there was a picture being taken.

Chapter Fifty

Sometimes things get worse before they get better, just hold on and learn the lesson.

"You've got to be kidding me?" Zyair said.

"Man, I wish I was. That young motherfucker was getting his dick sucked while my car was being vandalized. What's real crazy is that my car was the only one damaged which basically means I was targeted, that this whole thing was a set-up. Even when we tried to look at the video, I couldn't see shit. It's like the motherfuckers had their backs turned the whole time. Whoever did this had obviously been to the garage and knew where the cameras were located."

"Who would do some shit like that?"

"I don't know. Even when the police pulled the video and tried to enhance it, we couldn't make out faces and there was no license plate on the car."

"And it was two women?"

"Yeah." Thomas slammed his hand down on the table. They were in his den. "I still can't believe this shit."

"You see man, I told you not to be fucking with those money-hungry females you meet at the games and shit."

Thomas looked at him like that was the last thing he wanted to hear. He pulled out a chair and sat down.

Zyair stepped to the side of him and placed his hand on Thomas' shoulder. "Come on, get up and get ready for your party."

Thomas shook his head. "I don't even feel like having that shit."

"And that's what whoever did this wants. They want to fuck up your day. Shit man, a car is a material thing, you can always get. . . ."

Zyair knew when he'd said enough by the way Thomas looked up at him. "All right, all right, I'll shut up, but know this man, I got your back."

"I know you do."

They gave each other daps.

"But damn," Thomas said, "I wish I knew who it was."

"You need to figure that shit out later. Right now, you need to get ready for tonight."

Thomas stood up and looked at his watch. "You know what, you're right. Let me go get ready for tonight and I'll deal with this shit tomorrow." He knew it was easier said than done, but he had a houseful coming and needed to be prepared.

They half hugged one another and Thomas walked Zyair to the front door. "Don't be late."

"Tell that to the little lady," Zyair said, talking about Champagne. "Shit, you know how women are."

That Thomas did.

"Did you invite Alexis?" Zyair asked.

"You know it. At least that's something to look forward to."

"All right man, I'm out."

Once Zyair was gone, Thomas went to make a couple of phone calls. He'd had his car towed before coming home and needed to let his insurance company know what happened. He also needed to get a referral for an investigator to find out who fucked up his car.

Thomas knew that Zyair was right when he talked about his past choices of women. He usually picked the ones that were out for a party. The ones that just wanted to have a good time, sex, and money. Yes, he knew that most of them were all about the dollar. That didn't really bother him much because money came and went. If a few hundred dollars meant less of a headache, than so be it.

He went into his room and pulled out his phone book and his photo album. He went through them both trying to decide which one of these women were out to get him. This one female, named Shondell, he'd dealt with some time ago had taken to calling him, cursing him out and leaving obscene messages on his phone. He wondered if it was her. He doubted it because he could tell she was all talk. However, one could never be sure. He was going to have someone pay her a visit. Better yet, he was going to pay her one himself.

Chapter Fifty-one

Just ask a person what you want to know; don't assume they know what to tell you.

Champagne was on the phone with Alexis when Zyair walked through the door.

"Are you serious," she asked, motioning for Zyair to come sit next to her.

"Yeah, what do you think? I had the picture in my hand."

"Are you sure it was Thomas in the picture, Alexis?"

"Didn't I just tell you that?"

When Zyair heard Thomas' name, he mouthed, "What? What?"

Champagne put up her hand and told him to calm down.

"Are you going to his party tonight?" Champagne asked.

"Hell no!"

Even Zyair heard that through the phone.

"Well, I think you should go. You need to tell him what you saw and ask him what's up."

Zyair looked at Champagne and waited patiently for her to get off the phone.

"Listen," Champagne told Alexis, "Zyair just came in and we have to get ready."

"Don't say anything to him about this," Alexis told her. "I want to talk to Thomas first."

Champagne lied and said, "Okay, but you need to handle this as soon as possible and not wait around. You know like I know, you care for him more than you want to admit. And for all you know, that chick could be straight lying."

"I know, just don't say anything to Zyair."

Champagne didn't respond because she knew the second she was off the phone, she was going to tell Zyair.

"What's going on?" Zyair asked the second they hung up.

"Does the name Shondell ring a bell?"

"Shondell? Shondell?" He repeated the name, knowing that it sounded familiar, but he couldn't place the face. "I don't know babe, it sounds familiar. What does this have to do with Thomas?"

"Supposedly, she's pregnant with Thomas' child."

Zyair stood up. "Who told you that shit? Ain't nobody having his baby. He would have told me some shit like that." That was not something Thomas would keep to himself and if Zyair was sure of anything, this would be it.

Thomas always talked about how he wanted children and if he was about to become a father, Zyair would be the first to know because he would be the godfather. "How did Alexis hear about this?"

Champagne went on to tell Zyair about Victoria coming to Alexis and asking her for help. She then told him what took place when she got to Victoria's house.

Zyair just shook his head. "Damn! Thomas is having a bad-ass fucking night." He looked at his watch. "Come on. Let's get dressed and I'll fill you in on what happened to him earlier."

Alexis was sitting on her bed feeling all emotional and shit. She was stuck somewhere between anger, disappointment and jealousy. Anger because she felt played once again, disappointment because she really thought Thomas was trying to change and jealousy over actually seeing one of the women he was dealing with. She didn't expect to feel that way at all. *Does this mean I care more than I want to admit? Does this mean I'm falling for him? What about Shamel? Why would I sleep with him if I have feelings for Thomas?*

"Shit!" Alexis said out loud. Her emotions were starting to become confusing. The last thing she wanted to do was develop more than friendly feelings for Thomas. What she thought she wanted from him was to be friends with benefits. Could it be that she wanted more?

"Call him, talk to him," Champagne told her. "There are two sides to every story."

Alexis would do just that after she calmed down and got ahold of her emotions. What she wanted to do right now was lie down and get some sleep. She was mentally drained.

On the nightstand next to the bed was the *Sister Girls 2* book, she was almost finished reading. She reached over and picked it up because she recalled putting Gavin's card inside. She pulled it out and looked at it.

You know that boy is too young for you, she told herself. Alexis was not into young boys but she had to admit he was charming and maybe he'd help her get her mind off Thomas.

Alexis looked at the card. "Damn, why he gotta be under thirty?"

She decided to call him anyway, after all, what's a three to four year difference?

Chapter Fifty-two

Ask who when meeting, ask what beforehand and ask why when you're doing it.

He was kissing her between her thighs, running his tongue up the insides, stopping short of just where she wanted him to be.

"Why are you stopping?" Alexis asked him.

He didn't answer her. He just continued to let his tongue travel in circles on her thighs. As his tongue got closer and closer to her spot, Alexis started thrusting her hips toward his mouth, but he'd pull away.

"Stop playing," Alexis told him while feeling her vaginal walls clench and tremble. He'd been playing with her for over ten minutes and she was ready for him to either bring her to an orgasm with his mouth or get inside her, but he wasn't paying her any mind when she told him to stop.

His whole focus was on what he was doing. Suddenly, she felt his tongue on her clitoris, flicking back and forth.

Gavin surprised the hell out of Alexis. She didn't think he'd have skills like this, but he proved her wrong. Before she knew it, his fingers started to go inside her, first one and then another. He then climbed on top of her body and replaced his fingers with what she'd been waiting on, his dick.

"Wait," she stopped him. "Do you have a condom on?"

He pulled out so she could see that he did.

Damn, he's slick as hell. Alexis didn't even know when he'd put it on. She placed her hands on his buttocks and pushed him deep inside her.

"Put your legs up," he told her.

She bent her legs up until her knees were pressing against her chest. She closed her eyes and felt him even more as he lifted up and entered her. Their bodies slammed together repeatedly until she felt him stiffen and look in her eyes. He didn't even have to say it, she knew he was coming, she could feel him pulsating.

It was now official; she was a whore. She'd slept with three men in less than a month, something she never would have done before. If someone else had done it, she'd probably talk about them.

"What I am is in control," she said out loud.

Gavin turned over and yawned, "What did you say?" He asked with his eyes closed, taking in the moment.

"Oh, nothing," Alexis said.

He opened his eyes and said, "Yes, you did, you said something about control."

Alexis threw the covers back. "Are you hungry, you want something to eat?"

She wanted him to say no, to just leave, but she didn't want to be the one to initiate it.

"And she cooks too."

Alexis just looked at him. Obviously she was going to have to help him along with leaving. She'd do so right after a quick breakfast.

"Are you going to serve me breakfast in bed?" he asked.

Alexis gave him the "you have lost all your mind" look and Gavin got the message because he started climbing out of bed.

"Can I have a towel and wash rag?"

"Look in the hallway in the linen closet. It's near the bathroom. There's also an extra toothbrush in there." Alexis threw on a robe and went into the kitchen to make a quick breakfast.

As she was cooking she tried to recall how the conversation went from "Hey, I was hoping you'd call" to him eating her pussy, to him being inside her.

Damn, was his game that good? The obvious answer was yes.

"Hey beautiful." Gavin was standing in front of her looking like he was dipped in fudge. All he had on were his jeans. They were hanging slightly off his hips, not low like the youngsters but low enough where she found herself asking, "Aren't you uncomfortable without drawers on?"

Gavin just laughed. Before she could stop him, he was up on her hugging her from behind.

"Stop," she said playfully, while slapping his hands away. "Let's eat."

"What did you make?"

"Vegetable omelets."

"What, no meat?" Gavin couldn't imagine a breakfast without bacon or sausage.

"I don't eat meat."

They took their plates off the counter. Alexis grabbed two water bottles out of the refrigerator, handed him one and they sat down across from one another.

Alexis found that she couldn't look him in the eye. Suddenly she was embarrassed. Damn, how was she going to be a woman of the world if she couldn't handle what she was doing and what she was becoming.

"What's going on Alexis?"

She looked up at him. "Huh?"

"What's going on?"

"Why do you think something is going in?"

"You won't look at me. Are you regretting last night?"

"I . . . I. . . ." What was she going to say? *This is not me, this is not something I do often, sleep with a man on a first date. I've only done it a couple of times.* Hell, his being here in her home wasn't even a date, what it was, was a booty call. "This is not something I do often," she went ahead and told him anyway. "I'm not a whore."

Gavin took a sip of his water and sat back in his chair with his arms crossed. He looked her in the eyes, "I didn't think you were."

"How could you not? I call you to talk and next thing you know I'm asking you to come over and we're going at it like two horny teenagers."

When she said that, he laughed.

"What's so funny?" she wanted to know.

"Nothing."

"Then why are you laughing?"

"Because you're serious." He sat up in his chair and told her, "Sweetie, you need to relax. We are both adults and what happened, happened. Why dwell on it?"

Alexis decided she'd do just that, move on; pretend it wasn't a big deal. At least she had enough sense to use a condom.

After they finished eating, Alexis stood up, picked up their dishes and put them in the sink. "I have a lot to do today."

"Are you putting me out?" Gavin asked. Before she could answer he told her, "That's okay, I know you need to think."

She turned and looked at him. She started to say something but he stopped her by stepping to her and kissing her on the lips.

"Don't say another word, just know that next Sunday, I'm picking you up and we're going somewhere fun."

She wanted to protest, but the word fun was something she hadn't heard in a while and it sounded like something she needed at this exact moment.

Ten minutes later, Alexis was standing on the porch watching him get in his Navigator and pull off. She looked down the street and noticed a car with someone sitting behind the wheel. The windows were slightly tinted, so she couldn't see inside the way she would have wanted to, but she could have sworn they were looking her way. She put her hands up to her eyes to shield the sun and to see better but it didn't help.

Girl, you are seriously bugging, ain't nobody watching you. You just have a secret admirer, that's all. She tried to convince herself.

But someone was and he'd been paid to do it. He picked up the cell phone and dialed a number. He listened to it ring.

"Did she stay in last night?" the voice on the other end asked.

"Yes, but she wasn't alone."

There was a slight hesitation, then, "Find out who she was with."

It wasn't with Thomas that was for sure, because last night he'd been arrested.

Chapter Fifty-three

If you doubt it, ask. If you don't believe, do research. Take only your word.

Alexis was about to get in the shower, when she turned on the television. She was about to turn around when she saw a familiar face and that face belonged to Thomas.

What the hell? She picked up the remote and turned the volume up.

The newscaster was saying, "Thomas Wade, the agent for several well-known athletes was arrested early this morning around three a.m. for solicitation of minors."

Alexis dropped down on her bed staring at the television. *What the hell is going on?*

The newscaster went on, "The police received an anonymous tip that Mr. Thomas was having a gathering at his house and underage call girls were present when they arrived. They found several underage girls drinking, partying, and soliciting."

At that point, Alexis stopped listening. She was in shock. As she looked around for her phone, she heard it ring. It was under the bed. Alexis bent down to pick up the phone. She didn't even bother to look at the ID.

"So, your boy was locked up last night?" It was Shamel.

Not catching the tone in his voice, she said, "I know. I can't believe this. It can't be true. There must be some kind of mistake."

This was not what Shamel wanted to hear, he wanted to hear outrage and disgust. "How do you know it's not true? Shit, you never know what someone is capable of."

She knew he was right but her gut told her in this instance something was off. Even though Thomas was a known womanizer, she knew that he could get almost any woman he wanted. He didn't have to succumb to dating woman that were too young.

What Shamel was saying, Alexis wasn't trying to hear. She needed to get off the phone and find out what the hell was going on.

"Listen Shamel, I don't have time for this. Let me call you back."

"Call me back?" Shamel looked at the phone. He couldn't believe this shit. He wanted to go off, but he quickly pulled it together and asked, "Can we get together later?"

The last thing Alexis wanted to do was get together. "Not today."

"How about Sunday? We can go to brunch."

Alexis, unable to hold it in told him, "Shamel, I want to find out what happened with Thomas. Please let me call you back."

Shamel didn't respond. He just hung up.

Alexis then dialed Champagne's number, which was busy. *How the hell can a phone be busy when there is call waiting?* She hung up and tried again. This time it went to voice mail.

"Champagne, call me. I just saw the news. What's going on?" She hung up and sat on her bed. She looked at the ceiling and said a silent prayer for Thomas while wondering, what had he gotten himself into. She refused to believe even for a minute that he knew these girls were minors.

While Alexis was wondering what the hell was going on, Thomas was sitting in a cell wondering the same thing.

The gathering had started like all the other gatherings he'd had in the past. Him at the door, greeting people, Zyair mingling, making people feel at home, his assistant making sure she kept up with who came with whom so she could send out thank you cards, which was always important in the business he was in.

On the guest list were several well-known athletes, and quite a few up and coming athletes who were looking for new or better representation. Some came alone and some brought their wives.

There was also a list of women that were invited to these types of functions. It was a secret list that only a few agents had and only a few knew about. These women were high class, sexy, and fine. They knew how to entertain and make a man feel special. They knew how to make him feel like he was the only person in the room. They knew how to stroke a man's ego.

Everyone was on the bottom floor spread out between the dining area, the conversation room and the game room which had two pool tables and some old school video games like *Pac-Man*.

A couple of the women had just come in and asked him if they could get in the pool and the Jacuzzi.

He'd told them yes but not to let things get too carried away. He then gave one of the security men the look which meant, "Watch their asses."

Thomas was walking behind the bar when the bartender told him, "I'll make your drink, that's what you're paying me for."

"Nah, I've got it," he told him. He needed to do something other than talk to occupy himself and to keep from noticing that Alexis hadn't arrived. They needed to talk. He'd tried calling her several times but hadn't gotten an answer. Zyair had informed him earlier that Shondell somehow had gotten to her and fed her some bullshit.

Out of all the women from his past for Alexis to run into, she ran into the craziest one out there.

Shondell was the craziest and the freakiest. She could suck dick for hours, fuck for hours, and take it in every hole on her body. For a second there, Thomas thought he was in love with her. Until she started calling him all hours of the night, insisting he tell her where he was, and who he was with. That shit got old real quick and he had to let her go. Initially, she still continued to call and he wouldn't give her the time of day. It wasn't until he told her if she didn't stop calling he'd get a restraining order on her, that she finally stopped but not before cursing him out.

When Thomas first met Shondell he never would have taken her to be a crazy one. As a matter-of-fact, his first impression was of someone that was sophisticated and had her head on her shoulders.

She ran game on him like it wasn't anything. Obviously she knew he grew up in a foster home. That would not have been too hard to find out being that his clients are high profile and he'd given a few interviews himself. She talked about how she was raised by a lady she called her aunt, when the woman was really just a friend of her mother. Her mother was a schizophrenic who had lived in a mental facility since Shondell was a child. Knowing what it's like to grow up without parents, Thomas felt for her and after learning that she herself was a single parent he started to provide by giving her money here and there.

So between the sex she was giving him, which up until that time had been the best he'd experienced and his feeling like her hero, he got caught up. It's when she became sort of a stalker that he had to let her go. He hadn't heard from her in over three months when he ran into her at a night club. She was looking good as hell. Some kind of way; it may have been because of all the liquor he'd consumed, he ended up at a hotel and that night the sex was out of this world.

The second they walked through the door, she was on him, damn near ripping his shirt off his back. He had to tell her to hold up. She took a step back and looked at him while licking her lips. "Don't you miss having your dick in this mouth?"

That he did.

Then she had the nerves to turn around, pull up her dress, bend over and show him she wasn't wearing any panties. "What about this ass? Don't you miss having that dick in this ass?"

That he did.

Before he knew it, his pants were down and he was stepping to her. His mind was saying, "Thomas, what are you doing? Thomas, stop this nonsense right now. You know her ass is crazy." But his dick was saying something entirely different. His dick was saying, "Go for it."

When she started wiggling her ass, he knew that was just what he was going to do. He was holding his dick and rubbing it on the crack of her ass while she held her cheeks apart. He was teasing her. As much as he wanted to go there right at the moment, there was no way he would do that without a condom.

"Dip it in my pussy," she begged.

He wasn't ready to do that yet and especially not without a condom.

"I thought you wanted it in your ass." That was where he wanted to put it.

"I want it there too." She pushed two fingers inside her pussy and pulled them out and rubbed her clitoris.

Thomas reached into his back pocket and pulled out a condom. He'd taken to carrying them everywhere he went, just in case.

He bit it open, threw the wrapper down, and placed it on his dick. Once it was on, he dipped his dick in her pussy and pulled it out while sliding it down the crack of her ass. He then put just a tiny bit of his dick in her ass, causing her to wind her hips around, allowing her to open up wider and he'd pull out and dip it back inside her.

"Oh, you're trying to play with me? Is that what you're doing?"

Thomas pulled his dick all the way out and this time slammed it inside her pussy. They hadn't even gotten to the bed yet, she was bent over a table.

"Oh, fuck!" she cried out. "Fuck my ass like that."

And he would because he knew she could take it. He knew she would take whatever he gave her like a champ and want more.

He pulled his dick out of her pussy slammed it in once again and pulled it out real slow. He entered again until he had just the head in. He took one of his fingers and started playing with her asshole, circling it, dipping his finger in and out, he kept the tip of his dick in her pussy, moving slightly as he opened up her ass more and more with his finger.

Shondell was moaning and moaning. She was loving every minute of it. "Damn, I'm glad I ran into your ass," she told him. "Come on and give it to me."

This was the shit that got him in trouble with her before. She could talk shit and back it up, but she was also mental.

At that moment, he knew he needed to hurry up and do what he came to do so he could get the hell out. He pulled his dick out and opened another condom and put it on, threw the old one down and placed his dick on her asshole and pushed it in causing her to scream out.

"You knew it was coming baby, don't scream,'" he told her. "Take it, take it like you want it."

Take it she did. She pounded back on his dick like it was in her pussy, while rubbing on her clitoris and rubbing on his balls. Once he was all the way in and she could feel his balls on her ass, she started to grind.

"Give it to me," she demanded. "Give it all to me."

Thomas did just that. Before he knew it, his body started trembling.

Shondell started bucking even harder and ruined the moment talking about "I love you Thomas, I love you so much."

The second he came inside the condom, he took it off and held it in one hand, pulled his pants up with the other and walked to the toilet to flush it down. When he came out of the bathroom, Shondell was sitting on the edge of the bed totally naked.

"Come on, we're not done yet."

That I love you shit threw his game off and he was ready to go.

Thomas made the mistake of looking at his watch and that set her off. "Oh, so now you're ready to leave? You done fucked me all up in the ass and got your nut and you're ready to go. That's fucked up Thomas."

It was and he knew it.

"The least you can do is let me get mine and I promise I won't bother you again. All that love shit I said was in the moment. I'm over your ass. I just want your dick."

Thomas said the only thing he could think of to say, "I don't know if I could get hard again."

"I know how to make it happen."

Then Thomas and his weak ass allowed her to pull his pants down once again and suck on his balls.

"I only had two condoms," he told her.

"Don't worry about that I got it covered."

She reached over, opened her purse, pulled out a condom, opened it, and put it on him.

"We can do this real fast. Just fuck me hard, while I play with my clit."

He did as requested and it was over before it started, with both of them exploding with him inside her.

"Your work is not done," she told him while taking the condom and heading toward the bathroom. Normally he would have been the one to take control of the used condom. Working with athletes had taught him a valuable lesson. He'd heard one too many stories. But this time he slacked off. It wasn't until the next day when he replayed the scene in his mind that he realized what he'd done. All he could do at that point was hope she wouldn't do anything stupid.

That was the last time he saw her or heard from her until recently, when she started calling, hanging up or breathing into the phone once again.

When Zyair arrived a few minutes before everyone else with Champagne in tow giving him the evil eye, he had to know why.

"Man, that psycho chick you used to mess with knows Alexis and told her she was having your baby."

"What? Who?"

"Shondell."

"What! Where's Champagne, let me talk to her."

"Nah man, she went to the ladies room and I promised her I wouldn't say anything."

"Now why would you promise some stupid shit like that?"

"Because I want some pussy tonight."

Thomas just looked at him. He had to get in touch with Alexis and soon.

After calling Alexis for the fifth time and accepting she wasn't going to call him back or come to the gathering, he gave up. He needed to mingle with the guests. He'd visit her tomorrow unannounced. She was going to talk to his ass.

However, that wasn't what was in the cards for him.

For the past forty-five minutes, Thomas had been in his office talking to a potential client when he realized how late it was. It was almost two a.m. and he was ready to start sending people home. Any other time, it would have been over by now but he'd been so preoccupied with his thoughts and trying to conduct business that the time flew by.

The second Thomas arrived from the back office, his front door burst open with men in uniforms following.

"What the. . . ." Everyone stopped in their tracks to see what the hell was going on.

One of the officers stepped up. "Thomas Wade? We're here for Mr. Wade."

Everyone turned to face Thomas who had stepped up. "What is it Officer?"

"Are you Thomas—"

"Yes, yes, I am."

"And this is your residence?"

At this point Thomas' attorney stepped up. "Excuse me Officer. I'm his attorney and I would like to know what's going on."

Several of the officers by now had dispersed and were moving throughout the house. The officer who was speaking pulled out a search warrant.

"We have reason to believe that there are minors under the influence at this residence and that they are here soliciting." He waved his hands around to indicate the numerous men who were standing and watching what was taking place.

Thomas laughed at this. "I can assure you gentlemen that all the ladies here are of age."

From behind Thomas, he heard women fussing and talking about, "Get your hands off me. What do you want? I want my lawyer."

Thomas turned around to see what the ruckus was about and was shocked to see some women he didn't even know. Not only didn't he know them, but he had no idea who let these women into his home.

He took a step forward toward the girls. "Who the hell are you?"

One of the girls popped the gum she was chewing. "You know who the hell we are. You sent for us."

"All right, all right," one of the officers said.

"Oh, hell no. I don't know any of you. Who the fuck let these girls up in my house?"

No one answered. He looked at the girls again. If you looked hard enough and were experienced enough to see under the makeup, it was obvious these girls were either just eighteen or slightly under.

"You are under arrest. . . ." and so the story went.

So here Thomas sat, wondering just like Alexis "What the fuck was going on and who the hell would set him up like this?"

Chapter Fifty-four

Sometimes there is nothing you can do but wait.

Alexis hung up the phone. She'd just spoken to Champagne, who had informed her that Thomas' attorney was working on getting him out of the holding cell. It might not happen until Monday, depending on if they could find a judge.

"Fuck!" Today was Sunday, the day she'd told Gavin she would go out with him. That was the last thing she felt like doing but Champagne told her maybe it would be the best thing to get her mind off what was happening with Thomas.

Shamel tried to call her numerous times but she just let the phone go to voice mail. She had some other shit she was trying to deal with and he wasn't a priority.

Alexis went into her bathroom and turned on the bath water. She sat on the edge of the tub and questioned what she was doing. Alexis had contemplated calling Gavin all day and canceling their date. She would have if she hadn't misplaced the card with his cell phone number and she forgot to save it on her cell phone.

She wanted to stay home and find out what was going on with Thomas but Champagne already said there was no more information to give. *I kind of do want to go on this date. Shit, it ain't like I can concentrate on anything anyway.*

Alexis settled down in the tub, letting Calgon take her away.

Across town Gavin was finishing up a conference call at one of his shops. He was looking forward to this date since earlier this week.

Dating older women never made Gavin nervous. Successful older women were more his preference. They were more secure in themselves, comfortable in their bodies, and less likely to beg. They also had fewer inhibitions.

That night when she'd called him up, he was surprised. He was almost positive that he wouldn't hear from her after he gave her his number, but thankfully he was wrong.

Tonight he planned on taking her to Dave and Busters, a game lounge for adults and kids. He wanted to do something fun and different, to show her that life did not have to be so serious all the time. But first he told her to meet him next door at the bar called Honeys. On Sundays they had open mic and he had a treat in store for her.

A few hours later Alexis was walking into Honeys. The plan was for them to meet inside. On her way there, Gavin was kind enough to call and let her know that he would be running a few minutes late and that he'd left her name with the hostess.

Alexis had never been there before. That might have been because this whole hanging out thing was new to her. When she stepped through the door, she noticed that the crowd seemed to be professionals in their midtwenties and early thirties.

When Alexis gave her name at the door, the hostess smiled and stated, "We were expecting you."

She then led her to a table that was in the center of the floor with the best view of the stage.

As she took her seat she noticed that the people at the surrounding tables were looking her way and whispering. It made her self-conscious. She stopped a waitress and asked her, "Do I have something hanging from my skirt? Why are these people staring at me?"

The waitress laughed and told her, "They're trying to figure out who you are because that table is usually reserved for celebrities."

Alexis felt a little uncomfortable with all the stares and hoped that Gavin would hurry and join her.

"Would you like a drink or an appetizer?" the waitress asked.

"As a matter-of-fact, I'd like a Mojito."

The waitress nodded and walked away.

Alexis turned her attention to the stage where a band was setting up. *I wonder if Thomas is okay. I hope no one is doing anything to him. Okay girl, get him out of your head, you are here waiting on another man.*

Speaking of the other man, Alexis looked at her watch and wondered when he'd be there. He said a few minutes late it was now more like fifteen, damn near twenty.

The waitress returned with her drink. She placed it on the table. Alexis went to reach for her purse which she sat on the chair next to her, but the waitress stopped her and said, "Oh, no sweetie, it's taken care of."

"By who?" She looked around to see if another man was looking her way.

The waitress tapped her on the shoulder and pointed to the stage where Gavin was standing with a white rose and looking directly at her.

"I'd like to sing this song for the sexiest girl in the club."

"Who me handsome?" a voice yelled out in the crowd. Everyone started laughing.

"You too but I'm talking about that lady sitting right there." He looked directly at Alexis, which made everyone look her way.

He will not embarrass me this way.

That's just what he did when he started singing "Sweet Lady."

Oh my God, that's my song. How could he know that? Alexis closed her eyes and pretended that Tyrese was up on that stage singing to her, although Gavin wasn't too far from it.

I think I can worry about Thomas later.

Once the song was over Gavin stepped off the stage and walked over to the table. She stood up and they hugged.

"You like?" Gavin asked.

"I loved," Alexis told him and she did. "I've never had anyone sing to me like that before."

"I'm glad I was the first."

Gavin pulled out her chair. "Finish your drink and then we're going next door."

"Next door?" The only thing she saw next door was Dave and Busters and that was a game room.

"Yes, next door."

"To Dave and Busters?"

She must have been frowning because he told her, "Don't knock it until you try it. Watch, you'll have fun, you're with me."

Alexis wasn't really into arcade games but shit, she was willing it give it a try. Who knew, she just might have a good time.

After finishing their drinks and listening to the band play, Gavin stood up. "Are you ready?"

"Don't you have to pay?"

"It's on my tab."

Alexis smiled. "So, you have a tab here? You come here that often?"

"Nah, one of my boys owns the place."

"Well, good for him," she said while smiling.

"What's got you smiling?"

"It's just good to see black men succeeding."

Gavin knew where she was coming from because there was a time when he didn't think he'd make it out of the streets. He thought he would be a hustler for life, but fortunately after a four-year bid in prison, he wanted more for himself. He had stashed his drug money with an old girlfriend he could trust, someone that wouldn't do him dirty. When he was released, he did the right thing, cut her off a nice chunk and opened his first detail shop. Initially, only the other hustlers were his clients but he hired this smart female, who told him to offer specials to businesses and their employees. Once he did that, it was on and business started booming so much so that he had to open another and another and another.

They were walking through the door of Dave and Busters and since this was her first time here, she asked Gavin if they could walk around first.

"It's your night; we can do whatever you want to do."

As they walked around Alexis found herself feeling like a kid.

Eventually, she became overwhelmed because she didn't know where to start. "So, what do you want to try first?" she asked him.

"How about basketball?"

To basketball they went.

For over an hour, they played games. Come to find out, Alexis was more competitive than she realized. She even won a couple of small prizes.

Gavin watched her with amusement. It was obvious she was enjoying herself. Gavin asked her, "Do you want to get something to eat, grab a drink, or play pool? It's on you."

"Let's order something light and play a little pool."

As they were walking to the dining area, Alexis felt someone tap her on the shoulder.

She turned around and no one was there. "Mmm, I could have sworn I felt someone tap me on the shoulder."

"Maybe someone bumped into you and you thought it was a tap."

Alexis knew what a tap felt like. She turned around and scanned the crowd, trying to see if there was someone she knew on the premises.

They found a table, sat down, called the waitress over, and ordered appetizers and drinks. Alexis stuck with her Mojito, while Gavin ordered Hennessey.

Alexis just happened to glance at the television and on the screen was Thomas. Gavin must have been talking to her and she'd tuned him out because he touched her hand.

"Earth to Alexis."

She shook her head. "I apologize, I was watching the news."

Gavin turned around and glanced up at the television that was behind him. The commentator was talking about athletes and performers seeing underage girls and the kind of example they were setting.

"Why are you so into what they're saying?"

"Because one of the people they're talking about is a good friend of mine."

"Who? Thomas?"

Alexis was surprised to hear him say Thomas' name. "Yeah, how did you know?"

"I didn't, I was just guessing. Plus, he's from around here. As a matter-of-fact, he and I sponsored a few little league teams together. He's a decent guy."

Alexis didn't know what to say because all she was thinking was, *This is a small-ass world.*

"So, are you dating him?" Gavin wasn't one to beat around the bush. He wanted to know where he stood with her, if he even had a real chance.

Alexis didn't lie. "We've seen each other a few times."

Gavin knew what that meant. He knew because of the way her eyes looked and her body shifted when she said it.

"Are you two serious?"

Alexis looked him dead on then and told him, "If we were I wouldn't be here with you."

Gavin, relieved, raised his glass and said, "I'll drink to that."

The waitress came with their food and as they ate, they talked about themselves, how they grew up and where they saw themselves in the near future.

"I used to be holy and sanctified," Alexis told him when they got on the subject of religion.

"Get the hell out of here." Gavin just could not see it because when he thought of holy and sanctified, he thought of women in long dresses, no makeup, no jewelry, shouting in the aisles. "What happened, did you backslide?" he joked.

"I don't really know what happened. It's like all of a sudden I started living my life in a different way and started slipping away from the church."

"Do you not go at all now?"

"I haven't been. Sometimes I wonder if it'll make that much of a difference in my life if I did. Because honestly, when I was going, I wasn't that happy."

"Well, are you happy now?"

That was a question Alexis was really going to have to think about. There were moments when she was content. She thought she was happy when she was with Khalil and now, well, she was just going through the motions.

Before she got a chance to respond, the waitress approached with another drink.

"I didn't order that," Alexis told her.

"I was told to deliver it to your table by the gentleman over . . ." She turned to identify the person who sent the drink. "Where is he?"

Gavin turned to look in the direction she was looking in. He wanted to see who the hell was disrespecting him but no one was there.

"What did he look like?" Alexis asked.

"Tall, slim, brown-skinned."

Alexis and Gavin waited on a better description and she gave them none.

"Is that it?" Alexis asked.

"Well, that's all I could remember."

"Well, shit," Alexis said, "that's half the black men in here."

Gavin picked the drink up off the table and told her to take it back. Alexis didn't even stop him because she agreed.

Standing up, Alexis told him, "I'm ready to go."

"So soon?"

"I don't feel comfortable now."

Gavin told the waitress to bring the bill.

"Do you want to do anything else, go anywhere else?"

"No, I just want to go home."

The waitress returned, Gavin looked at the bill, pulled some cash out of his pocket and gave some to the waitress. "Keep the tip." He placed his hand on Alexis' arm. "What's going on?"

"I don't know Gavin. I hope I'm not being paranoid, but I think someone is watching me, that I'm being followed."

They were heading toward the door. "What? Are you sure?"

"No, I'm not sure. It's just a feeling."

"Is there anyone that has something against you, that's angry with you?"

"Not enough to stalk me."

"Do you want me to stay with you tonight?"

"No, I'm going to call my girl Champagne and see if she'll stop by."

"Well, I'm going to follow you home."

When they were standing in front of his car, Alexis turned around and kissed him on the mouth gently. "Thanks for showing me a good time."

Gavin took her hand and told her, "If you need me I'm here for you, as your friend or as whatever you want me to be."

Damn, this young boy not only has all the right moves but he knows just what to say as well.

Alexis climbed into her car and drove off with Gavin following close behind.

Chapter Fifty-five

Know when to go, know when to stop, and know when to pause.

Shamel was pacing the floor and his boys were watching him.

"Yo man, what's with all the pacing."

He looked at them. It was Big Tone, Ronnie, and True. He wondered how much he should tell them. Should he tell them he thought he was in love with Alexis? Should he tell them how far he was willing to go to get her?

Fuck it, they were his boys, if they said some wild shit and got out of hand, he'd just punch them in the fucking mouth.

"Yo, I think Alexis is the one. I'm considering making her my woman."

"Who? That chick you had Ronnie watching? The one who had that other ni—"

Shamel cut Big Tone off. "Yeah, man, that's the one."

Big Tone, his main homie, who was sitting down, jumped up and said, "Oh, hell no, are you serious man? What happened to players for life? What happened to getting all the pussy you can?"

"Yeah, man," True interrupted, "she must have put it on you."

Ronnie knew better than to open his mouth, so he just stood there. After all, Shamel paid his bills and he knew not to fuck with the man in charge.

"Ronnie, True, leave me and Big Tone alone."

True stood still, acting like he didn't want to move.

"Yo, I said step."

True turned and walked out of the room behind Ronnie.

Once they were out of the room, Big Tone asked, "What's up with your boy?" He was talking about True.

"He wants me to let him manage a club."

"So he's acting like a little bitch because of it?"

"Yeah, I guess so."

"You know you're going to have to handle that shit."

"Yeah, I know and I will, but that's not what I wanted to talk about."

"What you wanna talk about, this chick you got Ronnie following? What's up with that, man? Ain't no honey worth all the trouble."

Big Tone was Shamel's homeboy from childhood and he knew he could tell him anything. They went as far back as diapers.

"Yo dog, I guess I should have told you that I've been getting tired of this player shit. Ever since I spent the holidays with my family, I've been feeling like there's a void in my life. I want some little Shamels running around."

"Well, you can have that without getting serious with someone."

"I know, but I don't want to do it that way."

Big Tone, who was once married and vowed never to entertain that shit ever again saw that his boy was serious and decided that he would not clown him, but support his decision. "Man, if that's how you feel. You know me and my selfish ass. I felt that we were going to grow old banging pussy, smoking weed, and running these clubs."

"I'll still be doing that, but I'll have my main girl at home waiting for me."

Big Tone laughed at this because although Shamel spoke of change, he didn't think he was really ready for commitment.

There was a knock on the door.

"Speak!" Shamel yelled.

"It's me Shamel."

"That's shorty?" Big Tone asked. Obviously he recognized the voice.

"Yeah," Shamel answered.

"I thought you weren't dealing with her anymore."

"I'm not."

"Come on Shamel, let me in!" the voice yelled through the door.

Big Tone looked at Shamel who gave him the nod yes.

Big Tone went to the door and opened it. "What's up Diamond?"

"Hey Tone, what's going up?" she responded while looking at Shamel the whole time.

"I guess I'll leave you two alone." He walked out and closed the door behind him.

"What should I call you? Diamond or Shay?" Shamel asked.

"You can call me whatever you want."

"How about an underage liar?"

Shay stepped up to Shamel and wrapped her arms around his waist. "You mean to tell me, you honestly didn't know I was underage?"

He pushed her back. "Bitch, I ain't R. Kelly."

Shay dropped her arms. "Why I gotta be all that? Why I gotta be a bitch?"

Shamel turned and walked away from her. He went and sat behind his desk. He knew she didn't really expect an answer. "Why are you working here if you're still in school, what's up with your home life?"

Shay dropped her eyes and told him, "I don't have a home life."

"What, are you telling me you're homeless?"

Shay didn't answer him.

"How come you haven't been to school?"

"What are you, my father?"

Shamel didn't even bother answering.

"What the hell I got to go to school for? I need to make a living. What, you fucking Ms. Houston now? You don't want me anymore because of her old ass."

Shamel narrowed his eyes and told her, "Don't go there and who I'm fucking doesn't concern you."

Shay walked behind Shamel's desk and sat in front of him. She was wearing a jean mini-shirt with a yellow formfitting T-shirt. She opened her legs and he wasn't shocked to see she didn't have any panties on.

"You mean to tell me you're going to give up this sweet, young pussy for hers?"

"Close your damn legs girl. I got business I need to take care of."

Shay didn't listen. She placed her hand on her pussy. "Look at it Shamel." She put her finger inside and pulled it out. "You know you want to."

He looked and his dick got hard immediately.

"What are you gonna do about it?" Shay was teasing him. "What are you gonna do about this tight young pussy?"

Shamel didn't say a word. He just stood up, unzipped his pants, pulled out his dick, pushed her back, and shoved it in her pussy. Even knowing she was underage, he couldn't stop himself.

"Yeah, that's what I'm talking about. Fuck me Shamel."

Shamel placed his hand on her throat, "Shut up!" He continued to ram inside her pussy, making his dick go as deep as it possibly could. If he could have gone through her he would have. "Shit!" he called out as he pulled his dick out and came on her thighs.

"I knew you wanted this pussy."

Shamel pulled open the top drawer on his desk and pulled out a box of tissues. "Here, wipe off and let's talk."

Shay climbed off the desk and did as she was told.

Shamel fixed his clothes, looked at her and said, "I have something I need you to do for me."

"What am I going to get in return?" She wasn't doing shit for free, especially since he fired her ass.

"Don't worry about that. Just know that I'll take care of you."

"All right, what is it you want me to do?"

"It involves Alexis," he told her.

Shay rolled her eyes and said, "I should have known."

"I want you to go back to school."

"Back to school? For what?"

"Because you need your education."

Shay laughed out loud about that one. "You know damn well you don't give a damn about my education."

"I need you to do this so that no one's on my back about you. I don't want the police called and shit."

"Why would someone call the cops on me? I ain't nobody."

Shamel knew now was the time to throw on the charm. He touched her face and said, "That's where you're wrong. You mean more to me than all these hoes I got working up in here."

"Then how come I can't keep working here?"

"Because I want bigger and better things for you. I want you to work in my office, help me with my books and shit."

Shay may have been naïve when it came to him, but she wasn't that naïve. "So basically, you want to keep fucking me and make good with Ms. Alexis so you can fuck her too?"

Shamel was fed up with her asking questions, so he walked around her to the door, opened it and told her, "Get the fuck out and don't come back."

Shay didn't want to leave. She wanted Shamel any way she could have him and if that meant going back to school, she would but it would only be for a short while.

"All right, all right Shamel, I'll do it but remember you said you would take care of me."

He closed the door, "Come and give daddy a kiss."

Shay walked over to him slowly and wrapped her arms around him, "I love you Shamel. I'll do anything for you. You know that, right?"

Shamel could care less. He didn't want to hear those words from her, a high school student. He wanted to hear them from a grown-ass woman; a woman named Alexis.

Chapter Fifty-six

***Why be afraid of the Unknown? You
won't know if it's your cup of tea
unless you try it.***

Alexis waved to Gavin as she walked through
her door. He followed her home just as he said he
would. She didn't invite him in.

She pulled her cell phone out of her purse and
sat down on the couch. She dialed Champagne's
number.

"Hello?"

Alexis could hear people talking in the background. "Hey, where are you?"

"At a get-together."

Alexis was about to ask her, how could she be
at a get-together while Thomas was locked up, but
then again, Thomas wasn't Champagne's man,
Zyair was. *What am I so upset about? I don't go
with Thomas, we're not exclusive. There's no
reason for me to care so deeply.* Alexis tried to
convince herself, but she knew she wasn't fooling
anyone but herself. She found herself on more

than a few occasions wondering what Thomas was doing, who he was with, and if he was thinking about her.

"Why? What's up?" Champagne asked.

Alexis opened her mouth to speak but no words came out, instead she started crying.

"Are you crying?" Champagne asked once she heard a sniffle.

"No, no. I'm okay. It's just that . . ."

"Just what sweetie, talk to me."

"I . . ." She didn't know what she wanted. She didn't want to ask Champagne to leave where she was at having a good time and come sit with her miserable ass.

"Come where I'm at," Champagne said.

"Nah, I don't want to rain on your parade."

"Girl, come on. It'll take your mind off of whatever it's on and as you know there's nothing like girlfriends getting together. Plus I have someone I want you to meet."

Alexis looked around her empty house, then at her watch. It was still early and she didn't feel like being alone, so why not. Maybe the company of women was just what she needed.

"All right, where are you?"

After Champagne gave her the address, Alexis picked up her purse and opened her door. Before stepping out, she looked up and down the street to make sure there wasn't a car parked anywhere with someone sitting in it watching her. She was relieved to find that there wasn't.

Twenty minutes later, Alexis pulled up to the address Champagne gave her, parked and called Champagne on her cell phone. "I'm outside."

Less than ten seconds later Champagne was walking out the door, waving her in.

"So, whose house is this?" Alexis asked.

"Sharon's."

"Who's Sharon?"

"The girl I was telling you about."

"What. . . ." Alexis didn't even have to finish her sentence because it hit her, it was "the girl". "The lesbian?" Alexis whispered.

"Shhhh. Come on in and meet her. She's having a get-together."

Alexis followed her inside and prayed to herself that she wouldn't be uncomfortable or feel out of place. She'd never purposely hung around a group of gay women and wondered if anyone would try to come on to her.

When they entered the home, Alexis felt welcomed immediately. Some of the women in attendance approached her with hugs and introduced themselves.

"I'm Sharon," one of the most attractive women there said. "Make yourself at home. Any friend of Champagne's is a friend of mine."

"Thank you." Alexis followed her into the living room where over twenty women were gathered drinking wine and having a heated conversation.

"Does Zyair know you're here?" Alexis whispered.

"I'm here as a friend not a lover and all he needs to know is that I'm getting together with a group of women."

"She's very attractive." Alexis was talking about Sharon.

"Don't I know it."

Alexis just stood there and took it all in. She didn't even notice when Champagne walked off with Sharon.

"Hey, don't I know you from somewhere?" a voice whispered in Alexis' ear. She turned around to see who it was. It was a woman named Lana who helped her when she was out one night having a drink by herself.

Alexis knew she'd had one too many drinks but she didn't feel drunk, therefore she figured it was okay to drive home. Out of the bar she walked, but the second she stepped out the door, she felt herself stumble.

"Uh oh, maybe I am a little tipsy," she said out loud. "This is not a good thing." She felt on her shoulder for her purse and realized it wasn't there.

Just when panic was starting to set in, she heard someone yelling, "Ms., you left your purse."

Alexis turned around. "Oh my God, thank you. I was just about to panic."

"I tried to catch up with you before you walked out the door."

Alexis couldn't believe her luck. "Damn, I can't believe you actually ran out here after me."

"There are still good people in this world."

"I see that."

"I'm Lana," she told Alexis as she handed her the purse.

"Alexis." Before she could get another word out of her mouth, she felt herself heave.

Lana took a step back. "Are you okay?"

Alexis shook her head and ran a couple of steps down the sidewalk. She stopped and threw up. Embarrassed out of her mind, she turned around to see Lana looking at her.

"Want me to get you some water or something?" Lana asked.

"You would really do that?"

"Sure." Lana turned around and started walking in the direction of the bar door but she stopped and looked at Alexis. "Maybe you should come with me into the ladies room."

Alexis followed and was basically taken care of. Lana helped her clean herself up and sat around and talked to her until she felt well enough to drive home.

"Oh, hey. How are you?"

"I'm good, how are you?"

Alexis wondered how long they were going to stand there and say, "Hey, how are you?" So she was honest and said, "Shit, I've had better days."

"Anything I can do about it?"

"Do you always help strangers?" Alexis asked.

"Well, you're not a stranger anymore. So, again, is there anything I can help you with?"

There really wasn't, so what could Alexis say other than, "No thank you."

Alexis looked around the room and wondered if everyone was gay. Was she the only one in the room that slept with men?

"Who are you here with?" Alexis asked Lana.

"I'm a friend of Sharon's."

At the mention of Sharon, Alexis looked up for Champagne and noticed they were both gone. *I wonder where they went, are they making love?* After having that thought, she was surprised to find herself feeling a tinge of jealousy. *What the hell?*

"I'll be right back. I have to go to the bathroom." Alexis left her standing there and went to look for Champagne.

As she made her way to the back, supposedly in search of the bathroom, she peeked into a room that was empty. *For all I know they could be outside.* It was then she heard voices and if she wasn't mistaken, one of them was Champagne's.

The bathroom was next to the room where the voices were coming from. *I wonder if I can hear what they are saying if I go into the bathroom?* As it turned out she could. Not only could she hear what was being said but there was a door that connected to the other room.

Alexis made sure the bathroom door was locked and she cracked open the other door, hoping they wouldn't hear. If she got busted, she'd make up some kind of excuse. Whether it was believable or not, she'd deal with that when the time came.

"I can't see you in that capacity," Champagne was saying.

"Are we going to go through this again?" Sharon said. She stood in front of Champagne and pulled her to her so that their pelvises were touching.

"Go through what?" Champagne asked.

"Go through the whole I can't see you thing. You know you want to."

"I'm getting married," Champagne told her although she and Zyair still had not set a date. But there was no reason to tell Sharon that.

Alexis watched as Sharon kissed Champagne on the neck. *What the hell, am I becoming a voyeur? I wonder if Champagne is going to put up a fight?*

She didn't have to wonder because Champagne didn't. She closed her eyes and moaned instead.

"Come on, let me fuck you Champagne, let me do to you what your man does." Sharon then placed her hand on Champagne's pussy.

"You have company. You need to go entertain your company."

Alexis couldn't hear what Champagne said because there was a knock on the bathroom door. She had to quietly close the adjoining door.

After flushing the toilet and turning the water on in the sink, she said, "Just a minute." She looked in the mirror and found that her face was flushed. She took a deep breath, opened the door and walked out, letting the other person in.

When she entered the living room, Champagne was coming from the back and headed straight for her. She couldn't even look her in the eye.

Once she was up on her she said, "Let me follow you home, I need to talk."

Alexis looked at her friend who was obviously torn between her love for Zyair and her lust for this Sharon character and told her, "As do I."

They quickly said their good-byes to everyone and were on their way out the door when the female who assisted Alexis that night came up to them with a piece of paper in her hand.

She handed it Alexis, winked and told her, "Call me."

Alexis took it without saying a word.

When they arrived at Alexis' house, she was exhausted. It had been a long and draining day. It hit her the second they walked in. The last thing she felt like doing was having a conversation and it seemed like that was the last thing Champagne felt like doing as well.

"Girl, I'm tired. You mind if I stay in the guest room."

Thankfully, Alexis changed the sheets each time she slept in there with someone. "Where's Zyair?"

"I called him on my way here. He's at the courthouse. They finally got a judge to sign papers to have Thomas released."

"What the hell happened, Champagne?"

"I know what didn't happen and that's that Thomas was as surprised as anyone that those women were underage. He was surprised they were even there."

"You think he'll see me tomorrow?"

"I'm sure he will."

They were standing in the hall heading to separate rooms when Champagne asked, "Oh, how was your date with the young dude?"

Alexis smiled and told her, "It was really nice. I'll tell you about it in the morning."

"All right, love you."

"Love you too."

When Alexis walked in her room, she sat on her bed and thought about what she'd witnessed between Champagne and Sharon. She thought about how wet it made her and how fast her heart began to beat. She knew that she would have watched everything had something more gone down and if there wasn't a knock on the bathroom door.

Damn, was her curiosity getting the best of her? Would her openness and willingness to be this new sexual being allow her to sleep with a female? Was it something she could actually go through with?

Alexis fell asleep with these thoughts and perhaps that explains her having the dream she had, the dream about Lana entering her with a dildo.

"Come on, try it, you just might like it."

Alexis looked at her with the double-sided dildo in her hand. She wondered what she was going to do with that thing. So she threw up both her hands.

"Okay, you need to slow it down. I'm not ready for that. Heck, I thought there was more romance to this whole lesbian thing. You're acting like a man that just wants a slam bam thank you ma'am sex session."

Lana smiled at her and said, "My bad. I just wanted to get it started before you changed your mind. In the past, it has been my experience that you first timers are less likely to stop once I penetrate you with the dildo, but I'm sorry, lie back."

Alexis lay back and Lana started to kiss her. In one smooth motion, they went from kissing to Lana pressing Alexis' breasts together and sucking on both nipples.

Lana started to go lower and kissed Alexis from her breast to her belly button. She was giving every nook and cranny of Alexis' body attention, whereas, some men couldn't care less.

Before Alexis could catch her breath from the tender kisses, she felt Lana's cold tongue run the length of her vagina.

She placed her whole mouth over Alexis' clitoris and started to lick and suck and lick and suck. Alexis' body started to react to every stroke of her tongue.

Before she knew it, Lana had placed a finger inside her vagina and was sucking on her clitoris and working her finger in and out. Just as Alexis started bucking her hips, Lana stopped and reached for a double-sided dildo. She gently rubbed it up and down the lips of her vagina until she finally slid it in.

Alexis felt like she was going to cum immediately.

She heard Lana whisper, "Don't cum yet. Hold it. I want to cum with you." Lana lay so that her pussy was facing Alexis' and she put the other end of the dildo inside herself.

They both started playing with their clitoris until they exploded at the same time.

When Alexis woke up the next morning, her pussy was sticky and all she could do was smile, because she remembered every detail of the dream.

Even though she smiled, she speculated on the meaning of the dream. What did it mean, if anything? Was the dream because of what Champagne was going through, was the dream because she was around a bunch of gay women or was she starting to get curious as well?

Chapter Fifty-seven

Know your enemies as well as you know your friends. Know what motivates them to despise you so.

Zyair and Elliot Hart, Thomas' attorney, waited on Thomas to come from the back where the possessions he carried with him when he was locked up were being held. It had been a long-ass night and a half for him and he couldn't wait to get home to take a hot-ass bath. Being in a cell was not something he wanted to experience ever again. It was cold, it was dark, and there was a damp old smell to it that he knew was clinging to his body.

When he walked into the front of the county jail, he was surprised not to see any press. There sure was enough of it when he was getting arrested and when he was brought in but now that a brother was released, they were nowhere in sight.

Zyair and Elliot appeared to be in deep conversation when Thomas saw them waiting. Hopefully they were doing what he had been doing all night and that's trying to figure out who the hell was out to get his ass.

"I'm a free man!" he said by way of greeting.

Zyair was the first to stand up and give him a brotherly hug. "What's up man? You okay? No one bothered you in there, did they?"

Thomas shook his head and laughed. "Damn man, you're acting like I was in prison and shit. I was in a holding cell."

"You do know you're going to have to do damage control to keep your reputation, perhaps put out a statement and give an interview," his attorney stated.

"Yeah, but that shouldn't be a problem. People know me and they know that underage shit wasn't my doing."

"I didn't think it was," his attorney said. Although one could never be sure what a person was or wasn't capable of. This was one case where he had no doubt because when the ladies arrived Thomas was nowhere to be found, and when they were questioned all they said was they were invited to the party. They claimed not to know the name of the person that called them.

"Sir," one of the officers said, "We need you to fill out some papers."

"Man, I'll meet you out front," Thomas told Zyair while he and Elliot went to sign release papers.

Once done and standing outside, Elliot told Thomas, "We'll talk later."

"I'll call you tomorrow." Thomas needed the day to think.

"Let's make it before then."

"Let's not." A bath, some rest, and an errand were the only things on his mind.

All Elliot could do was agree. After all, he worked for Thomas not the other way around.

Once in the car, Zyair asked Thomas, "What the fuck is going on with you? Be honest with me man. Did you fuck with someone's wife or fuck someone over?"

"If I did, you would be the first to know. Not only that but messing with another's man property, those days are long gone. You know I'm trying to make an honest man out of myself."

"Well, it's obvious someone is out to get you, first the car and now this."

"You think I don't know that? You think I didn't run down the list of people I know and have done business with?"

"What about that female who told Alexis she was pregnant by you? Shondell?"

"Nah, man. I don't think she has the kind of contacts for some shit like this, but you best believe I will either be stopping by her crib or giving her lying ass a call."

"Do you think that's wise?" Zyair asked. "I think right now your concern needs to be clearing your name."

Zyair was right, that should be his concern but he had another concern and that was Alexis. He'd thought about her all night. Was she that upset by what she was told that she chose not to come to the gathering? If she was, that meant she cared for him more than he thought.

"Have you talked to Alexis? Does she know what went down?"

"Of course she does. Champagne stayed at her house last night. She said something about some dude following her."

Thomas didn't like what he was hearing at all. If he found out who this character was, he was going to get the beat down for real. Thomas knew what he had to do and that's call out the big dogs; the fellas from his past, perhaps even do some investigating. Damn, here he goes again investigating someone. He really didn't want to have to go there because Alexis was not happy with him about the first time. But at least she learned who Khalil really was.

The rest of the ride was silent except for the music playing in the background.

Thomas was thinking about Alexis and Zyair was thinking about DaNeen. He ran into her a few days ago and found that he couldn't get her off his mind. He knew just thinking about her was trouble but his mind didn't always do what he wanted it to. He was a good man, normally a faithful man who slipped that once and didn't plan on doing it again. It's just that something was going on with Champagne. She'd seemed distracted lately and he was feeling a little left to the side. They were going to have to talk about whatever it was and hopefully fix whatever it was. Then that way maybe, just maybe, his mind wouldn't wander.

Chapter Fifty-eight

Before you can face others, you need to face yourself.

Alexis was in her office with the door closed looking at the flowers Gavin had delivered to her.

That morning when she woke up, Champagne had already left. There was a note on the kitchen table. It said, *Hey girl, I didn't want to wake you up but I did want to let you know that Zyair picked up Thomas last night and I'll call you later.*

Alexis looked at the clock and saw that she had hours to go. She needed to see Thomas and speak with him. She needed to hear his voice and know that he was okay.

No, she hadn't forgotten about Victoria's mother. At this point all she could do was hope that the pregnancy story was a bold-faced lie.

Alexis' schedule was packed for the day. She had a meeting with the school superintendent. She also had to counsel a couple of students and get ready for a conference.

Normally, she tried to get out of going to the conference, but because her life had become somewhat of a mess and her mind was confused about who she was and who she wanted to be, she figured the getaway this conference afforded her was just what she needed. Plus, it was in Tampa, Florida, which meant she could extend her stay and visit Miami.

Alexis picked the phone up off her desk and dialed Thomas' number. On the first ring, someone knocked on the door. She hung up because she didn't want a half conversation with him.

"Come in."

The person who walked in surprised the hell out of her. It was Shay.

Alexis stood up and went around her desk to greet her with a hug, but when she put her arms out, Shay gave her a look that stopped her in her tracks. She quickly put her arms down.

"I'm glad to see you, Shay."

"Are you?"

"I wouldn't say it if I wasn't."

Shay just stood there, not saying a word, just looking around.

"So?" Alexis asked, waiting to hear what she had to say.

"So?" Shay repeated.

Alexis could see where this was going and if it was going to go anywhere, it meant she was going to have to take the lead. Alexis sat down on the couch that was against the wall. She crossed her legs and thought maybe she should wait Shay out, let her have the first words.

Shay cleared her throat and tried to think of something to say. *I don't fucking want to be here. If it wasn't for Shamel's ass, I wouldn't be.*

Alexis looked at her watch. "I don't have all day Shay. You came to see me, so there must be something you want to say."

Placing her hands on her hips, Shay told her, "I ain't got shit to say. I heard you've been looking for me and wanted to know what you wanted."

Fed up with the attitude and not wanting to play who can be the biggest ass, Alexis patted the seat next to her. "Come sit next to me."

"I can stand," Shay told her.

"I have been looking for you. I've been worried about you."

"I can take care of myself." Shay told her as she tried to picture Shamel with her guidance counselor. Shay thought about what transpired in the office with Shamel, how he fucked her and basically told her to "step off." It was their first time having actual intercourse and she wanted it to be different. She'd gone down on him a few times over the past three months and she was trying to build it up to be more. She was hoping that he would become her sugar daddy and take care of her, but after the way he treated her, she just didn't see that happening.

"How? By working at a strip club?"

Shay rolled her eyes. "I was doing just fine until you came in there. What were you doing in there anyway?" She wanted to see if she was going to tell her anything about Shamel but Alexis wasn't falling for it. She was a grown-ass woman and she wasn't going to give a child information about her life.

"That's not important, what's important is why you've chosen to go the route you're going. Why are you stripping? You're smart, Shay. You used to be an honor student. What's going on with you?"

"You're asking a lot of personal questions."

"That's because I care for you. You're one of the few students that have unlimited potential. You're special Shay, too special to be showing your body to any Tom, Dick, and Harry. You are a queen and you need to know that," she told Shay.

Shay looked at Alexis and saw the sincerity in her eyes.

"Please sit next to me."

For some reason Shay couldn't explain, she did just that.

"Talk to me. That's what I'm here for. Is something going on at home? Is there anything I can do to help out?" Alexis knew she was going out on a limb, but for very few students she would, and one of them was Shay. I went to the address in your files looking for you."

This threw Shay off. She didn't really know that Alexis was looking for her. "What!"

"I went looking for you."

"And what happened?" Shay wondered if her drug-addict mother answered the door. She was always fucked up. It could be by liquor or crack cocaine, whatever she could get her hands on. That's why Shay had to do what she had to do. That's why she stayed in motels with the money she made from stripping because most nights her mom had company and it was the kind of company she didn't want to be around because she was scared she might kill a motherfucker. Shay knew that she should share this information and that it was a burden she shouldn't have to carry herself, but she didn't and she wasn't sure when she'd be ready to.

"A woman answered the door." Alexis watched Shay closely to see if she would get some kind of reaction. She wondered if it was her mother. "She was intoxicated and she told us—"

Shay grew alarmed. Who the hell did she take with her? "Us, who's us?"

"A male friend of mine," Alexis reassured her. "We were told you don't live there."

Shay crossed her arms. "That's because I don't."

Alexis leaned into Shay trying to create intimacy. "Was that your mother?"

When Shay didn't answer Alexis knew her answer.

"Where are you staying? Who are you living with?"

Fuck! Fuck! Fuck! Shay did not come here to be grilled.

"Damn, how come you can't mind your business?" Shay stood up to leave but Alexis grabbed her arm.

"You are my business. I want what's best for you." Alexis stood up. She took both of Shay's hands. "Do you remember when I first started counseling you and I asked you where did you see yourself after graduating? You proudly said college, and that you wanted to be a lawyer?"

Shay did remember but that was over a year ago. That was before her mother stopped caring, again. There was a time when she had it together, but then she'd start getting high again and so the cycle went. Right now Shay didn't see college happening. She needed to survive.

"Do you remember how we mapped it all out for you?" Alexis let go of her hands and was surprised when Shay didn't move. She went to a file cabinet and searched for a file. Once she found it, she handed it to Shay. "Look inside Shay. Look at what you dreamed of no less than a year ago. That can still happen."

Shay didn't want to but she found herself opening the folder anyway and looking at the papers inside. She felt herself start to well up.

Alexis could see that she was having a small breakthrough. "Shay, all this is possible and so much more. You just need to let me help you."

I didn't come here for this. I didn't come here for this, Shay kept repeating to herself but Alexis' voice was overpowering hers.

"Look at you, you're smart, you're beautiful, you have more going for yourself than a lot of other students and you want to mess it up, you want to give up."

"I owe people money. I'm in debt. I have to help my moms," Shay told her.

"I'll help you get out of debt. We'll get you a part-time job." *What the hell am I getting myself into?* Alexis wondered but she couldn't stop. She felt like she needed to save this girl.

Shay couldn't stop the tears that were falling down her cheeks.

"What is it? Do you need somewhere to stay? Is that it?" Before she knew it, Alexis was saying, "You can stay with me until we figure something else out."

It was then Shay broke down. She sat down, placed her head in her hands and started crying. There was so much she wanted to say, so much pain inside her, but it was hers and she didn't know how to share it. All she knew was that Ms. Houston believed in her more than she believed in herself. It was a first. No one else had ever done that. No one else had ever told her the world was within her reach. She wanted to believe it.

This stripping shit paid the bills and allowed her to feed her mom but she wasn't responsible for her mother; she was responsible for herself. She did want out of the game. She just didn't know how she was going to escape it and here someone was offering her a hand.

I'm going to take it. I'm also going to tell her about me and Shamel.

Shay wiped her tears. She looked up at Alexis. "There's something I need to—"

Before Shay got a chance to finish her thoughts, Victoria came busting in the door.

"Ms. Alexis, I apologize. . . ." She stopped in her tracks when she saw Shay sitting there. "Oh, I'm sorry."

Shay stood up. "No, no that's okay. I'll come back."

Before Alexis could stop her, Shay was out the door.

Victoria looked at Alexis and asked, "Was Shay crying?"

Alexis didn't even bother to answer. She needed to go after Shay. "Why are you busting up in my office like that?"

"My bad. It's just that I wanted to apologize for my mother."

"Why are you apologizing? What your mother does has nothing to do with you." *With her lying ass, I hope.*

"I know. It's just that I got you all involved when you didn't really want to and well, I'm embarrassed."

Alexis had to ask. "Is your mom really pregnant?"

"I don't know. She said she is."

"Does she have anyone to help her out if she is?" What she was really asking was if Thomas had been around.

Victoria raised her eyebrows. "Why?"

Think fast. "Because I may be able to give her a number of someone that can help with doctor appointments and whatever else she may need help in."

Victoria thought this was strange. "My mother's not a child. She had me and she's taken good care of me."

"You're right, she did and she has." Alexis looked at her watch. "Listen, I have to go look for Shay."

"Is she okay?"

Of course, Alexis wasn't about to tell a student what was going on. "She's fine."

Five minutes later, Alexis was walking back into her office, alone. Shay was nowhere to be found.

Alexis had a few minutes before her meeting with the superintendent so she picked up the phone to call Thomas. She dialed the number and listened to it ring. She needed to find out what happened; if he knew who would set him up and to let him know that she believed in him and his innocence.

"Hello?"

"Thomas."

"Alexis?"

"Yes, it's me."

"Can I see you tonight?" he asked her. "We have some things we need to talk about."

"That's just why I was calling. I'll be by around eight o'clock."

After hanging up Alexis asked herself yet again, "What the hell am I getting myself into?"

Chapter Fifty-nine

Sometimes the best thing to do is give in, especially if it pleases the one you're with.

Alexis was sitting in front of Thomas' house trying to figure out what she wanted to say. What right did she have to ask him if what Shondell said was true? What right did she have to ask about what transpired the night of the party?

However, she needed to know. She had to know because against her will and against her better judgment, her feelings had gotten involved. She was starting to care for him more than she wanted to admit even to herself.

She looked up at the door and glanced at the window. She saw Thomas looking out the window and she knew he was probably wondering why she was sitting in the car. Did she need a moment and what for? They caught one another's eye and she looked at the door, which he had just opened. He waved her over and she put up one finger as in "wait."

She didn't want to be rushed and she wanted to come in on her own time. After counting to ten, she got out of her car, closed her door and walked in the house.

"Thomas?" she called out.

Thomas came from the back. The second they saw one another, they wanted to run into each other's arms like they do on television, fall on the floor and make wild passionate love. They didn't because this was reality and there were some things they each wanted to say to the other.

Standing in front of one another, they eyed each other up and down, at first with neither saying a word.

"How are you?" Alexis asked.

"It's all good."

"Is it?"

Thomas took her hand. "Come on, let's go into the kitchen."

She didn't protest.

Once in the kitchen, Thomas poured them each a glass of wine.

"I didn't know you drank wine. I thought you were a cognac, Hennessey man."

"I'm that and more," he told her as he sat down on a stool and pulled out one for her. "What's going on Alexis?"

"Shouldn't I be asking you that?"

"Zyair told me you came across Shondell."

Alexis didn't feel like beating around the bush. "Is she having your baby?"

"Would it matter to you if she was?"

Alexis placed her wine glass down and stood up.

"Where are you going?"

"I don't have time for games."

"Who's playing games? I just want to know if it would matter to you."

"I wouldn't be asking you if it didn't."

"Does this mean that you're feeling me on a deeper level?"

Alexis wasn't ready to admit it. "Is she?"

"The last time I slept with her was two or three months ago and it was that one night only."

"Did you wear a condom?"

"Of course. Do you really have to ask that question? You met her, she's crazy. That's why I stopped seeing her in the first place. Yes, we used to deal but it was just sex. Every now and then I'd help her and her daughter out. But when she started stalking and questioning me, I knew it was time to call it quits."

"How do you know she didn't poke a hole in the condom or something?" Alexis had heard of women doing this all the time, especially when the man involved was well-off. "Was it your condom or hers?"

"It doesn't matter," Thomas told her. "Just know that I'm going to get to the bottom of this."

Thomas didn't want to think about Shondell and the condom. That was the last thing he wanted to think about. What he wanted to think about was asking Alexis point blank to be his lady. After being arrested, getting his car destroyed, and having his reputation put on the line, he knew that it was time to cut out all the bullshit and settle down. The one he wanted to settle down with was sitting right in front of him.

Ever since they hung up earlier, Thomas had been rehearsing his I-want-to-be-serious speech. Well, not really rehearsing but going over in his head what he wanted to say.

"What are you going to do about her?"

"The only thing I can do; confront her."

Alexis stood up, "Let's go sit on the couch."

Good, this means she's staying and she's trying to get comfortable.

Once they were sitting next to one another, Alexis asked, "So what happened the other night?"

"You know what, I have no idea. What I do know is that someone is out to get me."

"Are you sure?"

"I'm not one to be paranoid or suspect shit for no reason. I know when something is up and right now something is up. I just need to find out what and who is causing this shit to happen."

Alexis leaned back on the couch and closed her eyes.

"Are you okay?" Thomas asked.

"I am. I've just had a long day, that's all."

Thomas moved closer to her and put his arms around her. He pulled her into him. "Alexis?"

"Yes?"

"You know I want to be with you, right?"

"Thomas, don't start this right now."

"Start what? I'm not starting anything. I'm stating a fact and that fact is that I want you to be my lady."

Alexis wasn't stunned. She knew that this was coming. She just didn't know that it would happen so soon.

She pulled away from him. "Thomas, how can you ask me that? You know I'm not ready to be in an exclusive relationship. You know my recent history. Hell, you played a part in me finding out about Khalil and how he played me out. You know it left me hurt and damaged."

"I do know these things but what he did has nothing to do with me. I'm not him."

"How do you know that you are ready for a serious relationship? How long have you ever been faithful to one woman?"

Thomas didn't answer.

"Exactly. Thomas, right now is not the time to be playing with my emotions."

"Why do you think I'm playing with your emotions? I'm asking you some real shit right now. I'm asking you to be my lady."

"I can't say yes to that. Right now I just want to keep it light. That's all I can handle." She was saying those words, but did she really mean them? Did she really want to keep it light? She wasn't even sure.

Thomas stood up in front of Alexis and started pacing. "You know what Alexis, you're right about me and you raised some very good questions. You're correct in saying I have never been faithful to one woman. Shit, I never tried. How do I know that I am ready for a relationship? Well, I'm not ready for any relationship. I'm ready for a relationship with you. I know this because when I wake up in the morning I think about you and whether or not we're going to speak. And when I think about who I believe will make me a better man by just being in their presence, all I see is your beautiful face."

He stopped pacing, looked at her and noticed that he had her undivided attention. "I adore you Alexis and what I haven't done in the past is simply because I haven't run across another you."

"Thomas, I'm not ready to make you any promises."

Thomas sat back down and placed his finger gently on her lips. "Nor am I asking you to. I want the ball to be in your court. I am relinquishing control and placing my heart at your mercy."

Alexis was blown away by what Thomas just said to her. Shit, he'd blown himself away by being so deep.

If he's running game, he is doing a hell of a job. If it's just sex he's after, hell, he was going to get that anyway.

"Thomas?" She wanted to distract him from this line of conversation. He was being so serious with her. Didn't he know the fear of being hurt was on the forefront of her mind?

"Yes?"

"Make love to me."

Thomas stood up but Alexis pulled him back down. "No, make love to me right here, right now."

Thomas looked her straight in the eyes as his hands touched her face. *Damn, I'm really in love with this woman.*

He moved his hands and pushed her back and started to kiss her. The longer they kissed, the deeper and more intense it became. Alexis had to pull away because there were so many feelings flowing through their lips.

She reached for his shirt and tried to pull it over his head but he told her he'd do it. He stood up and took off his shirt. She unbuttoned hers and unsnapped her bra. He pulled down his pants and she slid her skirt up.

"Oh, so it's like that."

"Yes, it's like that."

Thomas laughed as he bent down to pull her panties off, but not before rubbing her through the material causing her to moan.

"Do you want me to taste you?"

"No, I want you inside me."

Alexis reached out and touched his dick. She pulled it gently toward her. He knelt between her legs and let her guide him inside her pussy with her hands. They both closed their eyes until he settled inside her.

Slowly, he began to move inside Alexis as her pussy walls clinched around his dick.

"Whatever you're doing, keep doing it," he told her.

She started to work her vaginal walls even more, hoping he felt every squeeze. Thomas started pulling all the way out and going as deep inside her as he could go. He'd pull out slowly again and go deeper. Once he was in as far as he could go, he started moving his body in a circular motion.

The rhythm he had going was causing her to shudder. Alexis was feeling a sensation that she hadn't felt before. It felt like she was going to urinate. She found herself contracting her muscles and trying to pull away but Thomas wasn't going to let that happen.

Please don't let me pee on this man, Alexis thought to herself as she tried to pull away again.

"Relax, let it happen," Thomas told her.

Please don't let Thomas be into golden showers. "I feel like I have to pee," she broke down and told him.

Thomas laughed as he continued grinding into her.

"Stop Thomas, it's not . . ." She couldn't continue her thought process because suddenly she felt a tingling sensation that felt like pressure in her stomach that moved down to her vagina. Before she could stop, she found herself searching for his mouth with hers and as she felt her orgasm build up, she bit down on his bottom lip. Alexis arched her back, grabbed his ass, and pushed him as deep into her as she could as she felt wetness coming from her vagina.

Exhausted from what just happened, she looked up at him but he had his eyes closed and was on the verge of his own orgasm. She started to slowly move with him until finally he collapsed on her.

After a brief second or two, he looked at her and she asked, "What was that?"

Of course, Alexis didn't expect an answer. She knew what it was. It was the first time she'd had a vaginal orgasm; an orgasm strictly from dick with no clitoral stimulation. Something that she'd only heard about and never thought she'd experience because according to Oprah over 75 percent of women didn't.

It was then that it started to hit her and she knew. She knew that Thomas just might be the one.

Chapter Sixty

When you know it's over, don't look back.

Shay was nervous as hell. She was going to tell Shamel that after working with him and being available to him for three months she was through with him; that she decided to live her life right and that she was worthy and could no longer be his play thing sexually or any other kind of way.

He really shouldn't have a problem with it. He can have any girl he wants. Shay tried to trick herself into believing this but she knew Shamel. She'd been dealing with him for over a year and she knew that he would give her a hard time just because he could.

I have to try and better myself. Ms. Houston believes in me and truth be told, I believe in myself. She offered to help me in any way she could and the least I can do is take her up on that offer. If it doesn't work out, if I fail for some reason, at least I can say I tried.

Shay walked up to the club and stopped in front of the door. She had to go through with this.

It's his fault anyway. He's the one that sent me to her, talking about "Go back to school. I want you to work in my office." I can be a lawyer. Fuck working in an office.

No one was standing at the door because it was still early, so Shay opened the door and stepped in. After adjusting her eyes to the dim light, she glanced around and saw the usual suspects. The only person she didn't spot was Big Tone.

She didn't see Shamel so she asked the bartender, "Is Shamel here?"

He looked toward the back. Shamel was walking out of his office with someone that looked familiar. Once they were up on one another, she noticed that it was Karen, this girl from her biology class. Karen looked up and saw Shay looking at her. She quickly looked away.

Shay watched as Shamel popped her on the ass and told her he will see her tonight.

He looked at Shay and told her. "Follow me."

She does. *Should I tell him that Karen's underage?*

Once in his office, Shamel closes the door. "Did you go to school today?"

"Yes." *Maybe what I need to do is warn her.*

"Did you see Alexis?"

"Yes." *Maybe I should tell Ms. Houston.*

Shamel can sense something is up. "Why the fuck are you giving me one word answers? What's up?"

"I've decided not to deal with you anymore."
There, I've said it.

Shamel thought this was the funniest shit he'd
heard in a long time.

"What's so funny?"

"You're what's funny. What are you going to do
if you're not with me? Go work in one of those
hell-hole strip clubs where no one will look out for
you? You need me Shay and you know it."

Shay looked at Shamel like he was crazy. "I don't
need you. Ms. Houston said—"

Shamel got in Shay's face. "Said what? That you
got potential and that you could do better than
being a stripper? Hah, that's a laugh. That's what
she gets paid to say."

"She's a good person, Shamel. I don't know what
you have planned to do with her or to her, but I
don't want to lie to her. . . . She told me that I don't
have to dance anymore and that she would let me
come live with her and help me pay you all the
money that I owe you."

Shamel grabbed Shay by the neck. "You . . .
You told her my name? You told her you owe me
money?"

Shay put her hand over Shamel's and tried
to pull it away. "No, I just told her that I owed
somebody some money and I was dancing to pay
back the debt."

Shamel took one step back. The look in his eyes frightened Shay. She turned to walk away but he grabbed her arm and held on tight.

"Let go of my arm Shamel. You're hurting me."

"First of all, you silly little young-ass ho, I own your ass."

Shay tried to pull away but he was holding her too tight. "What the fuck is wrong with you Shamel? Are you crazy? Let me go!"

He didn't because something in him clicked. "I tell your dumb ass to do a simple task, go back to school, suck it up and act like a good girl. But no, you come back to me with this new life plan shit. I see you lack discipline, and it's my job as head of the family to see to it that discipline is enforced. You disobeyed me, and for that you must pay."

What the hell is he talking about? Whatever it was, Shay knew it was going to be brutal because of the look in his eyes. She'd seen him react physically to men in the club before. She'd seen him grab the women forcefully and she'd felt his hands around her throat and there was a look each time. The look he had now was it.

She started to scream but Shamel pulled her into him and placed one hand over her mouth and put his legs between hers in a way that she wasn't able to move.

He took off his thick leather belt with the other hand and raised it high. In doing so, Shay was almost able to escape but he grabbed her arm and started striking her over and over. He was hitting her everywhere, on her arms, her legs, and her face.

"Stop! Please stop!" Some kind of way she got loose and tried to run toward the door but he grabbed her again and started smacking her in the face with an open palm.

Suddenly he heard someone trying to get in the office with a key.

The only person that had a key was Big Tone.

Before he had a chance to stop him from entering, Big Tone walked through the door and noticed Shay on the floor bleeding with a belt next to her and Shamel with his arm raised.

"What the. . . ."

Shamel dropped his arm and looked at Shay then Big Tone.

"What the fuck did you do?" Big Tone asked.

"Get her out of here," Shamel said after kicking her.

"Get her out of here? Just what am I supposed to do with her?"

"I don't know and I don't care."

Big Tone reached down to help Shay up. He looked at Shamel and told him, "You fucked up man, you fucked up big time."

Big Tone half carried her to the bathroom that was attached to the office and in a low voice told her, "You need to go to the hospital. I'm going to drop you off."

Shay could barely speak. She was in shock and in pain.

"Just don't say who did this to you because if you do, you know what'll happen."

Shay knew that was a warning and it was one she wasn't going to take lightly.

Chapter Sixty-one

Sometimes you have to get involved. Don't think of it as a chore, think of it as a gift to the other person.

Alexis was home sitting on her couch, relaxing and thinking about the conversation she and Thomas had. She was seriously considering giving this relationship thing a try again. That meant she was going to have to call Shamel who had left her several messages, and tell him they couldn't go out anymore. As for Gavin, well, she enjoyed the time they spent together and she could see them being friends.

She was also on the couch wondering if she should call the police and report that she thought she was being followed. She didn't know what to do because she hadn't seen anyone and she was just going off a hunch. Well, more than a hunch. When she arrived home from Thomas', there was a note attached to her door that said, "How's Thomas?" That shit scared the hell out of her. She tried to call him but the phone went right into voice mail. She didn't leave a message.

Alexis was supposed to be at work but she called out. She just didn't feel up to going and had some things she needed to think about.

She'd left a message with the secretary and with Maya, telling them if they saw Shay to have her call her cell phone and that it was very important.

"Are you sure you want us to give a student your cell number?" they both asked.

She was sure she told them.

Alexis picked up the remote to turn the television on when her cell phone rang. She'd left it on the kitchen table when she made breakfast. She stood up to get it but it stopped ringing. Before she had a chance to sit back down, it started ringing again. This time she made it into the kitchen. Not even bothering to look at the caller ID she answered, "Hello."

"Hey sexy." It was Gavin.

"Hey you."

"I'm coming by the school to drop something off for my sister. Do you mind if I come by your office?"

"I'm not there today. I called out."

"Really? Well, how about having lunch together?"

Alexis figured she'd say yes, because it would give her an opportunity to tell him about Thomas. "I'd like that. Where do you want to meet?"

"How about I come pick you up?"

She saw no harm in it. Plus, if someone was following her like she thought, they'd see a man coming to her door and maybe, just maybe they'd go away. That thought alone made Alexis go to the window and look out. "That's cool."

"What time?"

When she looked out, she saw a car drive by slower than usual. She quickly closed the curtains. "The sooner the better."

Gavin could hear panic in her voice. "Is everything okay?"

"I don't know, Gavin. I think I told you before that I think someone is following me."

"Yeah, I believe you did tell me that."

"Well, I think the person is on my street."

"What! Are you sure?"

"I don't know. I just might be paranoid. It's just that I looked out the window and I could have sworn this car was driving by real slow like."

"What kind of car was it?"

That was a question she didn't have an answer to. "It was black."

Gavin waited to hear more but when she didn't say anything he asked, "That's all?"

"I don't know cars Gavin. The only thing I know about cars is how to drive them."

"I'm on my way over."

"You don't have to come right now. I'm in the house. I'll be all right."

Gavin wasn't hearing that shit. He was on his way anyway. "I'll see you shortly."

When they hung up the phone, Alexis looked out the window again and this time there was no car riding by and everything on the block looked normal. She also tried to call Thomas again but it went to voice mail. "Thomas, it's me, your . . . your. . . ." She wanted to say your woman but the words were stuck in her throat. "It's Alexis, call me."

She hung up and sat back down on the couch. While waiting she thought back to her childhood and her father, who she still had not called.

She thought about how he would tell her that, *"You determine your path and you teach people how to treat you."*

Back then when he would drop those bits of wisdom, it went in and out. Now that she was older, she realized he knew just what he was talking about.

She was here, in this place, unmarried, with no kids, and doing a job that she used to love, but now tolerated because of the choices she made.

That's right, the choices she made.

She knew it was now time to make new choices and the first one would be to commit to Thomas.

If she was honest with herself, she liked him all along, even when he was screwing a bunch of women. She just didn't take it anywhere because she knew better. She didn't want to set herself up for heartache.

Alexis shook her head because that's just what happened anyway. She ended up getting her heart broken by another man.

Please God let this be it for me. Let Thomas be the one. He sounded sincere in his words and I do want to take this chance with him.

Prior to meeting Khalil, Alexis was all into church. She attended every Sunday, went to Bible Study on Wednesdays and even attended prayer service. She was a Bible toting, scripture-quoting woman. *Maybe I need to go back to church. Maybe Thomas will come with me.* Although she tried to act like it was no big deal that she wasn't in the church anymore, she knew it was. Her being a female player wasn't really working for her the way she thought it would. She didn't feel complete. She didn't feel satisfied and she didn't feel she was being true to herself. She knew she was playing a role.

She thought about why she stopped attending church and what caused it. What happened? Khalil happened.

Initially he was going to church with her. Then one Sunday he said he wasn't going and asked her to stay home with him, which she did and then it happened another Sunday. The next thing she knew, she wasn't going at all. There was some guilt on her part but she was in love and she believed or wanted to believe that God understood.

I'm going to church this Sunday. I need to get back in the Word. God, I know you hear my thoughts. Please show me the right way once again. I promise I'll come back to you.

The difference this time would be that she wouldn't go overboard preaching to everyone and trying to save everyone. There was a middle ground in religion and she was going to find it.

There was a knock on the door, she looked out the window and saw that it was Gavin. She opened the door.

"I told you it wasn't necessary to come."

They gave one another a hug as he stepped in. He went to kiss her on the lips and she turned her head. It didn't go unnoticed but Gavin figured he'll leave it alone for now. "What kind of man would I be if I didn't come running when you said you think someone is following you."

"I just might be paranoid."

"I always say if you think it, there's a possibility it might be going on and that applies to almost everything." He followed her into the living room. "I rode around your block a couple of times. Nothing stood out."

Alexis felt a little relieved. "No black car?"

Gavin smiled. "There were a lot of black cars but no one was sitting in any of them."

Alexis sat down and Gavin followed her lead. "Gavin, I want to be honest with you about something."

Gavin did not like the sound of this, so he sat back and waited to see what she was about to say.

Before she could say a word, her cell phone rang. "Excuse me," she told him. She'd laid her cell phone on the coffee table after speaking with him. She reached over to answer it, but first she looked at the caller ID. It was the school calling. "Hello?"

"Alexis?" Whoever it was sounded rushed or panicky.

"Hello?"

"Alexis, it's me. Maya. Shay is in the hospital."

"What did you just say?"

Because of the alarm in her voice, Gavin stood up.

"Shay is in the hospital. They just called here asking for you. Something about her being beat up and they found your card on her."

"I'm on my way there." Alexis hung up and stood. "I have to go."

"What's going on? Where are you going? Is everything all right?" Gavin was throwing questions at her.

"My student, Shay. Maya said she's in the hospital and they found my card on her."

"That was Maya?"

Alexis started looking around for her purse. "I have to go. Call me later."

"Let me drive you."

"I don't know how long I'm going to be there."

"It doesn't matter. I'm coming with you."

Alexis didn't feel like putting up a fight. "All right then, come on let's go."

While they were in the car, Alexis figured she'd let Gavin know where her mind was as far as a relationship was concerned.

"Gavin?"

"Yes. Thanks for being my friend." She threw the word friend in there hoping he would get the hint.

Of course he didn't because he told her, "Well, I'd like to eventually be more than a friend."

Alexis turned in the seat to face him. "That's just not possible right now." She could see from the look on his face that he was hurt.

"For real? You're serious?" Gavin asked her.

"Yes."

"Damn girl, you're breaking my heart."

"I'm sorry. It's just that . . . Well, you know I've been dating other people."

He kind of figured he wasn't the only man in her life.

She continued. "There is one in particular that I'm thinking about seeing on a monogamous basis."

Gavin was disappointed but it's been his experience that if he stuck around long enough, the woman just might come around. "I understand and like I told you before I'm here for you as a friend."

Alexis wanted to reach over and hug him but in the car that wasn't possible so she kissed him on the cheek. "Thanks Gavin." She hoped that they would be friends for a long time because she genuinely liked him.

Finally they pulled up to West Point Hospital. As they were getting out of the car, Alexis said, "You know Gavin, this is probably all my fault. I asked her to change when she was not ready to change."

Gavin didn't understand how that could be Alexis' fault. "And? How is that your fault?"

"I think she got beat up because she was trying to start a new life."

They started walking toward the entrance.

"What are you talking about?" Gavin asked, still not getting it.

"My student Shay, the one I told you about that was stripping. She came by the office yesterday and we had a heart to heart. I convinced her to stop living the way she was living and I told her I would help her."

"And?"

"Maybe she went and told someone and they didn't want her out. Shit, I don't know."

"Damn, you really think someone would harm her because she wanted a better life?"

"Stranger things have happened."

"Damn, that's fucked up. Who would do some shit like that?"

"I wish I knew. Hopefully we'll find out."

Alexis and Gavin went to the front desk to find out what room Shay was in. After being given the information, they got on the elevator and pressed the appropriate button.

Alexis was nervous as hell. She didn't know what she was about to see. She looked over at Gavin. He told her, "I'll be in the hallway if you need me."

She was so glad she agreed to let him come along.

When they stepped off the elevator, they followed the signs until they found Shay's room. Alexis stepped inside, while Gavin waited by the door.

When Alexis pulled back the curtain she saw that Shay's right arm was held in the air by supports. Her face was so swollen that she could barely see her eyes. There was a bruise on her cheek shaped like a handprint. As Alexis got closer to her, she noticed handprints around her neck.

Alexis rushed to the bed. "Oh my God, baby! Who did this to you? Are you okay?" Alexis chastised herself for asking such a stupid question.

"I'm okay," Shay responded in a groggy voice. She was obviously drugged. She tugged on her hospital gown to pull it down.

Alexis took her hand.

"I need to know something," Shay said.

"What baby, what do you need to know?"

"Did you really mean it when you said that I can come live with you? I mean can I still come?"

Alexis couldn't believe that with all the pain Shay was probably enduring, all she cared about was if Alexis would still let her move in.

Alexis grabbed her left hand and looked her in the eyes. "I would like nothing more than for you to come stay with me."

Shay tried to smile. All she ever wanted was a place to call home and a semblance of a family.

Shay's moment was interrupted by the sound of Gavin's voice. "Alexis, can I come in?"

Alexis looked at Shay for permission. Shay nodded.

"Come in Gavin."

Shay immediately dropped Alexis's hand. "Gavin, did you say Gavin?"

"Yes."

Before she could say anything else, Gavin appeared and the look on Shay's face when she saw him caused Alexis to be alarmed. "Shay, what is it? What's wrong?"

It's obvious she recognized him. "You! You! Get out of here. Get out now!"

Gavin was looking at her like she'd lost her mind.

"What are you doing here? Get out, I don't want you here."

Alexis glanced from one to the other. "What the hell is going on?"

Gavin had no idea and he told her this. He then looked at Shay. "I don't know you, sweetie. How do you know me?"

Shay was almost in hysterics. "You don't know your own flesh and blood. I'm Shay, Cassandra's daughter."

Gavin looked like he was about to fall out.

Alexis asked, "Who's Cassandra?"

"Cassandra is my sister," he told Alexis while staring at Shay. "And that means you're my niece. You're little Shameka?"

Gavin was in shock. Alexis was sitting on the edge of the bed with her mouth wide open. "Are you serious?"

Shay started to cry. "Yes, we're serious."

Gavin didn't know what to say. All he could do was stand there and stare at Shay, while he repeated, "I don't believe this. I can't believe you're little Shay."

Shay allowed the tears to fall down her cheeks. "What happened to you? You promised me that you would always be there for me, but just like everyone else you weren't."

Alexis looked at Gavin. She too was waiting on an answer because he wasn't saying anything. He was just standing there staring. Alexis nudged him.

Gavin stepped closer to the bed. "I can't believe this. I am so sorry. You have no idea how sorry I am. I did tell you that and I meant it. But I got locked up for four years and when I got out I came looking for you and your mother."

"Obviously you didn't look hard enough."

Alexis didn't feel the need to interfere. Shay seemed to be handling this situation well enough.

"Yes," Gavin answered, "I have to admit I didn't look hard enough. I got so caught up in my own life that I neglected those I love. I know it's selfish and I swear to you I am so sorry. You have no idea how sorry I am."

Shay didn't say anything.

Gavin continued. "I should have been there for you. I will be there for you from this point on. You can come stay with me. I'll take care of you."

Gavin's apology was so sincere that Shay, Alexis, and the nurse who was standing at the door were all crying.

Shay looked away and Gavin placed a finger under her chin and turned her face toward him. "Please, just give me a chance."

Alexis interrupted. "Shay, I believe that your uncle means what he is saying. For the short time I have known him he has been a stand-up guy. I think you should think about forgiving him. There is nothing like family."

Shay was stubborn but she wanted to be loved more than anything in the world.

She placed her left hand in her Uncle Gavin's. "I hated the thought of you for so long. I'm scared to trust you. I always believed that no matter what, you would come rescue me, but you never came."

"I'm here now," Gavin told her. "Let me show you what it's like to be part of a family."

There was something nagging at Alexis and suddenly she realized what it was. "How come Maya never said anything?"

Shay looked at Alexis. "Who's that?"

"Ms. McMillan," Alexis told her.

Shay looked puzzled. "Why would she say anything?"

"She's my half sister," Gavin told them both. He then addressed Alexis. "We have the same father, but not the same mother. My father was a rolling stone as they say. Shay's mother has the same father as well but as kids we didn't associate. There's just too many of us."

Alexis was blown away.

"Princess, please let me be there for you," Gavin said to Shay.

When he called her Princess, Shay melted. That was the nickname he gave her before her mother started wilding out.

Without any assistance and what surely must have been painful, Shay sat up and held her arms out. Alexis got up off the bed and allowed them to hug one another.

"I'm going to leave you two alone for a little while. Shay, do you need anything?"

"Just some clothes, a toothbrush, a book or two—"

Alexis cut her off. "Hold up, hold up. I don't have my car. I came with your uncle."

When she said uncle, they both smiled. Gavin took his keys out of his pocket and handed them to Alexis. "Here, take my car and get what you need. I'm going to stay here a while." He looked at Shay. "If it's okay with you?"

Shay nodded.

"Are you sure Gavin?" She knew men didn't give up their cars that easily.

"I'm sure. I want some time alone with my niece."

"I'll be back sweetie," Alexis told Shay. "When I return, we need to talk about what you're going to tell the police."

"I'm not telling them anything."

Alexis didn't respond. She'd deal with it when she returned.

The second she was gone, Gavin asked, "Who did this to you? I promise that he will not hurt you again."

Shay, remembering that her uncle was always thought of as the bad seed or a thug knew that his words were true. But she also knew Shamel and she knew his ass was crazy. "I don't want to start any trouble. Can't we just leave it be?"

Gavin shook his head. "I can't do that. Whoever did this to you needs their ass kicked."

Shay turned her head.

"Either you tell me or I will find out another way."

Shay wanted to tell but she was scared. She wanted Shamel to get his ass kicked, but she didn't want Gavin to get hurt. Hell, she'd just gotten him back. He'd just reentered her life.

She turned back toward Gavin. "I don't want you to get hurt."

Gavin laughed at this. "Baby, I'm not the one that's going to get hurt. You best believe that."

Shay wanted to believe that. She didn't want her uncle hurt. Still, after what Shamel did to her, she did want him to pay. As a matter-of-fact, she wanted him to pay with his life. Although she felt this way, she found herself speaking in a low tone.

"I didn't hear you," Gavin told her.

She said the name again. This time Gavin had to put his ear near her mouth. She repeated the name in a low tone. "His name is Shamel, Shamel Walker."

Gavin knew he'd heard that name before. He tried to place it.

Shay continued. "He owns the strip club on Waters Street."

Oh, yeah, I know that motherfucker, Gavin thought to himself. He'd run into him a couple of times in the past, drug dealings, of course. "I'll be right back," Gavin told her.

"Where are you going?"

"In the hall to make a phone call."

Shay wasn't stupid. She knew just what kind of call he would be making. She just hoped he knew what he was doing.

Alexis was heading toward the parking lot. In her mind she was making a list of the items Shay needed when she noticed a note on Gavin's windshield. She looked around to see if she saw anyone hanging in the area. There was no one there. She looked back at the note and noticed her name on it. She took the note off the windshield and read it. It said, *Choose*.

Alexis turned the paper over in her hands, expecting to see more and wondering what the hell that meant. Panic started setting in because someone was fucking with her emotions, playing on her fears and she had no idea who.

She opened the car door and was about to shut it when she heard someone calling her name.

"Alexis! Alexis, hold up!"

She looked in the direction of the voice and saw that it was Finn. He'd left a couple of messages earlier that week telling her whenever she was ready he'd get her car fixed.

She waited until he was up on her. "Finn? Hey. I'm sorry, but I don't have time to talk. I have some things I need to do."

"It won't take long. I just wanted to tell you I'm still waiting to hear from you."

At the rate things were going, she doubted she would have the opportunity to call him at all. She looked around the parking lot again.

He followed her gaze. "Are you okay?"

"Yeah, yeah. Listen, did you see anyone put something on this car?"

"Nah. I saw you walking so I hurried up and parked to catch up to you."

"Oh, okay. Listen I have to go."

"You still have my number right?"

She was sure she did. "Yes."

"Call me. Let's get that car fixed."

"I'll do that." Alexis closed her door, started the engine, and left him standing there watching her, while she wondered who was at the hospital he knew.

It was then she heard her phone beep. There was a message. It must not have been able to connect while she was in the hospital. She reached over and pulled her cell out of her purse and pressed the button to connect to voice mail.

It was Shamel. "I'd like to see you tonight. I have something I want to ask you."

She hung up and told herself she'd call him either later if she got the chance or tomorrow.

While she had the phone in her hand, she tried to call Thomas. Again, there was no answer.

I will not panic. He's not with another woman. I won't think that. Shit, we haven't even gotten started yet. Shay, concentrate on Shay.

"Thomas, please call me. I need to see or talk to you." Damn, did she seem desperate already? She hoped not.

Chapter Sixty-two

Pick your battles slowly. Don't go charging in.

Thomas wasn't with another woman. He was wrapping up a meeting with his attorney. The charges had been dropped because there was no evidence that he ordered the girls to the house. Several people also came forward to say that he wasn't even around when they arrived.

Now, what he needed to find out was who the hell sent them and who the hell fucked up his car. He also needed to go and confront Shondell about this baby situation.

Please God, don't let this crazy woman be having my baby. That's the last thing I need right now especially since I believe Alexis and I are going to be together.

Thomas reached inside his glove compartment for his cell phone. It wasn't there. *Shit, where did I leave it?* He tried to retrace his steps in his mind.

Did he have it when he left the house? He believed so. Did he have it at the attorney's office? He wasn't sure.

He did remember calling Zyair as he was walking out the door.

Thomas turned the car around and headed back to his attorney's. *It has to be there.* Good thing he was only a couple of blocks away because when he pulled up, the attorney was walking out of the building.

"What's up? You're back?"

"Yeah, I think I left my cell phone in your office. Is your receptionist still there?"

"Yeah, just tell her to go in my office and look around."

"All right, thanks man."

A few minutes later Thomas was getting back in his car with his cell phone. He'd just heard Alexis' message and tried calling her back but his phone died.

"This is some bullshit!" he yelled out loud. *I'll call her after I leave Shondell's house.*

Thomas made the decision to just go straight to Shondell's house. He hoped she still lived in the same place. He would call her, but he deleted the number out of his phone and erased it from his memory purposely. Also, the way he figured, if he confronted her face-to-face, he'd be able to read her. *If she is pregnant, why would she tell Alexis and not tell me? Does she know what Alexis means to me?*

Before he knew it, he was in front of Shondell's door about to knock when it opened.

It was Victoria.

"Mr. Thomas? What are you doing here?"

"I came to see your mother."

Victoria looked behind her and stepped out into the hallway. "I don't think that's a very good idea."

"I need to speak with her, Victoria."

Victoria placed her hands on her hips. "About what? You broke up with her remember."

"Is your mother pregnant?"

Victoria grabbed his arm and pulled him away from the door. "Where'd you hear that?"

"It's not important. Is it true?"

"I think so."

"Did she tell you I'm the father?"

Victoria honestly didn't know who the father could be. She knew her mother slept around quite a bit, but she also knew her mother was obsessed with Thomas. As she stood there she thought about how they could have a better life if the baby was his, so she told him, "Yes, she told me you were the father."

Thomas didn't know what to say. *This shit could not be happening, not right now.* "I need to speak to her."

"She's 'sleep right now. Can you come back another time?"

Thomas didn't want to come back another time. He wanted to settle this now, but then again, he knew he needed to calm down. Too much shit had been happening and right now he was operating off pure emotion. Plus, he needed to call around and find out how soon he could take a paternity test. He wanted to get this taken care of as soon as possible.

"Tell your mother I'll be by in the next few days."

Victoria watched him walk away before going back inside the house.

His next stop was to the detective he'd hired to investigate who was fucking with him, but first he needed to call Alexis again. He looked at his cell phone which he'd placed on the charger and saw there were a couple of bars on it.

He dialed her number and once again her voice mail came on. *Where is she? She left me a message saying she needed to speak with me then why isn't she answering her damn phone?*

Less than ten minutes later Thomas was sitting in Mike Jones' office. Mike came highly recommended by several of his clients. He was told if there was some dirt, if some shit was going down, about to go down or someone was out to get you, Mike Jones, was the man with the plan. Thomas hoped so because he didn't come cheap.

Thomas was sitting in front of him. "Please tell me that you found out something regarding all these so-called coincidences that are occurring in my life.

Mr. Jones leaned back in his seat. "I think you're going to be very happy with what I uncovered for you."

"Well, spit it out." Thomas wanted this information so he could do what he had to do and if that meant fuck someone up, well, so be it. He was tired of this bullshit. Here he was, trying to live his life right and someone was trying to throw him all off track.

"Does the name Shamel Walker mean anything to you?"

Thomas repeated the name several times in his mind. "It rings a bell but I can't place it."

"He's the owner of several strip clubs and bars in the area."

Thomas looked at him and waited for more.

Mike pulled opened a folder that was on his desk. Inside were pictures.

Mike handed the pictures to Thomas. "Isn't that your lady friend?"

Thomas' first thought was, *There is no way he's talking about Alexis. How would he even know about me and Alexis? But then again, let his clients tell it, Mike Jones knows everything about a client before he takes them on.*

Thomas took the pictures and there it was in color, pictures of Shamel and Alexis.

Thomas stared at the picture. It hit him all at once. *This is the motherfucker me and Alexis kept running into. Don't tell me she's seeing this asshole. I can't believe this shit.*

Thomas looked up at Mike. Just as he is about to say something Mike's phone rang.

He looked at the ID. "Excuse me," he told Thomas, "I have to take this."

Thomas didn't say a word. He watched as Mike listened to whoever was talking on the other end.

Whatever that person was saying caused Mike to look up at Thomas in alarm. He placed his hand over the mouthpiece. "This is my associate. According to him, Shamel is on Alexis' porch."

Thomas jumped up out of his seat and was out the door before Mike could stop him.

Chapter Sixty-three

Keep your cool and never let them see you sweat.

When Alexis pulled up to her house she was surprised to see Shamel sitting on her porch. She looked around and noticed a car in front of her house. *What the hell is he doing here? Didn't I tell him once before I don't like pop-ups? Well, good this will save me a phone call. I'll let him know now.*

As she got closer, she noticed that he looked frazzled, not as together as he normally looked. He was sweating, frowning, pacing, and it looked like he was talking to himself. She also noticed a spot that looked like blood on the front of his shirt. This was cause for concern.

Why would he have blood on his shirt? What the hell happened? Is he hurt? Did he hurt someone? "Shamel, what happened? Are you okay?" she asked as she approached him.

He didn't answer her. He just looked at her.

"Are you okay?" she asked again.

"Where the hell were you?" he asked in a tone that was low and almost menacing.

It threw Alexis off for a second. His tone frightened her, but she told herself not to show it. "What's wrong with you? What are you doing sitting on my porch like this?"

"I've been waiting on you."

Alexis didn't like how he sounded. His tone implied that she should be at his beck and call. "Waiting on me? Waiting on me for what?"

"We need to talk about us, our relationship."

What the hell is he talking about? We don't have a relationship. And why the hell is he looking at me like that; like he's about to snap? Alexis knew without a doubt that she was making the right decision in not seeing him anymore. With the way he was acting now, she just had to figure out a way to tell him.

Alexis tried to get past him. "Shamel, you're scaring me. I think it's best if you leave." He didn't move an inch. *Okay, now why isn't he leaving?*

"I ain't going nowhere until you talk to me," he told her.

He has lost all his mind.

Shamel looked at the car in the driveway. "Whose car are you driving?"

"A friend's."

"What friend? Another man's? Is that where you were? With someone else?"

Alexis tried to get past him again but he stood up and blocked her path.

"Answer me. Where the hell were you?"

Alexis decided to try another tactic. "Shamel, why don't you call me later, we'll talk. I need to get back to the hospital. One of my students is in the hospital."

"Yeah, I know. I know about Diamond or Shay as you call her. I heard about her little incident."

How did he hear that? Was he behind it? With the way he was coming across at the moment she didn't know what to think. "Listen you need to move. I need to go in the house." Once again she tried to brush past him, but he grabbed her arm so tight that she told him. "You're hurting me. Let go of my arm."

He ignored the request. "Who the fuck you think you're talking to? All the shit I've done for you to get you."

Alexis looked at him like he was crazy. *What the hell is he talking about? What has he done for me?* "What are you talking about?"

He didn't answer the question. He just told her, "Open the door Alexis."

"No." She took a quick look around and hoped that someone saw what was going on and that they would come to her rescue because at this point that's just what she felt like she needed.

"Open the goddamn door!" He gave her a look that told her if she didn't he wouldn't think twice about hurting her.

"Please don't hurt me, Shamel. Talk to me. Tell me what's wrong. What's going on? Why are you acting like this?"

"I won't hurt you, I promise. I just want to talk."

Alexis felt like she had no choice but to do what he said. She moved past him and unlocked the door. "I'm expecting company soon," she lied.

"I thought you said you had to get back to the hospital."

She didn't answer, there was no need to.

She tried to walk through the door and close it on him but he pushed it open and stepped inside. Within the blink of an eye, he had a gun pulled out on her.

Initially she thought her eyes were deceiving her. It only took a second for her to realize this was real. Water formed in the corner of eyes from the fear she was feeling. She put her hands up as though she could protect herself from a bullet. *Please God, you promised you would protect your children from harm. Well, I need your help now.*

Alexis looked up at Shamel and in a calm tone asked, "What are you doing? I thought you said you wouldn't hurt me,"

She watched as he scanned the room while still holding the gun in his hand. "I'm not. I just want your cooperation."

"My cooperation? I thought you said you just wanted to talk." *Why is he doing this?*

"I do want to talk," he told her, "I want to talk about how I'm tired of you trying to play me."

Alexis glanced around the room to see if there was something, anything she could grab ahold of so she could fight back. "Play you? Why do you think I'm trying to play you?"

He pushed her on the couch and stood over her. "I'm not stupid Alexis. Don't you know I could have any woman I want? Don't you know that?"

She nodded her head. "I do know that Shamel and you could have had me." *Why did I say could have, why didn't I say, he can?* Alexis wished she could backtrack.

It was as if he didn't even hear her. "But I want you! You're the one I want!" He bent down and tried to kiss her, but she turned her head.

She didn't know what to say about any of this. She figured the best thing she could do was keep her mouth shut.

"Nah, but you want to fuck around. You want to mess with that nigga, Thomas. I tried to show you who he was; a pedophile but that's not enough for you. Oh, hell no, this shit will not happen to me again."

What does he mean, he tried to show me who Thomas was? Was he the one who set him up?

Shamel turned his back to her for a second. *This is my chance.* She tried to get off the couch but he turned back around too quickly.

He pushed her back down. "Where do you think you're going? You think you can get away from me like that? You think it's going to be that easy?" Still holding the gun in one hand, he started taking off his belt with the other hand. "You can't fool me. This shit happened to me before. Every time I love a bitch, she ups and leaves. I'm about to teach your ass a lesson. You think I beat Shay's ass; it's your turn."

When she heard this, her initial reaction was shock. *So, he's the one that did that to her.* Then she started to scream.

Champagne who had just pulled up and turned her engine off, heard Alexis screaming. She jumped out of the car and ran to the door and knocked.

"Alexis! Alexis! What's going on in there?"

Inside, Alexis could hear Champagne calling for her. She looked up wide-eyed at Shamel.

He put one finger to his mouth and placed the gun on Alexis' temple to stop her from calling out.

I can't believe this is happening to me. I can't believe I didn't know any better. I'm smarter than that, Alexis thought. *Please let her call someone. Please don't let her just leave.*

Champagne continued to call out and tried to look through the curtains. She couldn't see anything, but she was sure she heard screams. She was positive of it. She looked at the car in the driveway and at the car in front of the house. She wondered who the cars belonged to.

Inside the house, Alexis was staring at the door as Shamel stared at her.

Champagne ran back to her car and pulled out her cell phone and tried to call Zyair. He didn't answer. *Where the hell is he?"*

Champagne reached into her glove box and pulled out the gun she just picked up from the gun shop. She was actually stopping by to see if Alexis wanted to go to the shooting range with her later. It was a new hobby Sharon introduced to her. She had no idea whether or not the gun would come in handy. She hoped it wouldn't come down to that. But if it did, so be it. She looked at the gun and sighed. *The Lord works in mysterious ways,* she thought as she put the bullets in the chamber.

Just as she was getting out of the car with the gun in hand Thomas pulled up.

He shut the engine off and climbed out of his car. Immediately he noticed an unfamiliar car in Alexis' driveway and the gun in Champagne's hand. He knew some shit was about to go down, so he opened his glove compartment and pulled out his own gun.

Champagne ran up to him. "I heard Alexis in there screaming."

She didn't need to tell him anything else. He motioned for Champagne to go to the back of the house.

She nodded her understanding. As she ran toward the back of the house she glanced down the street at a car that was parked. For some reason it felt funny to her; a little off.

Down the street in the black car that was parked, an individual was watching with anticipation.

The second Thomas stepped on the porch, Gavin pulled up with one of his boys. Both of them got out of the car. Gavin was packing too. He and Thomas looked at one another. As they did, they heard Alexis scream.

"I'm here to help," Gavin told Thomas as he stood next to him.

Thomas instructed the man Gavin was with to take the back. He then turned his attention back to Gavin.

They gave each other the nod. Thomas put up one finger, two fingers, then kicked the door in. They rushed in, only to find Shamel with his pants open and the gun pointed at Alexis.

Her shirt was torn and tears were running down her face. When she saw them, she thought about getting up but the gun stopped her.

When Shamel heard them rush in, he didn't bother turning around. All he said was, "If you don't stay back, I'll kill her. I swear I will."

"Come on man, you need to let her go," Thomas told him.

"Why? So you can have her?"

"That's not what this is about. This is about me and you and you know it."

Shamel started laughing. "You really think that don't you?"

Champagne and Gavin's boy were standing back where Shamel couldn't see them. When they had arrived at the back door, Champagne recalled that Alexis kept a key inside the flower pot for emergencies.

They crept in silently while trying their hardest not to be seen or heard. However, Gavin spotted them out of the corner of his eye. He tried to let her know he was aware of their position.

Champagne backed up some when she heard someone else walk in the door.

"Shamel!" Big Tone had walked in the house. "What the fuck are you doing?"

Shamel had no idea what Big Tone was doing there. "How did you know I was here?"

"I always know where your ass is."

Shamel didn't like the sound of that. What the fuck was Tone doing keeping tabs on him? "What?"

Big Tone shook his head. "Man, I've been keeping tabs on you ever since you started talking about this girl. I knew this shit was going to happen again. This shit has got to stop and it needs to stop right now."

Everyone was watching this exchange and took note of the word "again."

"What matters right now is all these motherfuckers got a gun on you. You need to think about what you're doing."

"This shit ain't your business. It has nothing to do with you."

"It has everything to do with me, because if you fuck up, the business is fucked up and then I'm fucked. What you need to do is put the gun down."

Gavin, tired of the back and forth, stepped up with his gun pointed at Shamel. "Enough of this talking shit."

Shamel pressed the gun to Alexis' head. "All y'all motherfuckers need to get the fuck out of here or I'm going to shoot this bitch on the count of three."

Alexis could feel herself start to shake. She felt like she was having an out of body experience. It was as though she was a spectator watching this happen to someone else. She was in shock. Had her Lord let her down? Was He not going to come to her rescue? Was this her punishment for sleeping with three men? Is this how she was going to die, right here, right now in her home without even experiencing real love, without having children, without being married? Was this really it?

"All right, we're going to back up," Thomas told him.

"I ain't going no fucking where motherfucker. Shay is my niece, motherfucker." Gavin was ready for whatever.

"Gavin, please," Alexis begged. "Please back off."

Shamel started to count. "One."

Gavin looked at her, then at Thomas. It was almost as if they had a secret code. In the meantime Champagne and Gavin's boy were creeping up behind Shamel.

"Two."

"Please everyone. Calm down," Alexis begged.

Shamel shoved her in the face with the gun. "Shut up! Shut the fuck up!"

Big Tone yelled, "Shamel, behind you!"

Before Shamel could respond or say "three", Alexis pushed his arm away and rapid gunfire was heard.

TO BE CONTINUED